MICHAEL STEWART

Prodigy

FONTANA/Collins

ACKNOWLEDGEMENTS

Particular thanks are due to: ABC Television, New York; the Down's Children's Association, Birmingham; Dr David Geaney, Lecturer in Clinical Psychiatry at the Littlemore Hospital, Oxford; Professor Philip Graham, Professor of Child Psychiatry, the Great Ormond Street Hospital for Sick Children, London; James Hale; Dr Oliver Sacks; John Welsh, Director of the National Association for Gifted Children; and the directors of certain institutions who, due to the sensitivity of their work in clinical genetics, have requested to remain anonymous.

First published in Great Britain by
Macmillan London Ltd 1988

First published in Fontana Paperbacks 1989

Copyright © Michael Stewart 1988

Printed and bound in Great Britain by
William Collins Sons & Co. Ltd, Glasgow

this is for Martine

PART I

ONE

In the delivery room the lights were dim and the voices hushed. Green venetian blinds filtered out the sunlight. Beside the bed, the lamps were set low and carefully shaded. Flute music played softly in the background. There'd be none of the dazzle and din of a normal delivery suite at this birth.

Alex's breathing was coming quicker now, in short, panting bursts. Anxiety filled her hazel eyes. Her hand sought his and clutched it tight.

'Jake?'

'Take it easy,' he said. 'You're doing fine. Nearly there.'

He tried to sound calm but he was nervous, too; nervous and apprehensive. He'd attended plenty of births as a doctor but only one before as the father.

The obstetrician bent forward between Alex's raised legs. He nodded. Any moment now.

Jake squeezed her hand harder.

'Push again,' he urged.

With a sudden, sharp cry, she jabbed her nails into his hand as another long contraction bore down through her body. Her head thrashed back and forth on the pillows.

He leaned forward and peered in the half-light. Beyond the swollen stomach the mouth of the birth canal was widening. Quite suddenly the crown of a head appeared. The hair was fair, like the mother's, and tousled and glistening. Inch by inch the head came free. For a moment the face lay downwards, then with a small corkscrew motion the baby girl twisted onto her side. Another contraction squeezed out one shoulder, a second the other, then the arms and trunk. Tiny hands groped the air. Very gently the obstetrician slipped a finger under each arm and eased out the rest of the small body.

The baby took a sudden gasp of breath and let out a vigorous howl. At first her breathing was stertorous but within moments she had settled down to a regular rhythm of snuffles and grunts.

The doctor slid her up onto Alex's stomach. Jake's mouth was dry. This was the critical moment. The ultrasound scans, the amniocentesis, the gene-screen in the sixteenth week – all the tests had shown perfect results. But he'd not yet *seen her face*.

Would she, in spite of everything, have turned out like her brother?

Craning forward, he quickly scanned the tiny face with its wrinkled, flattened features, tight-shut eyes and rubbery wet cheeks. Then, very slowly, he let out a long breath. Thank Christ.

The obstetrician was beaming.

'You have a fine little girl!'

Jake returned the smile.

'Her name's Sophie,' he said.

He'd known she was a girl from the very first moment he'd set eyes on the tiny cluster of living cells on a slide under his microscope, nine long, tense months before.

Alex was straining to see, too, but the baby's face was pressed against her stomach and the tiny features were hidden. She looked up at him. Hope battled with fear in her eyes. He bent down and kissed her damp forehead.

'She's fine,' he whispered. 'Perfect.'

'Quite perfect?'

'A hundred per cent.'

She laid her head back on the pillows and let the tears stream silently down her cheeks.

Jake stroked the baby's back in a slow, rhythmic motion. Her body was slippery to the touch and her skin exquisitely soft. No caress had ever felt so intimate. The infant gurgled, wriggled, stretched her legs and sucked her hand, but did not cry.

She was perfect – unlike her poor brother Daniel. Jake had made sure she wouldn't inherit the defect by arranging an *in vitro* fertilisation. But Alex had never quite believed it would work. They'd known the chances of a second Down's syndrome child were normally quite high, especially for a woman in her late thirties . . . Perhaps she simply hadn't dared to hope.

He carried on stroking the baby for several minutes until the umbilical cord had finally stopped pulsing and the obstetrician had clamped and cut it. Then he picked her up and lowered her carefully into a basin of lukewarm water. Immediately the tiny body relaxed and the tightly wrinkled face began to open out as she returned to the state of weightlessness she'd known in the womb.

Quite suddenly, as she lay cradled in his bare arms with only her face above the water, her eyelids fluttered and she opened her eyes. She looked straight up at him. Impossible, of course, but she seemed to be *seeing* him! He couldn't tear his gaze away. Her eyes were immense pools of violet, their stare profound and unblinking. Alert, curious, yet somehow strangely knowing, they drew him irresistibly into their dark well.

He sat in the chair beside the bed. Alex lay with her child at her breast, her eyes closed. She looked tired but at peace. The obstetrician and nurse had run their routine post-natal checks, cleaned up and left. Distant hospital noises floated in upon the sluggish air, as if from a different world. Nothing existed outside this warm, dim-lit room.

Sophie lay sucking contentedly. Her eyes were open, though she couldn't *see* anything. And yet ... that first moment she'd opened her eyes ... had he been imagining things?

He leaned forward towards the baby and clicked his fingers softly.

Alex stirred.

'Leave her,' she murmured. 'She's hungry.'

The sucking was just a reflex. A newborn wasn't in need of food.

'She's OK. I just want to see something.'

He fluttered his fingers across the baby's field of vision. She stopped sucking. Yellowish milk escaped around her lips and two small lines puckered her brow into a 'V'.

'Sophie? he whispered. 'Watch.'

The infant twisted her head towards the sound. Slowly he passed his hand from side to side, quietly clicking his fingers as he did so. At first her eyes wandered randomly around. Then one locked onto his fingers and began to follow the movement. For a brief moment the other joined it in parallel, before both diverged and, losing their focus, wandered off in separate directions again.

The 'V' on her brow dissolved and her mouth lifted into a wonderful smile.

'That's enough,' said Alex, steering her nipple back towards the tiny mouth. 'You'll wear her out.'

'She loves it. Look at her.'

'You'll wear *me* out.'

'I'm sorry.'

He looked back at the child. His pulse drummed in his temples and his stomach had seized up taut.

12

Christ, he thought. *This isn't possible!* A newborn baby can't really see. It can't detect moving objects for several weeks. And it should be several more before it can focus both its eyes.

He checked his watch as he stepped out of the drab concrete Maternity Hospital into the ebbing September sunshine. Four fifteen. Tea-time on the paediatrics ward. Too early to call his father with the news, though: another hour before the afternoon nap ended with the first gin of the evening. Should he slip up to the labs? No, Helen would have it all under control there. He'd look in on his way home tonight.

He headed down the steep hill towards the Royal Infirmary. The whole city of Bristol lay spread out below, stretching across the broad valley, with tower blocks and white stone crescents and furrows of terraced houses rising up the slopes to the far skyline.

He thought about Daniel. The boy was now six, but he had a mental age of about two. Alex had been only thirty-two at the time and there'd been nothing to suggest he might be *wrong*. The first hint had been the obstetrician's sudden frown and his sharp, querying upward glance with its unspoken message, doctor to doctor ... *it needn't be allowed to live* ... Then he'd seen the face for himself, with its tell-tale flattened features, its slanting eyes and small, low-set ears. For a second he was judge over life or death, and his first instinct was to say, *Spare it the misery* ... How could he have even contemplated that – he a paediatrician, a man who'd given his life to caring for Nature's human tragedies? How? Because it was always other people's human tragedies he had to deal with. This one was his own.

They'd made the best of it. They loved Daniel dearly and did all they could for him. People sometimes called

13

him a lucky boy, having a consultant in clinical genetics for a father and a teacher of deprived children for a mother. But no one without a mongol child could ever know what it was like for the child – or for the parents, either. However bravely you battled on, eventually the sheer irreversibility of the situation wore you out.

But now there was Sophie: a fresh hope, a fresh start.

And yet, even that event had created its own disharmonies. From the moment he'd found a way of having another child without the defect, it had somehow become *his* child, and Daniel, by extension, Alex's. She blamed herself for the boy; she was the carrier of the chromosome disorder. He did all he could to persuade her it wasn't right, but the feeling persisted, present in the sub-text of all they said and did, and with the best will in the world there seemed nothing he could do to change it, except carry on and trust to love and patience to heal things.

Taking a deep breath of the dry later-summer air and hunching away the stiffness in his shoulders, he hurried on down the steep stone steps that led to the rear of the great hospital.

As he stepped out of the lift on the eleventh floor, he met a nurse from his ward coming off duty. Unlike the main paediatrics ward opposite, which dealt with the normal accidents and illnesses of childhood, theirs was smaller and treated complex congenital cases. This was his chosen field. Ever since Daniel's birth he'd been doing research work into genetic defects in children at the labs of the university's Department of Medicine, in parallel with his hospital work.

The nurse's face lit up as she saw him.

'Wonderful!' she said. 'Just what Daniel needs – a little sister.'

'Thank you, Susan. News travels fast.'

She smiled.

'Good news does, Dr Chalmers.'

He turned quickly in through the fire doors and, slinging his white coat over his arm, swept into the ward.

There were six children in at the moment. Three were seated at a large table in the centre, with two nurses. Louise, aged seven, was staring fixedly into her mug. Kevin, four, was beating the table with a plastic plate. And Denise, a Down's child about the same age as Daniel, was being fed at her high chair but, lacking the muscle tone to chew properly, dribbled out her food as fast as she was given it.

In a bed to the right, with a drip fixed in his wrist and being attended by Jake's stand-in for the day, lay Jeremy, aged nine, the small fair-haired haemophiliac who'd been admitted the previous week. He was being given replacement therapy for the missing coagulation factor in his blood.

Opposite, in a wheelchair, sat Gianni, the ten-year-old Sicilian boy with thalassaemia whose parents had flown him over for a treatment the hospital was pioneering. The university Genetics Research Unit had managed to engineer a retrovirus to remove excess iron in transfused blood; no one knew for certain if it would work, but without taking the chance Gianni was unlikely even to reach the age of twenty.

Lastly, watching television with her back to the room, sat Karen, the pretty eight-year-old with hypophosphataemia, another genetic blood disorder. She was now recovering from a bone-marrow transplant.

Then he spotted a row of sheets of paper strung across the windows, some upside down and others back to front but spelling in all the message, CONGRATULATIONS.

The nurses started to clap as he came in, encouraging those children who could to clap their hands, too. Gianni let out a whoop. Jeremy grinned. Kevin beat the table with his plate louder still. Louise broke her fixed gaze into her mug and beamed broadly. Only Denise, the small girl with the little slanting eyes and flattened face, didn't understand.

Jake went forward and took her hand.

Here is Denise, he thought; Denise is defective. There, barely half a mile away, is Sophie; Sophie is perfect.

It isn't *right*.

He was checking Karen's chart when his bleeper sounded. He called the switchboard from the sister's office. It was Helen, from the labs.

'Congratulations again,' she said warmly. 'You're a multiple father today.'

'How many?'

'A litter of six.' She paused. A different note entered her voice. 'Jake, maybe you ought to come and take a look.'

Twilight had fallen fast, bringing with it the first chill hint of autumn. In the Department of Medicine, lights burned in the corridors and the central heating was already on, mingling the odours of plastic and chemicals. The Genetics Research Unit on the fifth floor was empty. Herbert Blacker, his professor, was in Los Angeles, discussing the funding of a new research fellowship that would add greatly to the unit's resources. Ivan, the lab technician, belonged to a union and had gone home at five thirty; he'd left a drawing on the blackboard of a stork carrying a test-tube in a diaper.

But Helen, his research assistant, was still there.

16

She was twenty-five, ambitious and hard-working, with long dark hair and intense blue eyes.

The laboratory lay between Herbert's large, well-ordered room and his own small, chaotic cubicle. The central benches were laden with microscopes and test jigs and the special equipment for screening, probing and splicing genes. At the far end, beyond a partition, lay a honeycomb of Perspex cages where the rats, beautiful sleek white creatures, were housed.

The cages on the right held Herbert's larger animals, each the size of a small rabbit. The professor was looking into dwarfism, a terrible affliction in humans. He'd micro-injected the human growth gene into fertilised rat eggs and produced offspring that grew double the size at twice the rate. He had now achieved an almost complete understanding of the trigger mechanisms of the genes concerned and was confident of developing an ante-natal cure for humans within five years.

But Jake's own work was where the unit was making its name. In the cages opposite were housed his own high-IQ rats, ten in all, quartered in a complex of cages with labyrinthine passages, treadmills, see-saws, brightly coloured mobiles and interestingly textured toys, designed to provide an enriched environment. He'd had a major breakthrough just the previous year in isolating a cluster of human genes that coded for intelligence. These rats had been specially bred to express those genes. They were not just maze-bright but maze-*brilliant*. Genetic intelligence was a fiendishly difficult area but perhaps the most vital one of all, since so many congenital defectives – not just Down's syndrome cases – were mentally retarded as well.

Helen gestured towards an incubator cage.

'It may be nothing . . .' she began.

One of the two females of the bunch had given birth to six tiny pink babies. They'd been segregated from their mother in case she attacked them – possibly even devoured them, as sometimes happened – and they were being fed from an array of automatic dispensers.

A sudden chill prickled his skin and his throat went dry.

'What time were they born?'

'Around three o'clock,' she said.

'*Today?*'

'Of course.'

'My God!'

The young of rats are born blind and stay blind for several days. But five of these six babies had their eyes open. And as he moved a hand across the bars of the cage, five tiny heads turned.

TWO

Sophie was a happy baby who hardly ever cried. Mostly babies cried because they were bored. The trick was to keep their curiosity satisfied.

Sophie's curiosity was almost insatiable. At first, simple movement excited her most – her own fingers wiggling, the mobile above her cot fluttering, Daniel peeping in and out of view. Then she changed to textures, and for a good while she couldn't be drawn away from her pieces of wool and velvet, plastic and sponge. Soon she learned to grasp with her hands and her passion suddenly turned to crinkling tissue paper. A few days later she discovered that pulling a thick cord of plaited wool made a large, glittery disk above her cot rattle, and that kept her fascinated for hours at a time.

The days lengthened into weeks, and physically, too, she grew fast. She kept her violet eyes and her fine, golden hair. She kept, also, the small 'V' that furrowed her brow whenever she was deep in thought, only to vanish the moment she smiled. By the sixth week, in half the time it took the average child, she could raise both hands at will, and by the seventh she was reaching and grasping the rattle without using the string. By the eighth week, she could spread her fingers and touch her fingertips with her thumbs. In the tenth week she rolled her body over by herself, and in the twelfth, with Christmas just round the corner, she began to crawl. By now she was almost three months advanced.

Visitors began to remark on her progress. Only just

recently Herbert, his head of department, had come to drinks and spent almost the entire time up in her room. (What the hell had he been doing? *Examining* her? Why couldn't people stop poking their noses in all the time?) Still more uncomfortable was the interest shown by Graham, Alex's brother and a lecturer in the Psychology department. He came to dinner most Fridays and had become quite obsessed by the rate the baby was developing.

Jake did his best to laugh it off.

'She takes after her mother,' he'd say with a smile, and change the subject.

It happened again that Friday. He'd had to drag Graham down from Sophie's room for supper. Graham was a tall man with a ready laugh. He gave the impression of having extra arms and legs because of the way he twisted them into knots when he grew animated. A typical neurotic psychologist.

'That child is special,' Graham mused during a lull in the conversation.

'Every child is special,' responded Jake promptly.

'Every parent *thinks* so. But the average child is, by definition, average. Sophie, though, is absolutely—'

'Absolutely normal. OK?'

Graham shot him a quick glance.

'You're touchy tonight, Jake.' He paused. 'How do they get on, the two of them?'

Alex laughed.

'Better than you and I did, Gray. She won't be the first girl to have a dimmer elder brother.'

Graham chuckled, and Jake took the chance to ask him about his skiing plans over the New Year.

Sophie was advanced, yes, but all the same she was a perfectly normal baby. A baby just like any other. Daniel might need special treatment, but then he was a special case. Sophie wasn't. There was no call to treat her specially.

Alex felt the same, too, though for her own reasons.

She was emphatic that they should bring her up like any other child – shown no special favouritism and given no special privileges. Alex herself came from a comfortable middle-class family; her father, a Lloyds underwriter, had recently retired to the Channel Islands for tax reasons. Rejecting this privileged background, she'd gone into teaching deprived children in the East End of London. Now, after a good fifteen years of harsh realities, her Utopian fervour had lost its edge and she looked upon the injustices of the world with a more ironic eye. But when it came to her own children her principles were as clear-cut as ever, and she was determined not to slip into the temptation of favouring one against the other, or either against the general run.

That was fine by Jake. The less fuss people made of the child the better.

They spent the afternoon of the Saturday two weeks before Christmas decorating the house. By three o'clock daylight was already fading, and the holly and bells sprayed in artificial snow stood out sharper and brighter than ever on the darkening window-panes.

Jake was putting the finishing touches to the tree while Alex waited with Daniel in the corridor outside.

'Ready yet?' she called, her patience audibly wearing thin.

'Hang on just a moment.'

The Christmas-tree lights weren't working and he had to check each bulb in turn. At last he found the dud and replaced it. A galaxy of tiny coloured lights suddenly sprang to life, echoed tenfold in the gold and silver glass balls that festooned the branches.

21

From the baby bouncer behind him, Sophie let out a gurgle of delight.

'Fairy lights,' he told her. 'Good aren't they?'

For reply, the infant kicked and jigged up and down. She loved this contraption, for it held her upright and let her see everything going on around. She was in her favourite place, too – suspended from the beam that divided the kitchen from the living room; by twisting one way or the other she could see the whole of the large open-plan area.

After Daniel was born, these two rooms had been knocked into one large space. He could play in the main part while still being visible from the kitchen. Building-blocks and soft toys were piled untidily in a corner. One wall was painted as a blackboard and another held a panel of softboard on which were pinned brightly coloured cut-outs of animals and letters. Otherwise, up to the height he could reach, the room was clear of books, crockery, records and anything else that could be damaged or broken. The Christmas tree stood in a tub on a table, well out of range.

'Why are we waiting?' came Alex's chant from the corridor, accompanied by high-pitched, piglet-like squeals from Daniel. The boy was getting dangerously excited.

Jake swept up the remains of the tinsel, put the hammer and screwdriver safely away, straightened the cards on the mantelpiece and checked that the Chinese lanterns were securely taped to the paper chains. Then, switching on a tape cassette of carols from King's College chapel, he swung the door open.

'Wow!' gasped Alex theatrically. 'Look at that!'

She walked Daniel in, holding his hands above his head to steer him. The boy's muscle tone wasn't good and he went floppy unless he was supported all the time. He pulled away and stumbled into Jake's arms.

Jake lifted him up with a groan.

'You're getting heavy, Danny boy,' he laughed, bouncing him up and down.

Though he was shorter than a normal six-year-old, the lad had the Down's tendency towards plumpness. He was a lovely child, full of affection, and always clinging and hugging. He was mostly a happy one, too, and smiled a lot, despite all he had to contend with. His mouth was small, for instance, and his tongue tended to loll out, and this gave him constant difficulty breathing. He couldn't yet feed himself properly and dropped or spilled everything he held. He loved playing in the swimming-pool, but he had a common heart defect which meant that his play time had to be strictly rationed. He loved music – right now he was rocking back and forth in time to a carol – and he'd sit absorbed as Alex played him a simple tune on the small upright piano in the corner, but his flattened hands and stiff, stubby fingers prevented him from copying her. That made him frustrated, which in turn led to tantrums. He battled on courageously, but his need was so great.

Jake returned his hug.

'Like it?' he asked.

Daniel's reply was thick and indistinct, but his face wore a smile so broad that the slits of his eyes were almost closed. As he jigged up and down, he reached out to grasp one of the light bulbs. Jake had to steer him away: he wasn't very sensitive to pain and might easily burn or cut himself without knowing.

Daniel started to kick.

'Tell him *no-go*,' said Alex on her way past to the stove. 'He's got to learn.' No-go was the word for things, such as electric sockets and sharp knives, that were not to be touched.

'It's OK,' Jake replied gently, letting the boy down.

He led him towards the bay window. 'Come on, Danny, let's make some more paper chains.'

But Daniel still wanted to explore the light bulbs. He broke free and, clambering over, tried to get up onto the table. As Jake bent to lift him away, he let out an angry howl and lashed out with his fists.

'Tell him,' repeated Alex from the kitchen area.

That wasn't the way. The boy might have the strength of a six-year-old but he had the comprehension of a child of two. Jake looked around for a distraction and caught sight of the unbreakable plastic torch Daniel loved.

'Danny?' he called, flashing it at him. 'Look!'

Within a second the boy had forgotten about the Christmas lights. Crawling over to his father, he seized the torch in both hands and began playing happily with it.

Jake sank into the low sofa. Alex brought him a cup of tea. For a moment she lingered with her hand on his shoulder. He looked up into her face. These past years had taken their toll. Her hazel eyes were tired and ringed, and the smile-lines that streamed out at her temples had grown permanently etched into her skin, along with the worry-lines. Was her hair greyer than when he'd last noticed? Had the freckles across her nose joined together more?

'Let's go away for a weekend before you start back to school,' he suggested. 'We need a break.'

'You can, Jake. I've got too much to do, coping here.'

'That's just the point . . .'

He gave up; this wasn't the moment. Her mind was here, in the home. She was looking around the room, her face softened with contentment. Daniel, Sophie, the tree, the presents.

'Our first proper Christmas,' she said quietly. 'As a proper family.'

24

He thought back to the previous Christmas, when she'd been taking the fertility drugs and was waiting to go into hospital to try to conceive another child. And how he'd promised it would be all right. And then how . . . He flashed her a glance.

They exchanged a smile. He squeezed her hand.

'We're over the worst, angel. It's all going to be great from now on.'

'Yes, it is, isn't it.' She withdrew her hand and looked at her watch. 'Will you do Danny's tea or shall I?'

'Steady now! One . . . two . . . three . . .'

The sleek white rat sat on its hind legs on the desk-top, balancing a ping-pong ball on the end of its pink nose. Its tiny paws pedalled the air and its whiskers twitched as it struggled to keep the ball aloft.

'Four . . . five . . .' continued Jake, trying to keep from cracking up.

The rat suddenly lost its balance, and the ball fell and bounced away off the table. Helen, standing behind him, caught it and handed it back. Her sapphire eyes danced with amusement.

'You need never worry about a pension, Jake.'

With a laugh he clicked his fingers and the handsome young animal obediently got back onto its hind legs.

'A fiver he makes it to ten, OK?'

Just as he was positioning the lightweight ball on the tip of the small pink nose, the phone rang just a few inches away on the desk. The animal started in terror, scrabbled down the table-leg and shot off into a corner behind a pile of *Nature* magazines. Helen quickly shut the door before going after it.

Herbert was on the line. There was an edge of excitement in his usual dour tone.

'Jake? Can you spare a minute?'

Herbert sat on his hands on the edge of his large partner's desk, rocking back and forth, while Jake read the letter. The professor had a plump, round face. His eyes were heavily ringed from years of peering into microscopes, and he carried his glasses suspended round his neck by a length of stethoscope tubing.

Jake lowered the letter.

'That's big money, Herbert.'

'It's a big project.' The triumph in his tone was unconcealed. He held Jake's eye steadily. 'Well?'

'It's a big decision, too.'

'You mean, you need to think it over?'

No, of course he didn't. He should talk it over with Alex first, that was all. He knew what she'd say. She simply wouldn't *understand*. What the hell? Did he need her permission to accept the biggest break in his career?

Alex wanted to see him as the doctor he'd always been, not the scientist he'd become. She respected the one and mistrusted the other. He'd always intended to give up research work after a few years and go back to hospital practice full time, anyway. He'd been planning to make the move shortly, but this new opportunity had come up. The breakthrough in finding the intelligence gene had opened a whole new field and raised a thousand questions that cried out to be answered. Could he turn his back on the challenge? The money, the equipment, the resources, a major research fellowship backed by a major American pharmaceutical company – it was all here, on a plate. All he had to do was say yes. Which was he: a doctor serving men or a scientist serving *man*?

He handed the letter back to the professor.

'I'll get some substrate sent over to Stanford,' he said. Herbert smiled.

'That's more like it.'

'We'll need to start recruiting.'

'George can give you a few names, Jake.'

'I'll get Helen onto a data link, too.'

Herbert got up from the desk – he suddenly seemed very short – and moved round to his own side, where he slipped on his glasses and consulted his diary.

'There's a Faculty Board in the second week of January. Can you make it by then?'

Later, he wished he hadn't told her. At least, not in so many words. And especially not with her brother Graham there. As a fellow academic, shouldn't *he* have understood?

Graham lived a few streets away in the top half of a large Victorian granite house like their own. Divorced and without children, he was constantly dropping in for tea, supper, drinks or just a chat. He was two years older than Alex – she was herself five years older than Jake – and brother and sister were very close. Jake sometimes wondered if he'd gone all out for the post at Bristol University just to be closer to her.

Supper was over. Both children were in bed. Jake sat on the sofa, going through a pile of case reports. Graham sprawled in an armchair, bottle and glass in hand, clearly enjoying the tension in the atmosphere. Alex moved around the room, clearing up toys and books.

Graham addressed his sister.

'So naïve, these scientists. They're kids. They think the world's a sandpit to play around in. Can't see it'll end in tears. Know something? Einstein said that if he'd known relativity would produce the atom bomb, he'd have become a locksmith. What should you have been, Jake?'

'Don't be provocative, Gray,' said Alex.

'A vet?'

Jake bit his tongue and said nothing.

'But, Alex,' Graham protested innocently, 'you were telling me yourself about animal engineering. Like those super-pigs without any fat at all. What did you say happened to them?'

'Look, Gray, it's his decision—'

'They die from cold in winter. And those cows specially bred to produce double the milk: they only live half as long. You can't calculate all the costs before you start.'

Alex couldn't resist playing along.

'Jake can do anything.'

'Sure, *he* can draw an arbitrary line and say he won't step over it. But he can't commit the others. Knowledge belongs to anybody. What he's doing with animals today, someone else will do with people tomorrow.' He put on a whining voice. ' "Please, Doctor, make me a child who's got blue eyes, blond hair, who'll be college football champ and win lots of scholarships . . ." Designer kids!'

Jake looked up to see that Alex had stopped in the middle of what she was doing and was eyeing him with a worried, accusing frown. Graham had struck a sympathetic nerve.

'Gray's right, Jake,' she said with quiet force. 'It's only a step from Mendel to Mengele.'

Jake flushed with exasperation.

'For God's sake, Alex!' he snapped.

But he held back. There was no winning on this terrain. Alex had a set mind. Her world view was shaped by conspiracy theory. Science frightened her. The most innocent discovery was the thin end of some pernicious, dehumanising wedge. All he was really doing was messing around, making a few rats a bit brighter, a bit bigger, maybe live a bit longer. A pharmaceutical company would be backing the research, yes, but there was no suggestion of using the work for genetically enhancing *people*. That was just Alex's and Graham's paranoia. It was the world of cheap thrillers and sensationalist movies. The real world wasn't like that. Scientists were responsible men, they had families and loved ones, they respected their fellow beings as anyone else did. They just didn't go round tampering with human life.

Hear that, Alex? Frankenstein is dead! Dead. *Dead*.

He slammed down his papers and rose to his feet. He went over towards the kitchen. He had himself under control.

'Coffee for you, Graham? Alex?'

The week before Christmas was a nightmare on the ward.

Late one night, Jeremy, the nine-year-old haemophiliac and the joker of the pack, was playing pranks on the other children, swinging along the curtain rails from bed to bed like a monkey, when he fell and bruised himself badly. The coagulation therapy wasn't anywhere near complete, and for several days Jake was very worried about his condition.

Then Gianni had a sudden relapse and had to be moved into intensive care. The retrovirus seemed to be upsetting the regulation of his blood stem cells. The rate at which he deteriorated baffled everyone. In the early hours of one morning, Jake was woken by an urgent call. He hurried over to the hospital. The boy was failing fast and there seemed nothing anyone could do.

Later in the morning, a priest arrived. Gianni had

slipped into unconsciousness and his olive skin had that cold, greenish pallor Jake knew all too well.

Jake stood beside the parents while the priest administered the last rites. He'd seen those faces all too often, as well: drained, defeated, full of puzzled helplessness. The service was brief, almost hasty. The nurses had moved a discreet distance away, as if ashamed they'd failed their patient. A teddy-bear with bright eyes and a fixed smile lay tucked in beside the boy. The paper chains looping between the walls and the wisps of tinsel hanging from the strip lights celebrated that birth which had promised conquest over death.

'*Pax Domini tibi*,' intoned the priest as he sprinkled holy water on the boy's pallid brow.

A sudden burst of anger rose in Jake's throat. He remembered feeling the same welling rage at his mother's death. Rage for the rage she would not feel herself. A devout Catholic, she had made her peace with death, and she'd died with peace on her face.

He glanced at the boy's parents. They now wore a look of calm acceptance. The priest had taken charge of the boy's spirit and they, too, were at peace. Jake felt another surge of anger. How was it that they didn't see humility as humiliation, submission as subjection? As a young boy, he'd been fervent in his faith. Even now he only had to shut his eyes and he could smell the incense at the Mass to which his mother would take him every Sunday while his father stayed at home, reading the papers or washing the car. But, around twelve, he'd gone through his Age of Reason and rejected it all. Later, science kept God from the door and medicine kept his eyes upon earthly things. More recently, too, there was Alex and her influence. She was more concerned with getting things right down here on earth.

When the priest had finished anointing and blessing the dying boy, Jake ushered the small group out of the room. In the corridor outside, Gianni's mother gripped his hand. There were tears in her eyes. Tears of gratitude.

'Thank you, Doctor,' she said. 'Thank you for trying.'

'I'm only so sorry—' he began.

The woman held up her hand. She groped for the words.

'We are only humans, Dr Chalmers. We must keep to our human affairs. We cannot interfere in the divine plan.'

Leave unto doctors the things that are doctors', and unto God the things that are God's?

All very well, but where did you draw the line? Were arms and legs *human* things, and genes somehow *God's* things? Wasn't the first heart-transplant surgeon accused of playing God? Why was it acceptable to modify horses and dogs, cattle and crops, by selective breeding, while unacceptable to modify them by altering their genes directly?

Ah, Christ. Where was he? Stumbling about in unknown territory, beyond the borders of all the science and medicine that had gone before. He was lost, adrift without his bearings. He needed to get a fix on something. Where had his own faith gone? Couldn't he rediscover it and find some way of bridging the chasm between the small miracles that he performed every day in the lab and on the ward and the supremely great miracle that was needed to save a life like Gianni's?

The real nightmare, however, took place at the labs. It happened on the morning of Christmas Day.

Sophie had a temperature and Alex and he were up half the night looking after her. Then Daniel, who caught the excitement of Christmas even though he didn't understand it, got up at half past five and insisted on going downstairs and opening his presents.

31

It wasn't until mid-morning that Jake could take a break and slip over to the labs.

He hurried through the light crust of snow that had fallen during the night and let himself into the Department of Medicine with his electronic pass-card. The building was quite deserted. He took the stairs, not trusting the lift. A wan sun filtered in through the metal-framed windows and his heels echoed hollowly down the empty corridors that led to the Genetics Research Unit.

The moment he let himself into the main laboratory, he sensed trouble. In the corner, Herbert's rats were running back and forth in their cages, clearly ill at ease. Then he heard a muffled shriek from the dormitory room where his own rats were, followed by a vicious snarl. He hurried down the lab and flung the door open.

A scene of carnage and havoc met his eye.

Swinging gently back and forth at the bottom of the treadmill lay one rat, its eyes closed and its legs stiff and still. From the angle of its head, Jake knew at once that its neck was broken. Small tufts of white fur littered the floor and blood smeared the wood shavings. Behind, caught in a plastic play-tube, lay the half-devoured body of another. And there, hunched in a corner and baring bloodied fangs, cowered a third. Alive, and watching him.

Only two of the six offspring remained. Their coats caked with dried blood, they snarled at one another from opposite corners. The bodies of their four brothers lay eyeless and gaping on the bedding between them. The mother rat herself had been cornered in a maze and savagely mutilated.

Out of sixteen, only four were alive. And even as he watched, a fight broken out between an adult and one of the young ones.

He whipped the door panel open and made to pick up the adult rat, but the animal lunged forward and bit him viciously on the hand. Grabbing a glove, he hauled it out by the tail.

As the rat dangled in the air, twisting and snapping, Jake knew in that instant that everything had gone catastrophically wrong. His stomach heaved with horror as he realised what he was witnessing.

The gene trigger had failed. The whole process had been thrust into reverse. He was no longer looking at a highly evolved, civilised, laboratory-bred specimen but a sewer rat, a throw-back to a savage, primitive stock.

These rats had gone feral. Reverted to wild.

Almost at once another thought more horrific than the first struck him and froze his blood.

How old was this rat? Eighteen or nineteen months. What was that in human years? Twelve, perhaps thirteen.

Twelve, perhaps thirteen human years.

THREE

Why, of all days in the calendar, did he have to be late for lunch on Christmas Day? 'The lab clock had stopped.' What kind of feeble excuse was that?

Alex was seething. They had people round – Graham and his latest girlfriend, a student half his own age, and the recently widowed lady from two doors down, too. She'd spun out the gin-and-tonics as long as she could, but in the end they'd had to start without him. During the meal he struggled to be sociable, she could see, but he kept going off into his own thoughts, and there were embarrassing moments when the conversation passed to him and he had no idea where he was.

Even after the guests had left, he remained in this irritating, self-absorbed mood. He kept staring at Sophie, who had now recovered from her night's sickness, with a strange, haunted expression as if nothing else in the room existed, not the Christmas tree stripped of its presents, not the wrapping-paper and toys littering the floor, not Alex herself nor even Daniel. He simply wasn't *there*.

'Jake, are you all right?' she asked finally. 'Jake?'

'What? I'm fine.'

'You could have been a bit more with-it at lunch.'

'Sorry. I'm not . . . feeling too great.'

'What's wrong? A temperature?'

'No, no. It's nothing.'

After tea, he took Sophie upstairs and put her to bed. A while later Alex went up to the bedroom herself to kiss the child good night and found him standing over the cot, staring at the sleeping infant with the same strange, disturbed look on his face. Downstairs, he did his best playing with Daniel and his new trucks, and later he spent half an hour reading the boy nursery stories in bed. Then more friends came in for drinks and he made a supreme effort to be hospitable, but as soon as they left he withdrew into himself again. The two of them spent supper in virtual silence.

Early next morning, he was off to the labs again. He came into the kitchen in his duffel-coat to say goodbye.

'But it's Boxing Day,' she protested.

'Not in the animal kingdom,' he replied.

'And you're going out again this afternoon.'

'You can come too. Best party on the wards.'

'But the children—'

'Bring them.'

'That's not the point, Jake.'

He'd long gone and she was preparing the children's lunch when she suddenly understood. It all fell into place. Those trips to the labs when the rest of the world was on holiday, those late-night sessions when most people were at home with their families. That small present she'd seen on his desk in Christmas paper, with a card marked, *To Helen, with much love, Jake*. And now his distracted behaviour these past two days.

Of course. Helen.

She'd had her suspicions all along. Jake himself had said she was attractive, vivacious, bright. Alex had caught a glimpse of her at a concert one evening. She was a good ten years younger, too. Oh, God.

Daniel was banging a toy truck against the floor, Sophie was crying, the kettle was whistling, the phone had just started to ring . . . For a second she felt like walking out right there and then and slamming the door behind her. Let Helen cope with Daniel, look after Sophie, run the house and a full-time job *and* be bright and fun. Then she pulled herself together. No modern marriage could be blind to the likelihood of one or other partner being unfaithful at some point. Why else did one in three end in divorce? She'd often thought what she'd do if it happened to her. She'd ask him quite simply if he was in love with the girl. If not, the affair was unimportant and a mature, intelligent woman should be able to find a way of living around it. But if he was, their own relationship was dead, the family ties went by the board and she'd do well to pack his bags for him. She could cope by herself. Better being on one's own than living a lie together.

But now that it *had* happened, all the theory went out of the window. She felt vulnerable and afraid. Betrayed, too – had it been going on all the time she was having Sophie? And what now lay in store for them all?

She sat down with a cup of tea and stared out into the flat, purple-grey morning, watching the robins squabbling over scraps on the bird tray, and wondered where she'd gone wrong. Perhaps she'd been too dull and serious; certainly, life hadn't been much fun these past years since Daniel. The two of them were very different people, too: they looked at the world differently, wanted different things from life and disagreed over the really important issues. This new job of his, for instance. Helen wouldn't have given him a hard time; no, she'd have encouraged him, supported him. Perhaps she herself was too critical, too judgemental. What right had she to pass sentence on matters of conscience?

That evening, she made a special effort to be accommodating and show she was happy to talk about whatever was preoccupying him. But he wasn't to be drawn,

36

and the supper passed in an atmosphere of well-intentioned but disengaged fondness.

Later that night, on her way to bed, she looked in on his study. She found him sitting in his dressing-gown in a studded leather chair, staring vacantly into the shadows. A bottle of whisky lay half empty on the table beside him.

Standing behind the chair, she began gently stroking his hair. He let his head sink into the caress.

'About Herbert's offer, Jake,' she began. 'I know it's very important to you. If it's what you want, take it.'

He just shook his head.

'Those things I said the other day,' she went on. 'I know how science works. Turning the work down yourself won't stop someone else picking it up. At least if *you* do it, you can control it.'

'You don't need to say this, Alex,' he replied.

'I know, but I *mean* it.'

He looked up at her. In the half-light his angular face seemed longer than ever. She couldn't bear to see the pain and distress sunk deep in his dark eyes. Somehow she had to help him unburden his heart. She felt strangely calm now. They'd coped with far worse. Daniel and Sophie had forged bonds that couldn't be dissolved overnight.

'Tell me what's troubling you,' she said tenderly. 'It's better out in the open.'

He braved a smile.

'Just got rather a lot on my mind.' He patted her hand. 'You go to bed.'

'I'm not blind, Jake. We're grown-up people. We can work round problems, provided we recognise them.'

'There's nothing to worry about.'

'Jake . . .'

But she checked herself. She knew from his tone that there was no point in pressing him further. He was one of those men who appeared open and accessible on the surface but who hid their real selves behind layers and screens and found it very difficult to speak of their innermost feelings.

She went to the door.

'Well, don't be too long,' she said simply.

In the early hours she woke, aware that he wasn't there beside her. She lay awake for a while, listening for sounds, then finally put on her dressing-gown and went downstairs. The house was in darkness and he was nowhere to be found. As she passed the front door she noticed the chain was off. His duffel-coat was gone from the stand in the hallway.

Oh, God, he'd walked out. Literally, like that. Without a word.

She went into his study, half expecting to find a note on the desk. *Dearest Alex, This will come as a shock to you* . . . But there was only a pile of computer print-out lying on top, covered with a mass of calculations and diagrams that meant nothing to her. But as she was turning away, her eye caught a small ivory card in the letter-rack. The top half alone was visible, showing a simple black cross. She took it out. Under the cross, in Gothic print, was inscribed, 'Church of the Sacred Heart' and, beneath, a list of the times of services.

Puzzled as well as anxious, she went back up to bed and lay staring at the pattern of the street-light on the ceiling until, after what seemed like hours, she heard footsteps on the stairs and, without a word, Jake came in, undressed and slipped silently in beside her.

In the morning she came down to find Daniel dressed

and fed, Sophie changed and in her play-pen and the table laid for their own breakfast. 'This Week's Composer' was playing on the radio – Borodin, she guessed, though it was hard to make it out above the din – the scrambled eggs had turned to rock in the pan and a smell of burnt toast filled the room. Everything seemed perfectly normal. The night belonged to a different, fictitious world.

Half way through breakfast, though, Jake suddenly went quiet. Rising to his feet, he switched the radio to a French station and took it over to the play-pen. Sophie crawled forward and examined it intently, babbling quietly to herself.

Alex managed a bright smile.

'Uh-oh. Who have we been reading now? Not Dr Spock. Not Miriam Stoppard. I know: *How To Raise A Brighter Child*.'

'Alex, there's a serious point to this.'

'You've got to be joking!' she laughed.

'It's actually quite important she hears other languages.'

'But she can't speak her own yet!'

'Just listen!' He paused; Sophie was imitating a word the announcer had just spoken. 'Hear that?'

'So what? That's how children learn anyway.'

'Yes, but she'll now remember that sound.'

'She could learn it at school, like any other child.'

'School is too late,' he persisted. '*This* is her brain's peak growth phase. Now.'

Puzzled, she handed him his coffee. She tried to keep her tone light.

'It's not too late for all the other kids on this planet.'

'That's because educationalists don't know the facts.'

'You should be in politics, Jake.'

He wasn't smiling. He leaned forward, stabbing the table with his forefinger to emphasise the point.

39

'Did you know that half a person's intellect is already formed by the time they're *four*? By the age of eight, *eighty per cent* is fixed! All your secondary education can only make a twenty per cent difference. It's criminal to squander those early years.'

She smiled more tightly. She wasn't going to get through by teasing.

'I thought we'd agreed, Sophie's going to be treated just like any other child.'

He shot her a hard, defiant glance.

'You love her, don't you?'

'What a ridiculous question!'

'Then you'll want her to have the best possible start in life.'

'Of course, but—'

'The best possible start in life,' he repeated. 'No buts.'

Breakfast ended in a strained silence. Afterwards, she cleared away, washed up and then took Daniel on his morning visit to the toilet. When she came back she found that Jake had gone to his study. She poured another cup of coffee and took it in to him. Somehow she had to get through to him. She'd never known him in such an intractable mood before.

He was just coming off the phone as she entered the room. His voice was low and urgent. She guessed who he'd been calling.

'Sorry,' he said, refusing the coffee. 'I've got to get over to the labs.'

'That was Helen?'

'Nothing serious.'

She forced herself to sound casual.

'Bring her back. Christmas is no time to be alone.'

'Helen? She never eats lunch. Always on one diet or another.' He picked up the stack of print-outs and managed a smile. 'I won't be late this time. Promise.'

He leaned forward to kiss her, but she moved

40

and the kiss went awkwardly askew. He patted her on the shoulder in a comradely fashion instead and headed for the door. He hesitated briefly, as if about to say something, then with a small grunt he left. She stood watching him through the study window as he walked purposefully through the shallow snow to the car. He started up and drove off without a backward glance.

She stared after him for a moment, biting her lip. What should she do? Who could she ask for advice? On impulse, she reached for the phone and dialled Graham's number.

'Gray, I'm worried,' she said right away. 'I think Jake's having an affair with that girl in the labs.'

'Helen? Nonsense!' barked her brother at the other end. 'He's crazy about you. He *adores* you. And the kids.'

'You saw how he was at lunch the other day.'

'The chap's under a lot of strain. You're being paranoid, darling. Relax.' His tone was bright – too bright? How would he really know, anyway? 'Look, we'll talk about it at the Marshs' tonight.'

'I can't come. The children.'

'Get a baby-sitter!'

'You know Danny. If it's not Suzanne, forget it. I expect Jake'll be there, though.' She paused as an idea occurred to her. 'If you see him, keep an eye on him, will you, Gray?'

The streets were dark and cold and the air heavy with the threat of more snow. He'd looked in on the party for a few minutes earlier in the evening, but Graham had cornered him and started quizzing him about his job, his marriage, his ambitions. He'd had a drink or two, no more, then left. Drink was his father's way out; it solved nothing. He'd tried it the

41

other night at home, hoping that the alcohol would dampen his brain down and quieten the noise of his thoughts, but it hadn't. Now, as he walked through the empty, snow-grimed streets, it was worse than ever. Whatever he tried – whistling, humming, even talking aloud to himself – he couldn't seem to quash the clamour in his head, forever arguing, accusing, disclaiming, justifying. Could nothing silence a troubled conscience?

The sight of the rats, reverted to feral, constantly flashed across his mind. That morning, Helen had called to show him the Golgi stains she'd run on tissue from one whose brain she'd ablated to examine; it revealed two astonishingly bright, dense clusters of white specks, standing out amid the maze of other cells and their gossamer-thin connecting pathways. These hyperactive sites were the amygdala, the seat of the emotions of fear and rage. What in Christ's name did that mean for . . . ?

He walked briskly, without sense of time or direction. He passed lovers embracing in alleyways and youths hanging shiftlessly in doorways. He saw drunks brawling and hookers soliciting. From time to time a police car or ambulance sped past, sirens wailing, hurrying about more important business. This was someone else's world and he was living someone else's life in it.

What had he done?

Stumbling on, with the sad, hollow city centre behind, he steered his steps uphill towards home. As he reached the stolid granite houses of middle-class Clifton, he turned off his route and headed down a side-street. After a hundred yards, he stopped. The snow had all but blotted out the signboard: Church of the Sacred Heart. Twice since Christmas he had slipped surreptitiously into this church, though he'd only stayed for a moment, not trusting his motives or his responses. He held back on the step. Snow had begun to fall again. Flakes tumbled thickly from the purple-black sky, muffling the dim glow from the church windows and turning to a dazzling white shower under the street-lights. With sudden decisiveness, he hurried on up.

The church was empty and dark, lit only by electric altar candles. Loudspeakers with their wiring unconcealed hung from the columns, the choir stalls had been cheaply modernised and the font was built of plastic marble. The tawdriness shocked and disappointed him. But in the aroma of incense, dusty stonework and wood polish that rose giddily to his nostrils, the past twenty-five years slipped away and he felt himself once again the innocent, fervent boy of eight his mother had taken every week to Mass.

Genuflecting as he crossed the nave, he took a seat at the end of the front pew from where he could contemplate the figure of Our Lady. She wore a faint, mysterious half-smile, as if both saddened and amused by the frailties and struggles of the world. He slipped to his knees.

The clink of keys nearby finally broke his prayers. He looked up. A short, fresh-faced priest stood a few feet away, regarding him intently. He felt suddenly embarrassed and rose to his feet.

'I'm sorry,' he mumbled. 'You want to close up.'

'No hurry.' The priest eyed him thoughtfully. 'I've seen you here before.'

'I used to be ... I mean, I was brought up ...' He broke off.

'I understand.'

The priest stood, waiting patiently. How Jake longed to unburden his heart to him. Did he still have the faith? Did he have the courage?

'I wonder,' he began, 'if I could talk to you some time.'

The priest smiled.

'There's a pub where I often pay a pastoral visit on the way home,' he said.

It was eleven thirty by the wall clock. The labs were silent and still but for the knocking of an air-locked radiator. Apart from the low-level safety lights in the corridors, the building was dark.

Jake sat at his office desk, writing the letter by hand. He couldn't bring himself to use Helen's typewriter: he knew what he was doing to her career.

> Dear Herbert,
> I very much regret that, after considerable thought, I have come to the decision that I cannot participate in the new research project. I feel unable, consequently, to remain a member of the department and have taken steps to terminate my work in progress.
> I intend instead to devote myself to my work at the Infirmary, where I feel my energies are most needed. Above all, as I'm sure you will understand, I want to spend more time with my family and give our new child the time and care she needs at this critical stage.
> I can only say how sorry I am for the disruption this may cause you and the Department.
> Yours,
> Jake.

He wrote it out again, making minor changes, then left it in an envelope on Herbert's desk where the professor would find it when he returned after the Christmas break.

He returned to his own office. There he took out all the files on the human intelligence gene and, sheet by sheet, fed the whole stack into the shredder.

Next, he went to the main lab. He unplugged the power supply to the cryostat that stored the brain-tissue slices on which Helen had been working; by daybreak, they would have degenerated beyond use. One by one, he destroyed the histological slides and gene cultures by exposing them to high-level radiation, then went round the room with a glass dropper contaminating every phial and jar that contained any product of the research. Finally, having checked that nothing of any value survived, he took a bottle of chloroform, a hypodermic and a thick leather glove and went into the dormitory area.

The surviving rats, now three in number, had been isolated from each other. Skulking in the corners of their cages, they spat and snarled as he approached. As he drew closer, his skin broke out in a cold sweat. In the space of barely twelve hours, their coats had grown wiry and dark, their fangs had lengthened and their bodies taken on a coarse, feral shape. Nausea rose in his throat. *He* had done this. *He* had made this happen by tampering with things he didn't fully understand. The gene triggers had got jammed and the system had flipped. Generations of healthy evolution had been wiped out at a stroke. And there was nothing he could do about it: the decay was *built into their genes*!

He grabbed the first rat in his gloved hand. Holding the wriggling, snapping creature on its back, he aimed the needle direct for its heart and sank it in. Within half a second the rat was dead, with just its hind legs twitching as the nerves gradually stilled.

Then he went for the next.

He felt physically sick as he threw the heavy, limp

45

corpses into a plastic refuse bag and sealed the neck. He checked the labs one last time, then went down to the incinerator in the basement.

Alex glanced up at the clock as she heard the key in the latch. Ten past one. She'd called Graham around eleven, only to be told that Jake had left the party several hours before. She heard him stamping the snow off his boots in the vestibule, then a moment later the door opened. She was angry and hurt. Of course she knew where he'd been. Her stomach tightened with apprehension. What was he going to say? Was this *it*? She turned, bracing herself for the worst.

He stood in the doorway. His face was grey with exhaustion but he looked strangely calm, almost at ease.

He stepped wearily forward.

'It's all over,' he said in a dry, matter-of-fact voice. 'I've done what I had to.'

'Jake, I was so worried . . .' she began.

He hardly seemed to register.

'I've written to Herbert. I'm not taking the job. Or going back to the labs, ever. I'm finished with all of that.'

'Jake?'

'I'm going to concentrate on where I'm needed. Helping people. On the ward. And here.'

She hesitated for a moment, overwhelmed by the unexpectedness of the news. Then she went over to him and drew him against her. His cheeks were cold and his hands numb.

'You've come home,' she said quietly.

'Yes, I'm home.'

FOUR

Herbert stormed round the moment he returned from holiday and spent a brief, ill-tempered session with Jake in the study. He told him he was suspending him with immediate effect and instructing the university's lawyers to sue for damages. The Department had had to turn down the American funding deal and with it any chance of taking a leading role in the field of genetic enhancement. He himself was in serious danger of losing his job and Helen had seen five years of her career destroyed overnight. He hadn't come to argy-bargy, though, he said. He just wanted a simple answer to a simple question: *What the hell had made him do such a fucking stupid thing?*

'I couldn't go on,' replied Jake quietly. 'In all conscience, I could not.'

Herbert fixed him with a cold, venomous stare.

'Know what they say over there? "If you ain't gonna shit, get off the pot." Don't foul it up for other people. How does your conscience feel about George, and Francis, and Helen?'

'The alternative was even worse.'

An ugly curl twisted the professor's mouth.

'Jake, you're sick. You need psychiatric help. I blame myself: I saw the signs long ago . . .'

Jake let him rant on. He said nothing; there *was* nothing to say. After a while, still angrier for not having found a reason he could comprehend, Herbert left.

A few days later, a letter arrived from the faculty board confirming Jake's dismissal, terminating his research grant and requesting the return of his electronic pass-card. The same afternoon, a large carton arrived at the house in one of the Department vans. It contained the contents of his desk drawers, his photos of Alex and the children, his personal books and other effects. There was also a short note from Helen. She felt he should know that she was going to continue the work. It would mean starting at the beginning again and it would take time, and she might not succeed at all, but she had notebooks that she'd been keeping as a starting-point. She had to go on: as a scientist she had a commitment to knowledge.

I'll never forget what you once said [she added in a postscript]. 'Remember where the primordial apple came from? It came off the Tree of Knowledge. Science *is* knowledge, and it's man's inescapable condition to seek after it.' You can destroy the answers, Jake, but you can't destroy the questions.

Was he trying to reverse this inescapable human condition, to put the genie back in the bottle, to turn back the clock to a prelapsarian paradise? Since his talk with the priest, he'd begun stopping by at the church on his way home from the Infirmary in the evening – he'd even managed a Sunday Mass, giving Alex an excuse about a hospital Ethics Committee meeting – and, cautiously and with much self-doubt, he'd grown to find some comfort and reassurance in the promise of forgiveness and mercy.

He felt calmer and more resolved. The threatened writ from the faculty board did not materialise – most likely, they feared the publicity – and he threw himself into his work on the ward. At first he felt his colleagues there were avoiding him, and at one point the Administrator asked if he was sure he was fit to work – he meant, was he mentally fit? – but very soon the strange goings-on up the road were forgotten in the more immediate daily dramas of hospital life.

Partly out of habit and partly until a new schedule could be worked out, the morning hours he'd previously worked at the labs he now spent at home with the family. In mid-January, Alex's term started and she resumed her job. A week later, Daniel's special school went back, too. A mini-van came each morning to fetch him, returning him in the afternoon, when Suzanne, the young nanny, took charge until Alex got back. This meant that, during the mornings, Jake had Sophie all to himself. The pleasure and excitement he drew from her company grew daily. He played with her, talked to her and watched as her boundless curiosity drove her to learn and discover ever more of the world about her. Soon he came to look forward to those hours together as the best part of the day. Before long, he'd established a fixed routine: he spent Monday, Wednesday and Friday mornings until twelve mid-day at home, making up the hours by working later into the evenings.

The nightmare seemed left behind, and he'd make sure it never surfaced again. He'd keep it at bay by the sheer power of his love. Love and care would be her salvation.

Sophie was alert, playful, full of curiosity and perpetually inventive. Her smile radiated into his heart. When she sat, as she would, for ten or fifteen minutes at a time, totally absorbed in a problem she'd set herself, with her violet eyes locked in concentration and her brow furrowed in its characteristic 'V', he could do nothing but watch and wonder.

Her appetite for novelty was limitless. From the moment she could crawl, she was off, exploring her floor-level world. She'd collect objects – a cotton-reel, a plant leaf, one of Daniel's trucks – and arrange them on the carpet in interesting patterns. One day he noticed she'd separated the red and blue objects into two piles, and when he looked again she'd rearranged them, this time into piles of equal number. Could she have grasped the concept of category? Surely not: this was February, and she was still only five months old.

He brought her a small xylophone at which she hammered away, totally absorbed in experimenting with the various sounds she could make by hitting the wooden bars in different ways. One of the earliest toys he made for her was a set of three large cubes cut out of foam rubber and painted with dots like dice; she played at moving these round until she had lined them up and the dots all matched. Later, he gave her a set of smaller cubes, each painted with dots of the same number, from one to six, and one morning he found she'd put them in batches – numbers one and two on one side and number three on the other, or two and three on one side and five on the other ... There could be no doubt: she was discovering how to add and subtract.

She grew quickly bored with Daniel's building-blocks, which were blank and painted in simple primary colours, so he gave her others with letters and painted in subtler tones. He also made her a large jigsaw of a farmyard from polystyrene board, with each piece shaped like an object – an animal, a tree, a tractor – and separately coloured. He'd spent two painstaking evenings over it, but she mastered it within minutes and was bored by it at the end of the morning. It ended up in Daniel's toy chest, where it remained, tried once and abandoned. Another evening, he cut out the same picture but made the shapes unrelated to the design. When she'd worked that out, he made her yet another, this time without any design or colouring, just pure shapes. She puzzled over this for all of an hour before putting it together quickly and faultlessly. By then it was March, the frost still lay crisp on the ground all day and the child was barely six months old.

Anyone in his profession knew that the infant brain was preoccupied first of all with laying down the basic motor links in the cortex. Distinctions between mind and body hadn't yet become established. He could see she was just as eager to explore her body's capabilities, and so he rigged up a low bar along one wall in the living room on which she could pull herself up and down. He bought her a child's trampoline, too, on which, long before she could walk, she loved to jig and roll. But her favourite of all was the bouncer in the doorway, where she could exercise herself and at the same time observe what was going on around her.

As he watched her unfurling like the spring across the city, Jake felt a sense of wonder and elation he'd never known before. She was, simply, the most beautiful, the most exciting child he'd ever seen.

Alex saw this and was glad. Jake had truly come home. After Herbert's visit that New Year's morning he'd simply told her he'd been sacked. Nothing more had been said. For several weeks she'd seen him watch the post anxiously, but whatever he feared had never arrived. She'd heard rumours that he'd wrecked the labs, set the animals free, even started a fire in the building but, whatever truth there was in these, she'd decided she'd rather not know, content merely upon the main thing, the outcome: he had given Helen up, he was no longer involved in that dubious work and, above all, he was putting the family first.

To celebrate their tenth wedding anniversary, they spent a weekend at the end of March at a small hotel in Dorset, leaving the children with Suzanne. This was the first time they'd been away on their own since before

Daniel was born. The first buds were breaking in the hedgerows, the air was sharp with the cries of birds and the warming earth exuded the promise of renaissance. They ate well, slept late, took picnics into the country and made love in fields and barns. They read Thomas Hardy to one another and their silences were rich and full of contentment. The long dark years seemed to be behind them.

Those years had started brightly enough.

They'd met at a wedding. At the time Jake was a junior houseman at St Bartholomew's Hospital; he'd done his medical training alongside his physiology degree at London University. She was teaching at a secondary school in Hackney. She'd never imagined love could be like that. The summer passed in a delirium of happiness. One day in the autumn he said he'd been offered a job as registrar in clinical genetics at the Bristol Royal Infirmary; would she marry him and come with him? She said yes. They left London in the New Year and were married that March. She was twenty-nine, he twenty-four.

She took a job at a school in a deprived inner-city area. For two years they tried for children of their own. Eventually she became pregnant and, the very week he was promoted to senior registrar, she gave birth to Daniel.

Even now, at night, she still woke up with the memory of the first sight of that baby – the shock, the disappointment, the self-disgust, as she took in the meaning of that flattened face, the stubby nose and those small, low-set ears.

Jake was wonderful. He explained everything very carefully. Down's syndrome, he said, was caused by an extra chromosome, but no one knew exactly how it occurred. Sometimes it had to do with the mother's age – she was only thirty-two – and sometimes it could be inherited. They could undergo tests to find out, but did they really want to know? If one of them turned out to be responsible, wouldn't that be hard to live with? It only really mattered if they wanted more children. And did they?

She remembered the day she made up her mind to find out. She was feeding Daniel, but his body was slack and he kept slipping off the nipple unless supported all the time. What would his life really be? All children needed brothers and sisters, but didn't he even more than most?

A friend of Jake's in Pathology ran the tests. When the results came through, Jake brought the photos home. Each plate showed a number of small, striped, maggot-like shapes, arranged in pairs. Chromosomes, he said. His own were fine, a perfect set of forty-six. Then he pointed to Daniel's: the boy possessed *three* number 21s when he should have had two – a Translocation 15/21. Then he showed her her own. The fault was clear to see. One of her 21s was somehow attached to one of her 15s. There it was, in black and white, betraying her as completely as a fingerprint on a murder weapon. She was the carrier.

What were the chances a second child would be normal?

'About one in five,' he told her. 'We could always test the foetus at sixteen weeks, though, and abort if it wasn't all right.'

Abort it? she protested. But life began at fourteen days!

'Yes, Alex,' he persisted gently, 'but what kind of life can a child like Daniel really expect?'

She knew. By then she'd read up. The boy would be backward. He'd catch infections. He probably wouldn't live to thirty. But he could still be a very happy person and live a fulfilling life. Jake knew better. He'd seen loving parents driven to despair, heard them secretly

53

confess they wished their child had never been born. But she couldn't condone the killing of an unborn child. All they could do was make the best of the child they had and give him all the love and care they could, knowing they could never have another.

The tragedy deeply affected Jake and spurred him to action. He persuaded Herbert to fund him in a special research project, and he arranged with the hospital board to allow him to work part time only at the Infirmary. From then on, he spent his mornings at the university labs and his afternoons on the hospital ward. Down's children, like many others with congenital disorders, were mentally retarded. The task he set himself would strike at the root. He'd go for the genes that coded for intelligence and the trigger mechanisms that switched them on.

And so his hunt for the intelligence gene began. Alex watched the months turn into years with nothing but frustration to show for his efforts. It was hard enough to define intelligence and harder still to analyse it in terms of brain chemistry, but almost impossible to isolate the genes responsible. It was like looking for an ant on Mount Everest. Finally, just before Daniel's fifth birthday, he announced triumphantly that he'd cracked it. He'd isolated the most promising human gene string and micro-injected it into fertilised rat eggs. Super-bright rats had resulted.

Meanwhile, Daniel was becoming less manageable as he grew bigger, and Alex had her own work problems at school. Jake was spending more and more time at the labs, often not returning home till nine or ten at night. He'd managed to take a couple of weeks off that summer and they'd rented a house by the sea, but Daniel caught a cold and was so temperamental in his unfamiliar surroundings that they'd had to come back after a few days. She was on the point of breaking down. For five years she'd kept control of herself, always been cheerful and smiling. She'd given Daniel everything, but everything still wasn't enough. He was a happy, cheerful child and coped with his disabilities bravely, but in the end the obstacles were insuperable. She'd sunk her whole self into caring for him, leaving nothing for Jake, let alone for herself. Her life was out of balance, and she began to realise bitterly that there was only one thing that could restore it: giving Daniel a brother or a sister.

They tried adopting, but the fact of Daniel weighed against them. The issue slowly grew out of all proportion until everything, from the mortgage to the marriage itself, seemed to depend on getting another child.

Jake dropped his research for a time and threw his energies into finding a solution. Eventually he came up with the answer: an *in vitro* fertilisation, based on a test he'd devised that would *guarantee* only a normal child.

Alex agreed to try it.

Five days after her next period, she went on a course of clomiphene citrate to make her multiple-ovulate. Eleven days later, she went into hospital. There, six ripe eggs were surgically removed from her ovaries. Jake then fertilised all six, and the process of life had begun. Here came the trick. When the six embryos had each divided into four cells, and while it was still possible to extract one cell without disturbing the embryo, he removed one cell from each and tested it for the presence of the extra chromosome.

One of the six was good.

The next morning that good embryo was implanted in her womb and the rest destroyed.

She watched anxiously for signs of a period, but soon she knew the new life had taken. Jake had been able to tell from the chromosomes that it was a girl. He named her Sophie, the Greek for 'wisdom'. And as the weeks stretched into months and the miracle unfolded within her body, Alex blossomed with a joy she'd given up for lost.

By the fourth week, Sophie had a heartbeat.

By the fifth week, Jake said, she was two millimetres long and had begun to develop a rudimentary spine and nervous system.

By the sixth week, limb buds had appeared. Small depressions had formed where her eyes and ears would go. She was over six millimetres long, and growing fast.

By the seventh week, she could move her head. (Most babies, Alex had read, did this in the eighth. Surely he was bluffing.)

By the tenth, she was as long as a little finger and all her essential organs were present and functioning.

In the twelfth, she gave her first kick. (There was no doubt about that, though the book said week sixteen was the norm.)

In the thirteenth, he said her diaphragm muscles were producing a breathing sequence. Her limbs were properly formed and all the joints moved, her fingers and toes were unwebbed and all the nails were growing. (Alex laughed. How could he possibly tell? This shouldn't happen for another three weeks.)

In the fourteenth, the scans showed she could frown and squint when a bright light was shone at her, and grimace at an unpleasantly loud noise.

In the fifth month, she could already hear well. She kicked to the beat of music and moved in response to Jake's voice. These functions were still reflexes, he said, but by now the cortex was developing – the motor, sensory and visual areas, in that sequence. She'd have a fair chance of survival in intensive care if she had to be born now.

56

In week twenty-four she gave the first clear sign of developing consciousness. He tapped once on Alex's stomach and Sophie kicked back, once. He tapped twice. She kicked back twice. He rewarded her with some flute music. (Alex read that most babies' brains weren't mature enough to support consciousness, let alone lay down the first thin slivers of memory track, until well into the seventh month.)

Then, as the thirty-seventh week opened, Sophie made it known that she was ready to be born.

From the first, Daniel loved his baby sister. He'd crawl up to her cot and stare at her, gurgling at her and making her laugh by mimicking her expressions. He wasn't allowed to touch her, though: he meant her no harm, of course, but he couldn't control his movements well enough to be safe.

When she was a little older, they'd play together on the floor, talking to one another in a special kind of babble, a private language composed of sounds and half-words all their own. Sophie might be six months old and Daniel six years, but she was better company for him than any of his friends at the special school, better perhaps, too, Alex sometimes thought, than either of his parents.

Sophie was a lovely child: lively and always smiling, and so easy to manage after Daniel. She was all they could ever have hoped for.

FIVE

Those three mornings a week, from nine to twelve, Jake worked at home with Sophie. It *was* work, though Alex at first scoffingly called it play. Without really meaning to, he found he was transferring onto the small child the enthusiasm he had previously put into his research. Home, Alex was soon to remark wryly, was becoming his new lab.

Almost every day he came up with a new idea to enrich the baby's development. Towards midsummer, for instance, he was reading a study of the psychological effect of colour on learning and, that weekend, he decided to paint her nursery a pale eau de Nil. He was half way through when Alex looked in. She stood in the doorway, frowning.

'Don't you think yellow would be more cheerful?'

'Yellow's too restless.'

'That green is like a gynaecologist's waiting room. I suppose it's another crackpot Steiner notion?'

This was a standard gibe. Mongols, she claimed Rudolf Steiner had believed, were throw-backs to the apes. His evidence was based on the 'simian line', the deep crease running across the palms of primates and Down's children alike. In her vocabulary, the name was shorthand for all that was bigoted and misguided.

'Green is good for thinking,' he replied calmly.

'Come on, Jake, this is a nursery!'

'The nursery is where we have to start.'

'Start what? Conditioning her? Give the poor child a chance!'

From there on the conversation ran on well-oiled

but parallel tracks. The only variation was the level. The high road took them along the nature versus nurture debate, the lower and dirtier road carried them right into the heart of the Sophie versus Daniel conflict. This time they kept to the high ground.

'She'll get a perfectly good start just by coming from this home,' Alex continued, locked on course. 'Background is nine-tenths of the battle.'

'That's simply not true, Alex. In terms of a person's intelligence, environment barely counts for a third. Heredity is by far the dominant factor.'

'Then why bother painting her environment green?'

'Because—' he checked himself abruptly. 'Because that's all we can do anything about.'

Her hazel eyes danced mockingly.

'For heaven's sake, she's a *person*, not a puppet! Spend a day at my school, then you'd see the real facts. Kids from poor homes do worse, the kids from well-off homes do better. And you're saying the poor ones are inferior *genetically*.'

'Maybe they are, in certain cases . . .'

'Jake!'

'Look, let's just agree: middle-class homes produce brighter children.'

'I'd like to know why,' she persisted, 'if it's not because of the home environment.'

'A child that's born dim will always be dim. Give it an enriched upbringing and it'll learn to compensate; it'll be more confident and cope in the world better. But put it in a deprived home with no books around, no encouragement to learn and no real parental love or care, and it *can't* compensate. Two negatives don't even make half a positive.'

'So let's fight for better housing and better schooling, then, and a fairer chance for the ones who are less fortunate.'

'Yes, Alex, of course we must do that, too.'

She glowered silently for a moment, then turned to leave.

'Your brush is dripping. Dimwit.'

On the low road, the debate became more personal and bitter. The fact was, Sophie was such absorbing company it was impossible not to be enthusiastic about helping her develop or to enjoy sharing her discovery of the world. It simply wasn't the same with Daniel.

A small room, in former times a pantry and now a boxroom, led off the living room. Jake decided to transform it into a place for Sophie – she'd just play in it now but later it'd make an ideal study for her. Over the space of two weekends he put up shelves from floor to ceiling, which he filled with books; he built a desk with a hinged lid and adapted a high chair at which she'd soon be able to sit properly. On the lower shelves he put her counting-bricks and jigsaws, her abacus and other favourite toys, interspersing these with books – not that she could read yet, of course, but merely so that they'd become familiar by association.

Alex watched mistrustfully as all this went on. He was rigging up a mirror in the old fireplace, at child level, when she finally broke her silence.

'Danny will smash that,' she pointed out casually.

This had to be tackled sooner or later.

'I've been thinking,' he began. 'Maybe we should discourage him from coming in here.'

'Oh, no, Jake. We're not having first- and second-class areas in this house.'

'I was thinking in the longer term.'

'I know exactly what you're thinking: Danny will hold Sophie back. *Retard* her. Right?'

'Let's be honest, Alex.'

'No, let's be clear what we are. We're a family, Jake, not a bunch of Fascists.'

He could see the storm clouds looming. One day

they'd break, and God help them all then. The issue was as old as time. Did you hold back the stronger to let the weaker catch up, or did you give them their head? Should schooling be like a handicap race, or like life itself, where the fittest survived best? Alex wanted everyone to go at the pace of the slowest, reduced to the lowest common denominator, while he wanted to see the lowest raised to the level of the highest. She called him élitist; he said her way produced only mediocrity. The issue penetrated the very heart of their family.

As a compromise, he could always put the mirror somewhere else. But the study itself?

'Tell you what,' he offered, 'I'll take the door off its hinges. That way, they'll both be in the same room but they'll have their separate areas.'

'Apartheid,' she muttered with unconcealed disgust and turned away.

Around the time the schools broke up for the summer holidays, Sophie turned ten months. She was tall for her age, lanky even. Her hair had darkened to a burnt-gold colour and her face had already lost some of its infant chubbiness, but her deep-set violet eyes were as curious and knowing as ever. She'd learned to stand without help at seven months and now, able to get about partly crawling, partly walking, she set about exploring the garden by herself. She'd climb down the shallow stone steps backwards and strike fearlessly across the lawn to the large weeping willow at the bottom. There, on a low bench under the spreading skirt of the tree, she kept a collection of her findings: old tennis balls, empty snail-shells, birds' feathers.

On fine mornings, Jake would spread a rug on the lawn and lie beside her and they'd talk and play together. She was already showing a mathematical bent: she loved undoing take-apart toys and putting them back together again. Nothing, not even a bird

61

flying squawking past or a sudden breeze fluttering the pages of a journal he'd be reading beside her, would break her concentration. This was especially striking. Even children a good few months older could not normally focus their gaze on anything for more than a moment before their attention was diverted. An actual physiological fact lay behind this: the part of the visual cortex dealing with objects in the centre-field simply developed later than the part dealing with the periphery.

In the last week of July, Sophie spoke her first proper words.

Alex would often take her shopping in the afternoons, leaving Daniel behind with Suzanne. She'd sit her at the front of the trolley as she wheeled it up and down the supermarket. Each time she put something in the basket, she'd say its name and Sophie would try and copy the sound. It had become a game. But this time Sophie remained oddly quiet, just watching as the tins and packets went in one by one.

'Tea,' Alex announced routinely. 'Coffee powder.'

The little girl puckered her forehead, but still she said nothing.

'Razors for Daddy,' Alex went on, reaching for a different shelf. 'Baby lotion for Sophie.'

She moved round to the canned-foods section and took down a tin of spaghetti rings in tomato sauce. This was for Daniel, a passive eater who found soft food easier. Before she had a chance to say its name, Sophie suddenly piped up. Her voice was as high and clear as a bell.

'Spaghetti,' said the ten-month-old child. 'For Danny.'

At first, Alex was almost too stunned to move. She couldn't believe her ears. She reached forward into the basket and held up a packet of tea. 'What's this, darling?'

'Tea.'

'And this?'

A pause.

'Coffee powder,' said the child, her eyes wide with delight.

Bending down, Alex picked her up and stood there amid the swirl of shoppers with their trolleys and shop girls with trays of refills for the shelves, hugging her precious daughter to her.

That evening, she made her repeat the names of all the items in front of Jake. She caught his eye and grinned with sheer pride. Yes, they had their differences, but what did they count for when such a joy united them?

Shaving in the bathroom with the sunlight streaming in, Jake heard the front door slam and Daniel shuffle across the gravel outside as the driver helped him to the waiting bus. A moment later, Alex came hurrying up the stairs and looked in. She was dressed for school – a white cotton jacket over a tight-waisted, striped dress.

'See if you can't get back before Danny's bed-time for once,' she said. 'And have a look at the paddling-pool while you're sunning yourself out there. It's got a leak.'

He reached forward and kissed her, leaving a daub of shaving-foam on her nose. She pulled back; she had no time for play.

'Don't forget the window cleaner's coming,' she went on. 'And phone the insurance.'

' 'Bye, angel.'

' 'Bye, drone.'

A moment later, he heard the front door slam again and her car start up. He was rubbing his face dry when he heard a small burbling sound behind.

Turning, he saw Sophie in the doorway in her blue dungarees, clambering towards him. He swept her up in his arms and stood hugging her tight against his chest, relishing her baby smell and the feel of her small, lithe body in his arms. He was about to put her down when suddenly, in a clear, high-pitched voice, she spoke her own name.

'Sophie,' she said, and bubbled with laughter.

'Right, then, Sophie,' he said, jigging her up and down. 'What does milady want to do this morning? Shall we go outside and—?

'*Sophie*,' repeated the child in a more insistent voice.

He craned his neck so as to see her face. She was looking over his shoulder and pointing. Pointing at herself in the mirror over the basin.

A sudden tremor chilled his spine.

'Who is that?' he asked carefully.

'Sophie. Me.'

Her face broke into a broad beam of delight.

He held her closer to the mirror. Their eyes met in the glass. Pointing to her ear, he spoke to her reflected image.

'Whose ear is that?'

'Sophie's ear.'

'Whose nose?'

'Sophie's nose!' And she trilled with laughter.

But he didn't laugh. His throat was dry, his pulse drumming. My God, he was thinking. This is extraordinary! This child already recognises herself in a mirror!

He knew what that meant: she knew she was *herself*, a thing different from other things, a distinct individual in a differentiated world. That was a highly evolved perception. Except for chimps and a few other higher primates, animals couldn't recognise themselves in that way. While a cat, for instance, could tell apart the things it saw – it could tell a dog from a bird and one dog from another – it couldn't actually tell *itself* from the dog or the bird. In a way, it *merged* with its world. Humans uniquely possessed this consciousness of self, but it only developed gradually and seldom much before the age of two.

But Sophie was not yet one.

As he stood there, rooted to the spot, watching the baby girl slowly moving her hands over her face and exploring the new person she'd discovered, a profound realisation dawned on him. He'd been spending all this time with the child and lavishing all this attention on her simply because he found her so thrilling to be with. She was so quick to learn, so inventive and so insatiably curious that just to be in her company was rewarding in itself. In return, he gave her all the love and care of which he was capable. But that was not enough. Love and care had given Daniel a happier life, yes, but done nothing to *cure* him. How could he rely on that to carry her over the terrible hurdles ahead? No, the answer lay in her *mind*. The human mind had incredible powers to overcome the body's genetic destiny. Daniel, of course, didn't possess a mind of any useful power. But Sophie absolutely did. Of all the developing intellects he'd known, Sophie's was the most extraordinary. Her real hope lay within herself, in developing and harnessing the prodigious power locked up inside that golden head of hers. *This* was his duty. But he'd have to do it alone, for the worst of it was, he couldn't tell Alex.

Yet this way it might, just might, turn out all right.

Alex was busy giving Daniel his bath. She greeted with a wry glance the bunch of flowers he brought home from the Infirmary and left him to deal with them. While she went down to make supper, he put the boy to bed. He sat reading to him until he fell asleep, then tucked him in loosely, for the night was hot, and kissed him good night. His skin always smelled good – partly it was the ointment he had to have, especially after a bath, to stop it getting dry – and when he slept, in spite of his difficult, snuffly breathing, his slackened features seemed to take on a strange, beatific smoothness. How wrong it was that having *extra* genetic material in their cells caused such children to *lack* abilities. Perhaps, after all, they had something extra that normal people didn't. Such as peace of mind.

In the kitchen later, over the chilli con carne, their latest money worry came up again. Their house, a large Victorian structure, was built on one of the steepest streets in Clifton. It had been subsiding for years, but recently the plasterwork had begun to crack alarmingly and the doors and windows at the back barely opened any more. The builder's quotation was astronomical. What could they do? They simply didn't have that kind of money spare, especially now that his research grant, small though it was, had long since dried up. And there was his father, too, a constant drain on the family resources, which, quite reasonably, Alex resented.

'Jake . . .' she began.

He knew what she was going to say.

'There's a visiting consultant's post going at Bath General,' he intervened quickly. 'The pay is good. Just two evenings a week.'

'Evenings? What about the mornings you fritter away here with Sophie?'

Here we go again, he thought. Should he let it pass?

'Alex,' he responded patiently, 'what goes on in these first eighteen months is absolutely critical to her whole life.'

'And the house falling down about us isn't critical to *ours*?' She shook her head in annoyance. 'I thought your Jesuits said it was the first seven years, anyway. Or are we going to be without a roof over our heads for the next six?'

66

'I'm talking about brain development, not behaviour.' He spoke into his wine-glass to avoid her eye. 'A fellow at Cambridge I know did an experiment on newborn kittens—'

'I don't want to hear.'

'He reared them in cages with only vertical bars. When they were grown up he put them in cages with only *horizontal* bars. What happened? The cats kept walking into the bars. They simply couldn't *see* them. They hadn't developed the right detectors.'

'Sophie is a human being, not a cat!'

'I'll give you a human example, then,' he continued calmly. 'Did you know, seven out of ten children in the world suffer from chronic protein deficiency? It completely destroys their ability to learn. They don't develop it then, and they can never make up for it later.'

She pushed her plate away.

'It's disgusting to think of us in the West, living off the fat!'

'Alex, you're missing the point.'

She turned on him with an accusing glare.

'I'll tell you the *real* point. You're favouritising one at the expense of the other. It's all very well pushing the boat out for Sophie, but what about Danny? *He's* the one who needs the special attention, if anyone. Where were you in the first eighteen months of *his* life? Inventing *him* clever toys, reading *him* proper books, making *him* listen to languages on the radio? Did you give him his own study or paint his bedroom those crackpot colours?'

Red and white blotches had appeared among the freckles on her cheeks. Her anger radiated off her like that.

'I was working in the labs,' he replied tightly, 'trying to find a cure for cases like him.'

'Cases! That's exactly what he is to you – a *case*!'

67

Her lower lip was trembling now. 'Why can't you give him an equal share of . . . of *you*?'

'I love him, you know I do.'

'You don't love him! Sophie's only got to come into the room and you're off like a shot over to her. You think he can't *feel* that? You only love Sophie because she interests you. She's responsive, she's fun, she's your toy. You love her *qualities*, not the child herself!'

He clenched his teeth to check his own rising fury.

'That is simply not true, Alex,' he said.

'It is, and you know it! Oh, *God*!'

She buried her head in her hands. He could see her knuckles whitening as she clutched her hair in her fists. If only he could take her back to the beginning of it all, to unpick everything, to explain what he'd done, to make her understand, perhaps even forgive . . . But what could he say now?

He shook his head, despairing.

'This is quite terrible,' he said quietly. 'Our children are dividing us.'

She spoke from behind her hands.

'Yes, Jake. Because we are dividing our children.'

That night he stayed up late, working on an article he would submit to the *British Medical Journal* on the link between sleep patterns and learning in infants, using data from his observations of Sophie over the past months. It was after two o'clock before he went to bed. Alex was asleep, her face hidden in shadow. A full moon cast the pattern of the window across the sheets. Undressing quietly, he put on his dressing-gown and went over to look out.

In the garden nothing stirred. City traffic rumbled on in the distance. At the foot of the lawn the great willow stood motionless, caught in a web of greenish lunar light, its leaves sheened like tarnished silver. He stood, transfixed by the tree, his head swimming from the black nectars of the night. Even now, when most creatures were in repose, the restless chemistry of life was going on, ineluctably, in every leaf and cell. It could only do what it had been *made* to do; it was innocent. But man was free to choose. Therein lay his original sin. There could be no blame without choice, and no choice without blame. But what of the man whose choice had already been made *for* him? Determined in advance? Genetically?

He thought of Daniel, and of Sophie. Finally, he turned away. He'd go and see the priest and, one morning when Alex was at school and Suzanne out shopping, he'd take Sophie down to the church and secretly have her baptised. She had to be absolved of the sin born into her. Then she'd be free to make her own way, to choose her own destiny. If she could.

PART II

Eight years later

SIX

Jake waited in the Volvo, listening out for the school bell. For the fifth time he checked the dashboard clock: they were late out today. He returned to the physics textbook he'd taken out of the university library. 'The Hamiltonian function H,' he read, 'is the total energy expressed as a function of the generalised co-ordinates q_i and the momenta p_i.' He rubbed his forehead. It was becoming harder and harder to keep more than a step or two ahead of Sophie. Twenty years ago this had been like his mother tongue, but the brain circuits had been steadily atrophying. God damn it, when was someone going to discover something really useful like a macro-molecule for memory?

He looked up. A pale March sun was already sinking behind the bare trees that surrounded the playground. His was the only car in the car park and he the only parent collecting his child. The children who came out at this time of afternoon were the older ones and they went home on bicycles – some even on motorbikes.

At last, from deep inside the low-built modern school the bell clanged and, a moment later, the first boys and girls burst out through the swing doors, their scarves and satchels flying. Some hurried straight to the bicycle racks, others hung about in small groups, gossiping and tussling over class notes, while still others broke off into couples, in the way of sixteen-year-olds.

Sophie came out last, walking alone.

She wore school uniform – blue gingham dress, white knee-high socks and crested blazer – and her fair hair was swept back in a pony-tail. She was tall for eight and a half and as leggy as a young foal, but her classmates were all a good deal bigger. She looked so different, so apart, yet secure in her own separateness. As she passed, one boy with drainpipe trousers and slicked-back hair drew apart from his coterie. He stepped out in front of her and, checking that no one was looking, passed her an exercise-book. She flashed a sympathetic smile up at him and slipped the book into her case. He returned to his friends, a triumphant smirk on his face.

She caught sight of the car and ran forward.

'Hi, Dad.'

She threw her case into the back seat, climbed in after it and leaned forward to give him a kiss.

'Hi, darling,' he said.

'Sorry we're late out. Jerry got caught fooling around and Mr Sykes kept us all in.'

'I'll have a word with the Head.'

'No, don't, Dad.'

He bit his lip, flushed with annoyance. Typical of these imbecile teachers, penalising the whole class for one pupil's misbehaviour! He heaved a breath to calm himself. At the end of this term, when she'd taken her O levels, he'd insist she move to another school again. They'd simply have to find the fees. And if they couldn't, he'd damn well apply to the local authority for permission and teach her himself at home. Alex would just have to go along with it.

He started up the car.

'The boy you just spoke to,' he said. 'Isn't that Jerry?'

She read his meaning instantly, as always. She sat forward, between the front-seat arm rests.

'It's all right, Dad. It's no problem.'

'Problem or not . . .'

'But I feel sorry for Jerry. He really hates maths.'

'You've got your own work to do.'

'It'll take five minutes to write it out. I've done it in my head already.'

'Five minutes is five minutes.'

She sighed.

'Yes, Dad.'

He had to smile.

'No, Dad, you mean.'

She'd take no notice, of course; she'd do Jerry's homework for him while the boy himself, no doubt, slummed it in some coffee bar in town with the other school tearaways. Alex would approve, though: she'd call it a lesson in caring – conveniently ignoring the fact that in the long run a child was actually hampered by having his homework done for him . . .

He pulled out into the traffic and glanced at the dashboard clock again. They'd have to cut fifteen minutes off her swimming time.

He handed her a paper bag from the front seat.

'I got you some books. I thought we'd take a look at Heisenberg this week. You know, the idea we talked about: how measuring a system changes the system itself.'

'Yup.'

'And don't say yup.'

'Nope.' She ruffled through the bag. 'Hey, there's something else here.'

'I got you a couple of tapes, too.'

'Great! It's my sonata – opus a hundred and six, number twenty-nine. But they're both the same?'

'Yes, so you can compare.'

'Mum says Alfred Brendel's best.'

'Listen to the Gilels and make up your own mind.'

'OK, I will.'

She began reading the notes on the tapes. After a moment he looked up and caught her eye in the rear-view mirror. She'd put on her thin dark-framed glasses to read and her long, oval face wore a serious expression.

'Dad?' she began. 'We did the inner ear in biology today. I couldn't see what damage loud music could do to the cochlea or the nerves.'

'It affects the tympanum, in the middle ear. Bring Gray's *Anatomy* when we get home and I'll show you.' He reached behind and patted her knee. 'It's why Walkmans aren't particularly good for you. You don't want to end up deaf. Think of your music.'

'Think of Beethoven.'

'I'll get you a book of Beethoven's letters. Going deaf was sheer torture.'

Her seriousness gave way to a playful smile; this was going to be the argument game.

'I bet he'd have had a Walkman instead of a trumpet thing.' She laughed. 'Imagine!'

'Then he'd have gone deaf all the earlier.'

'But Danny's got one,' she said sweetly.

That struck home.

'Yes, but Danny isn't so . . .'

'Isn't so what?'

He sought for a way to put it. Of course she knew what he really meant to say. She could have said it more clearly and honestly herself.

'Things like that aren't so . . . critical for Danny. It's more important he enjoys himself now, day to day.'

Daniel had been quite ill recently. They'd managed to keep him at home and look after him there, and he'd recovered well enough, but it had been a worrying portent of trouble ahead.

She nodded.

'I know,' she said quietly. 'I didn't mean it.'

She fell silent and immersed herself in the new books.

He drove on. They'd reached the swimming-pool and he was pulling in to the kerb when he glanced up into the mirror again and saw her rubbing her eyes hard under her glasses. She'd complained of a funny spell the other day, but she'd clammed up when he'd pressed her further. Was she straining her eyes, or could she be getting migraines?

'Feeling all right?' he asked.

'Yes, of course.'

'No more . . . funny things?'

'No,' she replied quickly and firmly.

He hesitated for a moment, but decided to leave it there. He switched off the engine and, reaching for her swimming things, climbed out of the car. She followed more slowly, lost in her own thoughts. As they came up to the plate-glass door to the new university Olympic-size pool – a perk he'd managed to wangle, although he was no longer officially connected with the Department – she took his hand. Her face was pale and there was a strange edge of anxiety in her voice.

'Dad, can we visit Lizzie after?'

He glanced at his watch. They'd made good time. Perhaps a quick in-and-out trip to the hospital would be all right. Lizzie, a girl in the same class, had apparently been riding her bicycle through the school gates a couple of days before when she'd suddenly had an epileptic fit. She'd fallen in front of a car, and crushed her arm and leg badly. They were keeping her in for tests, though when he'd dropped in that morning he was puzzled to learn the EEGs hadn't shown any unusual spike formations or other signs of electrical malfunction in the brain. Sophie felt very bad about it and blamed herself, though, of course, it wasn't her fault.

Yes, they could fit it in – provided there wasn't a problem on his own ward across the corridor and he was called over to deal with it.

'Of course we can. But don't forget your piano practice at six.'

'Thanks, Dad.'

He sat on the battered leather sofa in his study, taking Daniel through a book of *Superman* comics. The boy lay resting against his chest, while he went through the story, picture by picture. Daniel loved this book; he'd insisted on it every day for several months now, and was beginning to remember the story.

Through the open door, from the living room, came the rhythmic rise and fall of scales – octaves and double thirds, melodic, harmonic and chromatic, hands separately and together, and then the whole cycle repeated again a semitone higher: C, C sharp, D, E flat . . . Sophie was taking her Grade VIII exam the following month. Right now, Alex would be in the kitchen area, preparing the children's supper. From time to time she'd intervene to correct a note or a phrase, but that happened less and less now. She'd started her off as a small girl of four on the simple pieces she taught at school, but by now Sophie was far too good for her – and soon she'd have outstripped the piano teacher at her own school, a retired concert pianist. But they weren't pushing her. She did her hour's practice a day, no more. As a child herself, Alex had been forced to do six hours at the keyboard before her exams, and she wasn't going to impose that cruel regime on Sophie. For his part, Jake agreed; Sophie's music had its place, just like her swimming and gym, but it wasn't the really important thing.

Daniel looked up as the scales ended and the opening phrases of the Mozart sonata took over. He wriggled upright, flapping his hands as he did when excited.

'Sophie's tune,' he said. 'I want to.'

'Let's listen from in here, Danny.'

The sofa was soft and deep and the boy couldn't haul himself up. A small frown of frustration spread across his face.

'Dada,' he pleaded.

Jake pointed to a picture.

'Look at this, Danny! What could Superman be doing there?'

Daniel looked from the book to the door and back again.

'He's going *whoosh*!'

'And in this one?'

It was hard work, and painful, too, to be constantly depriving the poor lad of what he wanted to do. But it was the only way. He was fourteen, wilful and lusty. He could get about on his own perfectly well now, but he had little sense of co-ordination and no idea of his own strength. He'd only have wanted to hammer away at the bottom of the piano while Sophie was practising, he'd have had to be pulled away and then he'd have started screaming. Alex had subtler ways of deflecting him, but sometimes he himself had to resort to palliating him with small diversions and deceptions. How could that fail to be patronising?

The hands of the clock laboriously inched their way to seven, and the hour was up. At last he closed the comic book and, taking Daniel by the hand, led him into the living room.

Alex looked up from beside the piano and, catching Daniel's eye, put her finger to her lips. Jake held back in the doorway. Sophie was finishing her piece in a flurry of arpeggios. She sat on the high piano-stool, her back perfectly straight and rarely glancing at her hands. Alex stood behind her, following with the music; Sophie never needed music, for once she'd read it, she remembered every note and marking.

The final chord rang out. Jake clapped, and Daniel copied. Sophie got up and dropped a small pretend curtsey.

Alex put the music down.

'Much better,' she said. 'Just watch the tempo at the end. Don't run away with it.'

'I didn't that time, Mum,' said the girl, closing the piano lid.

'No, but you still tend to.'

Sophie was about to say something, then she caught Jake's eye.

'Yes, Mum,' she said simply.

Alex glanced briefly towards Jake.

'She's all yours,' she said, and reached out her hand to take Daniel's. It seemed like a swapping of prisoners at a frontier. 'Supper time, Danny. Are you hungry? Sophie, get him a clean bib from the airing cupboard, there's an angel.'

Sophie skipped out of the room. Jake took the cutlery out of the sideboard and began laying the table for the children's meal. He could see Daniel at the stove, hugging his mother's waist while she served out a helping of steaming casserole and mashed it soft.

Sophie returned with the bib and helped her brother on with it. He was heavy and awkward in build but, despite the six years between them, she had almost caught him up in height.

'It's still too hot, Danny,' she said, tying the last string. 'Let's go and sit down.'

She led him away by the hand, as meek as a lamb, and sat him down at the table in his special chair. Sitting in her own place next to him, she began chattering away in Abacus, the special language she'd made up with him. This had evolved from a game Jake had once played with her in which words were spoken backwards, but she'd developed it into a whole language of its own, complete with complex grammar and syntax and a seemingly limitless vocabulary. She'd begun writing it down, at night and in great secrecy, and had already filled several exercise-books. One he imagined might be a diary. He'd chanced upon these recently: she had pulled a muscle in her back at gym and he was laying a board between the mattress and the base of her bed when he found the books hidden there. Daniel couldn't keep up, of course, and the times they spoke it now were more like lessons than real conversations. But it was wonderful to see his face fill with delight as he grasped something she'd said and she, in turn, understood his reply.

'Oh, do talk sensibly,' pleaded Alex as she put the bowls down in front of the children. 'Sophie, I want you to tidy your room before you go to bed tonight. It's a disgrace.'

'It's a waste of time, Mum. It only gets untidy again.'

'You manage to keep your study tidy enough.'

'That's different. Everything's got its place.'

'Then give things their places in your bedroom.'

'But . . .' She checked herself. 'All right, Mum.'

Jake was by the sink, pouring himself a whisky. He added an extra slug from the bottle. What did an untidy bedroom *really* matter? It didn't mean an untidy mind. He couldn't help glancing up at the wall clock. Time was so precious, how could you spend it like that?

'It's OK,' he said quietly. 'I'll do it while you're doing Daniel's.'

Alex didn't turn. They hardly seemed to look at each other these days.

'No. Sophie will do her own room. It's her mess.'

He bit his lip. They'd vowed they would never fight in front of the children – never even disagree, either, if they could possibly help it.

He make a mock salute.

'Yes, *ma'am*,' he said with a tight laugh.

At eighteen months, Sophie could read the headlines of the newspaper. By two years old, she could
read almost fluently. She developed an obsession with
counting; once she spontaneously recited the number
of books of each colour in the study and, on another
occasion, she told her uncle Graham exactly how many
squares there were on the check jacket he was wearing. Jake never made her recite multiplication tables,
using cube models instead to let her · work out the
numbers by herself. He tried never to *tell* her things
but rather, through a Socratic question-and-answer
method, encouraged her to discover the answers for
herself.

He'd allow nothing that might discourage her curiosity. Once she was sitting in her high chair and threw
a cup on the floor; she clearly found the effect so fascinating – the noise and the broken fragments – that
he handed her another, and then another. Alex came
in and lost her temper. It was after that that he made
her vow they'd never fight in front of the children.

Curiosity was a basic drive in children, like hun-
ger. A 'good' child was a child who'd been trained to
suppress it. Even animals possessed it: monkeys would
work on puzzles for ages without a reward, rats would
take a long but interesting route to get to food rather
than a short, boring one, and many lab animals could
be motivated by the simple reward of a view out of the
window. It was all just common sense.

At six, Sophie was writing programmes on her
computer terminal and had devised a new table of
logarithms using a base of twelve, rather than ten.
By seven, she had already outgrown two schools and
was on her third. Now, at eight and a half, she

was working at the level of an average child of six-teen.

She talked quickly, in short bursts. Sometimes her mind outstripped her words and she'd speak in a kind of bouncing shorthand, alighting on phrases and leaving out the connections and the ends of sentences. Jake teased her, calling this 'kangarooing'. She had invented her own method of speed-reading and possessed an almost photographic memory. As for subjects, she was equally good at music and maths, though she found the imaginary world of numbers and concepts the more exciting to explore. Above all, everything seemed so effortless. She never had to struggle to comprehend; at most, she merely tilted her head to one side and thought for a moment, her brow puckered in its 'V', and quite spontaneously she grasped the point. She saw it all as fun. She laughed as she discovered something new and she was eager to share it with Jake. *He* was the one putting on the pressure, fixing the schedules, counting the minutes; she had time for everything, for Daniel, for her mother, for music and swimming and the inevitably few friends she had at school.

People were calling her a prodigy. The word was spreading. Interest, too much interest, was being taken in her. There had already been a reporter from the *Bristol Chronicle* and phone calls from the sensational-ist Sunday press. Even Graham had been pressing to study her as a case in developmental psychology. So far, Jake had managed to put off all of them, firmly but tactfully, but how much longer could he hold out? That summer she was set to become the youngest child in the country ever to pass her O levels.

Of course he was proud of her, but he had a duty to protect her. Publicity would only interfere with her work. Before, he'd been adamant that people should see her as a perfectly normal child. She wasn't going to become some peep-show creature of the salacious Press. Yes, she was bright. Brilliant, even. But she was not *abnormally* brilliant. She was just an ordinary child who'd been allowed to follow where her curiosity led and was having fun along the way. She'd achieved nothing more than any other child could have achieved, given the same degree of cultivation and interest of her parents.

Above all, there'd been no further hint of the storm clouds that had loomed so threateningly that first Christmas. She was growing up fine. A hundred per cent fine.

She waited until the house was quiet. Mum had been in to check over the room and say good night; Dad wouldn't be up for another hour. She was very sleepy, but this had to be done.

She tiptoed across the room, careful to avoid the boards that she knew creaked. Climbing on a chair, she reached up onto the roof of the wardrobe, the new hiding-place she'd found, took down the three exercise-books and carried them back to bed. There, by torchlight, she began to write her diary.

Visited Lizzie in hospital today, she wrote in fluent Abacus. *They've put a plate in her left arm. She's left-handed and they don't know if she'll be able to take exams ...*

She screwed her eyes to shut out the tears and sank back into the pillows as she recalled the event.

She didn't mean to do it, she thought. It just happened.

Lizzie had been teasing her all afternoon, calling her a snotty little swot and names like that. That was nothing – she was used to that. But after school, in the playground, Lizzie grabbed her bag and went all through it, tearing up her exercise-books and ripping out pages from her notebook with the new theorem she was inventing for Dad. She couldn't do anything – Lizzie was fifteen, and half the class were there, laughing too – so she did what Dad said to do. The rational thing in the circumstances. Do nothing.

She stood really still, right there in the middle of the playground, just staring at her. Then she began to get a funny metal taste in her mouth, like when you lick a copper coin. And then this strange pumping feeling in the front of her head ... in and out, in and out, as if her lungs had got up into her forehead. The background around Lizzie gradually went more and more blurry until everything was blotted out except her head, which was outlined by terribly bright blue and yellow rings. She couldn't break the stare. She'd got locked on. And it was getting tighter all the time.

She half saw Lizzie chuck her bag into a litter bin and go over to the bicycle racks. She wheeled her bike to the front gates and got on. The funny pulsing grew stronger. It seemed to be pushing out of her head, a long, shaft-like thing, reaching right across the space between them, like a huge, long, invisible steel tongue. She saw her ride into the road. Half way across, Lizzie began to wobble. *She was pushing her off balance!* She didn't see what happened, but she heard it: the tyres screeching, the bicycle clattering across the road and that horrible crumpling sound ...

Sophie switched off the torch and curled up tighter under the covers. She was shaking badly. They'd said Lizzie had had a fit, but it wasn't that. *I* did it, she thought. What is wrong with me?

SEVEN

Alex stood alone in the staff room, staring out across the empty playground. Pale scars criss-crossed the sooty brick walls where obscene graffiti had been scrubbed out. Cans and sweet wrappers eddied around the litter bins in the quickening April breeze. A fluorescent plastic traffic cone still sat crookedly atop the high wire-mesh fence, and on the trunk of the long-suffering chestnut, standing in the centre like an island amid a sea of tarmac, the bark bore the weals of a lifetime's abuse.

Twenty-five years spent teaching kids like these, and what did she have to show for it?

Behind a breeze-block wall stood the garbage tanks where she'd caught Dennis and Rick sniffing glue. The brightly painted panels above the ground-floor windows opposite were still scorched and blackened from the fire that Dillon broke in and started one weekend. And there, in the hidden nook behind the boiler house, was the spot where Loretta was found trading her sexual favours. What would become of them? Had she done anything to steer them away from growing into junkies, arsonists, hookers? Or had she merely *coped*? Held back a tide but not reversed it?

And what of her own life? Seventeen years of marriage, two children of shockingly opposite abilities, a husband she felt growing further away from her every day?

Daniel's future was a worry. He only felt secure in familiar surroundings and was easily upset by changes in routine. He wasn't happy even when Jake arrived back late from the hospital. He'd never grow up and leave home like any other child. He'd be dependent all his life.

And what of Sophie, too? She was dangerously isolated at school. In the holidays she hardly ever saw friends. She didn't *have* many friends, for she found those of her own age too childish and the older ones were primarily interested in boyfriends, while at any age there was no one really to match her mind. Graham had once asked her who her best friend was; she'd replied, 'Dad'. She needed other children around her. That was something Jake never saw, something he didn't want to see.

Things with Jake were, frankly threadbare. She loved him, in a well-worn way. Sex between them had dwindled to an occasional, perfunctory act. There wasn't much companionship, still less a meeting of minds. They were simply cohabitees of the same house, co-wardens of the same children. She cared for him, for how his work was going, how he felt, whether he was happy and fulfilled or angry and frustrated. But was caring enough? She cared about Graham slipping into middle-aged bachelorhood, she cared about the boy next door, laid up after a motorbike accident, she cared about the kids in her class and their hope of a worthwhile life . . .

And she was beginning to care about someone else, too.

Arthur ran the history department. He was fifty, ten years older than Jake, and his wife had died six months before, leaving him with four children aged from seven to fifteen. Lovely, normal children, too; she'd been to tea to meet them. Of course it was absurd even to think of it, but . . . Well, just suppose. Sophie was young enough to form an attachment to

87

a new father. It might even do her good. But Daniel would always be the problem. It would be unthinkable to move him to a strange house and a strange family.

What was she thinking of? This was ridiculous fantasy. She didn't even have that kind of relationship with Arthur. And she wasn't going to, either. Not for her the lies, the alibis and all the other sordid deceptions of infidelity she'd seen and so abhorred when Jake had been involved with Helen. And yet, what were she and Jake waiting for? Were they staying together only for the sake of the children? For *Daniel's* sake?

My God. At forty-six, what kind of questions were these?

She turned away abruptly, angry with herself. This wouldn't do. The clock above the door read three forty. She had a meeting with the head, next term's textbooks to take home with her and the weekend's shopping to do before Suzanne left at five. No time for fanciful speculation.

Gathering up the remaining things from her locker, she headed decisively towards the door.

She arrived home to find that Daniel had a high temperature and Suzanne had put him to bed. He lay in his large, wide cot, restless and perspiring and, despite his fever, deathly white. Even his tongue, hanging slack from bloodless lips, was pale. At the first glance, a terrible, sick panic gripped her. *Had it come back?* This was just how it had started before. They'd caught it in time and dealt with it before it could take a proper hold, but they'd been warned it might only have retreated and still be lurking, dormant, deep in the cells of his bone marrow. And then it wouldn't be a case of four weeks in bed at home: it would mean hospital and the full, awful treatment.

She gave him some aspirin dissolved in Ribena,

his favourite drink, knowing it would do no more than help ease the symptoms. She checked her watch. Jake wouldn't be back for a good hour. She couldn't get hold of him now: he'd be in the car, taking Sophie to her swimming, playing his idiotic number games with her and talking in algebra.

'Mumma,' whimpered Daniel, reaching out for her.

She hugged him closer.

'Daddy will be home soon, darling, and we'll have you right as rain.'

His skin was cold and damp, just like before. She was stung with shame to recall her thoughts earlier that afternoon.

After a while, his breathing grew slower and deeper and he fell asleep. She tucked him up gently, careful not to let the sheet cover up his face, for his sinuses were bad, too, and he could only breathe through his mouth. She quietly drew the curtains and, placing a light kiss on his forehead, she left the room. A moment later she returned with the baby alarm and plugged it in so that she could hear him downstairs. From the airing cupboard she brought out a pile of spare pyjamas and the rubber under-blanket, and from the back of the bathroom cabinet she took out the special plastic bowls and mugs they'd used last time, brought them downstairs to the kitchen and sterilised them. She knew they'd be needing all this again.

At three minutes to six, with the usual unnerving precision, the Volvo scrunched on the gravel outside, two doors slammed and a moment later Sophie burst in, her jersey on inside-out and her fair hair streaming wet. Jake followed with her swimming things.

'I broke my underwater record, Mum!' she cried. 'Any biscuits? I'm starving. Where's Danny? I got him a badge for his collection.'

'He's upstairs. Jake—' She caught his eye.

Sudden anxiety flashed across his face as he read her meaning. He turned to Sophie.

'Get started on your practice, angel,' he said, moving back to the door. 'I'll be right down.'

He slipped out of the room and she heard him bounding up the stairs. Stuffing a biscuit in her mouth, Sophie went over to the piano and pulled out her music.

Alex laid a hand on her shoulder.

'Sophie,' she said quietly, 'not tonight.'

The girl looked up sharply.

'What's the matter with him, Mum?'

'Just a temperature.'

'I'm going up to see him.'

'No, darling. You settle down and do your homework. I'll bring you something to drink in a while.'

'But Mum . . .'

'Be a good girl, now.'

She waited until Sophie had gone into her study then, closing the living-room door behind her, she went into the hallway. Jake was coming slowly downstairs. He looked very shaken. He stopped a few feet from her. His fingers whitened on the banister.

'I'd better call and get a bed ready,' he said.

She caught her breath.

'Oh my God.'

'It may be nothing. Don't let's jump to conclusions.'

'Jake,' she whispered hoarsely. 'Tell me he's all right.'

'Let's wait for the tests.'

'What are his chances if . . . ?'

'About fifty-fifty.'

He came down and folded his arms around her. It was the first time they'd held one another like that since . . . since the last time Daniel was ill.

She shut her eyes, not wanting to read his face. They stood there, clinging together, trying to draw comfort and sustenance from the shreds that remained between them.

'It's bad, isn't it?' she said finally.

He nodded.

'It could be the worst.'

'Jake, I'm afraid.'

He took her by the shoulders.

'You mustn't be. We've faced up to this already. He'll get the very best treatment that's going. Alex, look at me. Think positive. Have faith.'

As she looked up, the living-room door caught her eye. It was a fraction open. Beyond the crack, she fancied she saw fleeting movement.

Sophie lay in bed, unable to sleep. Through the open curtains, above the canopy of the willow tree, she stared out at the stars and automatically began picking out the constellations. How far away was the Pole Star? If you travelled backwards at the speed of light, where would you end up? Could you make a Rubik's cube with four dimensions? What about 45369? It was the number on the phone at the swimming-pool. A nice, friendly number – 213 squared. And 8741! That was a good one! She'd trumped Dad in the prime-number game with 8741.

She shut her eyes. *Stop!* Stop the thoughts! She wanted to think about Danny.

It's bad, isn't it? . . . It could be the worst.

They were going to take him away. Why did Mum and Dad pretend?

She slid out of bed and stood for a moment on the landing, listening. The house was silent and dark. Tiptoeing quickly down the corridor, she crept into her brother's room. He lay asleep, snuffling in his usual way. In the glow of the night-light he looked as pale as a fish.

91

Poor Danny. It wasn't fair. She had so much, and he so little. Why did even that little have to be taken away from him?

Careful not to wake him, she lowered the safety rail, climbed up into the wide cot bed and snuggled in beside him.

Jake took Daniel in with him the following morning. The boy looked tired and desperately white and he could barely stand. At the hospital, they put him in a wheelchair and brought him up to the main children's ward on the eleventh floor, opposite Jake's own, where he was put to bed and given a series of blood tests. Every time he had a spare moment, Jake slipped across the corridor to look in on his pale, sick child. *Wait for the tests*, he kept having to tell himself. But in his heart he knew the answer; he was a doctor, practised at weighing a case. He was a father, too, though, and had a parent's inextinguishable hope.

That afternoon, after her gym and before her tea, he took Sophie to visit her brother. She insisted on going home first to collect his toys; she knew his favourites. He was excited to see her and flapped his hands so much that the sister was afraid he'd dislodge the drip in his arm.

Afterwards, in the car on the way back, she sat without a word, bolt upright and very still. They were in sight of home when she finally spoke.

'Dad,' she said, 'you'll never let him be sent away, will you?'

'Sent away? Of course not.'

'Promise.'

'He may have to stay in for a while, but then he'll come home. Like last time.'

'Promise,' she repeated.

'He's going to be all right, darling. I promise.'

Two days later, Jake received a call from Pathology that the results were through. The doctor's face said it all as he handed him the computer print-out. It *had* come back, with a vengeance. Acute lymphoblastic leukaemia. Cancer of the white blood cells.

They began treatment at once. The hospital had treated Down's cases with the illness before, for they had a genetic disposition to it. With the radiotherapy and chemotherapy, Daniel grew thin; he felt constantly sick and his fine, straw-coloured hair began to fall out. Alex and Jake took turns sitting with him, playing with him and trying to keep him cheerful. It was heartbreaking to see the helplessness in the boy's eyes and the underlying puzzlement that though they were doing all this to him they couldn't seem to make him better.

The days became weeks, and all the signs were good. Then, towards the end of May, with the great willow in the garden a bright sappy green and the white lilac by the shed in full bloom and the first dog-roses breaking out along the tottering old brick wall, Daniel was allowed home.

Alex's term had begun once again, and she was busier than ever with the approaching exams. Discipline always suffered in the summer, and for most of the school-leavers, who didn't care about exams anyway, the term was merely a nuisance to be suffered until real life began in the real world. It was disheartening still to be sending out young people who could barely read and write, for whom literature meant comics and letters were primarily of the French kind. On top of this, there was Daniel. His convalescence was slow, and it had its set-backs. At school, Arthur was very supportive. Several times he supervised her class when she was called home urgently. He volunteered

93

to take over her committee duties, too, and contrived in many other small ways to ease the burden of her work there.

At home, she threw herself into reorganising the house around Daniel.

First of all, she swapped his room with Sophie's, which was closer to hers and Jake's and next door to the bathroom. Sophie obligingly took down her astronomy charts and an old good-luck card from Daniel in his childish scribble, the poster of Jacqueline du Pré playing the cello and the small plaster bust of Beethoven, and replaced them with his bold Mister Men posters and his pictures of cars and railway engines and inter-galactic warriors.

A problem arose at once over her music practice. Her Grade VIII exam was set for ten days' time. Daniel slept – or Alex tried to get him to sleep – as much of the day as he could, and so piano playing was out of the question.

'I'm cancelling her exam,' she told Jake. 'I'll get her booked in for September instead.'

'You will not!' he objected. 'She's all keyed up for it.'

'It's only an exam, Jake.'

'Sophie will take that exam. It's scheduled.'

'Damn the schedule! She can take it another time. It'll mean learning new pieces, but that'll be good for her. Widen her repertoire.'

'Just a minute, Alex. That child has devoted all this time to your music—'

'*My* music, I like that!'

'— when she could have been studying her physics or her biology.'

'I know she'll be disappointed, but children have to learn to handle disappointments. Don't look like that. I've made up my mind. I won't have her playing in this house until Danny's better.'

'In that case, I'll get her a practice room at school.'

'Don't be silly. Who'll teach her? Who'll take her through her aural tests?'

'Alex, I hate to say this, but I don't think there's much more you can give her. As for aural tests, she's got perfect pitch anyway.'

It stung, and she resisted the impulse to fight back on the same level. But Sophie and Daniel were what mattered, not their own egos. She fought to keep her tone under control.

'You're putting her under too much pressure,' she said. 'She'll crack up. Blow a fuse.'

'Alex, the brain isn't some kind of fuse-box. You can't overload the synapses like that. Believe me.'

'I don't give a toss about your brains and synapses. I'm only interested in people. *People* can be overloaded. And I can see one child who's being pushed dangerously close to the edge.'

She lost the issue. Jake made arrangements with the school and from then on, between five and six, Sophie practised in one of the rooms at school, by herself. Her swimming or gym hour followed between six and seven, after which she came home for supper and her evening's work. Three days went past in this way until Alex could bear it no longer. Arranging with Suzanne to stay an extra hour, she went to the school herself and coached Sophie there every day up to the exam. She couldn't let her down.

But the problems didn't end there.

Daniel was in constant discomfort and, though he tried to be brave, he cried a lot in the night. For a while, they had him sleeping in their room and moved him back when things seemed to be getting better, but it meant that she and Jake were up on and off throughout the night. More than once she heard Danny crying, but by the time she got to his room she'd find Sophie already there, soothing him quiet. Sophie soon began coming down to breakfast with grey rings round her eyes and her face wan from lack of sleep. She always wanted to be the one to take her brother his meals and drinks and begged to be allowed to sleep in the same room so that she could be there when he needed her. Just when he seemed to be getting better, he developed a nasty cough which made it hurt even to breathe, and back came the difficult nights.

Over breakfast, the day before Sophie's music exam, Jake was going through a chemistry exercise with her when she literally fell asleep over the book. While she was getting ready for school, he came back into the kitchen and shut the door. His face was like thunder.

'She's got her music tomorrow,' he said. 'And her O levels three weeks after that. This won't do.'

Alex nodded. It wouldn't do at all. But their solutions were bound to be different.

'Let her drop physics and biology for now. There's no need for her to take all five at once. She'll be the youngest in the country to take just one. Or won't that satisfy your pride?'

'Let's not go into that,' he responded tartly. 'Right, now. I think we should move her bed down to her study for the time being. And discourage her from running up to see to Danny all the time.'

'Visiting times for Danny? This is a *home*, Jake, not a hospital.'

'I'm talking of a few weeks only. A few very critical weeks.'

'No, Jake.'

'What do you mean, no?'

'What it sounds like. No way. Nix. Negative.' She held his eye fiercely. 'Danny's coming along extraordinarily well, you said so yourself – well, he was till just now. And it's largely due to Sophie. You know how she is with him, how she makes him laugh and forget he's ill. If anything's driving him on to get better, it's wanting to get up and go outside and play with her. These are critical weeks for *him*.'

'But just look at the child! Bags under her eyes . . .'

'Then ease off the pressure.'

'I'm *not* pressurising her. She does it because she wants to. Because she loves it.'

'Then I suggest you discourage her from overdoing it.'

He shook his head in rage.

'Christ, Alex, I don't understand you!'

She shook her head, too, but in despair. She said nothing, for there was nothing left to say.

The next day, Jake arranged to swap shifts with a colleague and take the afternoon off. Alex wasn't able to get away; she wanted to get back to Daniel as soon as school finished, for his cough was getting worse.

He collected Sophie from school after lunch and drove her to the hall where the Royal Academy of Music exams were being held. On the way there she sat in silence with her eyes shut and her brow puckered in concentration, every now and then drumming out a phrase on the back of the marbled and leather-bound set of Beethoven sonatas he'd given her at Christmas. He led her into the waiting room and reported to an old invigilator whose hands were so crippled with arthritis that he could barely write down her name. Beyond the oak-grained double doors, a Schubert impromptu was coming to a sticky end. A moment later, heels scurried down the boards and a boy came out, red-faced and close to tears. The invigilator nodded to Sophie.

Jake got up and accompanied her to the door.

'Good luck, darling,' he said, kissing her on the head.

'I hope I don't need it.'

'Your music!' called the invigilator after her.

She smiled.

'I really hope I don't need *that*.'

Jake paced up and down the long, narrow room. It seemed an inordinately long time before she began. Then the first notes sounded – scales, arpeggios, broken chords, rippling effortlessly up and down the keyboard. The invigilator looked up, startled. Aural tests followed, and various spoken questions and answers. Another silence fell, the stool scraped on the platform, there was a. muffled cough and then the commanding opening chords of the great 'Hammerklavier' rang out.

Jake sat spellbound. She'd played the sonata in front of friends at home and at concerts at school, but never like this. The resonance of the grand piano in that hall couldn't be compared with the sound of the upright in their living room, of course, but here was another dimension he'd never heard in her performance before. Her playing was full of such passion, such feeling, such . . . *anger*? Was it Beethoven's anger, or hers?

The invigilator was standing with his ear to the gap between the doors. As the Adagio sostenuto went on towards its full twenty minutes without interruption from the examiners, Jake began to realise that they, too, were under the same spell. They were no longer judging the music but listening to it for sheer pleasure. The hands on the wall clock steadily moved on. The next pupil arrived and took her seat. Sophie's forty-five minutes were long up, but she was still playing. The clock passed the hour, then another quarter, before the punched notes of the fugue broke open into a series of jerky leaps and trills that finally came together again in four emphatic tonic chords. As the fourth rang out and gradually died away, he heard a sudden sharp exclamation, then another, and a burst of applause spontaneously broke out across the hall.

He took her for large cream tea in town, where she sneaked a chocolate meringue to take back to Daniel. Afterwards, they visited the city museum to look at fossils. The afternoon was warm and they had time to spare, so they went for a stroll in the park and played the syllogism game. They walked hand in hand round the pond, stopping to watch the swallows skimming the surface to drink, and on to the botanical gardens where she found an example of a stem with a helical arrangement of leaves. She might only come up to his chest and her whole hand be enveloped in his, but it was easy to forget she wasn't much more than eight and a half. Sometimes he felt she could be any age, that they were brother and sister, even.

It was nearing six o'clock when they wended their way home. As they pulled up in the drive, the front door opened and Alex came out, her face drawn with worry. Sophie ran forward and hugged her mother.

'It went fine, Mum,' she cried. 'And I didn't hurry the ending. How's Danny?'

'She was brilliant,' endorsed Jake. 'They gave her a standing ovation.'

'That's wonderful!' exclaimed Alex. She released herself. 'Tell me all about it in a minute, sweet. Hurry along inside just now. You'll find Suzanne in the kitchen.' She held Jake back until the girl had gone inside, then she gripped him by the sleeve. 'Where on earth have you been? You left your bleeper behind, too.'

'What's wrong?'

'Danny. Dr Blythe is here. He says it's a lung infection.'

He picked up the referral letter and saw the spry,

silver-haired family doctor to the door. They shook hands in the porch.

'I'll see what I can wangle,' he said.

'It's better coming from you,' agreed the doctor. 'Let me know if you need anything more from me.'

'I will. Thanks for coming out, Frank.'

He returned slowly to his study. He'd have to pull strings to get Daniel into the clinic. Where should he start? Maybe he'd try the Hospital Administrator first.

He sat down at his desk and began dialling. The number was engaged. Alex came in and stood opposite, her hazel eyes large with anxiety.

'Who are you calling?' she asked.

'I'm going to try and get him into Bath,' he said, trying the number again.

Her expression sharpened.

'Bath? Whatever for? Dr Blythe said he'd be all right here. He can be an out-patient and get all his home comforts.'

'It's the best clinic in the country for what he needs.'

'Hang on, Jake. He's Dr Blythe's patient. We can't go against his advice.'

'He's our son, too. Frank agrees with me, anyway. He's given a referral note.'

He pointed to the letter and started dialling again, but she put her finger down on the cradle. Suspicion crept over her face.

'He clearly told me Danny would be all right here. You talked him into it!'

'Don't be absurd. He didn't think we could get him in. And maybe we can't. Now, if you don't mind . . .'

She kept her hand where it was. The malevolence in her look took him aback.

'You pulled rank. Senior consultant against a humble GP.'

'Alex, be reasonable. Why should I want to send Danny miles away if we could have him here with us?'

'Because you want to get rid of him! You want him out of Sophie's way!'

'That's a vile thing to say!'

'It's true! You want him away so he won't disturb her precious studies. It's been the story all along. The separate rules, the separate areas, the business about the bed, the piano . . . You treat him like a leper, Jake. You don't want him to *contaminate* her!'

He rose to his feet. She stood her ground, glaring her vicious accusation defiantly at him. Christ, he couldn't help it. He lashed out at her, catching her across the cheek with the flat of his hand.

'Don't ever say that again!' he hissed. 'I love that boy just as much as you do. I know my job. I'm sending him where he'll get the treatment he needs. Where he's concerned, he comes first. No compromises. Get it?'

Sophie paused on the half-landing. She'd been coming downstairs from Danny's room when she'd heard raised voices in the study. She knew what that meant. She stood there, her knees turning to water, wanting to drown, to disappear, to go away for ever, because it was her fault they were quarrelling, because *she* made them quarrel and without her there they wouldn't. Please, Mum, please, Dad, she cried to herself, stop.

She'd have gone and hidden in her study, put on a tape and shut it out of her mind as she usually did, but that meant going right past the study door. She was stuck on the stairs there. One voice inside her said, Go back, don't hear, don't try and know. But another, more insidious voice urged her, Go on, listen, find out.

She took a step forward.

'Why should I want to send Danny miles away . . . ?'

'Because you want to get rid of him! You want him out of Sophie's way!'

With a small cry she pressed her hands to her ears and ran back upstairs. She rushed into her bedroom and threw herself on her bed.

God, she prayed, make me disappear.

When Dad came into her room later, she was sitting on her bed, looking through a periodic table of elements. He sat down near her and told her Danny had caught something in his lungs and had to go away for a while. An ambulance was coming later in the evening to take him to a special place in Bath. It was the best thing for him. The logical, reasonable thing to do in the circumstances.

She acted normal. She agreed. Of course, the best was the logical thing.

She couldn't eat supper and gave up homework after only a few minutes. She crept up the back stairs to Danny's room and stayed with him, holding his hand while he wrestled with his cough, until she heard the ring on the front door. From the window she saw the ambulance in the street. She slipped quickly out of the room and reappeared downstairs just as two men in uniform, carrying a stretcher, were crossing the hall.

She waited by the front door as they brought Danny down. She held his hand on the way to the ambulance. As they carried him inside, he gave her a big, cheeky grin and said the word in Abacus for going on holiday.

'Come along, laddie,' coaxed Dad. 'We'll soon have you all set up and ready to go.'

'Dad,' she implored, 'let me come too.'

'It's best not, darling.'

'Mum?' she appealed.

But Dad answered for her.

'We might be hours,' he said, patting her on the head, 'and I want you bright and sharp in the morning. Don't worry. We'll have plenty of time for visits later.'

She ran up the steps and into the ambulance. Pressing her face close to Danny, she whispered, in their secret language, 'I love you, Danny.'

Mum held her hand as they stood on the pavement, waving the ambulance off into the night.

'Come along,' Mum was saying as she led her back to the house. 'There's *On The Road To Rio* on television later. Have your bath and we'll watch it together.'

She stood by the open window. The midnight flowed coolly through her hair. To the right, the sky was smudged with orange above the city. To the left, inky darkness. In the centre, at the foot of the garden, stood the weeping willow tree, its skirt reaching to the ground all round and stirring slightly, as if it were moving from one foot to the other. In front spread the lawn, a black-velvet pool, reflecting nothing.

Where was Danny now? In a strange bed, with strangers all around him?

It was all because of her he'd been sent away. Because of her work. Mum had said so.

But Dad had *promised*. How could he have let her down?

As she stared out at the willow tree, she began to notice a strange yet familiar metallic taste in her mouth and her forehead started to pump, in and out, in and out, slowly at first but more and more powerfully. The low-hanging fronds of the tree stirred rhythmically. No, something was stirring behind them, *within* them. The pulsing grew more forceful. She couldn't drag her gaze away. She was locked onto a small patch that grew brighter, while the rest became more blurry. It

103

seemed to sway back and forth, back and forth, in time to the pumping under her skull. The fronds were now swishing crazily, as if someone was violently shaking the whole tree. Then suddenly they parted. And as they parted, they grew still. From the opening emerged a head, shoulders, arm, leg. The figure of a boy, crouching. Dark-haired, angular, animal-like. He looked around furtively. He didn't see her at first. He looked about him again, then abruptly stood up and stepped out into the open. Onto the black-velvet lawn. He took a few steps forward, then looked up. Straight at her. Into her. For ever. And he smiled.

He wasn't anyone she knew. And yet she knew him. And, strangely, she knew his name, too.

Valentin.

EIGHT

Jake silenced the alarm before it could wake Alex and dragged himself wearily out of bed. He'd spent a good hour with the Director of the clinic, then stayed late into the night at Daniel's bedside until they'd eventually had to give him a dose of Seconal to send him to sleep. He hadn't returned home until the first hint of dawn. But he was satisfied: they couldn't hope Danny would be better cared for anywhere.

He put on his dressing-gown and went down the corridor to wake Sophie – though, as often as not, she'd already be awake and reading. He tapped on the door and looked in. She wasn't there. Her school uniform hung where Alex had left it the night before. A pile of books lay unopened by an unmade bed. He glanced at his watch: six thirty-five. Perhaps she was already downstairs and starting her study-hour early. Funny, though: her reading glasses were on her desk.

Rubbing his eyes, he padded down the stairs, across the hall and in through the living-room door. On the left her study door, which they'd put back the previous year, was closed.

'Morning, Sophie,' he called, opening it.

The response came from the kitchen area behind him.

'Morning, Dad.'

She was sitting at the kitchen table, in her dressing-gown, drawing. She covered up the paper as he approached. Wednesday was differential calculus; perhaps she was redoing her schedule linear programme instead.

'Let me see,' he said. She held back. She was never normally reluctant to show him things. 'Come on,' he insisted with a laugh.

It was a strange, haunting picture of a boy standing against a black wall – or maybe it was a night scene, for the background was blacked out by thick scribbles of wax crayon. The boy's face was blank.

'I don't think you should be ...' he began, but checked himself. He softened his tone. 'That's very striking. Who is the person?'

'Nobody.' She turned it face down. 'It's for Danny.'

He went to the sink and filled the kettle.

'Danny sends you big hugs. You wouldn't believe the room they've given him! He's waited on hand and foot like a prince. It'll be a terrible come-down back here.'

He looked up. She hadn't moved. Normally – unless she was working, and then nothing could break her concentration – she was always jumping up and down or playing with her pony-tail or doing that double-jointed trick of hers, standing on one leg and holding the other foot high into the small of her back.

'I'll bring you in your tea,' he said. 'Go along now, darling.'

'OK, Dad.'

She rose and walked dully round towards the study.

'Set up DIFFCALC, and I'll be right along,' he called after her.

He made the tea and took it into the small, book-lined room. The pale morning sun filtered in through the window, brightening the dark green stained book-shelves and the rows of encyclopaedias and reference books.

Sophie was sitting at the desk, doodling with a felt-pen. Her textbooks stood in the piles where she'd left them the night before and the computer wasn't even switched on. He felt his annoyance rising.

'Come along, darling. You see? That's why I didn't want you going out late last night. Right, are we ready?' He switched on the terminal and logged on, then keyed in the letters, DIFFCALC. 'Now, we got to the equation starting delta-dash . . . Sophie?'

'Yes, Dad. I remember.'

'So, how do we complete the equation, given a value pf p . . . ?'

He could sense she wasn't with him. He looked up. Her oval face was even paler than usual and set in a hard, marble cast. He reached forward for her hand, then felt her forehead. It was cool, but normal.

'Are you all right, darling?'

'Fine, Dad.'

He glanced at the work schedule pinned to the side of the bookshelf by the window. It showed a grid with the days of the week broken down into half-hour slots and, against each, a subject title and a progress target. This had been her idea: she'd written a special linear programme for it. She loved order and system.

'Nineteen days left, that's all,' he said.

She turned her large violet eyes on him.

'Dad . . . ?'

'What is it?'

'Nothing.'

She looked down and began doodling absent-mindedly again. This wasn't like her at all. Something was wrong. Was it that she missed her brother? Taking down the work schedule, he rubbed out the two-hour inorganic chemistry slot on Friday afternoons and the biology of Sundays and inserted in their place the name 'Danny'. Then he pinned it back up again.

'We'll have to stick to the rest of the programme, won't we?' he said. 'Or else one of those'll have to go.'

* * *

He drove back from Bath into a spectacular sunset. He thought of a blind child he'd met at the clinic and felt a moment's familiar rage at the injustices of life. He'd had a serious word about Daniel with the consultant in charge of his case. The boy was being kept stable by drugs, but his illness had weakened his already poor resistance and the prognosis was, frankly, worrying. He wasn't telling Alex how worrying, of course. She'd driven over and spent the morning at the clinic, bringing Danny his space posters and a big box of toys to make his room seem a little more like home. They'd exchanged a word on the phone at lunch-time – a brief word, for neither could pretend his relapse was not a terrible blow. As a doctor, he knew too well how seriously the infection could develop; as a parent, though, he could only feel the child's pain, and simply hope.

Peals of laughter greeted him from the kitchen as he opened the front door. He went in to find Alex and Sophie sitting over the cassette player, recording a tape for Daniel.

'Hi, Dad,' cried Sophie. 'Come and say something. Mum's been doing a Suzanne impersonation.' She exaggerated the young nanny's lisp. ' "Sit up, Danny-boy, and draw me a nice big house." Hang on, you can hear.'

She wound the tape back and replayed it. The two of them fell about in fits of laughter. He looked around the room. A pile of Daniel's clothes lay on the ironing board and two irons, one a child's model, sat cooling on the work-top. Her satchel lay unopened on the table and beside it was spread a batch of Polaroid snaps of mother and daughter pulling funny faces.

Alex pressed the microphone on him.

'Come on, Jake,' she said. 'Say something.'

He hesitated. The clock on the wall read eight fifteen: Sophie's supper break should have been over half an hour ago, and it didn't look as if they'd even started yet.

'Be a sport, Dad,' urged Sophie.

He looked from one to the other. Of course he'd play the game. With a smile, he reached for the microphone. Sophie pressed the Record button. He cleared his throat.

'There once was a young lad called Danny,

'Who had a girl called Suzanne for a nanny . . .'

He faltered and, with a laugh, Alex took back the microphone.

'When asked, "Is she nice?"

'He replied in a trice . . .'

She looked helplessly towards Sophie. Without a second's hesitation, the young girl leaned forward and yelled into the mike,

'She's an awful lot nicer than Granny!'

Her hand flew to her mouth to suppress her laugh. Jake caught Alex's eye and they cracked up. Granny was Bettine, Alex's mother, a tart, uptight woman who stood on her dignity. He remembered one time she came to tea; Sophie was two and a half and made up some silly lines of verse for her – how had they gone? —

'Darling Granny Betts,

I love you very much;

If you were a rabbit,

I'd put you in a hutch.'

The woman had been deeply offended and demanded an immediate apology from the little girl.

'That's enough, now,' he said, still smiling. 'Shouldn't you be doing some work?'

Alex laid a hand on her daughter's.

'Supper won't be long, darling.'

Sophie reached for her satchel.

'Tell Dad I did the pastry,' she said. 'First time ever.'

He waited until he heard her study door close, then he turned sharply to Alex. She held up a hand.

'Don't,' she warned.

He reached for her arm but she moved out of the way.

'For God's sake, Alex, she's only got two and a half weeks!'

She cast him a pitying look.

'Your trouble, Jake, is you can only *listen* to a child through a stethoscope. She's very upset about Danny, can't you see? Give her some time and space to herself, let her go and visit him when she wants and she'll get over it. But if you crowd her like you do . . .'

She shook her head and bent to open the oven. A rich aroma of steak pie filled the room. He went to the sideboard and poured himself a whisky. He stood, swilling it round in the glass before swallowing it abruptly in a gulp.

Sophie waited until she heard Uncle Graham's foot-steps reach the bottom of the stairs, then she closed the book on endocrinology she'd been pretending to read and lay back against the pillows. Staring up at the ceiling, she began automatically patterning the flecks in the wood-chip wallpaper . . . She shut her eyes tight.

She'd seen Danny that afternoon, Friday. She'd told him, in Abacus, that she wasn't going to take her exams. She'd make herself fall sick or, if that didn't work, she'd just not write anything on the paper. Dad would be terribly upset. And that would be her fault, too.

She'd wanted to tell Uncle Graham just now; he'd been very clever, talking as if he really *understood*. But he'd only go and tell Dad, and Dad would laugh and

110

say, 'Nonsense!' Yesterday, Dad had found her in the study, reading *The French Lieutenant's Woman.* He'd been shocked. She was letting herself down, he'd said; letting *him* down, too. But she was really letting *Danny* down. She'd tried to explain, but he'd brushed it aside. 'Danny's being sent away because it's best for him,' he'd said. But she knew better. She'd heard what Mum had said. What could she do? Whatever way she turned, she was letting someone down.

That morning, she'd decided she'd just pretend to work. She'd make it look as if she was reading or doing calculations, while in fact she'd be thinking of something completely different. She'd tried it all day, but logically she knew it wouldn't work. She was only cheating herself. If Dad was taken in, she might just as well be studying properly, anyway. If he wasn't, he'd be even more upset when he did find out. One part of her knew she was being true to Danny by pretending, but another part knew, too, that pretending wasn't going to bring him back.

After a while she got up and fumbled in the back of her sock drawer for the exercise-books she'd hidden there. She hadn't written her diary for ages. Where should she start? Perhaps with that strange boy she'd seen creeping about the garden the other night.

'I don't know,' said Graham, knotting his fingers round his wineglass.

Jake pushed his plate away, unfinished. His stomach felt tight.

'Good thing you're not a doctor, Graham. "Don't know" wouldn't wash.'

Alex stacked the plates.

'Well, *I* know,' she said firmly. 'The girl's been overdoing it, and this is a perfectly natural reaction. I'm blue in the face telling him, Gray; it's laying up

111

trouble for her. Force her now and she'll crack up later. It's a known fact. This could be the first sign.'

'It's not a fact, actually,' her brother corrected her mildly. 'I was looking at a study of fifteen hundred gifted children, done by a bloke called Terman in California over a period of *fifty years*. The gifted ones had better brains and better bodies than the control group, they were more successful in their careers, they were healthier, more athletic, and even had fewer divorces and committed fewer crimes.'

Alex gave a derisory laugh.

'Statistics always hide individual cases. Bright sparks burn out later. Mathematical prodigies lose it in their twenties. Look at John Stuart Mill: he had a mental breakdown at twenty. Or that chess genius, John Nunn: he was out of a job at twenty-six. Or that American, Boris Sidis—'

'To me,' remarked Jake quietly, 'individual cases always say "special pleading".'

Two red spots appeared high on her freckled cheeks.

'You might like to know one thing they all have in common,' she retorted. 'They all had tyrannical fathers. Mozart, John Stuart Mill, Pitt the Younger, and what was that piano prodigy I was reading about whose father beat her all the time, Ruth Slenczynska or something—?'

Graham held up his hands, laughing.

'Alex, please! I hope you're not suggesting Jake *beats* the poor girl?'

'He *brow*beats her.'

Jake let it pass. Alex's experience of teaching children was ramming unwelcome facts down unwilling throats. She never understood that Sophie loved her work, she did it because she found it fun – or she had, till just recently.

He refilled their wineglasses.

112

'I heard the president of Mensa on the radio the other day,' he said in a quiet, factual tone. 'He was saying the hypothesis about burning out is an absolute myth. The real problem is the fire often doesn't get started in the first place. Too many potentially gifted children are lost before they even get to primary school, simply because they've had the misfortune to be born into a deprived environment. I don't mean lack of money, Alex, or even love. It doesn't matter whether you live on a council estate or in an affluent suburb: it's whether there are books around, whether curiosity is fed and whether the child is encouraged and stimulated to stretch itself even further.'

Graham was nodding judiciously.

'You're right about the burn-out myth,' he said, 'but Alex has a point about the psychological dangers. You're dealing with a child with a level of emotional development of eight or nine but the mind of a child twice that age.'

'Exactly,' agreed Alex at once.

'However,' continued her brother, 'you can avoid the dangers if you are aware of them.'

'Precisely,' said Jake.

A tense silence fell between them. Jake felt angry and hurt. He was tired of fighting Alex on every front all the time. If only she'd be more supportive, rather than always attacking and undermining him. If only she could think of Sophie as the actual child she was, with her thirst to know and discover, rather than wanting to hold her back in the cause of some outmoded egalitarian ideology. Sophie herself knew what was best for her. He'd watch over her and see she didn't overdo it; he loved her so completely, how could he conceive of letting her do anything that could possibly damage her?

But now there was this hiccough. Could she be

trusted to know what was best for her in *this*? Should he intervene, or leave her to it?

Graham was eyeing him intently as he looked up. He could have been reading his thoughts.

'Give it a day or two, Jake,' he said gently.

She sat staring out of the study window into the garden. The door was ajar and she could hear Mum washing up the Sunday lunch. Through the open window she could smell honeysuckle and roses and feel the warmth of the summer-afternoon air. At the foot of the freshly mown lawn stood the willow tree, like a giant waxy grass skirt, and to the right, by the tottering old brick wall, the large laurel bush in which Danny and she had once built a house. A buzzing distracted her thoughts. A large bumble-bee was caught between the sash panes. She watched it for a moment, beating itself so persistently against that invisible wall, and wondered if it knew anger and despair. Reaching for her pencil mug and a postcard, she quickly scooped it up and let it out.

Dad's footsteps were approaching across the living room. She sat down quickly and flipped the pages of her biology book forward a chapter or two.

She knew that look on his face – cheerful, pretending nothing was different, *hoping* nothing was different.

'How's it going, darling?' he asked.

'OK.'

'Here, let me see.' He took the book and nodded with approval, then turned back a few pages. 'That's an interesting view of the spinal cord. What are those disc-shaped particles in the nuclei of the epithelium?'

'The same as in the neuroglia cells,' she guessed.

'Yes, but what are they?'

She fumbled, looking down at her hands. This was awful.

He put the book down and drew up a chair beside her.

'Sophie, let's try and look at this thing logically. Exams are simply a means to an end. Passing your O levels is a necessary condition of reaching your goal. You can't hope to end up teaching at Cambridge unless you go through the necessary gates, one by one.'

'I know, Dad.'

He looked earnestly into her face.

'We all have our ups and downs, our moods, moments when we feel like giving up. You're ninety-five per cent home. The last five per cent is often the hardest, and you really have to push. It takes a lot of will power and self-discipline. You have got that, Sophie, abundantly. You must use it. Do you see?'

'Yes, Dad.'

He paused and dropped his gaze to his hands.

'I know what you're going through. My mother died a few days before my scholarship exams to university. I wanted to give up. I nearly did. But then I thought, What would *she* have wanted? So I buckled down and gave it that last five per cent.' He looked up into her eyes. 'I don't want to push you, darling. I want you to push yourself. Just this last lap.'

She nodded. What could she say? He didn't need to preach like this. She knew what exams meant. But that wasn't the point.

He stood up and stroked her head.

'Let's see how you get on now. We'll have another look in an hour or so. If it's going all right, there's no reason why you shouldn't come to see Danny with me later.' He went to the door and, turning, added, 'If I'm being hard, it's for your own good, darling. Because I love you.'

115

She waited till he'd left the room, then she turned back the pages to where she'd left off before. She read a paragraph but the words stuck on the page – she couldn't *see* them any more. She tried again, and a third time. Pushing the book away, she leant forward on the desk, put her head on her arms and quietly sobbed.

She watched from the landing window upstairs as the Volvo estate rolled down the gravel driveway, paused to check all was clear, then took off down the street. She clenched her fists. She felt like howling. All right, she hadn't done the work, but how *could* he go to see Danny without her?

She stamped downstairs as noisily as she could and barged in through the kitchen door.

Mum was putting on her gardening apron.

'Cheer up,' she said. 'You can come with me tomorrow, I don't care what your dad says.'

That wasn't the point, either. She blundered through the living room and kicked her study door open.

'Come on outside,' Mum called after her. 'Give me a hand. You could do with some sun.'

She didn't reply. She sat down at the desk and put her forehead in her hands. It was aching, throbbing. She swallowed; there was that funny taste again, too. She clenched her teeth. How *could* he have gone off without her?

After a while she made another attempt at the biology. It seemed to make a little more sense this time, but it just wasn't what she wanted to do. She wanted to be visiting Danny.

A sudden movement out of the corner of her eye made her look up out of the window.

It was him. The boy the other night. Valentin.

He was standing by the large laurel bush over by

the brick wall. He wore jeans, a red and blue check shirt and tatty old trainers. His eyes and his hair were dark, almost black. None of this surprised her.

He grinned and gave a small wave.

She got up and came to the window.

'Hi!' she said. 'How did you get in?'

He nodded his head towards the brick wall. He must have used the lawn-roller leaning against it to climb down. She looked across the garden to the far side. Mum was kneeling on a mat, weeding a flower-bed. She had her back to them. She got up and moved her mat a few feet along, but she didn't turn round.

Valentin had shrunk back into the bush, but now he came forward again. Still grinning, he reached into his back pocket, took out a small object and held it up to her, gripping it between his thumb and index finger. It was a smooth white pebble, just like the one she'd found on a beach once and given to Danny for his collection. With a sudden, deft movement, he whisked it away with the other hand, but when he opened that hand to show her, it was quite empty.

'Do that again!' she said, genuinely impressed.

Winking mischievously, he tossed the pebble in the air like a coin. Instead of catching it, he let it fall on the grass and reached into his pocket and, with a magician's flourish, produced another, identical stone.

This was brilliant!

'Hang on,' she said. 'I'm coming round.'

Knocking the biology book onto the floor in her eagerness, she ran down the hall and out through the back door into the garden and hurried round the side.

But he had gone.

Where? She felt a sharp pang of disappointment. She peered into the depths of the bush, but he wasn't there. She tried to climb onto the lawn-roller to look

117

over the wall, but it rolled forward at the lightest touch and she slipped off. You couldn't get over a wall using that.

Across the lawn, Mum looked up and caught sight of her.

'Sophie,' she called. 'Fetch me the secateurs from the shed, will you?'

'OK, Mum,' she answered with a sigh.

Just as she was turning away, something white caught her eye in the grass. It was the pebble. She picked it up. It was *exactly* like the one she'd given Daniel. Slipping it into her skirt pocket, she skipped down the path to the tool shed.

Pools of twilight mist hung in the low-lying land and strayed across the narrow country lanes. Trees that seemed distant one moment loomed close the next, and the bends in the road came up with sudden unexpectedness. The motorway from Bath to Bristol was blocked with roadworks and jammed with week-enders returning home, and Jake had left it at an early junction and struck across country.

He opened the window to fight off tiredness that came sweeping over him in waves. The onrush of air briefly braced him. He inhaled deeply the cool evening scents from the bristling thorn bushes and the cow-parsley overbrimming the roadsides. Above a green cornfield he caught sight of a kite hovering. A pair of starlings tore across in front of him, chasing off a marauding crow. On the road itself a pile of feathers marked where a pheasant, too old or too slow or too ill, had fallen victim to a car.

Ah, God. If only life could be as simple as Nature intended it. Man was the victim of his own ingenuity. Who really gained from all that love and care for the Dannys and Karens and Giannis of this world? The surgeons and doctors and nurses who could sleep comfortably at night, safe in their distinction between natural and unnatural causes? The parents and relatives who could sit at the supper-table with the empty chair and the empty place and feel reassured that they'd done everything possible? Or the poor children themselves? They *knew*. They knew they were different, that they were *wrong*. They could tell that the cheerfulness, the cajoling, the jollity around them was all false. You could make the best of a bad job, yes, but the job would always be bad.

Snap out of this! he told himself. He knew this mood. He was tired, harassed, worried, under pressure; that often brought on depression. A good night's sleep, some better news from the clinic in the morning, some sign that Sophie had pulled out of it, that was all he needed. He rubbed his face. The skin felt like someone else's. He glanced at the dashboard clock: eight thirty. He'd get home and have a damn good drink. He'd better step on it.

The air was getting chilly and he was winding up the window with one hand while steering round a gentle left bend when, without any warning, a figure—

Christ!

—a boy darted out. Right in front of him. Came from nowhere. Sprang from the ditch, from the hedgerow, from the air, the earth itself. A dark-haired boy. Wearing jeans, checked shirt, trainers. His face indistinct, a kind of blank, too quick to catch. Their eyes met. Horror flashed between them. Jake rammed his foot on the brakes. The boy leaped forward out of his way, but not fast enough. He was going to hit him!

He swerved wildly. The car lurched, lost balance, slewed round, hit the bank, spun back, toppled forward, fell side over side over side, the glass shattering, metal screeching, skidding, skating, all in a gentle slow motion, while he waited for the crash, the crunch, the crump, and then the pain, wherever it would be, pray God no, not now, not yet . . .

NINE

Am I alive? Yes, I can blink.

Where am I?

Upside down, chest pinned against steering-wheel, forehead pressed against shattered windscreen.

Try speaking aloud.

'Jesus bloody Christ!'

Speech and memory circuits undamaged. Next, the limbs.

Left hand OK. Right arm, *ouch*. Left leg hurts. Can't feel right leg.

Spine intact. You can move.

I can't.

Move, for God's sake, you stupid bastard! Get the hell out of here! Smell the petrol. The thing's going to blow up!

My legs are trapped. They'll have to cut me out . . . firemen with blow-torches . . . stench of burning flesh . . . I could still do the ward round from a wheelchair, propel myself by the hands across the floor from bed to bed in an orange-box on wheels like the cripples in Cairo . . .

On the passenger side, the roof had been stoved in onto the dashboard. The driver's window was shattered but the frame still roughly held. Above, he could see the twilight sky. He wriggled – *Aagh!* my shoulder! Come on, body, pump out the endorphins! – and squirmed up through the gaping hole. He heard the back of his shirt rip on the jagged glass and dimly felt it slice a gash in his flesh. Clambering out, he dragged himself through the brambles and out of the ditch until

121

he was clear. The car lay nose down, steam rising from the front, the back wheels still turning. Arse over tip (or is it *tit*?). He felt sick, overzapped with adrenaline. He shivered, though it wasn't cold: normal shock reaction, the body scrambling its sugar resources . . .

Now the final inventory. Would Dr Chalmers care to raise his right arm? No, we have a problem. Ah, I can feel it. Collar-bone broken, one end all but spiking through the skin. That's nothing. Undo a shirt button and ease the hand inside somehow, to form a sling. Blood streaming down face, hair caked and clotted, shirt collar drenched. That's not serious, a cut scalp always bleeds a lot, looks awful but isn't. Skull intact, and brain no more stupid than before. You ain't gonna be a vegetable, Jake Chalmers! He laughed aloud. Not a cauliflower, not even a Brussels sprout, no, sir! An ugli fruit, maybe . . .

Shut up. Get to a phone. Tell Alex it's all right, you had a puncture, you'll be late. Tell Sophie to carry on without you. You'll be right home. Tell her you love her.

Christ, that boy! I didn't hit him, did I? No, you didn't hit him. Where is he? Gone to get help?

Lights. A car. Flag it down. Stand up. Too fast. Everything swims, giddies, swirls, goes black.

An ambulance took Jake to the Royal Infirmary, his own hospital. X-rays showed he'd also fractured his left ankle. They set it in plaster, strapped up the collar-bone and stitched the deep gash in his back. He'd been bloody lucky. If he'd hit a tree, he'd have been killed; if he'd had a flimsier car, he'd have crushed his skull; a few millimetres deeper and the glass would have punctured his lung. But then, again, if he'd stayed on the motorway, or if he'd stopped on the way to phone home, or if he'd passed that spot a few seconds earlier, or later . . . If this, if that. Life was a blizzard of near misses; you only ever saw the ones that hit.

It was near midnight when they'd finished with him. They wanted him to stay in but he refused. Alex collected him and drove him home. She bathed him and put him to bed with a large brandy and some pain-killers.

Early in the morning she went to Sophie's room and told her the news. Sophie came rushing into the bedroom. She froze when she saw him. He was a pretty dreadful sight, yes, but not *that* bad! He'd never seen a look on her pale, oval face like it – not just shock but something closer to . . . *fear*? She hung back just inside the doorway, wide-eyed, tormented, then without a word she ran forward, threw her arms around him and hugged him tight.

Before he could stop her, Alex had called Frank Blythe over. The doctor ordered him to stay in bed for a week; Jake promised he would, without any intention of keeping the promise. Sophie brought him up breakfast and later came back in, dressed for school, to say goodbye. He hauled himself over to the window and watched as the small girl walked over to the waiting car. She looked up and caught his eye. She hesitated, then rushed back indoors, ran upstairs into the bedroom and without a word kissed him again, extra hard.

He stood at the window, waving, as the small pale face at the back of the car disappeared out of sight, then, throwing off his dressing-gown, began painfully climbing into his clothes. Hobbling on a walking-stick, with his trouser-leg slit to accommodate the plaster, he made his way by taxi to the hospital. The odd minor fracture wasn't going to stop him.

Around midday, he collapsed. The staff nurse sent for a consultant from Emergency. By the time he surfaced he was in Radiology. A scan showed a hair-line fracture in his skull, which would heal in time, but nothing more serious. Against all advice, he discharged himself and took a taxi home. He put himself back to bed. He'd be fine. What good was a physician who couldn't heal himself? Shivering despite the electric blanket and the hot summer afternoon and in pain despite the pharmacopoeia of tablets he'd collected from the dispensary, he lay in bed waiting for Alex to return with Sophie. She was off to visit Daniel after that, and then she had a staff meeting that would go on late. Good. He'd have a chance to talk to Sophie properly. Perhaps Alex was right after all and he was putting too much pressure on the child. Exams, science, career: you only had to brush with death to realise that none of it mattered in the end, only the beautiful fact of being alive.

For the first two periods Sophie sat composing Danny a letter in Abacus. The language used a twenty-four-letter Greek alphabet, but with several Arabic characters and two Hebrew vowels, too. He could only speak a few words and certainly couldn't read it, so she wrote the letter phonetically in English for someone at the clinic to read out to him. The rest of the class was busy writing a mock Additional Maths paper. She'd already done it in her head in a few moments and couldn't be bothered to write it down. What was the point, if she wasn't going to take the exams anyway?

Even so, it was hard to concentrate. She kept finding herself staring at the empty desk in front of her. Lizzie's desk. She'd been angry with Lizzie and look what had happened. Now the same with Dad. It was all her fault. She was a danger, a menace to people.

She made things happen without meaning to. Poor Dad: how could she make it up to him?

Taking a sheet of paper and without referring back to the exam paper, she quickly scribbled down the answers. Then she reached into her desk for her Gray's *Anatomy* to fill in the rest of the time before break.

Jake lay propped up in bed, his arm in a sling and his ankle in a cardboard carton under the sheets, which Sophie had made into a small tent. She sat cross-legged on the bed, tapping at the computer keyboard on a table she'd drawn up close. On the floor lay the tray with the supper she'd brought him up. The window was open onto the night; a car backfired in the distance, an owl hooted, a moth blundered around inside the lampshade on the bedside table, but nothing broke her concentration. He smiled to himself. This was more like it.

The keys clattered in small bursts. He could hardly follow the pace of the calculation. Suddenly she leaped back with a flourish.

'QED!' she cried.

He looked at the last few lines of the equation.

'Well done, darling.'

'Three minutes seventeen,' she beamed.

'Could be a record.'

Tilting her head, she cast him a wry smile.

'With that sling, Dad, all you need is an eye-patch and a parrot.' A distant look flashed over her face. 'Lizzie got a parrot for her last birthday.'

'Sophie, I hope you're not going to say what I suspect you are. Parrots are horrible, raucous, messy creatures.'

'I wasn't thinking of that.'

Her small oval face had clouded over and a perplexed frown puckered her brow. She toyed with her pony-tail, her eyes fixed on the coverlet, before abruptly looking up.

'Dad,' she asked hesitantly, 'can you make something bad happen by thinking it?'

'What do you mean?'

'There's a boy at school who . . . well, he has this idea that he *made* Lizzie's accident happen. They'd had a fight in the playground and he was thinking horrid, angry thoughts, and then she got run over.'

He reached for her hand. It was cold as marble.

'If you believe in positive thinking,' he replied, 'I suppose it's only logical to believe in negative thinking. We all have the power to heal ourselves, in body and mind. Possibly we can cause our own illnesses, too. Do harm to ourselves by thinking it. But not to other people.'

'Faith healers work on other people,' she objected. 'Couldn't you have . . . I don't know . . . faith *harmers*?'

'By definition it's a matter of faith, not fact.'

'But if it works?'

'There's a lot we don't know, Sophie.'

'That doesn't mean we *can't* know. Aristotle thought the blood was just there to cool the heart.'

He smiled.

'Knowledge changes, yes, but the principles of verifying it don't. The fact is, there simply hasn't ever been a single case of mind over matter that has been scientifically validated.'

'Maybe there's something wrong with the principles.'

He searched her anxious, puzzled face. What was in her mind? Was she trying to say something about *his* accident?

'Sophie, you've got to be careful here. Don't confuse the so-called paranormal with the normal. The supernatural is not natural. Your faith healers who perform miracle cures: it's the patients who cure themselves,

126

by their own mind power, not the healers by some transmitted power from outside. If you look deeper, there's invariably a perfectly rational explanation. No so-called paranormal event has ever been replicated in a laboratory under proper test conditions. The whole area is nonsense, dangerous nonsense. It belongs to the world of superstition and myth we left behind with the Enlightenment.'

She was nodding slowly. It was vital to guide her thinking correctly. On one level, she possessed an extraordinary mind capable of effortless feats of memory and calculation, but on another she was only a child of eight and three-quarters, inevitably lacking experience of life and vulnerable to the lure of the magic of a child's imagination. She must not be allowed to confuse the real with the unreal world. She, of all people.

She had turned back to the terminal and was keying in another equation.

'Dad,' she began in a different tone, 'what if we introduce a random variable there . . . ?'

Alex stepped out of the taverna into the balmy night air. Arthur followed, shutting the door on the blaring *sirtaki* and the smell of grilled lamb and oregano. She closed her eyes; she could have been twenty-one again, in Poros (or was it Paros?), with the sea plashing on the beach and the resinous scent of pines giddying her like a forbidden narcotic. A lorry roared past dangerously close and Arthur drew her back by the elbow. No, she was forty-six and this was Bristol. What did she think she was doing?

She glanced up at him. An attractive man, she thought: lean, fit, hair greying at the temples. A brave man as well, bringing up four children alone, but beneath it all a lonely man, too. He was a careful, receptive listener. She'd opened up too freely about her problems at home. She could hardly blame the retsina.

'I'm sorry,' she said. 'All I've done is go on about *me*.'

'I'm pretty fond of the subject,' he smiled, walking her to her car. 'I'd suggest a drinkable coffee somewhere, Alex, but I know you've got to get back.'

'Maybe next time.'

As they reached the car, she turned and kissed him on the cheek, then again, lightly, on the lips. She felt an adolescent's gaucheness. She wasn't very practised at this.

She fumbled for her keys.

'That was very nice. Greek food is always best outside Greece.'

He held the car door open.

'Don't forget to ask Sophie about Wales. It'd do her the world of good.' He cast her a long, concerned look. 'Call me if ever you need anything.'

'Thank you, Arthur. And thanks for the evening. You're very kind.'

She shut the door. She didn't catch his reply.

She drove home fast. Her hands was shaking. What was she up to? She wasn't ready for an adventure; she had enough on her plate already. And yet. She was still a woman. What about the walking holiday he was taking his four children on? Should she send Sophie with them? He was right: it would do the girl the power of good to get away from her books and do something completely different. Maybe she'd go along herself, too. It would be the perfect chance to be together.

Stop it! How could she be thinking like this? She had Danny poorly in a clinic and Jake laid up in bed. Shame on her! Maybe things were all her fault; perhaps she hadn't been giving Jake what he needed.

She ought to try harder, at least one more time, before she could declare an irretrievable breakdown.

She rose early the following morning. She chose the floral summer dress Jake liked and put on a touch of make-up. She brought him a bowl of yellow roses from the garden, with a cup of tea and his mail. She opened the curtains, switched on Radio Three and woke him with a light kiss.

'How did you sleep?' she asked.

'Like the innocent.' Wincing as he moved, he reached forward for the letters.

She sat down on the bed and took them first.

'I'll open them for you,' she said. 'You shouldn't use that arm.'

'Muscles need exercise or they atrophy.'

'Even so.'

She bit her lip. This wasn't going to be easy. She went through the small pile one by one. The first she recognised from the large, shaky handwriting. 'Your father.'

'I'll deal with it later.' He smiled. 'Pity, I won't be able to sign cheques.'

'Here's one from the insurance.' She opened the letter. 'The car's a write-off.'

'So was the driver almost.'

'At least the car's replaceable.' She moved to the next. 'This one looks like a circular. Forwarded from the Department. Shall I open it? Jake?'

He was far away in his own thoughts.

'That boy. I *would* have known if I'd hit him, wouldn't I? I can't remember that much.'

She laid her hand on his.

'You must stop worrying. The police said there was no one else involved. You must have missed him.' She opened the circular. 'Some Neurological Association conference in Oxford.' She was just putting it aside when a name caught her eye. She looked more closely. 'Wasn't Helen Lorenz *your* Helen? Seems she's now at the University of Chicago.'

'Let me see.'

'She's giving a paper. "Genetic Coding for Intelligence". That was your work, Jake!'

He whipped the leaflet out of her hands and read the rubric with a growing frown. Alex watched, perplexed.

'What's wrong?' she asked. 'Is she plagiarising you?'

'It's okay.' He slipped the paper under a magazine on the bedside table and gave a short, unconvincing laugh. 'I remember you once said that I might turn the work down myself but that wouldn't stop someone else picking it up. Well, it seems you were right. Any other fan mail?'

'Just a billet-doux from the electricity board.'

'That I will deal with later.' He struggled to sit up. 'I'm getting up.'

'You're doing no such thing. Lie back down. I'll bring you breakfast. Any special requests?'

'I placed my order last night.'

'I see. Well, I'd better go and check Room Service is working.'

'She's got it taped. Four minutes for the egg, half a sugar in the coffee.' He grinned. 'Nothing like being spoiled.'

She forced a bright smile in return and went to the door. As she was leaving, she saw him reach for the conference leaflet. Oh, God: Helen again. Did all this have to be raked up?

On the half-landing she met Sophie coming upstairs, carrying a laden tray. The young girl stopped, cast her a thoughtful glance and handed her the tray.

'You take it in, Mum,' she offered.

130

'No, darling,' she replied. 'You made it.'

She hung back on the stairs as Sophie entered the bedroom. Through the half-open door she listened as the two began their usual quick, animated repartee. A desperate sinking feeling gripped her. Father and daughter were so close; they had a bond she could never share, an understanding that quite excluded her. It made her attempts to communicate all the more painful, and pitiful.

Abruptly she turned away and hurried down the stairs to the utility room, where Daniel's clothes were lying in large piles for washing, mending and ironing. As she fed a heap of his dungarees into the washing-machine for Suzanne to sort out later, she tried to fight down a rising sense of hopelessness. Here she was, with the news on Danny getting worse, cleaning clothes which in her heart she somehow knew he would never wear, while up there the other two ... Defiant, angry, helpless, with tears filling her eyes, she began cramming more and more clothes into the machine, towels and shorts and sweatshirts, forcing them in, one upon another, until she could hardly shut the door.

Wednesday was a revision day and Sophie stayed at home. It was raining and the house bore a June chill, and she studied upstairs in the bedroom with Jake, snuggled under the duvet alongside him and surrounded by piles of books.

As her watch bleeped one o'clock, she put down the copy of *Mind* she was reading.

'Come on, Dad, time to strap you up.'

With a groan he sat up and took off his pyjama top. Standing behind, she unwound the thick crêpe bandage and, readjusting the cotton-wool padding, tied it up again, but tighter. Dad had read the article,

131

too, and was going on about language and whether it was a uniquely defining feature of man. Were the chimpanzees using American Sign Language actually *speaking*? She wound the bandage round his mouth to silence him, making the words come out muffled and indistinct.

'There,' she said. 'You can't speak, so you can't be human.'

In response, he laughed and growled and whimpered like an ape. She was opening the drawer of the bedside table for the sticking plaster to hold the bandage in place when a leaflet fell out. She picked it up.

'What's the Neurological Association, Dad?' she asked.

He spun round, letting out a cry as the sudden jolt hurt his shoulder.

'It's nothing,' he said shortly, taking it from her.

She tweaked his ear.

'Nothing?'

'Just about some conference, darling,' he said. 'No, the point about those chimps Washoe and Sarah—'

'You're changing the subject.'

'*You* were. I was talking about whether the chimps are forming meaningful new concepts or just responding to conditioning.'

'Come on, Dad, let's see,' she teased, reaching forward.

'No!' he snapped, then his tone softened. 'Have you pinned the bandage? Thanks. Right, I'm going to get dressed. Can't bear slugging around in this bed a minute longer.'

She glanced out of the window. The rain had stopped and the sky was brightening.

'I'll make some sandwiches and we can go for a walk round the garden.' She saw him look at his watch. 'An

132

hour maximum, Dad. We can talk in sign language. I'll teach you.'

The mossy stone steps down to the lawn were slippery from the rain and she had to hold his arm to steady him. His walking-stick sank into the turf as he went, leaving a trail like a peg-leg. The sun had come out, and mist rose silkily off the grass. They made one circuit, then another. On the third, they fell silent. As they passed the laurel bush, she thought back to Valentin's trick with the pebble. It *had* been Danny's – she'd realised that when she'd gone to add it to his collection – but the other one? Pure magic. What was he doing right now? Lunch break at school, probably. It would be nice to know his phone number.

Dad broke the silence. He was regarding her carefully.

'That friend of yours at school,' he began in a casual tone.

'Which friend?'

'The one you said was worried about Lizzie. Did they say anything else? Like about having ... funny feelings?'

She felt a flush rise to her face, betraying her.

'No. She didn't. She said she'd been making it up anyway.'

His easy smile wasn't echoed in his eyes.

'I thought you said it was a boy.'

'Oh, did I?'

'You did. I remember.' The pause lengthened. 'Darling,' he went on finally, 'you would tell me, wouldn't you, if there was something ... *wrong*?'

The note in her voice was transparently false.

'Nothing's wrong, Dad,' she replied lightly.

'If ever there is ...'

'There isn't.'

He smiled, almost apologetically.

'Good.' He walked on a few paces, swiping at the buttercups. 'My goodness, how the rain brings the lawn on! I only mowed it on Saturday.'

'Sunday morning, Dad.'

'Oh yes, so it was.'

She caught his eye and raised an eyebrow.

'You remembered, Dad?'

He laughed and went on to talk about the puzzle of memory. How were memories stored if they weren't located in particular places in the brain? He seemed quite keen to do the talking, while she walked beside him, interjecting the odd comment now and then. Her thoughts were elsewhere. Had he found her out?

TEN

'Dr Romberg will be right along.' The nurse smiled, ushering them into the consultant's office. 'Do take a seat. Coffee? Something for the young lady? You're Sophie, aren't you? I've read about you.'

'We stopped on the way, thanks,' replied Jake.

'Taking O levels at your age! Just think of it!'

'Thank you, Nurse.'

Alex cast him a look that said, That wasn't very nice. What could he do? This was going to get worse; already three national papers had phoned asking to run features on Britain's youngest-ever O-level pupil. There were only ten days to the first exam and Sophie was working smoothly and confidently. He was damned if her attention was going to be distracted – damned, too, if the truth about her was to be distorted by sensationalism. The photographers were sure to be at the school gates on the first day, note-books out and flashbulbs popping; he'd have a word with the Head and see if there wasn't a back way in.

He watched Alex casting a critical eye around the room with its leather and teak furniture and ultra-modern equipment. That's private practice for you, Alex, he thought; you only get the very best when you pay for it. Would you give Danny any less?

Sophie stood scanning the shelves. From time to time she took out a book and skimmed through the pages.

'Sit down, darling,' said Alex. 'It's bad manner rummaging through people's books.'

'Just a tick, Mum. Dad, have you seen this?'

She was showing him an old copy of *Scientific American* with Pribram's article on the neurophysiology of remembering when Dr Romberg walked in. The doctor instinctively shot her a reproving frown, then realised.

'Feeding the insatiable mind, eh?' he chuckled.

Sophie blushed and went to put the magazine back.

'I'm sorry,' she muttered.

'Take it, my lass, and keep it.'

He ushered the three of them into chairs and perched on the front of his desk, his hands thrust in his white coat and a look of grave concern on his smooth pink cheeks.

'There's good news and bad news,' he began. 'The good news is that Daniel is stable. And we think we've found the right antibiotics.'

He shot Jake a questioning glance. Jake understood.

'It's all right,' he said quietly. 'Sophie knows all the facts.'

'The bad news,' continued the doctor, hesitantly at first, 'is it looks as if the leukaemia was only in abeyance.'

Sophie caught her breath. Alex cupped the child's hand in hers.

'I really don't think Sophie should . . .' she began.

'It's all right, Mum,' said the girl.

The doctor looked to Jake for confirmation, then resumed.

'The lung infection means his blood is short of oxygen. If the leukaemia takes hold again, he'll have still fewer red blood cells to carry oxygen round his body. Now, the antibiotics may do their job and tackle the general toxaemia. But Daniel is already very weak, and if they don't, we will have to consider blood transfusions.'

'Is there a problem with that?' asked Alex quickly.

'Daniel's blood group is a very rare one. We've had red-cell clotting on all our stock samples.'

Alex looked puzzled. Sophie leaned towards her.

'He means,' she whispered, 'there's an antibody in Danny's serum which attacks the antigen in the red cells in the blood they want to give him. That makes it clot, and so it's no good.'

Dr Romberg listened, his eyebrows rising. He nodded.

'Precisely. So one turns to his immediate family. Your husband, Mrs Chalmers, has already given me details of his own blood group, and it's not compatible. I'd like to take samples from you and your daughter.'

'Of course. And then?'

'If we need to, we'll know we can give Danny a transfusion which could save his life.' His hand reached for a bell. 'I suggest the nurse does it right away. Then you can go and see the patient.'

Jake held Sophie's hand tight as he led her into Daniel's room. This was going to be a shock.

The boy lay propped up on pillows. He was breathless, feverish and deathly white. Small flecks spattered the front of his pyjama top where he'd coughed up blood. Behind the bed was pinned a small collection of get-well cards. Vases of flowers and a whole Noah's ark of cuddly animals covered every available surface, and from the windows a fine view stretched over spacious, well-kept grounds. He seemed to register very little of this.

Sophie went over and, taking his hand, whispered in his ear. His face, twisted with pain and discomfort, gradually softened into a smile. He struggled to sit up but she eased him back.

'Lie still, Danny darling,' she said. 'I'm right here.'

Jake caught Alex's eye and nodded towards the

door. Quietly they left the room and waited outside in the corridor. After a short while, he went back in. Daniel was sitting up, playing pat-a-cake with his sister. A faint colour had returned to his cheeks and he looked livelier than he had for days.

Before long, though, he began showing signs of tiring. Jake reached forward and touched Sophie on the shoulder.

'Time to go and let him rest, darling,' he said softly.

'But, Dad—'

'You'll come again on Sunday.'

They said goodbye. Alex promised she'd be back in the morning and spend the whole of Saturday there, and Jake would get over somehow, too. Sophie gave her brother a long kiss and whispered something in their secret language. As they left the room, Jake turned. Daniel's eyes were filled with tears and his expression was so forlorn that Jake went back in and hugged him tight, telling him everything was going to be all right and he'd soon be back home, sleeping in his own room, with all his own toys, having Mum cooking all his favourite food, and playing in the garden with Sophie, splashing around in the paddling-pool together . . . all those things Jake himself so desperately wanted to believe.

She sat on a rug beneath the shade of the great weeping willow tree, watching the needles of sunlight flickering through the fronds whenever the breeze stirred the leaves. The funny taste in her mouth had gone and her head had stopped hurting. This was a perfect hideaway, cool and secret and beautiful. So far from that terrible place where they'd sent Danny – where *she*'d sent Danny. But everything now would be all right. She was going to save him. She'd told him so, she'd whispered it in his ear: they were going to take her blood and give it to him to make him better. She'd *promised*. She'd told him over and over until he understood, and that made him very happy. Then they'd had to go, and he'd looked so sorry, so helpless. She hadn't cried, though. Crying wouldn't get him better. It was, as Dad always said, illogical.

She looked over to Valentin.

The boy sat a few yards away at the foot of the tree. He had his back to her and was whittling away at a willow stick with his penknife. He was going to make the shed at the back of the tree into a proper house. It was good to have him there.

She was returning to her book when she heard Dad's voice calling.

'Sophie?'

He called again, this time closer.

'*Psst!*,' she hissed. Valentin looked up, quite casual. She nodded urgently towards the shed. He shrugged. 'Hurry!' she whispered.

He clambered to his feet and slouched off into the shed. She heard the door close behind him just as Dad parted the fronds. He carried two mugs and a plate of biscuits.

'Brought you some tea,' he said, sitting down beside her. 'How are you feeling? Headache gone?'

'Fine, thanks.'

'Sitting in the sun probably did it.'

She took a biscuit.

'Dad, will they come here or will I have to go there?'

'For what?'

'For the transfusion.'

He smiled and patted her knee.

'Don't let's jump the gun, darling. They haven't done the tests yet. Let's hope it won't be necessary, anyway.' He reached for the book before she could say any more. 'Now, let's see, where have you got to?'

139

She knew Valentin wouldn't come out while Dad was there and she couldn't keep him cooped up for ever. She rose to her knees and brushed the crumbs off her skirt.

'Shall we go indoors and work there?'

'If you like.'

He picked up the tea and the rug. As she followed, she shot a glance over her shoulder. Valentin was at the dusty shed window, watching.

Alex hurried through the pouring rain to the front door, laden with shopping from the car. She dropped the latch-key and, bending too quickly, cracked the bag with the Rioja, smashing the bottle on the stone step.

'Hi! I'm home!' she called. 'Sophie, come and give me a hand, would you, angel?'

Jake hobbled out of the living-room door, a pencil tucked behind his ear and his glasses on their string round his neck. This place was getting like a school crammer, she thought. Putting his walking-stick under his arm, he reached to help her with the bags.

'Don't be silly, love,' she said. 'You can't possibly.'

'Sophie's in the middle of a tricky theorem. Hey, something's dripping.'

'Wine. You could fetch a cloth, though.'

She wiped the floor, wrapped the broken bottle in newspapers, then took the shopping into the kitchen and began to unpack. Jake put on the kettle.

'How was Danny today?' he asked.

'Stable, so Dr Romberg said. Does stable mean good or bad?' She pushed past him to the cupboard with an armful of tins. Why was she still buying the boy's spaghetti? 'He missed you.'

'I can't be everywhere, Alex. I've only just come off duty as it is.'

She'd tried not to sound reproachful, but his defensive reaction by now seemed a reflex.

'I told him I'd drive you over tomorrow.' She caught his expression, 'Oh, I forgot. Tomorrow is the conference. Tomorrow is Helen.'

'It's damn difficult, the clinic being so far away.'

She bit her lip. Whose idea had *that* been? she wanted to ask. Instead, she busied herself putting the coffee and tea away in the cupboard, letting the silence lengthen.

'Romberg has the results of the blood tests,' she continued eventually. 'I'm not compatible. But Sophie is. I'll tell her at tea.'

'I don't think we should,' he said quickly. 'Not yet, at least.'

'But she's been asking to know.'

'It may not need to come to that.'

She stopped unpacking. There was something in his tone she didn't like.

'What are you saying, Jake?'

'Just that her exams start in six days' time and giving blood takes a hell of a lot out of a child.'

'She will do it if she's needed, even if it means scrapping her bloody exams.'

'Of course, Alex. *If* she's needed.'

His tone still left her uneasy, but she forced herself to brighten. She'd resolved to try and stop bickering.

'I've got you a steak tonight,' she said. 'And liver for Sophie, as you said. Liver for iron, isn't it? Good for the blood. She'll be needing plenty of that.'

She couldn't help it. The words came out by themselves, the tone was ineradicable. What hope was there when the mistrust went so deep?

'. . . conclusively establishes the site of the HIG, the

141

human intelligence gene, on the distal portion of the long arm of chromosome thirteen. I believe this takes us a major step forward in our understanding of intelligence and gives us hope of an early cure for a wide range of disorders, from mental retardation in childhood to senile dementia in old age. Thank you, ladies and gentlemen.'

A brief silence was followed by prolonged, thoughtful applause, which Helen acknowledged with a series of brief nods. It was a brilliant performance: brilliant work, based on damn good earlier research – mainly *his* research, of eight years before. But she'd gone that crucial step beyond; she'd taken their work and seen it through. Listening to the clapping rippling round the amphitheatre, Jake couldn't help feeling a touch of professional regret. This could have been his, and more.

He sat alone, far at the back. Through the window he could see the Gothic spires and towers of the Oxford skyline. Below, in the well of the hall, the neuroscientists were thronging the lectern at which Helen had delivered her paper, grabbing copies of the text on the near-by table and pressing through the crush to speak to her.

He waited until the hall had finally emptied and Helen was left alone, collecting up her papers, then hobbled down the steep steps.

She looked up. Immediately she was on the defensive.

'Ah, Jake. I wondered if you might turn up here.'

'Hello, Helen.' He swung his plaster cast down the last step. 'Yes. I'm very interested in what you've been making of our work.'

'Now look, I've credited you in the footnotes—'

'Not interested like that.'

'Oh, no?' She held his eye in defiant disbelief.

She'd changed. She wore her dark, wavy hair shorter. Her dazzling blue eyes were sharper, quicker, wiser, less trusting. Her complexion seemed creamier, her jaw wider, her cheekbones more defined, her mouth harder, grittier and her whole bearing more challenging. She'd gone American.

'You're looking good, Helen,' he said with sincerity.

'Better than you.'

He smiled.

'Helen, that was a terrific talk.'

'I'm glad you think so,' she said, continuing to assemble her papers. 'I've always respected your judgement,' she added with a trace of sarcasm.

This wasn't working. He felt uncomfortable.

'Helen, can we go and talk somewhere?'

'Talk away here,' she said, packing her briefcase.

'Where are you staying?'

'Jake, what exactly are you after?'

He spotted a hotel key in her briefcase just as she was snapping it shut.

'I'll see you in the bar at the Randolph at six thirty.'

The bar was already filling up. Ten, fifteen minutes passed, and she still hadn't appeared.

Finally she arrived. The hand she offered him was cool and scented. She sat down, placed a small evening bag on the table between them and ordered a vodka martini. She lit a cigarette. When the drinks arrived, she signed the tab before he could protest.

'I should be thanking you,' she said with an ironic smile. 'For leaving the field to me.'

'I'm happy you found so much of our work useful.'

'Our work? You destroyed all our work, if I remember.'

'Helen, I'm not here to—'

'My work is all original research, Jake. I hope,'

143

she added carefully, 'you're not meaning to stake a claim?'

'Believe me, no.' He meant it, but she eyed him dubiously. 'I just wanted to ask you something you didn't mention in your paper.' He leaned forward. 'Those rats of ours. The ones that went feral. When you duplicated our work and tested it, what happened?'

' "Our work", as we'll hypothetically call it—'

'For Christ's sake, Helen! I'm not out to muscle in on you! I finished with research eight years ago. You can get a Nobel Prize, I don't care. I just need to know something. It's very important to me. For my peace of mind.'

She weighed him up briefly, then leaned forward and reached into her evening bag. There was a small *click*.

'Off the record, then. Jake, you were a fool to pack it in when you did. Yes, I got the same problems with the rats we had. They flipped at around eighteen months, like an inbuilt time-bomb. But we quite misinterpreted the evidence!'

He caught his breath.

'You mean, they *weren't* reverting?'

'Absolutely not. I'm not sure how to put it, but they were expressing their real natures. Supremely intelligent rats, *behaving supremely like rats.* The intelligence gene seems to have made them extra-capable of expressing their urges and instincts. When hungry, they were doubly clever at getting food. When threatened, they became doubly aggressive, and so on. What made them go apparently wild was, quite simply, *anger.* Anger at being shut up in a cage, anger at being made to perform all those tests, at being handled, examined, injected . . . Their rage was so powerful it actually modified their appearance. Their coats turned brown,

144

the hair went coarse, just like primitive rats – but they were *not* primitive rats. They were still highly intelligent creatures, only they were repressed and expressing their repression in this extra-powerful way.'

'You checked this, of course?'

'What do you think, Jake? Once I'd worked it out, I had a special hundred-cubic-metre living-area built for them, replicating their natural world as far as I could. And I left them alone. Then they were fine.'

But a light frown had settled on her brow. He leaned further forward.

'Perfectly fine?'

'Well, I could eliminate their anger at being imprisoned,' she admitted, 'but not the aggression and hostility that arose naturally between them as individuals in a group.'

'And how did that express itself?'

She reached for her drink.

'The thing is, of course,' she continued finally, more to herself, 'rats don't have *minds*. Nothing to mediate their instincts, nothing to temper their urges. You'd expect odd things to happen.'

'Odd things?'

She looked up sharply, then smiled.

'As you used to say yourself: testing human genes in animals, what does it really tell you? You must test like on like.'

'But no one's surely—!'

'Jake, you know better than to ask that.' She paused. 'I work in America, not Britain. All research ultimately has a commercial, *human* end-use.'

'But *is* anyone?' he persisted.

'Not as far as I know,' she replied. 'Yet.'

'And the rats,' he pressed her again. 'There's no doubt whatever they were not reverting?'

'I've told you. None whatever.'

They fell quiet. He sank back into the seat. This was wonderful news, better than he could ever have hoped for. He felt years of anxiety lifting from his shoulders. The time-bomb still ticked, but explosion would take the subject a leap forwards, not backwards.

He flagged a waiter down with a ten-pound note; he wasn't going to let her get away with this one. She looked at her watch.

'I shouldn't. Harry Gottlieb will kill me. Why do colleges dine so absurdly early? It's almost as bad as in the States.'

'See him in the morning. Let's have dinner together.' He cast her a long look. 'It's good to see you, Helen.'

She smiled.

'Good to see you, too, Jake.'

Alex lay in bed, unable to concentrate on her book. She'd been to see Danny; things were no different. She'd sent Sophie to bed early; the poor girl looked pale and exhausted. Jake had called saying he'd missed the last train and was going to stay overnight at the Randolph Hotel. As she reached to turn the light out, her eye fell on the honeymoon photo on the bedside table. Funny how you stopped noticing things. People, too: you could live with somebody for so long that they became, somehow, invisible. You had to *work* at seeing them. In the early days, when he'd gone off to conferences, they'd always phone last thing at night, just to touch hands, to renew contact.

She leant over and picked up the phone. She'd call and say goodnight. Directory Enquiries gave her the number of the Oxford hotel.

'Dr Chalmers, please,' she said when she was connected.

There was a long pause. She could hear pages being turned.

146

'We have no listing for Dr Chalmers, madam,' came the eventual reply.

Puzzled and worried, she was about to replace the receiver when a terrible suspicion entered her mind.

'Is there a Dr Lorenz staying?' she asked. 'Dr Helen Lorenz?'

This time the response was quick.

'Yes, madam. Putting you through.'

She slammed the receiver down and flung herself back on the pillow.

Oh God, why did she have to find out like this?

Jake had missed the last train by moments and, having called Alex from the station, he'd sauntered back through the warm night to the Randolph. He'd felt too elated to sleep: Helen had silenced his deepest terror. The hotel was full and he'd ended up at a bed and breakfast near by, catching an early train back home to Bristol in the morning.

He left the taxi waiting outside the house and hurried in to shave and change before going to work. As he came in through the front door, he found Alex and Sophie in the hall, preparing to leave for school. Alex was busy packing a pile of corrected homework. She cast him a strange, hostile glance, then went on with what she was doing.

Sophie ran up and hugged him.

'Hi, Dad,' she cried. 'How was the conference?'

'Couldn't have been better.'

Alex looked up. 'I bet it couldn't,' she said tersely.

'You missed a great supper,' Sophie went on. 'Mum and I went to Sainsbury's and we made a huge fish stew, French style. We left you some.'

'Why weren't you working?' he said, kissing her head.

'I was, kind of. I stood behind those check-out

147

tills, adding up the numbers as they came up on the screens. I did three at once. No mistakes.' She picked up her satchel. 'It's good about Danny, isn't it? Me being compatible, I mean.'

He shot Alex a glance of annoyance. She returned it defiantly. She turned to the child.

'Hurry up, angel, or we'll be late.'

' 'Bye, Dad,' said Sophie at the door. 'See you later.'

' 'Bye, darling. We'll look at that theorem again tonight, OK?' He reached to give Alex a kiss, but she brushed past him. 'Don't worry about me, love, I've got a cab waiting outside.'

'I'm sure you can take care of yourself, Jake. Come on, Sophie.'

He stood on the doorstep, waving them off. What was wrong with Alex? Hot one minute, cold the next. Still, he hadn't got time to think about that. If he didn't hurry, he'd be late for his morning round.

She sat at the kitchen table, watching Mum's face harden as she listened to the doctor at the other end of the phone. Finally, having said hardly a word herself, Mum put the receiver down.

'What did he say?' she asked.

'He has high hopes.'

'Come on, Mum, what did he *really* say? When does he want me in?'

'They're watching to see if the infection spreads. If it doesn't respond to the antibiotics, they'll need you then.'

She felt a twinge of panic. What if something went wrong too quickly and they didn't get her there in time?

'Mum? He will be all right, won't he?'

'Of course he will, darling. Dad says Dr Romberg is the best in the country. Now, when you've finished the

148

chapter, give me a hand upstairs with Danny's room. I thought we'd change it round for him.'

Sophie pushed the book aside. It was Saturday morning and exams started on Monday. Anything she didn't know by now she never would.

'Let's go and do it now,' she said.

Uncle Graham came by for supper that evening. He'd been to the clinic. Dad had still been there; he'd hired an automatic car, which he could drive without using his injured foot. She could see Uncle Graham wasn't going to tell Mum the latest news in front of her, so she made an excuse and left the room, but stood outside the door, listening.

The antibiotics weren't working, he reported. They were giving it until the morning, and if there was no improvement they'd call in his sister and begin the transfusions.

She went on upstairs, happy. It meant they were going to save him; *she* was going to save him.

Jake followed Dr Romberg into the corridor, glancing back through the small window at the pallid, comatose boy. The sight of a child suffering was a pain that grew sharper every time. Sunday morning: how much longer could it last?

He caught the doctor's eye.

'I'm sorry, Jake,' said the man simply.

Jake shook his head sadly.

'A transfusion won't even help.'

Dr Romberg nodded. 'Not with the carcinoma developing like that. If it were only a question of the infection . . .'

'Yes, if only.'

What could he say, what should he think? As a doctor himself, he knew this was the only way, but as the father his heart cried out to do something, *anything*.

'We both have been here before, many times,' the doctor was saying, 'and it only gets worse. We vaunt our great medical achievements, but really they're very puny. We can't create life, and we can't cheat death. Not much to show for three thousand million years, eh?'

Jake turned to the door. He wasn't in the mood for other men's philosophy.

'I think,' he said quietly, 'I'll go and sit with him a bit longer.'

Alex sat beside Daniel's bed, holding his hand. Though it was ten at night, the sky was still light – abnormally light in the way it was around midsummer. This was her shift. Jake would be at home, giving Sophie her last-minute coaching for her first exam in the morning. A gentle breeze through the open window fluttered the handful of cards on the wall above the boy's bed. Get Well Soon, they read. A wish or a command? Neither seemed any use now.

Daniel stirred. His bloodless face was frightened.

'Mum? Mum?' he called.

'I'm here, darling,' she replied, pressing his hand tighter and moving close so he could see her with his half-open eyes. But could he? He didn't seem to be focusing any more. His head rolled from side to side, his tongue lolled slack and every now and then he broke into a meaningless babble that sounded like the private language he shared with Sophie.

Suddenly his breathing grew short, too short, in small, desperate, panting gasps, like a fish suffocating out of water. Oh, God, not again, the poor lamb. This had been going on too long. Couldn't they *do* something?

She hurried out to the corridor and hailed the

150

young night doctor. The doctor came in, felt the boy's pulse and checked the equipment around him.

'Give him the transfusion,' she implored. 'Get my daughter in. Look, he's suffocating from lack of oxygen.'

'Dr Romberg says a transfusion is not necessary now.'

'What do you mean, not necessary *now*?' she hissed. 'Where is Romberg? Let me speak to him!'

'Dr Romberg is not on call,' replied the doctor and began checking the boy's pulse again. What was the stupid man doing? Checking he was really dying? 'I'm in charge.'

'Well then, *do something*.'

'We're doing everything possible, Mrs Chalmers. I appreciate it's very distressing for you—'

'Where's your phone? Show me where your phone is.'

'Dr Romberg is ex-directory.'

'I don't give a damn about Dr Romberg. My husband's a paediatrician. He's got more experience than the lot of you put together. I'll get him over. He'll bring Sophie. And then we'll see what's necessary and what isn't.'

Jake put his foot flat on the accelerator. He'd left Sophie studying magnetons, with a neighbour babysitting. The motorway was clear and in no time the signs for the Bath exit came up. He raced through the city, ignoring speed restrictions and jumping traffic lights. At the clinic he grabbed his stick and hurried in past the empty reception desk and down the corridor to Daniel's room.

Alex looked up as he burst in. Her face said it all. She sat there, white-faced, her eyes bloodshot from weeping. Daniel lay with his head on one side, very

151

still, very peaceful. Aghast, he reached for the boy's pulse, then lifted his eyelid.

There was no doubt.

Sophie looked out at the starry sky. Wherever God was, would He hear her?

Dad had gone to see Danny, but they hadn't asked for her. That must mean he was getting better. Please God, she prayed, say that he was. Tell Danny she loved him. Tell him she'd get her exams and he'd be very proud of her, and then she'd spend the whole summer looking after him, and they'd play in the garden or in his room or wherever he liked, and she'd let him meet Valentin and together they'd make the shed into a special house, just for him, and people couldn't go into it without his permission, anything he wanted was OK, only just let him be better.

ELEVEN

Jake had laid out four breakfast bowls, with four spoons and four plates, before he realised. He steadied himself, feeling a wave of emptiness wash over him. God, it was going to be hard. His eye fell on the telephone message pad on the wall where Danny had scrawled his initials in red felt-pen; behind, in a wall-cabinet, lay the boy's special bottles and beakers and, hanging on a hook by the sink, his plastic bib. With a lump in his throat, he picked up the suitcase they'd brought back from the clinic with his son's things in it. He caught Alex's eye as he opened the broom-cupboard door and heaved the suitcase in. She was grey with worry. Were they doing the right thing?

On Sophie's place at the table he propped up the good-luck card Danny had made with his finger-paints the week before and asked him to give to her on the day. The big day. What else could they do? To tell her now would destroy her chances. She'd go to pieces and blow the exams. Time enough later to break the news. And yet, he couldn't be sure it was right.

The doorbell rang. He caught his breath.

'Oh Christ! I forgot!'

'Send them away!' hissed Alex. 'Say she's not well.'

'We can't!' he whispered back. 'You know the Press. Hide her away and they'll make her out to be some recluse freak. I've said no to the nationals and TV as it is. One evening paper, that's all.'

The doorbell rang again, more insistently.

'I'm going,' said Alex. 'I'll tell them it's cancelled.'

'Don't.'

'Jake, we *can't*! It's sick.'

'It was fixed up before we *knew*. We'll have to go through with it now.'

He left her glaring at him and went to the door. A young woman reporter with a wide, sympathetic smile greeted him. She held out a card with the name Laura Abbott and introduced her companion, a lanky photographer named Phil.

'We'll have to make it quick,' said Jake, showing them into the living room. 'Sophie mustn't be late.'

The reporter gave an understanding smile and looked about the room. Pale sunlight fell across the blackboard with Danny's last scribbles on it and reached the corner where his toys lay neatly arranged by Suzanne. Were they going to be able to live all week surrounded by his things, *pretending*?

Laura picked up a coloured alphabet block.

'Her brother's?' she asked. 'Can we get a picture of them both?'

Danny's not here. He's . . . in hospital.'

'Oh, I'm sorry.'

'Just a routine check-up.' He swallowed, his throat dry. 'Do sit down. I'll get some coffee going.'

He found Alex in the kitchen area, making toast. She shook her head.

'I thought you were so against the media interfering,' she said.

She was right, but now it was different. He no longer had those fears. Sophie *was* a perfectly normal child, and very much herself.

'I'm proud of her. So should you be, Alex.'

In the archway leading to the living room the reporter cleared her throat. At the same moment, the door from the hall opened and Sophie came in. She wore her blue gingham dress and her fair hair was in a pony-tail.

'Morning, Dad. Morning, Mum,' she said. Then she saw Daniel's card. 'How was he?'

Alex blanched but forced a smile.

'He's resting, darling,' she said.

'Can we go and see him after exams today?'

Jake intervened quickly. 'We'll talk about that later. Sophie, this is Laura Abbott, from the *Bristol Evening Echo*.'

'Oh yes,' she said, shaking the reporter's hand. 'I read an article of yours on the weather. Actually, it *can* rain when the temperature's below freezing. It's called glaze.'

'You *are* a bright young thing, aren't you?' said Laura.

'Is that a question?'

She sat down and helped herself to cereal. Jake drew up a chair for the reporter. Alex brought over the coffee and retired to stand at the stove; she wasn't having anything to do with this.

'A *very* bright young thing,' continued Laura. 'I'm sorry to hear your brother's in hospital, dear.'

'Dad says the Bath Clinic's the best in the country. They're going to make him better.'

The reporter made a brief note on a pad, then signalled to the photographer.

'May we have a picture? "Genius Goes To Work On Weetabix." ' She smiled. 'This is a big day, Sophie. Nervous?'

'She enjoys exams,' said Jake. 'They're a challenge.'

'How do you feel to be the youngest child ever to take so many?'

'I feel great,' replied Sophie.

'Being the youngest isn't important to her,' interposed Jake again. 'It's how she measures up to her own standards that counts.'

155

'Or your dad's standards?' Laura went on. 'Does he cram you, Sophie?'

'She only does what she wants to do,' said Jake, growing heated.

'Does your dad do your thinking for you, too?'

Sophie held the woman's eye levelly.

'No one's ever forced me. I only do what I want. I just enjoy exploring things. I don't see it as work. And, by the way,' she added quietly, 'don't call me a genius. I'm not. I'm just *me*.'

A brief silence fell while the cameraman popped away with his camera. Laura sipped her coffee thoughtfully, then returned to her questions.

'Sophie, do you feel you're having a normal childhood?'

Jake had to break in.

'Of course it's perfectly normal! She does gym, swims, goes to the cinema . . .'

'But you don't have many friends, Sophie.'

Sophie eyed her coolly again.

'It's not easy when the rest of your class is twice your age. But I have friends.'

'Who's your best friend, Sophie?'

'Danny. And Dad. And Mum.'

'Danny,' echoed Laura, tapping her pencil on the pad. 'Tell me, if you were one of our readers, let's say, and I showed you a family with a somewhat backward son and a prodigy for a daughter—'

'What are you saying?'

'Well, wouldn't you call it a bit . . . odd?'

Jake stood up, his jaw clenched. He could feel Alex in the background, bristling.

'I think it's time we called a halt,' he said tightly. 'Sophie has got to get ready. Miss Abbott, Phil, thanks for coming along. I hope it has been useful. Alex, would you?'

'Very useful,' said Laura, rising. 'Come along, Phil.' At the door, she turned back to Sophie. 'Good luck, Sophie.'

'Thanks,' responded the girl. 'And by the way, the answer to your question is no.'

As Alex showed the visitors out, Jake turned to Sophie. 'Well done, darling.'

She laughed.

'She's the one who's odd, Dad. Imagine deciding on the answers before asking the questions! She wouldn't get very far in exams.'

Jake walked slowly across the car park to the main entrance of the Infirmary. His ankle seemed more painful than usual. He felt empty, hollow. However certain the fact of death, the event itself always came as a shock. He tried telling himself Danny was better off where he was, but that was only to comfort himself. For the boy the suffering was over, but not for those he'd left behind.

He took the elevator to the eleventh floor and paused for a moment at the window overlooking the city. Yet again he asked himself the question: had he done the right thing in not telling Sophie? She was so cool, so reasoned. Look at the way she'd handled that reporter. She'd absorbed everything he'd ever taught her about weighing up her feelings and thinking them through logically. Could she have coped with the news? Maybe yes, but he couldn't take the risk with the exams coming up. He'd been right. They'd face her with the truth after they were over. She'd see the reasonableness of withholding it from her, afterwards.

Decisively, he headed off to Sister's office. As he entered, a nurse handed him a clipboard.

'Morning, Dr Chalmers.' She paused. 'We're all so sorry about Danny.'

He tried a smile.

'It seems bad news travels fast, too, Susan.' He took a deep breath and applied his mind to the case-sheet. 'Right, what have we got today?'

Alex drove quickly, afraid she'd be late to meet Sophie from her first day's exams.

She'd managed well enough all day. Then, as she was closing her locker to go home, the pain hit her harder than ever: no Danny to go and visit, no Danny to take a treat to, a cream bun or a new sticker or a comic. A whole limb of her being had been amputated, half the point of her life had been lost. Arthur had been in the staff room – just the two of them, alone. He'd said very little, just held her to him and let her weep silently against his chest.

She arrived at Sophie's school to find Jake's hired car already there. Round the corner by the rear entrance, the last of the class were coming out, and Jake and Sophie were standing by a chestnut tree, poring intently over the exam paper.

Sophie's face lit up when she saw her mother.

'A real cinch, Mum!' she cried. 'All the questions Dad predicted.'

'Hello, love,' said Jake as she came up. 'Know what? She answered the lot in twenty minutes!'

'And wrote an algorithm to solve question ten.'

Alex hugged the child. 'That's brilliant, darling. Now, why don't we all go off to tea somewhere?'

'Let's go and see Danny, Mum,' implored Sophie.

Alex looked over to Jake: he could field that one.

'But you've got to revise for maths tomorrow,' he said.

'Come on, Dad, I don't need to.'

'Anyway, he's not to be disturbed. He's resting.'

'Still?'

'Doctor's orders. I really think it's best we leave visiting till Friday and all the exams are over.' He steered her towards the gate. 'Now, tell me how you tackled the one of conductivity.'

Alex followed, a step behind. Lying was folly; it would only backfire. They could break the news gently, but they should break it all the same. Would they pretend, on Friday, that he'd died that morning? How would they explain the funeral, arranged for the following day? The funeral – that was another issue. Why did it have to be a burial, not a simple cremation? Why had she given in to his absurd Catholic dogma? How could she have allowed herself to become complicit in the whole cruel and crooked business?

Jake was laughing now, telling a funny story. He turned to share the joke with her, but saw her face and turned back to Sophie. How *could* he? It was one thing to put on a brave front but quite another to act so ... so shockingly. Was he really grieving underneath? You'd think he was positively glad that Danny was gone.

Their two cars were parked side by side. Jake got into his and pushed the rear passenger door open.

'See you back home, love,' he called to her. 'Hop in, Sophie.'

Alex stood by her car, feeling redundant.

Sophie climbed in and slammed the door. She turned to wave, then hesitated, and a thoughtful look flashed across her face. Jake was about to pull away when she leaned forward to stop him. She threw the door open, jumped out and ran over to Alex's car.

'Race you home, Dad,' she cried. 'Come on, Mum, we'll show him.'

On Monday, he'd told her that Danny was resting.

On Tuesday, the excuse was that the boy was undergoing a biopsy. On Wednesday, he was recovering from the biopsy. That evening Jake purportedly went to visit him, taking a message from Sophie, written phonetically in their special language, which he had to read out. He drove to the sea front and sat drinking in a pub for two hours, filled with anxiety and shame.

To kill more time, he went for a drive round the new dockland marina and then made a circuit back home across the city to Clifton, stopping for a moment outside the Church of the Sacred Heart and pondering if he could somehow offload the risk along with the sin. This was absurd. A farce.

Alex was waiting for him in the hallway as he returned home. Her mouth was set hard and her hazel eyes burned with cold ferocity. She beckoned him into his study and shut the door. From behind a row of books she took out a newspaper. She handed it to him without a word.

It was that evening's *Echo*.

'DOUBLE TEST FOR GIRL PRODIGY' ran the headline, under a photo of Sophie eating breakfast.

Oh, Christ. They've found out.

Plucky child prodigy Sophie Chalmers, 8, (pictured above) [read the body copy] faces a double ordeal this week ... On Monday she became the country's youngest O-level candidate, sitting a total of five subjects ... This comes just a day after her brother Danny, 14, died in hospital after a prolonged illness ... Enjoying a healthy breakfast, Sophie said she 'felt great' ... She talked of Danny as her 'best friend' ... So it's bravery as well as brains young Sophie will be needing this week ...

'I'll warn the teachers,' he said shortly.

'For God's sake!' cried Alex. 'We've got to tell her *now*!'

'Alex, there's only two days to go. She's got additional maths tomorrow, and chemistry on Friday. Tell her now and she'll blow them both.'

'But it'll be all over the school in the morning!'

'I'll get the Head to speak to them in assembly. We can see she turns up late.'

'Don't be ridiculous!' She snatched the paper back. 'I'm going to, right now.'

He blocked the door.

'You will *not*! This is all she's ever worked for. It's vital to her future! She mustn't be thrown off course.'

'She's got plenty of time! What's the *point* in doing everything at half the age of anyone else? Where does it get her in the end? It just means she misses out on her childhood. And her parents are forced to lie to her. Let her take the maths and chemistry next year – next *term*, even. Give her a few months to get over Danny. Send her away to camp for the summer. I know a walking party in Wales she could join during the holidays, yes, that's exactly what she needs, a break, fresh air in her life, not being force-fed in this hothouse here . . .'

He waited until she'd worked herself speechless, then he slowly reached out and took back the newspaper.

'I'll ask the Head his advice,' he said quietly. 'Maybe she can take her exams in a room on her own, with a separate invigilator. Alex, I'm only thinking of what's best for her. Believe me. Trust me.'

The Head was a politician. He wasn't going to interfere in a decision that was for the parents to take, but it had come to his attention that Sophie was writing her

161

papers so fast and finishing them so quickly that she was putting off her neighbours in the exam room and they were complaining that they couldn't concentrate properly with her there, and so he was prepared to let her sit the remaining exams in a separate room. The following morning, therefore, with four papers to go, Jake took her to school himself – Alex refused to be party to the deception any longer – and chaperoned her into the special room set aside for her. In the corridor outside, he had a quiet word with the invigilator, and left for the hospital with a great sigh of relief. With luck, it was going to work.

At lunch-time he collected her and took her to the cafeteria in the park where they had fun playing the prime-number game and competing to see who could invent the most absurd chain of syllogisms, returning her just in time for her afternoon exam.

At four thirty sharp he was once again at the school. He waited in the corridor outside her special room as time ticked by. At ten to five, she finally came out. She was white-faced. Behind, the invigilator threw him a helpless, apologetic gesture. Swinging her satchel over her shoulder, she marched on ahead without a word, out into the sunshine and across the playground to the car park. He hurried to keep up with her, his questions about the exam and how it had gone totally ignored.

At the car, she turned and faced him, squinting her violet eyes against the sun.

'Dad,' she said in a half-whisper, 'did you have to treat me like a child? Didn't you trust me enough to tell me?'

'You mean, you . . . ?'

'The tea-lady said how sorry she was for me. I asked her why. She told me.'

He felt as if he were drowning.

'Sophie, darling, you must understand—'

162

'I do understand, Dad. I just think there was no need to pretend. You could have told me on Sunday, when it happened.'

He reached to take hold of her. She didn't move away, but he couldn't touch her; he felt sullied, impure, covered with shame.

'We were going to wait till the exams were over,' he said desperately. 'We knew how you'd feel, it's a terrible thing for anyone to have to cope with, child or grown-up, terrible for your mum and me, too, and, well, we thought it better to wait till you had time to cope with it properly, rather than letting it upset your exams . . .'

She held his eye.

'I said I understand, Dad. It's perfectly reasonable. Shall we go now?'

He stood there for a moment, too stunned by her reaction to move.

Alex watched the child picking at her food. She laid an arm on her shoulder.

'Try a little more, angel,' she coaxed. 'Spaghetti's your favourite.'

'Mine?' queried Sophie. It had been Danny's.

'Yes, well. You need the nourishment.' She paused, troubled by her strange composure. 'I think you're being a very brave girl, Sophie.'

Sophie pushed her plate away and regarded her mother coolly.

'Crying is pointless,' she said. 'You cry for yourself, not the person who's died. What good is it to them?'

In the background, by the sink, Jake grunted his approval. Alex searched Sophie's pale face for some expression she could comprehend, but the girl returned her stare blankly. What was going on behind those eyes? When would the real outburst come? This calm was unnatural, almost shocking.

'Yes, I suppose you're right,' she fumbled. She reached for the plate. 'Darling, try a little apple crumble.'

Sophie got up and pushed her chair in.

'No thanks, Mum.'

'Well,' Alex tried more brightly, 'only a couple more papers, and you're through. Then I think we ought all to sit down and think of where to go for a jolly good holiday. Eh, Jake?'

'Absolutely.'

'Mum,' said Sophie going to the door, 'you don't need to be like this. Let's get the funeral over first, then see.'

'Yes, love, one thing at a time.'

Jake added his smile. 'Sure you're all right, darling?'

Sophie turned at the door.

'I wish you'd both stop making such a fuss. Danny's dead and that's that.'

'Yes,' agreed Alex, shocked, 'but one mustn't be afraid to admit one's feelings.'

'Feelings let you down. Facts don't. Isn't that so, Dad?'

With that, she left the room.

Alex turned to Jake in silent horror. What kind of a child had they brought up – had *he* brought up? An automaton, conditioned to feel nothing when her own brother died? A repressed emotional cripple, trained to rationalise away what real feelings she did have?

Jake was shaking his head, half in wonder.

'Cool kid,' he remarked. 'Amazingly balanced.'

She glared back, stunned.

'*Un*balanced, if you ask me, and heading for trouble.'

She checked herself and fell silent. This wasn't the moment to open the floodgates. Not quite yet.

*　　*　　*

Friday: exams over, wrote Sophie in her secret diary. *A confusing question in chemistry, but the rest a walkover. Dad and Mum took me for tea at the Grand Hotel afterwards. Dad called for fizzy orangeade and made pretend it was champagne. Not very funny.*

It's Danny's funeral tomorrow. Poor darling Danny, it was my fault he was sent away.

She looked up as a sudden, chill breeze stirred the curtain. The night was hot and sultry. She could feel thunder on its way.

I could have saved him, but they didn't tell me.

Footsteps! She flicked off the torch and quickly hid the exercise-book under the covers. When Dad came in, she was breathing slowly and rhythmically, as if asleep.

He stood over her for a long while, then lightly kissed her head.

'Sleep tight,' he whispered and, closing the window a notch, crept back out of the room.

She slept fitfully. At one point she woke, stifling a scream: a huge hand, a claw, was poised above her bed, ready to grab her and punish her for what she'd done. She forced herself to lie still and reason it out: just a bright full moon and restless clouds throwing patterns across the wall. She dozed off again. Then Dad was showing her a picture – it was Mantegna's *Deposition of Christ* – and the picture came alive, and she was suddenly there, in it, and gradually the dead figure of Christ turned into Danny, all pale and bloodless, and he saw her and held out his hand to her, and she knew what he needed, and suddenly they were in hospital and she was connected to him by a plastic tube in her arm and a nurse was pumping her blood into him through the tube, it flowed a rich dark red, but however much she gave he still went paler and paler . . .

165

She sat up with a start, shaking and sweating. Her head was throbbing painfully. She didn't dare go back to sleep.

Slipping on her dressing-gown, she tiptoed down the corridor to Danny's room. Dad had told her she could have it back now, but that was wrong: it should stay Danny's. They would make it into a spare room, give his toys to the children's ward at the Infirmary, throw away his scribbling-pads and his collection of pebbles, along with his clothes and the piece of blanket he carried everywhere and couldn't be separated from. Somewhere still had to stay his.

Taking his huge cuddly Yogi Bear and as many of his crayons and pads as she could carry, she hurried down the back stairs and, pausing in the kitchen for a candle and matches, slipped out through the back door into the garden. The gravel hurt her bare feet, but soon it gave way to grass and the lawn spread before her. Thunder growled in the far distance, and the wind seemed to quicken. For a moment clouds obscured the moon and she had to pick her way more slowly. Then, just as she reached the foot of the garden, a bright flash of lightning threw the towering willow tree into stark relief, making the cascading fronds seem to leap out towards her. She counted slowly to eight before the first thunder rolled angrily across the sky.

She pushed in through the great tent of the tree and made her way in the flickering half-light to the wooden shed. Inside, she lit the candle and put it on the ledge by the window, she laid the crayons and paper on the desk beneath the bookshelf and propped the teddy-bear on the foam-rubber mattress she'd covered with an old candlewick bedspread to make a couch.

The first rain had begun to fall, striking the canopy of the tree far above with a sound of rustling tinsel and forming into thicker drops that smacked onto the tin roof of the shed. The fronds stirred uneasily in the rising wind. The candle flickered. Another flash of lightning sizzled the boughs and bounced off the thirsty ground. Before she could count to three a violent thunderclap burst above her head.

Hurry, Danny, she cried. Hurry or you'll get wet! Come in here, where it's safe, where it's home.

He was out there. She knew it. He'd come.

She peered out of the window. Her forehead was now pumping painfully. The fronds swished back and forth, but no Danny stumbled through. He wasn't there. He wasn't anywhere. He'd never come.

She felt as if she'd explode into a billion fragments. Sinking back on the low bed, she curled up in a tight ball and wept as the wind rose and the rain swelled. It was all her fault. She'd sent him to that place; she could have got him back, but she didn't. She could have saved his life with her blood, but she hadn't. Now he was gone. For ever. And she could never make it up to him, never bring him back.

Danny, Danny, I'm sorry!

At first, with her hands over her head, she didn't quite hear the tapping on the window. It grew more persistent until finally she looked up. Through tear-blurred eyes, she saw a face. Not Danny's face. But she knew it well. Completely.

Valentin.

She stumbled to her feet. As she slipped the catch, a gust caught the door and flung it wide open. Valentin stood in the doorway, looking at her. He knew everything. He understood everything.

He opened his arms. She fell into the embrace. He was everything in the whole universe melted into one. She hugged him, sobbing with joy and pain. As

she looked up into his face, he smiled down into hers.
Then slowly he turned to the window and stared out
in the direction of the house.

TWELVE

Alex started the car as Jake climbed painfully in. In her rear-view mirror she could see Sophie's small, wan face at the window of Jake's study. Why should the child come to the church if she didn't want to? Suzanne would bring her along to the funeral afterwards. She glanced across at Jake, sitting beside her in a black suit and tie, ashen-faced and tight-lipped.

'She's old enough to decide for herself,' she said tartly, pulling out into the traffic. 'If you ask me, the whole idea of a Requiem Mass is quite wrong, too. None of the congregation ever met Danny. I don't want to share my grief with strangers.'

Jake turned away and looked out of his window.

'If you believed in the soul, you'd understand.'

'Pity you didn't train Sophie to believe, too.' She couldn't help the sarcasm. 'What a disappointment.'

'Yes, it is, actually,' he replied, turning to face her. 'I'd like to think she grew up with a belief in something beyond this material world and its values. I could have wished for more support from you, too, Alex.'

'You're two people, Jake.' She glared at an oncoming driver, hooting at her for no apparent reason. 'One moment reason and logic is everything, the next you're asking her to believe unquestionably in all that absurd religious claptrap. You're all screwed up. I can't cope.'

'Alex, drop it for once, please? Our thoughts should be with Danny.'

'A bit late for you to claim to care about him now.'

'Alex!' he warned.

'It's true.' She felt the tears pricking her eyes. 'You

never really loved him! You never had *time* for him. He was just an encumbrance to you, getting in Sophie's way and holding her back.'

She turned the corner into the street where the Church of the Sacred Heart stood and pulled up by the kerb a short distance away. She couldn't go in to the service like this. She opened a window for some air and looked out across the street. Sunlight danced on the pavement, two young boys were setting out to go fishing and in the chestnut tree above a pair of pigeons was noisily mating. On the day they were burying their only son.

Jake had leant across her and turned the engine off. He spun her round by the shoulders and shook her. He was white with pain and rage.

'I loved Danny!' he hissed. 'I loved that boy! Christ, if you say that once again . . . !'

She watched the fury contort his face and felt the spittle fleck her cheeks, but she made no move to resist. She was far away from it all. It didn't matter any more who this man was or what he wanted her to believe. He was a stranger.

Sophie watched at the window until the car had disappeared, then turned and looked about her. She caught sight of herself in the mirror over the mantelpiece; how strange she looked in the plain dark grey dress with the white collar that Dad had given her. The receipt had still been in the bag; he'd bought in on Tuesday, for today.

This dowdy grey was all wrong! Clutching her handwritten letter tightly, she ran upstairs to her bedroom and, throwing off the dress, she pulled out all her brightest clothes – her pink baseball sweatshirt, her harlequin pants and the shoes she'd painted silver during the craze she and Danny had had for spraying things. That was how he knew her, and that was how she'd go to say goodbye.

She came back down to Dad's study. She could hear Suzanne in the kitchen, preparing refreshments for the mourners afterwards, with Radio One playing loudly in the background. She locked the door behind her. This business was private. She took her letter over to the desk where Dad's typewriter stood. She'd better type it out, to make sure.

Carefully, one finger at a time, she copied out the message in phonetic Abacus.

Darling Danny, [she began]
I miss you so badly. I keep on finding things I'd like to tell you and show you. I hope you're better now, not hurting any more and doing all the things you've always wanted.

It's all my fault, I'm to blame they sent you away. I could have got you better, too, but Dad didn't tell me in time.

I'm so terrible sorry, poor darling Danny . . .

She paused to open the window. A dull throb hammered away inside her head. The day was close and heavy, despite the previous night's thunder. She returned to the typewriter and continued until both sides of the paper were covered, then looked around for an envelope.

She was searching through the desk drawers when, underneath last year's desk diary, she came upon a photocopy of a typescript. She caught sight of the title page. 'Genetic Coding for Intelligence' it read, 'by Dr Helen S. Lorenz, University of Chicago, Ill'. The date was the day he'd gone to Oxford. So this was what he'd gone to hear at that conference he'd been so reluctant to talk about. She took it out and

171

skimmed through it. She couldn't make such sense of the technical terms, but the letters HIG kept cropping up . . .

She glanced at the desk clock. They'd have to go in a few minutes. Puzzled, she slipped the paper back; she'd come back to it later. Eventually she found an envelope, folded the letter inside and in bold letters on the front wrote 'Master Danny Chalmers'. She looked at it from a distance. It needed something more formal, some kind of a stamp. Her eye lit upon a stick of red sealing-wax in the desk tidy. She'd seal it, like a love-letter in a Shakespeare play.

Unlocking the door, she hurried across the hall – Suzanne was now in the utility room, emptying the dryer – and into the kitchen. As she opened the broom cupboard and was reaching for a box of matches on the shelf, a suitcase tumbled out. Danny's case. From its weight, she could tell it was full. Of what? She slipped the catch open. Inside· were all his things, his pyjamas, his jerseys, his special piece of blanket, his Mickey Mouse towel, his bright orange baseball cap, all smelling of his own special smell, of powder and ointment and hospital.

She stifled a cry. He was still here! Danny, Danny, how could they be burying you?

She heard Suzanne's footsteps tripping across the hall tiles to Dad's study; they paused, then came towards the kitchen. Blinking back the tears, she quickly closed the suitcase and pushed it back in the cupboard just as the nanny came in.

'Ah, there you are.' Suzanne's smile faded as she saw the clothes Sophie was wearing. Her eye lit briefly on the matches in her hand. 'What on earth are you doing?'

'I'm going like this.'

'You can't possibly!'

'I am, and that's that.' She dodged past the nanny and skipped back to the study.

'We're leaving in one minute,' Suzanne called after her. 'I'll want you changed properly by then.'

Sophie locked the door behind her again and lit the stick of sealing-wax. The flame lengthened, the wax sputtered and a thick coil of black smoke rose to the ceiling. The smell made her head ache even more. Carefully she poured a large pool of wax on the back of the envelope, then pressed a penny coin into the molten liquid to make it look like a proper seal. She hadn't quite finished when she heard Suzanne outside in the hall.

'Sophie? Hurry up! We'll be late.'

'Coming,' she called back.

The door handle rattled.

'Sophie?' The nanny's voice was sharper. 'What are you doing in there? Hurry up, now!'

Blowing on the wax to harden it, Sophie hurried to the door and unlocked it. She slipped out and closed it quickly behind her.

'What's that dreadful smell?' Suzanne demanded. 'And look at you! This isn't a party, you know.'

'Well, it should be. Danny would have liked that best. Don't worry, Dad and Mum won't mind.' She tugged Suzanne's sleeve. 'Come on. Let's go quickly.'

The boy stepped out from the laurel bush. He knew she wasn't there, in the house. Nor anyone else. He'd watched the cars leaving.

The French windows onto the garden were locked. So was the side door. He could fix the sash window in the kitchen with his penknife if need be, but he knew there was an easier way. He carried on round the side until he found it. A window, wide open.

He climbed in.

173

This was the father's study. His heartland. This was the place to strike.

Books lined the walls from floor to ceiling. He pulled one out. *Clinical Genetics*. Tiny handwritten notes filled the margin. He ripped out the page and dropped it on the floor. He skimmed another page, and tore that out, too. And another, and another, then he snapped the spine and tossed it after the rest. On the *Anatomy* book the marbled end-papers tore like cardboard, though the leather binding resisted and made him quite angry. He pulled the guts out of the antique gilt-edged Descartes and tore the bird plates out of the Aubusson. The pile in the centre of the room was growing nicely.

He took out the drawers of the desk and up-ended each in turn onto the heap. From the desk-top he picked up the photo of the man and the girl together, threw it onto the floor and stamped on it. A single sweep of his arm cleared the mantelpiece. A blow from the bronze bust of Einstein shattered the mirror above it. The old pedestal globe in the corner gave in at a kick.

His eye caught a box of matches on the desk.

The first match went out in a small spiral of smoke. The second caught the edge of a page of the Descartes but the flame died as it reached the stitching. He crumpled up twenty or thirty pages into small balls and, leaving plenty of space for air, laid them in a careful pile, heaping the rest on top. The third match caught. The flame spread. The more it spread, the stronger it grew. Fat, greedy tongues soon began to lick high up the pyre. The flames grew redder, lustier. The yellow-white smoke thickened. He began to cough. The heat was growing intense. He backed away to the window. Hauling himself through, he dropped noiselessly onto the gravel. He listened. In the distance a car backfired, in the next-door garden a radio played noisily, some way down the street an ice-cream van chimed. A normal summer Saturday morning. Except for the dangerous crackling coming from inside this house and the blackening smoke coiling out of the window.

Jake walked slowly the few yards from the hearse to the graveside, keeping step with the other three bearers. The coffin felt tragically light. He remembered when his mother died how he'd lifted her into his arms and felt such a shock at finding her as light as a sparrow. Life was more than the sum of the parts; it had a substance of its own.

Gradually they lowered the coffin onto the straps laid ready on the grass at the edge of the short grave. The priest came forward, swinging his censer. The rest of the group gathered round: Graham, Frank Blythe, a nurse from the clinic and a colleague from his ward at the Infirmary, Alex's parents, Miles and Bettine, who'd flown over from Jersey, and Suzanne and Sophie. His own father had not come.

He reached out and took his daughter by the hand. He smiled; he knew why she'd changed out of her new dress, and she was quite right.

The ceremony was short. Under the arch of the sky, after the enclosed gloom of the church, human life and death seemed so small. A gentle breeze carried away the priest's words as lightly as the smoke from his censer. The sun grew higher and hotter. A small lizard darted from behind the upturned earth and scampered into the open grave. High overhead a gull circled, crying mournfully.

' "Forasmuch as it hath pleased Almighty God of His great mercy," ' intoned the priest, ' "to take unto Himself the soul of our dear brother Daniel here departed . . ." '

He stifled a rising sense of outrage. How could a perfect deity allow this to happen? Was it not for us to know? Be quiet, he told his restless mind; be humble and respect the unanswerable.

Soon the priest gave a signal and the coffin was slowly lowered into the ground, earth returning to earth, ashes to ashes.

Jake stepped forward and bent to pick up a handful of earth. With a momentary hesitation, he threw it onto the coffin. The falling earth clattered onto the lid with a dry, hollow rattle.

'God be with you, Danny,' he muttered quietly.

Alex followed, tossing hers in with a swift, distasteful movement, then retired quickly to her place. Next, Sophie came forward and dropped a white envelope into the grave. One after another, in turn, the mourners followed Jake's example. Then the undertakers took up their shovels. One load after another thudded on the coffin, each one ringing less hollow than the last, until the earth began to fall with a soft muffled patter.

Sophie stood beside him, ramrod stiff, her hand unyielding in his. As the pile of earth diminished, he looked down at her. The faintest smile had softened her set expression. He followed her gaze. There, at the corner of the grave, was the small lizard, escaping.

Sophie walked slowly down the cemetery path between Mum and Uncle Graham. She felt empty, unreal. None of this was really happening. Mum held her hand, saying very little. Only Uncle Graham seemed to need to cheer everyone up.

'I thought the priest rather rushed it,' he was saying. 'Still, that's the religion of the rosary for you — say the words and let the meaning take care of itself.'

'Gray!' whispered Mum reprovingly.

'It's true,' her brother protested. He turned to Sophie. 'You're very quiet, young lady.'

She shrugged. Why did adults always have to be saying something? She wanted to be alone, to think her own thoughts. Mum squeezed her hand.

'Don't take any notice, darling,' she said. 'You know, I think you deserve a good holiday. How would you like that?'

'OK, Mum.'

They walked on in silence until they reached the large Victorian Gothic gatehouse at the main entrance to the cemetery. There they met up with the rest of the party. While the grown-ups stood in the bright sun, deciding who was going in which car, she looked around. She wanted to sit somewhere on her own, away from them all.

Just then a movement deep in the shadows of the building caught her eye.

Valentin! What on earth was *he* doing here?

The boy was beckoning her urgently. Glancing to check that the others were all absorbed in their conversations, she slipped quickly round the back of the group and followed Valentin to the side of the building, where he disappeared inside the door of a small concealed passageway. She hung back in the doorway while her eyes grew accustomed to the dark.

There was something odd, something wild about his look. His denim shirt was torn and streaked with black and there was a funny smell she couldn't place at first.

'What's wrong?' she whispered at once. 'Something's the matter. Something's happened.'

The boy reached into his trouser-pocket. With a flourish he took out a box of matches. She caught her breath and went icy cold with horror. She recognised that box of matches.

'Valentin!' she exclaimed. 'What have you been up to?'

He didn't reply, but she knew that he didn't need to. She already knew what it was, only it lay hidden like a half-forgotten memory that took time to rise to the surface. Slowly the thought took shape in her mind: something terrible ... at home ... with the matches ...

All at once she grasped it.

'Valentin, you ... *did you?*'

The boy slowly nodded his head.

'Where's Sophie?' asked Jake, toying with his car keys.

'She's not in the car?' queried Alex.

'She was here a moment ago,' said Graham. 'I'll take a look.'

Jake waited in the sombre group, exchanging a few short words with Alex's parents, while Graham went round the side of the gatehouse. A moment later, Sophie came running out. She tore straight up to him and tugged him by the sleeve.

'Dad, Dad, let's go home!' she cried.

'Yes, darling. Miles, you'll follow us?'

'Hurry!' she persisted.

The older man flashed him an understanding glance and patted the child's fair head. 'You've been a brave girl,' he said with feeling. 'We're all very proud of you, bless you.'

But Sophie pulled away and ran over to the car and jumped in. Jake turned to his brother-in-law.

'Gray,' he called. 'You're taking Alex?'

Graham didn't seem to hear at first. He stood staring after Sophie with a perplexed frown.

'What? Uh, yes.'

'Dad, come on!' called Sophie from the car.

Tossing his walking-stick in, Jake climbed in and

178

started the car. In the rear-view mirror he could see the child was white and fearful. Had Graham said something to upset her? On the drive home, she remained fixedly silent. He could feel her impatience every time he slowed down to let the car behind catch up.

As he turned into their street, he saw fire engines. Three of them. Lights still flashing. Hydraulic ladders extended. Thick smoke rising from the roof of a house. And men in black protective clothing and yellow helmets running everywhere.

Christ, the old lady next door!

He speeded up, but as he came closer he realised whose house was on fire.

With a cry of horror, he drove the car into the kerb and jumped out. He'd hobbled three paces towards the charred building when he suddenly froze. He turned. Sophie was standing beside the car, wide-eyed and ashen-faced. The realisation slammed him sickeningly in the stomach.

She had *known*!

THIRTEEN

Jake walked slowly downstairs, avoiding the firemen's hoses and stepping through the sooty marsh they'd made of the carpets. It could have been worse. The blaze had brought the study ceiling down and, with it, half of Sophie's bedroom floor. The windows of the spare room were blown out and the flame had scorched the curtains and frames. The main bedroom, the nanny's overnight room and Danny's room were filled with the stench of smoke but were otherwise undamaged.

Downstairs, the kitchen and living room had survived, and Sophie's study beyond was untouched, but the hall was devastated. The grandfather clock lay in ruins among broken furniture and ornaments and the splintered fragments of the study door which the firemen had axed down.

His own study was wrecked. Choking with the acrid smoke still rising from the smouldering timbers, he picked his way across the saturated carpet and took stock of the horrific scene. The smashed mirror; the bookshelves, buckled and charred and strangely half-empty; the desk overturned and its drawers scattered across the room; and in the centre, among the pile of ashes and debris, the remnants of scores of books. He stopped to pick up a leather book-spine – Descartes, *A Discourse On Method* – and tossed it back. Face up, by the window, lay the shattered remains of the photo of Sophie, aged three, sitting on his knee, learning algebra.

Outside, in the hall, he could hear the neighbour

repeating his story for the tenth time to whoever would listen. 'There I was, bedding in the dahlias, when I smelled this odd smell. "Funny," I said, "the Chalmers' got an incinerator?" The smoke was awful. Better nip this in the bud, I thought. So round I popped, and blow me down . . .'

'Quite so,' came Alex's father's brisk reply.

In the kitchen, he knew, Bettine had her sleeves rolled up and was making mugs of sweet tea for the firemen; she'd grown up in the Blitz and understood her priorities in a crisis. Suzanne was setting up a table in the garden. Alex was running up and down stairs, firing instructions left and right. Graham was prowling in the drive outside, hands behind his back, like a sleuth looking for clues. And Sophie was nowhere to be seen.

He shook his head. What a bloody awful mess. And today of all days.

He looked up as the police inspector entered, making notes on his pad. The officer gestured with his pen to the pile of smouldering books in the centre.

'That's where it started, sir. Or should I say, *was* started.' He looked at Jake pointedly. 'Clear case of arson.'

'But how did they get in?'

The inspector pointed to the side window. Like the rest, the blaze had blown out the glass and burnt through most of the frame.

'Anyone you know bears you a grudge, sir?'

Jake went into the garden to find Alex. There were immediate practicalities to discuss. They'd have to find her parents a hotel; they'd need to make a full statement to the police and list the damage for the insurance; they'd have to decide which rooms they could still use and how they'd cope until the place was repaired. The carpets would have to be taken

181

up as soon as possible, emergency glaziers brought in to board up the windows and electricians hired to render the power supply safe. The consequences were endless.

He found her by the rose-bed, talking intently to Suzanne. She looked up as he came over. Her face was grey with concern.

'Suzanne,' she said quietly, 'tell Jake what you've just told me.'

The nanny hesitantly began to repeat her story. She'd seen Sophie go into the study with a box of matches, she said, just minutes before they'd left. When she'd gone to get her, the door was locked. Had she seen inside? No, Sophie had rushed out too quickly and hurried her off, but she did remember noticing a distinct smell of burning . . .

Jake caught Alex's eye. Oh Christ, he thought. Pray it's not true. Not *this*.

'Where is she?' he asked hoarsely.

'In the shed at the back of the tree, I think,' replied the nanny.

He led the way down the lawn, oppressed by a dreadful certainty yet trying to persuade himself it would turn out to have been an accident, an oversight, a match inadvertently left smouldering . . . He brushed through the leafy curtain of the weeping willow and headed through the cool shade to the old wooden shed standing against the back wall. He tapped at the door. There was no reply. He tapped again, then opened it.

Sophie sat on a mattress on the floor, hugging her knees, her pale, oval face dead of expression. She registered no reaction when he stepped forward. Alex and the nanny hung back just inside the door.

'Darling, I have a question I must ask you,' he began. 'I think you know what it is. I want you to answer honestly. But whatever you've done, if you have, we will all still love you just the same.'

The small girl kept her violet eyes on his but her lips tightly shut.

He drew a breath and gritted his teeth.

'Sophie, did you start the fire?'

She said nothing; there was hardly a flicker in her face.

Alex spoke from behind him. 'Come on, angel,' she said. 'It's just to stop the police looking for anyone else. Nobody will be angry if it was you.'

Sophie's face remained blank. Jake knelt down beside her. She shrank back on the couch.

'We just need to know, Sophie. Was it you, or wasn't it?'

Very slowly the child began to nod.

'Say it,' he persisted. 'Yes or no.'

When she spoke her voice was small but defiant.

'Yes. Yes, I did it.'

He caught his breath. 'Jesus Christ!'

Behind him came Alex's warning voice, 'Jake . . .'

'But why, Sophie *why*?' he couldn't help exclaiming. 'What was the point?'

Alex shot him a fierce glare and moved between him and the small girl. She reached forward and took her in her arms. Sophie didn't resist, but remained cold and unresponsive.

'It's all right, angel,' said Alex comfortingly. 'You've nothing to be afraid of. We understand. It'll all be all right.'

Jake stood back. He clutched at the shelf to steady himself. His mind was in a turmoil, yet through it all he kept thinking of that strange, ominous remark Helen had made, *You'd expect odd things to happen* . . .

Oh God, was it starting? Was this the beginning? And what would it be next?

*　　*　　*

183

'We can handle this,' snapped Jake. 'You keep out of it, Graham.'

The three stood huddled in the utility room, between the washing-machine and dryer and the baskets of ironing. It was the only room in which they could be alone. Alex's parents were in the living room, tidying up after the firemen; Suzanne was mopping the tiles in the hallway; he'd left Sophie upstairs in Danny's room; and a small team of carpenters and electricians were at work, making temporary repairs to the main damaged rooms. Despite the hammering, drilling and shouting, he dared not raise his voice too loud in case Sophie was on the landing, listening.

Alex's hazel eyes blazed.

'We *can't* handle it, Jake! She needs help.'

'No,' he said flatly.

Graham plaited his legs. 'That child is seriously disturbed,' he declared. 'She absolutely must see a psychiatrist.'

'With all due respect, Graham,' he said curtly, 'you're an academic, not a practitioner. I am closer to the clinical needs of children than you.'

Alex intervened quickly.

'Jake,' she began again in a tone of contrived patience. 'Our daughter has set fire to the house. Now, we don't know why. We assume it's to do with losing Danny, coming on top of the stress of the exams, but that's only speculation. Even if we did know for sure why, we're in no position to deal with it.'

'I'm saying no. Flatly no.'

Alex rounded on him.

'Ah, I begin to see why you refuse. Because she went for *your* room, Jake. Your precious little creation was going for *you*, and you can't face up to that. That's what you're afraid will come out.'

'Rubbish!' he scoffed, but in his heart he felt the

184

knife-blade twist. Yes, he had thought of that, and it hurt. 'Now, *that's* speculation.'

Graham looked at his sister.

'All the Act requires is the signature of one parent and the family doctor,' he remarked quietly, 'and the matter is in other hands.'

Jake flared up. 'If you think for one minute . . .'

Alex held up her hand.

'There'll be no need to go that far,' she said, quickly. 'We're only talking of routine professional psychiatric help. Right, Gray?'

Her brother nodded.

This was a conspiracy, Jake thought wildly. Sophie didn't need that kind of help. He wasn't having anyone tampering around with his daughter, groping into her perfect mind with their clumsy, inadequate theories, clambering around her personality with their sick, grubby thoughts . . .

He turned towards the door. The matter was final.

'No one is going to interfere with that child,' he said. 'That's final. Absolutely and categorically.'

A restless wind had risen, stirring the great tree from cope to hem. Sophie sat on a rug on the ground beyond the shed, weaving willow leaves and humming to herself while she waited. Before long, as she'd somehow expected, she heard a crackle of dry twigs behind her. She turned.

Valentin stood there, by the wall. He was casually stroking the neighbours' black and white cat, which arched its back and nuzzled into his hand.

She stood up. It was awful, like getting rid of part of herself, but she had to do it.

'Go away!' she hissed. 'You're mad!'

He grinned faintly and went on stroking the cat.

'It was a stupid thing to do!' she went on. 'I had to

185

cover up for you, or they'd have sent the police after you. You're crazy, Valentin. You've got to go. I don't want anything more to do with you!'

The grin faded and such a look of deep sorrow and betrayal came over his face that she hesitated, biting her lip. But he *had* to go. He was mad, irrational and she was afraid of what he might do next.

He began to back away. She felt tears starting at her eyes.

'Go on! Go away. Leave me alone. Don't come back. Please *Please*.'

He shot her a final glance, then slipped away into the undergrowth, leaving only the startled cat eyeing her with flattened ears and bristling spine. Abruptly the creature took flight. Darting along the wall, it jumped down and vanished in the opposite direction.

Graham stepped noiselessly back to the parting. He hadn't seen her, for he'd kept the tree-trunk between them, but he'd heard it all. And seen the cat flashing past his feet. Taking care not to make a sound, he slipped out from under the tree and hurried across the lawn until he was well clear before slowing down and taking stock.

He'd caught her that morning at the cemetery, talking to herself oddly. At first he thought she'd probably invented an imaginary friend – many children did, especially after losing a brother or a sister, and it would make sense for Sophie to compensate for the loss of Daniel in that way. But now he'd seen the cat, he realised it was more than that. The first case suggested merely a mild form of schizophrenia, but this looked more serious: she was transferring the blame for her own actions onto an external object, and that was often a sign of a profound neurotic disturbance.

186

This was best kept within the family. He'd speak to Alex and see if the money their parents had placed in trust for their grandson couldn't be put towards the repairs, thereby avoiding an insurance claim and a fuller investigation. But first, there was Sophie to consider. It was time the child was taken away from this atmosphere, away from the pernicious influence of an obsessive father.

Alex took towels from the airing cupboard, sheets from the linen chest, and from the laundry room she brought jerseys and skirts, slips and socks. The stench of the smoke had permeated everything; she'd have to wash it all again at Graham's. She collected Sophie's toothbrush from the children's bathroom and, from her own, some make-up, her pills and the travel hair-dryer, and then added in the photo on her dressing-table of the whole family around the Christmas tree two years ago, before all of this had started. The suitcase was filling fast. Sophie's school uniform and all her clothes in her bedroom had been destroyed. First thing on Monday morning, she'd take the child into town and fit her out with an entire new set. They were going to make a completely fresh start to everything.

Sophie's bedroom door hung on one hinge, shattered by a fireman's boot. She glanced inside. Blackened joists lay exposed through the gaping hole where the floor had fallen in on the study below. Footprints crossed the scorched and sodden carpet; one set looked like Sophie's. The bed and counterpane, the small desk piled with books, the astronomy charts on the walls, all were soaked and begrimed. Nothing there could be salvaged.

She filled her arms from the bookcase on the landing. Novels, biography, history, gardening: it would

187

do Sophie good to get away from all that turgid, heavy maths and science. Exams were over, she'd done all that was expected of her, and more, and now she was free to enjoy the last weeks of term and, after that, a proper healthy holiday. That was what she really needed. Graham had retailed worrying stories of what he'd witnessed; he'd spoken of transference and paranoid delusion and other alarming conditions. He was right about one thing, though: it was imperative to get the child away from this atmosphere. She'd take her on the walking expedition with Arthur and his children. If a complete change didn't do the trick, then she'd take her along to see a psychiatrist.

As she was finishing packing the second suitcase, she heard Jake's footsteps approaching. He stopped in the doorway. She braced herself.

'I'm taking Sophie away,' she said shortly.

Jake's expression hardened.

'What the hell are you on about?'

'I'm taking her away from here. Graham is putting us up. For the time being.'

'Now wait a minute . . .'

'Don't, Jake!'

She snapped the lock shut and swung the case off the bed. He stepped forward to intercept her. She glared at him defiantly.

'It's the poor child's only hope. Look at what you've made her into! She breaks all these records to gratify your absurd pride, and for what? I warned you she'd crack. Well, now she has. She's got to get away from this place, this unnatural, suffocating hothouse!'

Graham had appeared in the doorway behind Jake. His face was set with determination. She beckoned to him.

'Gray, take these cases, would you?' She could see

Jake was knotting his jaw, his face reddening. 'Jake,' she said in a more reasonable tone, 'be realistic. This house is in a total shambles. It's not fit to live in. Sophie's bedroom is a complete wreck. The whole place stinks. The electricity isn't even working properly. We've got to move out, anyway, till it's sorted out. And Gray has kindly offered to put us up.'

She paused: 'us' could include him, too, but it was obvious she'd packed only her own and Sophie's things. He could come if he insisted, but she didn't imagine he would. Something positive might yet emerge from the day's calamities. This could well be her chance to take the first step in the break.

It had all happened so quickly. Alex's parents had gone on ahead to get Graham's flat ready. Suzanne had driven off to the shops in Alex's car to buy provisions for the weekend in the new place. Graham was loading the suitcases into his own car and standing guard with the doors open and the engine running while Alex fetched Sophie. The girl allowed herself to be taken by the hand and meekly led away. She offered no resistance and raised no query; she seemed too wrapped up in herself to care what happened to her. White-faced, eyes cast down, muttering to herself and occasionally smiling or frowning in some profound interior dialogue, she shuffled down the steps and across the gravel to the waiting car.

Jake watched from the hallway, paralysed. Why was he powerless to stop it? How could he stand by without intervening? Of course, Alex was right about the house being uninhabitable in its present state. But something else, something deeper within him, had clamped a brake on any action.

He needed time to work it all out.

He went out onto the doorstep, he even gave a

189

small wave, but Sophie sat unmoving in the back seat, silent and lost, as the car pulled away and disappeared down the street.

Why was she rejecting him? Why did she bear him such hostility? He'd tried questioning her, reasoning with her; he'd told her no one blamed her; he'd reassured her they loved her as unequivocally as ever. But she'd kept tight-lipped and remote.

Why?

He walked slowly round the house, lonely and in despair. In a single day he'd lost everyone he loved. He sat on the stairs, his head in his hands, close to tears. The evening was drawing in and, with the windows open for airing, the place was growing chilly. Eventually he got up and went into the kitchen, but the light was on the circuit that had fused. Groping around in the growing twilight for the whisky bottle, he poured himself a large tumbler, then hobbled out onto the lawn and stared up into the darkening sky. A star, perhaps the Pole Star (Sophie would know), shone alone and bright. Where did the answer lie? Certainly not up there. He walked slowly down to the foot of the garden and brushed in through the willow tree. In the shed he found some pencils and pads of Danny's, and the Yogi Bear teddy. The sadness welled up afresh inside him for the son he had lost. And for Sophie, who had lost her brother. This little place would never be the home she'd meant it to be.

But how did a child's grief translate itself into hate, and hate into arson?

He strolled back through the dew-damp grass and, refilling his glass, went to inspect the ruins of his study. The debris of books, the scorched walls, the charred furniture: *what was it saying to him?* If you listened with patience and love, couldn't you eventually

190

work out the secrets of a child's mind? You didn't have to be a psychiatrist to hold the key. Pray God, not.

He shivered. For a flash of a second he saw his mother's face at the window of the clinic, the rain streaking the pane, her grey eyes so lucid, so knowing and so fearful of what she knew. And he, a boy of ten or eleven, craning his neck to catch the last glimpse through the rear window of the car as his father drove off, and knowing, although just a boy, that she was not mad, not deluded, only the drugs and the men in the white coats were making her so. Eventually they'd discovered that her disease was organic, not psychotic, but by then it was too late. She'd spent the next six years until her death in a private nursing home. And he'd vowed to become a doctor.

He went upstairs and looked in Sophie's bedroom. It was a shambles. Nothing was left that could afford a clue. On the way back down, he glanced briefly into Danny's room; plenty of work had to be done there, too. As he was closing the door, something projecting from the top of the wardrobe caught his eye. One of the boy's comics, he guessed; he'd add it later to the pile going to the Infirmary. Then he stopped abruptly as a thought struck him. How could Daniel have reached up there? He had been far too unsteady to stand on a chair. He went back in.

It was an exercise-book, written by Sophie in her strange, secret language, a bizarre amalgam of Greek, Hebrew and other characters he didn't recognise. As he studied it, he saw it was organised in sections, each headed with a configuration that suggested a date. He'd been right: it was a diary. A secret diary. A key to the child's innermost thoughts and fears?

Trembling with both shame and anticipation, he took the book downstairs to Sophie's study, one room untouched by the fire. A few minutes assured him that this was a highly complex language and he wasn't going to be able to decode it easily. Would she have drawn up a dictionary? With a memory like hers, she wouldn't need one but all the same she had a strong sense of order and was forever compiling lists. The computer was the obvious place to start.

He switched on the machine and riffled through her diskettes, calling up the index on each. Was there a file, ABACUS? No, nor anything remotely like it.

He was about to give up when he noticed, on one diskette, that the capacity available was given as fifteen per cent but the amount taken up by the files shown only added up to sixty-two. Twenty-three per cent of the disc contained something not listed!

But what? What file name? He tried Dictionary, Lexicon, Grammar, Syntax, then various combinations of her name, her date of birth and their address, but each time the machine replied, DOCUMENT NOT FOUND. He fetched the bottle of whisky. It was growing dark outside. At one point Alex telephoned briefly to ask him to bring Sophie's satchel in the morning; when he asked to speak to Sophie, he was told she was in bed, asleep.

He returned to the problem. It had begun to obsess him. He doodled words on a pad, looking for links. Both SOPHIE and ABACUS had the same number of letters. What if you wrote them one above the other?

$$\begin{bmatrix} S\ O\ P\ H\ I\ E \\ A\ B\ A\ C\ U\ S \end{bmatrix}$$

Was there a hidden equation there? What if you re-notated the words, giving consonants the value 1 and vowels the value 0? You'd get a number expressed in binary.

$$\begin{bmatrix} 1 & 0 & 1 & 1 & 0 & 0 \\ 0 & 1 & 0 & 1 & 0 & 1 \end{bmatrix}$$

Then, add or subtract? He tried subtraction:

$$[0 \quad 1 \quad 0 \quad 1 \quad 1 \quad 1]$$

He keyed in the digits.

The reply flashed up: DOCUMENT LOCATED. TYPE USER I/D.

It worked! But he was only half way there. She'd made it almost impenetrable. TYPE USER I/D. Her user identification could be absolutely anything. He toyed around with various ideas. The decimal for 010111 was 23, a prime number. He tried PRIME NUMBER, but received the snappy reply, INVALID USER I/D. He tried everything he could think of until the table-top was littered with sheets of paper. Finally he sat back, groaning in despair. It was no good. He'd never get into the file.

He was staring numbly at a sheet of scribbles when it occurred to him that a line of digits could also be read vertically, as a column, and when you did that it made what looked very like a hexagram, reminiscent of the code used in the ancient Chinese book of prophecy, the *I Ching*. Writing '– –' for each zero, he quickly produced a workable hexagram which, when he checked in the book, bore the title *Ch'ien*, meaning Obstruction. The computer rejected both words. He tried to think himself into the girl's mind. She loved puns: was she

193

indulging in some fun here? *Chi'en–chien*? Or, better, making a pun *on* the pun?

With a mounting pulse, he tapped in the instructions again.

Command: REVISE DOCUMENT
Reply: TYPE DOCUMENT NAME
Command: 010111
Reply: DOCUMENT FOUND. TYPE
      USER I/D
Command: DOGGO
(Christ, it worked!)
Reply: FORMAT CHANGE REQUIRED?
      YES/NO
Command: NO
Reply: FILE 010111: ABACUS WORD
      LEXICON SYSTEM
      LOG-ON TIME: 23.43 HRS.
      PROCEED

He stood by the French windows, looking out into the night. In the distance, a church clock struck one. His muscles ached with the strain of the day and his head throbbed from an excess of whisky.

So that was it. Her rage, her grudge, was because of Danny.

Poor darling Danny, it was my fault he was sent away . . . I could have saved him, but they didn't tell me.

How could she be so deluded? He wanted to rush over to her immediately and take her in his arms and tell her she'd made a terrible mistake, it was all a mis-understanding, none of this was true.

But other worrying references arrested his thought. Who was this Valentin, this strange boy who had crept into the garden, uninvited, one night? That was unthinkably dangerous. Then there was the business about Lizzie. His guess had been right that Sophie blamed herself. And similarly over his own accident, too. Her reasoning was clear: one moment she had a hateful thought about Lizzie and the next the girl was run over. A simple confusion of a temporal event with a causal connection. But what of these funny headaches? And those strange questions she'd been asking lately? Was it a simple matter of migraines or growing pains, or was there something more deep-rooted and sinister inside her mind ... something, *that* thing, perhaps at last starting to express itself?

He shuddered. Setting fire to your own home was not the retaliatory act of a normal, angry child: it was an overreaction, uncontrolled and excessive. Look at the sheer ferocity of the act itself, at her ruthless indifference to the outcome and her cold admission of guilt without any shame or apology. This did not belong to the Sophie he knew but to the Sophie he feared. Once again, Helen's words in the Oxford hotel bar came back to him: *What made them go wild was, quite simply, anger ... expressing their repression in this extra-powerful way.* Oh God, dear God.

What came next? Would it get worse? He couldn't tell. No one could, for no one had ever been here before. All he knew was that, whatever the cost, he had to get Sophie back home where he could watch over her, where he could take care of her and see to it somehow that this, the worst of all his nightmares, never, *never* came true.

He fell asleep in a chair and slept fitfully, tormented by fearful waking dreams. Somehow ... But how?

At dawn, he struggled out to his car and headed over to Bath. It was Sunday and the roads were empty. Dr Romberg was not at the clinic, just as he had calculated. He persuaded the duty nurse to release him two small plastic phials, the blood samples Alex and Sophie had given. They were only half full, but that was enough. The clinic wouldn't be needing them any more. But he might.

He stopped at the Infirmary on the way back. He tossed the phial labelled *Mrs A.F. Chalmers* into an incineration bag. But he took the other one to the small labs on the ground floor. There he spent an hour meticulously preparing the sticky, reddish-black liquid for freezing. Then he went home, packed it carefully in insulating material and hid it away, unmarked, in a safe place where it would be stored at a permanent temperature of minus eighteen degrees Celsius.

He'd have something to work on in an emergency. Just in case.

FOURTEEN

Alex woke with a sickening jolt. Where was she? What was this room with the striped blue blind and the bed the wrong way round? Then she remembered. God, what a nightmare. She lay for a moment, adjusting to the unfamiliar surroundings. The flat was silent, and only the occasional car passing in the street outside disrupted the early Sunday-morning peace. Her travelling alarm-clock told her it was six fifty. Automatically she sat up – seven o'clock was time to start getting Danny up. The realisation hit her a moment later. Would she ever get over it? She climbed quickly out of bed. Keep busy, keep active, that was the way to avoid succumbing to grief.

Slipping on her dressing-gown, she went to look in on Sophie. The boxroom they'd made into a makeshift bedroom for the child was empty. The covers were thrown off the bed but her clothes still lay draped over the exercise bicycle and her overnight case still shared a corner with a pair of skis and several dusty tennis racquets. This wasn't going to be easy; you couldn't watch a child the whole time.

She found Sophie sitting on her feet on the sofa in the main room, deep into a book. As she came over to kiss her, she caught a glimpse of the title: *Handbook of Abnormal Psychology*. She checked an impulse to ask if she should really be reading this kind of thing.

'Have you been up long?' she asked.

Sophie said nothing. Oh dear, the child was still in this mood: she hadn't spoken a single word all the previous evening.

'It's very early,' she went on. 'You need your sleep. Don't you? Well, I know you say you only sleep to dream, but you're a growing girl, and growing girls need their sleep.'

She sat down beside her and stroked her fair hair. The child didn't respond but merely went on reading as if no other world existed but her own.

Alex cast her eyes around the carelessly untidy bachelor sitting room. Journals and textbooks lay open face down, records out of their sleeves were scattered on the floor. Ultra-modern Italian chrome and leather chairs were set alongside heavy old mahogany furniture and ornate gilt-framed mirrors. Unwatered areca plants jostled for living space with the essays and theses that spilled from the bookshelves and spread across the threadbare rugs. Already a small thicket had sprung up around Sophie.

'I have a plan, darling,' she began again. 'The forecast's sunny. Let's take a picnic and go to the seaside. Or we could visit that National Trust house just outside Bath, you know the one I mean. Would you like that? Sophie?'

It was like talking to the deaf and dumb. The child wasn't actually reading, she could tell.

She stood up.

'I think a cup of tea is what we both need, don't you? And then some breakfast. I got Suzanne to buy your special croissants. Sophie, are you there? Speak to me, darling, please.'

Sophie didn't move. She seemed made of stone. It was awful, watching the poor child in such torment. She took hold of her by the chin and turned her to face her. Sophie didn't resist. Her violet eyes were empty, lacklustre, distant.

'Sophie, listen to me,' she said insistently. 'It doesn't matter. No one's blaming you, no one's going to hold

198

it against you. It's all forgotten. Do you understand? *It's all right.*'

The child gave a faint, almost imperceptible nod, but when Alex released her hold, she dropped her head again and went back to reading her book.

Alex drew up slowly at the junction and peered cautiously round the corner at the line of cars parked outside the church. Good: Jake's hired car was among them. She'd guessed rightly that at a time like that he'd be drawn to the comfort of his religion. She glanced at the dashboard clock; she had a good twenty minutes clear before Mass was likely to end. She let out the clutch and drove off purposefully.

What *was* she going to do with Sophie? The child was so silent and subdued. Graham had said that she was seeking to be punished, symbolically. Like all children, he said, Sophie subconsciously expected punishment for doing wrong. To deny her punishment by being instantly forgiving was, in her eyes, to deny the act she had committed, and that in turn denied the significance and the reality of what she'd done – even to the point of casting in doubt her own actual existence. *Ago ergo sum*: my existence lies in my actions; deny my works, deny *me*. That, he claimed, was the basis for this impenetrable stone wall of silence.

Alex shook her head. Neat theorising, clever sophistry, but utterly crazy! Typical Graham. Jake was right about one thing: psychologists made lousy psychiatrists. The sooner she got the child fixed up the better. Maybe Arthur would have some suggestions; she'd tackle him when they went to tea that afternoon.

She arrived at the house to find a skip parked in the street outside, filled with charred floorboards and window-frames and rolls of sodden, blackened carpet. A cement mixer ground away in the front drive and, inside, a small army of bricklayers and carpenters was busy at work. God knew how much it must be costing. Jake had refused to touch the trust money. Was he planning to take out another mortgage on the house? She didn't know. Was that any longer a worry of hers?

Stepping through the tangle of power cables and taking care to avoid the gaps in the floor where the boards had been taken up, she hurried in with her empty suitcase.

Sophie opened the boxroom door an inch and listened. Mum and Uncle Gray were in the dining room down the corridor – in some dispute, she could tell by the tone of their voices. She slipped her supper tray onto the oak chest and, pinning back the PRIVATE notice that had fallen off the door, went back inside and turned the lock.

She lay curled up on her bed, staring at the ceiling. Mum had collected her computer from home and a load of books besides, but she couldn't summon any interest in them. She was too confused to do anything but keep very quiet and do nothing.

Everything was her fault. Lizzie got run over. Dad had a car accident. Valentin climbed in and started the fire because she'd made those terrible accusations that night she'd heard about Danny. Even leaving the window open was her fault.

Why, too, were Mum and Dad quarrelling? Why had Mum left Dad behind at home? Why had she taken the photos from her dressing-table and other things they wouldn't be needing if they really were only going away for a few days? What was she doing with that man Arthur? Why did she smile and look funny when he came into the room? Why had she kissed him in the kitchen like that, obviously thinking no one was looking? And what had she herself done to Valentin,

200

her only real friend now that Danny wasn't there any more? Had he really gone off for good? *Why?*

All because of her.

Maybe if she never said another word, she'd get smaller and smaller and shrivel up and wake up one day to find she'd simply disappeared.

Jake went round the rooms spraying air freshener in the hope of masking the smell of fresh paint and the underlying odour of smoke and burnt plastic still lingering deep in the fabric of the house. He filled the hall and kitchen with flowers cut from the garden and rearranged the furniture to give the place a homely feel. Until the paint fumes went, Sophie would sleep in Daniel's room, her original bedroom, and Jake had covered its walls with fresh posters and bought a new desk and an anglepoise lamp. By the time it was all finished, he was exhausted; he'd driven himself to the limit. But he was elated, too, for in a mere three days he'd rendered the house habitable again. All that remained now was to go and bring his family back.

He cleared out the car – there'd be all the clothes and linen to collect, too – and drove the short distance to Graham's flat. As he turned the corner into his brother-in-law's street, he pulled up sharply against the kerb. A car stood parked outside the house. In the passenger seat, with her back to him, sat Alex. She was engaged in an intense conversation with a man he'd never seen before. Jake held back, appalled and yet fascinated, too. After a moment, the man leaned forward and kissed her. She responded, briefly but warmly, then got out, exchanged a final word of some kind of agreement and hurried off into the house. The man started the car, turned it in the street and drove off past Jake. Jake hid his face but caught a glimpse of a lean, tanned man with grey hair and an intent, serious frown. Who the hell was this?

He gave it a minute, then rang the street door bell. Alex's voice crackled over the intercom.

'Arthur?'

'It's your husband.'

'Oh. Jake. You want to come in?'

'Of course I do.'

The buzzer sounded and he pushed the door open. Alex met him at the entrance to the flat. She looked flustered and stood defensively just inside the doorway.

'Arthur, eh? Friend of Graham's, is he?' He forced a cheery tone. 'Well, Alex, I've done it! Fixed up the whole place like new. You'd never believe anything had happened. The car's outside, we can go when you're ready. Where's Sophie?'

'Sophie's down the far end. Jake . . .' She bit her lip. 'Look, come in. We can use the sitting room. Gray's out.'

She led the way into the main room and closed the door behind her. A look of pain flashed across her face and she touched him briefly on the arm. A sickening dread swept through him. He knew what was coming.

'Jake,' she began in a quiet, controlled voice, 'we are not coming back.'

He listened, stunned, to the inventory of reasons. Their marriage was an empty sham. There was no love left, only habit. No trust left: she knew all about his infidelities. And no respect: he'd forfeited the last remains of that during these past months with Danny. Danny had been the only reason she'd stayed with him, and now that he was gone there was nothing to keep them together. It was best they separated.

A host of objections arose in his mind. What infidelities? Who was that man he'd seen her with just now? And Danny – was she still going on about that nonsense? The boy could never have stayed at home, and there had never been any need for Sophie to give her blood . . . But he had no chance to utter these, for her final statement shook the breath from him.

'Sophie can stay here for the time being,' she went on in a matter-of-fact tone, 'until I've made other arrangements—'

He grabbed her arm and spun her round.

'Oh no! Sophie stays at home.'

'I've been trying to tell you, Jake,' she replied patiently, 'that that house is no longer *home*. Not mine, not hers. Please don't make an issue of it. There's nothing you can do.'

'And where will you take her? Shack up with that man you were with just now? No, Alex. Her place is where it has always been. If *you* wish to leave home, that's your look-out. But the child stays.'

She shook her head.

'Wrong.'

'Right, Alex.'

She looked down at the carpet. 'I didn't want to have to tell you, Jake, but I've taken legal advice. Custody of the child would go to me as the mother. She'll be in a proper family situation, with other children . . .'

He felt the rage welling uncontrollably.

'I don't give a damn about legal advice!' he shouted. 'That girl is not going anywhere!'

'Jake, be reasonable—'

'I've never been unfaithful – *never*. Can I say the same about you and . . . Arthur? Is that his name? Who the fuck is he? Or should I ask Sophie? You are the one who is leaving me for someone else. The judge would find *you* unsuitable, not me.'

203

'Let's keep to the point,' said Alex tightly. 'The point is Sophie and what's best for her. You've overforced the child and she's paying the price now. Look at her! She hasn't uttered a single word since she's been here. A court would only need a psychiatric report and . . .'

Losing Sophie was inconceivable. In that instant he knew, with utter certainty, that he would go to the limit, commit murder if need be, to keep her.

'I'm warning you, Alex!' he hissed savagely. 'If you dare take her away . . .'

Something over his shoulder had caught her eye and she pulled away sharply. He followed her gaze across the room. Sophie stood just inside the door, barefoot, wide-eyed, ashen-faced. She hesitated for a moment, her eyes filling with tears; then she ran forward with her arms held out in desperate pleading.

'Mum, Dad,' she said in a high, shaky voice, *'Please . . .'*

It had to come to it. There was no turning back. Only one way through presented itself.

While Alex went to make tea, Jake sat quietly on the sofa with Sophie, holding her hand and explaining the truth about Danny. Remember what he'd always said, *facts fight fears*? She had no rational cause to blame anyone – not him, and certainly not herself. This had been a traumatic time for them all, but she always had her *mind* – hadn't he taught her how to reason herself through grief, anger and despair? She had a brilliant career ahead; they'd work together next on winning a scholarship to university. The way lay wide open to achieving all her ambitions. He'd be there to help her, to steer and guide her along the path.

From time to time, Sophie nodded and answered in monosyllables. Was he getting through?

Alex brought in a tray of tea and sat the other

side of the child. On a pretext, Jake left the room for a few minutes. He didn't want to be present while Alex made her plea. He was already ashamed enough that he'd made a pitch at all, but what other way was there? Only one person could fairly decide Sophie's future. Sophie herself.

He paced up and down in the kitchen, appalled and horrified at what he and Alex were letting happen. What the hell might it do to a child, only just bereaved of her brother, to be called on to make a choice which meant losing a parent, too?

What would he do if Alex proved the more persuasive? How could he possibly live without his Sophie?

Finally, sick with dread, he went back into the sitting room.

Sophie was sitting bolt upright on the sofa, looking down at her bare feet. Her face betrayed nothing. Alex stood up and went over to the mantelpiece, forming the third point of a triangle. She looked ashamed of the whole distasteful business yet smugly confident of the outcome.

'Tell Dad what you just said, angel,' she gently prodded the child.

Sophie swung her heels, neither speaking nor looking up.

Jake stepped forward. His heart was breaking. What cruel madness was this? He couldn't put the poor child through any more of this torture. Anything at all was better than forcing her to make the choice, to condemn one parent publicly against the other.

He cradled her fair head in his hands.

'It's all right, darling,' he said. 'You stay here, with Mum. I'll be just round the corner. We'll see each other every day and we'll still work together just as we were always going to and everything will be fine, you'll see—'

He broke off, the tears rising in his eyes. He kissed her head and went to the door. There he turned.

Sophie had raised her head and was looking at him with her big violet eyes, fixing him with the same unblinking stare as she'd given him that very first time he'd held her in his arms as the newest of newborn infants. She reached out a hand.

'Wait, Dad,' she said.

Sophie lay in bed, unable to sleep. The night was hot and the sour smell of burning, mingled with fresh paint, still hung in the air. She'd finished writing up her diary by torchlight under the bedclothes and now lay staring out at the starry sky, thinking, however hard she tried not to, of that afternoon. Had she done the fair thing? Mum had Uncle Gray and also that man Arthur. Dad had no one. She hadn't been able to bear thinking of him alone in this big house.

She tossed off her blanket but she was still too hot. Eventually she got up and stood at the open window to cool herself. The house cast a pool of shadow across the lawn and, at the foot of the garden, the willow tree stood as motionless as a ship of the dead, its great sails unstirred by the slightest breeze. She felt older, sadder. Was this what growing up was like? Would things ever be the same?

Something moved within the tree, briefly shaking the fronds. She held her breath. Could it be Valentin? Had he come back? Oh please, she prayed, let it be him.

But the minutes passed and Valentin did not appear. The leaves stilled and the tree grew calm again. He'd gone for good. She was on her own now.

'Helen? Your mail, honey.'

Helen looked up from the microscope as the internal

messenger boy handed her a sheaf of letters. He hung back expectantly. She threw him a smile.

'Thanks, Jethro. No, I'm busy tonight again – sorry.'

'No harm in tryin',' he grinned back. 'Have a good day.'

She skimmed the envelopes: drug-company circulars, conference proceedings, a letter from Gottlieb at the Max Planck Institute, and one from England, postmarked Bristol. She flipped it over; it was from her mother.

She stretched. Her back and her eyes ached from poring over the microscope at a new batch of DNA fragments she'd been cloning. She could use a break. Switching the machine off and glancing to check that all was going well with the gene-splicing instruments, she rose from the bench and, with her electronic pass-key in hand, went for a coffee in the main laboratory concourse.

She opened her mother's letter first. Inside, she found a press cutting from the previous week's *Bristol Evening Echo*, with a note clipped to it saying, *Thought you might be interested in this*.

The article was about Britain's youngest-ever O-level pupil. Sophie Chalmers. Jake Chalmers's little girl.

She read it carefully, twice. She thought back nearly ten years to the extraordinary lengths to which Jake had gone over the conception, how he'd battled to obtain permission from the Ethics Committee and how, with six fertilised ova of his wife's, he'd stayed up all that night, screening the embryos so as to find one free of the Down's problem. It had been a triumph: a perfect child had been born. But shortly afterwards he'd had his breakdown and behaved in that unforgivably stupid way. She'd severed all links with him and lost all knowledge of the child. Occasionally his name had

207

cropped up during the gossip at some academic conference, but she'd studiously avoided following it up. But Sophie: there had never been any mention that the child was uniquely and prodigiously gifted.

She thought back to their recent meeting in Oxford and recalled how desperately anxious he'd been to know what had happened to her rats after the stage that he'd reached, when the animals had apparently reverted to wild. What was it he had said? *I just need to know something. It's very important to me. For my peace of mind.*

A cold shiver ran up her spine, and it was not from the air-conditioning.

For a long while she sat there motionless, just staring at the photograph, at that intelligent face and those wide, knowing eyes.

PART III

Four years later

FIFTEEN

'Twenty-eight, twenty-nine, thirty . . . *sprint!*'

Sophie shot ahead, her primrose-yellow tracksuit quickly swallowed up in the early-morning dark. Jake caught up with her behind the park café, now bleakly shuttered up for the winter. She was jogging on the spot, waiting. She smiled and shook her head.

'See what it does to you?'

'Don't go on at me,' he wheezed.

They walked for the next thirty paces.

'Tell you what, then,' she said. 'Have an AHH screen done. If it's high, you give it up. Deal?'

'Deal,' he laughed.

When the count reached thirty, they broke into a jog again. Their feet crunched crisply on the frosty track as they followed the path round the frozen pond. In the cold pre-dawn light Jake could just make out the prints of ducks and moorhens criss-crossing the surface, stiff with ice-locked bottles and other litter. A low wind moaned in the fir trees, scattering tiny scintillas of frost into the air. His nose and throat burned with cold, his chest and lungs scorched. She was right about his smoking; he'd taken it up around the time of the divorce, the same time as she'd begun having her funny turns again. But that had all been cleared up now, and everything was wonderful. Nice idea of hers, screening for the genetic marker for lung cancer. But a far nicer idea if he were to pack it in altogether, anyway.

They ran another circuit, walking, jogging and sprinting in turn, then headed through the tall, wrought-iron gates of Tyndalls Park and down the wide residential street, past houses with lights now coming on in upstairs bedrooms, past the paper-boy swathed in scarves and the milkman blowing on his mittened hands, past the first cars with dipped head-lights, crawling along the icy road, and finally into their front drive, round the back of the tall, granite-stone building, in through the back door and into the warmth of the kitchen with the central heating full on and the porridge oats already bubbling thickly on the stove.

Her fair cheeks apple-red and her violet eyes shining with exhilaration, she turned and threw her arms round his neck.

'That was great!' she laughed.

He held her close, feeling her chest rise and fall against his own. She was tall and long-limbed and carried herself with complete self-assurance. It was easy to forget she was only twelve.

He lightly kissed her forehead and, breaking the embrace, steered her towards the door.

'You go ahead,' he said.

'No, it's my turn to do breakfast,' she protested.

'I've got it all organised. Go and have your shower. Take a fresh towel from the airing cupboard.'

At the door, Sophie threw him a worried frown.

'Dad, you look dreadful. Please don't peg out just yet.'

He laughed. 'Not till I see you get your doctorate.'

'Not even then.'

'I promise not. Go on, now.'

She left the room. He heard her bounding up the stairs two at a time and, a moment later, Shostakovitch playing on the radio. Gradually regaining his breath, he went over to the sideboard to lay the table. On it sat an ashtray, bristling with the previous night's cigarette stubs. With a swift movement, he swept it into the waste bin and tossed in after it the packs on the shelf he held in reserve. He didn't need them any more. Sophie had been fine for a good eighteen months now.

Their house had become a home for two: two place settings at meals, two pairs of wellingtons by the back door, two coats hanging in the front hall, two bicycles in the porch. There were still two studies with separate collections of books but also, in the large bay of the main living room where Daniel's play-pen had once stood, two desks set back to back, each with its anglepoise lamp, desk-top computer and orthopaedic reading chair. The wall on which the boy had had his blackboard was now fitted with shelves and held yet more books – chiefly the textbooks which Sophie was studying for her biochemistry finals at the university in the summer. On the wall opposite was fixed a white Perspex board, at present full of scribbled calculations in chinagraph pen on a new idea they'd had to measure the sodium permeability of a cell membrane. Beneath were housed the hi-fi equipment and a comprehensive library of compact discs. The piano still stood in the opposite corner, though she played it less often now. After winning a distinction in her Grade VIII, Sophie had gone on to gain a licentiateship from the Royal Academy of Music, but when, almost immediately afterwards, she won her university scholarship she elected to throw all her energies into her academic work.

Jake, for his part, had thrown all his energies into Sophie herself. After her O-levels, he had sought around for a school capable of giving her what she needed. He'd investigated everything. The Bath Project. The Cognitive Research Trust in Cambridge. The National Association for Gifted Children. He had researched the facilities in the States, too, where a far greater importance was attached to developing talented children: the John Hopkins University, where he looked at their Talent Search programme for kids of twelve to sixteen; Philadelphia and the Institute for Human Potential there; the Missouri Experiment; Hunter College campus school, in Spanish Harlem; Columbia University Teachers' College, with their centre where two- and three-year-olds learnt Japanese, studied thermodynamics and knew all about stellar evolution. He corresponded with parents of other gifted children – the Susedik family in Concord, Ohio, and Dr Rhea Seddon, one of the first American female astronauts, and the parents of David Huang, the prodigy from Houston, Texas, who'd read fluently at two, mastered BASIC at four and gone on to become America's youngest college student . . .

Eventually he realised that Sophie was more brilliant than any of these. Believing, perhaps arrogantly, that no one had a better idea of helping her reach her full potential than himself, he wrote to the local education authority, invoking the 1944 Education Act, and insisted that she leave school altogether and thenceforth receive her education at home, with him. After a difficult exchange of letters and interminable visits from social workers and educational psychologists, he was granted permission. This all took place during that first summer after Alex left home. Sophie was not quite nine.

The following summer, at the age of nine and three-quarters, Sophie took her A-levels in maths, biology and chemistry. A year later, she won a top scholarship to Bristol University to read biochemistry. A minor furore broke out over whether a child of eleven was too young to enter university, and the faculty was split. The national press picked it up. Under headlines like 'Set Sophie Free, Dr Chalmers!', articles appeared dubbing Jake a 'puppet-master' and accusing him of forcing his young daughter and denying her the right to her own childhood. Hack psychologists and TV-doctors joined in the debate, warning of emotional and social trouble in store and appealing to the authorities to intervene to save the abused child. Where were the friends of her own age? they demanded. She wasn't allowed any; friends were a distraction. Where was her mother? Driven from the house by this maniac child-manipulator ... From that moment on, Jake refused to have anything to do with the media. He turned away reporters, he put the phone down on interviewers, he rejected all approaches from magazines, including *People* and *Time*. Even Helen Lorenz, who wrote twice asking if Sophie could take part in a survey of high-IQ children she was running, received a polite but firm refusal. Jake was having no more outside interference. Sophie was not public property.

He took to driving her to her lectures every morning on his way to the Infirmary. At lunch, he'd pick her up and, if it was cold, they'd go to a coffee shop near her Department; in summer, he'd bring the sandwiches he'd made before they left and they'd sit on a bench in a hidden corner of the campus grounds, discussing her tutorials or an experiment she was conducting. In the afternoon, he'd take her to the library or the labs and return to the hospital before meeting her once again at five o'clock for their afternoon exercise hour in the university swimming-pool or on the badminton courts. Sometimes they'd stop off at an art exhibition on the way home, and very occasionally they'd go to the early show at the Clifton cinema, but they'd always be back for supper at eight, which he would usually prepare, and follow that with two more hours' study before going to bed.

As the months slipped into years, Jake felt an intimacy developing between them that filled him with more joy than he could ever have imagined. They spent more and more time in each other's company, until they grew quite inseparable. Fewer and fewer things were allowed to interfere in the harmony of their life together. Alex came to visit on Wednesday afternoons, after school, and stayed until just before supper; Sophie, in turn, went to Alex and Arthur's house every Sunday afternoon for tea. Otherwise, people hardly ever came by. A Mrs McAndrews, a quiet, orderly, Scottish widow, came in to clean the house and do the shopping, but as she worked alternate weekdays only, from ten till four, she didn't often cross their paths. Graham had given up his weekly visits, though he still turned up occasionally for a drink in the hope, it seemed, of discovering something more about his exceptional young niece. In particular, perhaps, in the hope she'd show some sign of those pyschological disturbances he'd said he'd witnessed, so that he could justify becoming more closely involved with her; but that was long over now. Neighbours fabricated excuses to pry, and each time she passed another academic landmark at half the age of anyone else in the country, there were always journalists and reporters buzzing around, but as time went on Jake found still better ways of avoiding public interest. Increasingly, he closed the doors upon the world outside. Each was all the other needed. They were complete unto themselves.

Jake took two mugs of tea upstairs and, tapping on her bathroom door, reached in and left one beside the basin. Through the frosted glass of the shower cabinet, he glimpsed the long, slender young body.

'Tea up,' he called over the music. 'Don't be long.'

'Thanks.' Sophie turned the shower off and slid

open the glass door. 'Pass the towel, could you?'

He handed it to her and lingered for a second, amazed at the exquisite lissom beauty of her naked form. When would the shame arise to mar the modesty, when would adolescence threaten the trust? And would the hormonal flood, with all its tempestuous awakenings, threaten to bring on its tide the onset of that dangerous change he had witnessed in those laboratory creatures . . . at an equivalent age, in human years, of twelve or thirteen?

He reached forward and kissed her dripping hair. The answer was no. Everything was going to be fine. Perfect.

True, there had been a hiccough at the time of the divorce. He'd been careful to keep her ignorant of Alex's attempts to gain custody through the courts, but the loss of her mother from the home was bound to be traumatic. For a while he'd been seriously worried that she'd react in the same extreme way as she had over the loss of her brother. He'd watched her very carefully; he'd even, to his shame, taken to hiding the matches. One Sunday afternoon she'd been round on one of her first visits to her mother's new home when Arthur had fallen off a ladder while painting a ceiling, and Sophie, who'd been the only other person in the room at the time, had once again blamed herself for the accident. That night, under pressure, she'd opened her heart to him, confessing her deepest worries. It had taken him most of the night to reassure her that there was no way, mentally or physically, she could have *pushed* the ladder from ten feet away. They'd worked it through rationally together and she'd ended up seeing it for what it was: nothing. It was a milestone in their relationship. From that moment her trust in him, her love for him, began to flower in a way it never had before. She told him everything. He became her closest friend, her *confidant*. She referred to him less often as 'Dad', as though their relationship was more equal than between a child and a parent. Her diary, which again to his shame he surreptitiously checked from time to time, ceased to be coded in her secret language but was written in normal English instead.

For his part, he matched her unconditional love equally, but not, if he were honest, her trust: he could not reassure himself in the way he had reassured her, for there were things he knew that she did not, and must not. And yet, the months passed with no further setbacks to spoil the mood of openness and ease, until he, too, felt that the bad, worrying times must all be well and truly behind them. She was, indeed, absolutely fine. He had to rid his mind of any other thoughts.

She'd stopped in the middle of towelling herself and was looking at him oddly.

'Feeling all right?' she asked.

'What? Oh, just daydreaming.'

'It's hardly day yet.'

'Dawndreaming, then,' he smiled. He opened the door; he'd better get moving, too. 'See you downstairs.'

As he was locking the front door a snowball thudded softly into the back of his neck. He spun round and, ducking, scooped a handful of snow off the porch steps. Sophie had disappeared; a trail of footsteps led behind the car. Aiming carefully, he lobbed the snowball in a high arc and watched it soar through the crisp, wintry, morning air. There was a muffled cry and she emerged shaking snow out of her fair hair, smiling.

'Pax,' she pleaded, secretly gathering another handful.

'C'mon out with your hands up,' he bawled.

She laughed and brushed her hands free.

218

'Cheat,' she teased.

'But *you*'re the cheat!'

'Cheat for seeing.'

He climbed into the car and leaned across to open her door.

'Some new irrationality principle? I don't think I know that one.'

She grinned and, settling herself in beside him, began to read by the small light he'd rigged up over the passenger seat. From time to time as he drove through the cold grey streets, he glanced across at her. Her straight fair hair was swept back into a bunch, with wisps falling free at the front and following the oval line of her jaw and a fringe that all but concealed the 'V' that still puckered her forehead when she was deep in thought. She wore a striped woollen scarf, a padded denim jerkin, thick needlecord jeans and fleece-lined ankle-boots. She carried her books in a lightweight sports bag with a special pouch he'd made for her pencils and erasers and her small computer diskettes.

They'd been talking the previous night about the puzzle of eidetic memory and she sat skimming the Russian neurologist Luria's classic case study, *The Mind of a Mnemonist*, and comparing it with a short story by Borges he'd given her, *Funes, the Memorious*. Had it been his doing, he often asked himself, that she'd steered away from pure mathematics and towards the chemistry of life, his own subject? Was it his subconscious ambition that she would take over where he'd left off? Carry a brighter torch, and further? Maybe. But that course was fraught with peril, too. One day, sooner or later – and more likely sooner than later – she would begin to ask the same question he had asked thirteen long years before. She'd begin to look at herself, and wonder. And then she would have to be told, or else, with a mind like hers, she'd be bound to work it out . . .

After a while she reached into her bag and took out a calculator.

'It's just possible, I suppose,' she murmured.

'Total photographic recall?' he queried.

'I meant the capacity of the human memory store. Ten to the eleventh bits. The same as a thousand *Encyclopaedia Britannicas*.'

'More, if you allow for redundancy.'

She nodded. 'Either way, I think the really interesting thing isn't remembering but forgetting. Don't you?'

He shot her a quick glance.

'One can choose to forget, or so the phrase goes,' he responded carefully.

'But you still *know* you know.'

Was she thinking of Danny? Of the days before it had ever occurred to her she herself might have a problem? Of the years when they'd all been one family? He let silence fall.

He drove on until they reached the biochemistry labs, a bleak post-war building of rain-streaked concrete that rose all of a piece out of the grey and grubby slush of the pavement and forecourt. Yellowish lights already burned in many of the windows, some of which still bore sagging paper chains and tired sprigs of holly left up since Christmas.

She leaned forward to kiss him.

'See you at lunch,' she said, throwing the door open. 'And don't look so worried. Everything's great.'

Her expression was so impish that he drew her back towards him and hugged her hard.

'Hey.' He released her. 'Watch the steps, Sophie. They're bound to be icy.'

'You watch your RNA,' she teased.

It was a family joke: worry and anxiety reduced

220

the rate at which RNA was synthesised in the brain's cells, the reverse of what was needed for learning and healthy activity.

'Go on, off with you!'

With a laugh, she slammed the car door and joined the stream of older students picking their way through the snow. At the steps she turned to wave, then slipped. She recovered, only to slip on the next step. She continued clowning until she reached the top step, where she turned back again, but just as she was miming a bow she actually did slip and sat down in the snow, brimming with laughter.

He waited, as was their ritual, until she'd gone indoors and her face had appeared at the first-floor window, then, still smiling to himself, he let out the clutch and pulled away down the narrow lane. She was so vivacious, so playful, for all that she was serious and thoughtful. God, he loved her.

He was driving past the Department of Medicine building, his own former labs, towards the Infirmary down the hill, when he noticed a car he recognised, drawn up outside the front, its exhaust puffing thick white smoke into the frosty air. It was the grey Rover saloon of Herbert Blacker, his old professor. Herbert was standing on the kerb, opening the passenger door. A woman wrapped in a silver-fox coat and knee-length leather boots emerged. The professor was reaching forward to help her out just as Jake passed. He'd driven past by the time he realised he knew that long, dark hair. He shot a glance in his rear-view mirror. The woman was already striding purposefully across the pavement and up the steps with the gait of one who was familiar with the building. He knew that stride. Yes, and he knew the woman.

It was Helen Lorenz.

* * *

Jake had a meeting of the Parents' Committee in the early evening and, having dropped Sophie back home, he drove back to the hospital. Herbert Blacker's work on dwarfism was paying dividends, and already one undersized small boy named Roland was showing markedly improved growth. It was tough, Jake found, no longer having any part in the research going on at the university, but it was inescapable; the professor had maintained his vow, and for the past twelve years he'd kept the Department's doors emphatically closed. Though cut off from the means of doing research of his own, Jake could still take advantage of the results of their genetic work, as could all the other medical centres around the world, but scarcely a week passed without a question occurring to him that he might have been able to answer had he access to the lab and its equipment.

For instance, he had a baby in at the time with PKU, a condition resulting from a deficiency in the gene responsible for converting phenylalanine, one of the amino acids essential for nutrition, into tyrosine, the next stage in its normal metabolism. In theory, the baby could grow up healthy on a strictly controlled diet, but too much or too little of the amino acid left in the blood could cause brain damage, and designing a diet to give exactly the right balance was as tricky, and as critical, as defusing a bomb. The child would be impaired all its life and probably die at around forty. Now, a sad feature of the syndrome was mental retardation and he, if anyone, knew the locus and behaviour of the human intelligence gene. For a second he considered tracking Helen down and asking her advice, but he thought again. Her letters had already shown an uncomfortable interest in matters better left alone. Why was she in Bristol? Why was Herbert giving her the royal treatment. Was she on a fleeting visit, or was there some deal afoot?

No, he was a doctor now. He'd do better to leave problems of science to scientists. Or maybe, one day, to Sophie?

He returned home to find the hall lit and the aroma of roast meat filtering through from the kitchen. He pushed open the door. The table, cleared of its usual clutter of books and print-outs, was laid for a feast: the damask tablecloth they hadn't used since their last Christmas as a family, candles in silver candlesticks no longer dull with disuse but gleaming brightly, the crystal glasses that had been a wedding present and which Alex had neglected to take with her, and the bone-china plates Jake's mother had left him, which had somehow escaped the depredations of his father on his decline into bankruptcy and ruin.

Sophie stood by the table, lighting the last of the candles. At the sight of her he caught his breath; for a split second he imagined it was Alex standing there, the Alex he'd first met as a young woman. She wore a long black dress with high shoulders and lace trimmings and she had her hair pinned up with a paste diamond clip. Did he detect a hint of lipstick and eye-shadow, too?

Her face gradually fell as she waited for his reaction.

'Don't you like it? she asked.

'You look perfectly ... amazing,' he said, awestruck. 'Where did you ... ?'

'Drama Club. That fancy dress party's on tonight – you know, you saw the invitation. Everyone was going as Romeo and Juliet. I though I'd be an Edwardian *grande dame*.'

He fought off a momentary flush of hurt. She might not even have reached her teens but she was a student on the same level as the others and it was important she felt part of that world so far as she wanted to. If that meant going to student parties on her own, then she had every right and, provided she behaved sensibly, he wasn't going to stand in her way.

He glanced at the clock: eight fifteen.

'When shall I take you?' he asked. 'You don't want to miss the fun.'

She smiled and took his hand.

'Don't be silly. I'm staying here, with you. We're having our party, here. You wouldn't have enjoyed it, and I've no intention of going without you.'

'But, angel . . .'

'What would I do? Dance with all those boring men? I'd far rather be just us. Wouldn't you?'

He gave her hand a squeeze and moved towards the door.

'I'd better dress for dinner, then, hadn't I?'

SIXTEEN

The woman huddled deeper into her fur coat – the car had quickly lost its warmth without the engine running – and pondered the tall granite house fifty yards down across the street. This was utterly crazy. She'd twisted the Dean's arm into allowing her a sabbatical term, she'd flown all the way across the Atlantic, she'd talked her old professor, Herbert Blacker, into giving her use of the laboratory facilities under the pretence of research into chimpanzee intelligence genes, and here she was, a mere few steps away from her objective and without the faintest idea of how she was going to achieve it.

The house stood like a fortress, set back from the road by a short driveway and screened by thick evergreen bushes. Behind those walls, the most astonishing human experiment ever conceived was going on. She was convinced of it – she'd followed the trail from the newspaper in Bristol to the clinic in Bath – but she needed proof, and the proof itself lay secure inside. She'd waited for over three years for this moment. She'd written to Jake; he'd replied to her first letter, rebuffing her, and ignored her second. He would clearly have nothing to do with her. How the hell did she think she'd get beyond the doorstep? She *had* to find a way. Her whole professional future hung on it: rejection if she failed, acclaim if she succeeded.

She watched as a pale sun gradually sank behind the bare trees and, one by one, the street-lights flickered on. She was on the point of leaving and taking the problem back to the hotel when she heard a car start up in the driveway. Two headlamp beams filtered through the shrubbery, and a moment later a blue Volvo rolled out. Jake was driving; he was alone. The car pulled up at the road. A young girl ran out after him and tapped on his window. She handed him some papers, waved him off and, casting a brief glance up and down the road, disappeared indoors.

So that was Sophie.

The woman waited for a full minute. Then, with a mounting pulse, she stepped out of her car and crossed the road. Herbert had told her that Alex had left Jake: with any luck, the girl would be alone. She went up to the front door and rang the bell. A light came on in the hall. The door opened on a chain. A pale, oval face appeared in the gap. Large, intelligent eyes scanned her intently.

She gave a friendly smile.

'Hello. You must be Sophie. I'm Helen. I used to work with your father years ago.'

The girl nodded.

'Helen Lorenz. Genetic Coding for Intelligence. The Neurological Association. Oxford. June, three years ago.'

Helen took a step back. Her mouth went dry.

'Why, yes. You . . . know about it?'

'I never got to read it. Hang on.' She unchained the door. Smells of baking, washing and furniture polish wafted through. She smiled apologetically. 'Dad believes in all this ironmongery. Can I do anything?'

'I was wondering if he was in.'

Sophie shot her a puzzled look.

'D566 PJO, the red car, wasn't that you?'

'Uh, yes.'

'But you saw him leave just now.'

'Oh, was that him? It's been a long time.' She

smiled again, more brightly. 'Perhaps I could leave him a note?'

'Of course. Come in.' Sophie led her into the hall. 'I'll get you some paper.'

The girl went through a swing door; Helen followed. The room resembled a study more than a kitchen. Beyond a large, circular pine table spread with books lay a further room with two desks in a bay window back to back, each with a small computer. One was switched on; the screen was full of figures and a sheaf of print-out lay beside the keyboard.

'You're working,' she said sweetly. 'I'm disturbing you.'

'That's all right.'

'Or maybe I could wait?'

'He's on an emergency call-out. He could be ages.'

'I don't mind waiting, if you don't.'

Sophie hesitated, toying awkwardly with a wisp of hair.

'I want to get this program done before he gets back . . .'

'Please, I needn't disturb you. I'll just sit here and you go on with what you're doing. I mean it.' She put her bag on the kitchen table and slipped off her coat. Sophie took a step back and, with a shy, embarrassed smile, returned to her computer.

Helen let her settle down for a moment, then cleared her throat.

'May I get myself a glass of water? No, no, leave it to me.'

She filled a glass from the sink and, checking she was out of sight of the girl, opened the freezer door of the fridge and rummaged around for ice. *Quick! Is it there?* Ice-trays, a bottle of Polish vodka, a pack of frozen beans . . . nothing else. She sat down and sipped the water. The wall clock whirred, the tap dripped, the computer keys clattered softly in the further room. She felt uncomfortably hot and tense with anxiety. *Where the hell else could it be?*

Judging the moment carefully, she went to the living room entrance.

'I wonder if I could use your toilet?'

Sophie turned. 'Of course. Down the corridor on the left.'

'Thanks. I'll find it.'

Taking her handbag, she left the room and went down the corridor. Her heart was pounding furiously. She turned on the light of the small lavatory but shut the door without going in, then she slipped on down through a door she guessed must take her into a utility room. Steeling her nerve, she switched on the light.

A chest freezer. Could this be it?

Listening for any sound from the kitchen, she quickly opened the lid. Frosty vapour rose from inside. She got to work fast, working her hands beneath the frozen chicken and joints of meat, the packets of tarts and flans and the tubs of ice cream, until she reached the bottom. It wasn't there! It *had* to be! A sudden muffled explosion brought her heart leaping into her mouth and she drew back sharply; it was only the central-heating boiler firing. Trembling violently, her fingers burning with frost, she scrabbled through the trays again. Just as she was moving the plastic ice cream tubs aside for the second time, she noticed that one at the bottom felt lighter than the rest. In a flash she'd prised it open. Inside, embedded in foam wadding, lay a small polythene box, taped round the sides with what she identified at once as heavy-duty laboratory tape. Without a second's hesitation, she slipped the box into her handbag and, replacing the tub exactly where she'd found it, closed the lid and hurried back into the corridor. As she passed the lavatory, she pulled

228

the chain, turned off the light and shut the door noisily.

Back in the kitchen, she put on her coat and went over to where Sophie sat.

'Look, I don't think I should stay any longer.'

'You're very welcome,' replied the girl.

'As you say, he could be ages. Would you tell him I called, and I'll be in touch with him?'

'Certainly.' The girl rose and took off her glasses. 'I'll see you out.'

'No, I know my way.' She reached forward and touched the child on the hand. 'Thank you for being so kind.'

She stepped out into the cold twilight and, controlling her pace, walked unhurriedly down the drive and across the road to her car. Once she'd driven well away from the house, she pulled up under a street-light. Her hands shook so much she could barely undo the tape. Inside, wrapped in more insulating padding, lay a small, unmarked plastic phial. Even in that poor light she could tell from the colour what it contained.

She drove straight to the labs. After four years, it was anyone's guess if the glycerol citrate had held up. What if there had been a power cut in the meantime? She'd have to take every possible precaution in thawing it. You could never be too careful when reconstituting frozen blood.

Alex looked up from her armchair at the two children in the small back garden, fighting over the snowman they were building. Tom, the ten-year-old, short and wiry and built like his father, was rubbing snow into Rachel's face and the thirteen-year-old girl was fighting back with a plastic spade. In a moment there'd be screams and tears. Should she intervene? No, children had to learn to work out for themselves that personal freedom had its social limits. Actually, this was the first moment she'd had to herself all week and she was determined to finish the Sunday review section before the next interruption. She glanced at the fancy onyx and gilt clock on the mantelpiece. Sophie would be arriving any minute.

Curled up in the other armchair sat Mandy, lost in a romance magazine. Her boyfriend was coming to pick her up, and they'd go to some coffee bar in town and sit and smoke, or maybe go to one of her friends' flats and listen to loud rock music and get up to God knew what else. Still, that was normal for a girl of her age and aspirations. She'd left school the year before and got a job in the telephones; she was happy and contented enough, and her only troubles seemed to be boyfriends. She had no point of contact with Sophie, nor Sophie with her; they passed one another by, politely, like two ships happening to ply the same stretch of water. With Rachel, Sophie had nothing in common either, except her age. She made an effort to talk to her on the same level and show an interest in ponies and in the clubs she was forever organising, but after she'd gone, Rachel would call her stuck-up and patronising. What would have happened if Sophie had come to live there, after all? Would they really have made a family?

Arthur was out, taking his Sunday-afternoon climbing class at the local boys' club. He'd be back for tea. Did he purposely arrange to be out when Jake came to deliver Sophie? She couldn't blame him if he did. He'd had a terrible time over the divorce, too. Jake had behaved like a madman – lawyers, affidavits from so-called 'experts', even a private detective. Absurd nonsense, but the reaction of a desperate man. He'd been ready to go to any lengths to keep the child. The case should never have got to court in the first place. With a twinge of pain she recalled the headlines of the local paper: 'Child Prodigy In Tug Of Love'. The accusations that had echoed round that courtroom still lingered indelibly in her memory, but in the years that had passed she'd grown to forgive him – or, at least, she'd found a means of living around the past and getting on with a life in the present. They communicated now with the practised pleasantness of two neighbours who shared a common garden fence that united yet divided them and of which each could only see their own side. Arthur, however, who'd supported her with fierce loyalty while suffering his own anger and shame, had never been able to forgive and forget.

The doorbell rang. Mandy was at the door in a flash. 'Alex,' she called in a flat voice, 'it's for you.'

Not for me, she wanted to cry, for *us*. She went to the door. Jake stood there in his sheepskin jacket, a forced smile on his face.

Sophie stepped forward.

'Hi, Mother.'

'Hello, darling,' she answered, kissing her. 'Come into the warm.'

' 'Bye for now, Dad.'

'See you later,' Jake called after her. 'Have fun.'

Alex steered her daughter indoors and was closing the door when she hesitated. Jake's face wore a strange, almost sad look. Suddenly he reached forward and squeezed her arm in a moment's tenderness, then turned abruptly and hurried off down the path Arthur had cleared of snow that morning, and out through the low gate. There he paused again and, with a small wave, climbed into his car and drove off.

Sophie was standing behind her.

'Dad misses you,' she said in a factual tone. 'We both do.'

She felt a brief pang of remorse. She *had* done the right thing, hadn't she? Arthur had needed a wife and

231

his children a mother. Jake needed a wife, maybe, but not *her* as his wife, and as for their child . . . well, their child at least had her mother who was alive and lived just a short drive away.

'Well, darling,' she said, helping the young girl off with her anorak, 'what's been happening?'

'You'll never guess who came round yesterday. Helen Lorenz. You know, Dad's old assistant. Dad was out, but she came in for a bit. She seemed very nice . . . What's the matter? Mother?

'Nothing, sweet. Come and help me make some tarts for tea.'

Seven fifteen, and she wasn't back yet. Jake refilled his whisky-glass and went back to the notes he was writing up on the boy he was treating with the drug developed by Blacker's department. He couldn't concentrate. She was three-quarters of an hour late. He reached towards the phone, but checked himself.

This paranoia was absurd. Sophie had elected to stay with him of her own free will, rather than leave with Alex. When he felt on top of things, such as that very afternoon, he regretted what had happened and almost wished Alex would come back. When the doubts ate away at him, however, he knew he only wished her back so as to remove the threat that one day Sophie might change her mind and leave him. All the evidence pointed against it, but he could never feel absolutely secure. What happened during those hours she spent at Arthur's every week? She always shrugged it off; she hadn't much to say about the other children, and nothing really stimulating ever seemed to happen there. Intellectually, she might be able to resist any pressure they might put on her, but she was still only twelve, with the emotional development of a child of that age. Every Sunday, as he waited for her to come

232

home, he had this sneaking anxiety that the phone might ring and Alex would tell him that everything had changed and that his precious Sophie had finally opted to stay there.

To find reassurance, however, he had only to look around the house at all they shared, at the books they'd read together and discussed, at the desks placed back to back, at all she'd done for him – the old rummer for his whisky that she'd bought with her pocket-money from an antique shop, the paintings and drawings she'd done for him, the article she was working on for the *Journal of Neuroscience* in which she acknowledged her debt to him. She worked for herself, to satisfy her own curiosity, but the exams she sat, the awards she won, the records she broke as the youngest or the brightest, these, he knew, she did for his sake, for the pride she knew he took in her achievements. How could he doubt her?

He must just relax. Everything was fine. Her tutors were tipping her for a congratulatory first in her Finals in the summer. All he had to do was keep her, and himself, on an even keel, and see that there was as little outside interference as possible. Helen's turning up at the house like that was worrying, but she hadn't been in touch since; perhaps she'd only been on a flying visit and had gone back to the States. *Don't worry.*

He'd just returned to his report when he heard a car door slam in the street and, a moment later, a key turn in the front-door latch and Sophie's high voice, slightly out of breath, in the hallway.

'Dad? I'm back.'

'In here,' he called back.

She skipped into the study and put a polythene bag on his desk.

'I brought you back some tarts. A bit carbonised, I'm afraid.'

233

'Just as I like them,' he smiled.

She came round the back and, wrapping her arms round his neck, peered over his shoulder. 'How's it going?'

'I'd like your opinion. Pull up a chair and I'll read you what I've written so far.'

Instead, she leaned forward and flipped quickly over the pages one by one – she could absorb the most complex information in seconds – then stood back and took a tart out of the bag.

'On page seven you contradict what you said on page three about the Jacob-Creutzfeldt agent,' she said with her mouth full, 'and there's an inconsistency at the bottom of page nine. But otherwise I'd say it's fine. What are we having for supper?'

Helen had barely slept or eaten for three days. Herbert and his team had come at nine and gone at five, but she had paid no attention. The wall clock told her it was just after eight – was that morning or night? The metal-frame windows shone like black mirrors, reflecting the familiar laboratory in every detail. For the tenth time she glanced at the timer on the autoradiography machine. Any minute now, the X-ray plates would be developed.

Five millilitres from the blood sample had provided enough white cells for the experiment. Once purified, she'd treated it with a restriction enzyme, then subjected it to electrophoresis on an agarose gel slide so as to separate the DNA fragments according to size. Next, she'd denatured the DNA with alkali and transferred the fragments to a nitrocellulose filter, which she'd then exposed to a specific radio-actively labelled gene probe she'd designed in Chicago and brought over with her. It was a complex process, but one she'd repeated countless times before.

234

Only not, she knew for sure, on a sample quite like this.

A *ping* told her the X-ray film was ready. Drawing a deep breath, she took it out of the machine and carried it carefully over to her bench. One glance under the microscope told her everything.

She gasped.

The gel showed two distinct lanes. The left lane carried her own stain, as a control; the other was the sample she'd acquired from Jake's house. As she expected, a large, dark-stained blob was apparent in both lanes on a ten-kilobase fragment. But just below, in the right lane only, a second, identical blob stood out clearly.

That sample contained *two* of the same gene!

She walked round the room and, opening a window, took deep gulps of the cold night air before returning to the bench. But no, she wasn't imagining it. There, in black and white, as clear as if it were printed in letters a foot high, was the proof of what she'd suspected. A thrill of triumph shot through her. She'd been right!

There was only one way it could have come about, and she had worked out how.

She stood back from the bench, suddenly very cool, very resolved. She knew exactly what she needed. Should she approach the girl direct? Or perhaps the mother? No: she'd keep both those options for later, in case. Besides, the man had nearly destroyed her career. Now he could do something to help it. Something considerable.

She reached for the phone and dialled.

The voice at the other end sounded brisk.

'Jake Chalmers here.'

'Hello, Jake,' she said. 'It's Helen.'

'Now look, Helen—'

'No, you look, Jake, and listen. This is rather important for you.' She held up the plate as she spoke. 'I've got something here I think you should see.'

That night, Jake's world fell in.

The second he'd put the phone down, he checked the deep-freeze. Yes, the phial had gone. The truth was out.

He managed to persuade Sophie to go to bed early – Monday was always a big day for her – so that she wouldn't be around when Helen came over. He went upstairs to say good night and found the child already asleep. He stood for a while staring at her pale, innocent face in the moonlight. How would he tell her? How *could* he tell her?

Oh, Christ.

And Helen: what would she be after? Could he dispute her results, deny her conclusions? No, she had the essential evidence, and she'd have made sure the test results were faultless. Could he appeal to her to lay off it for Sophie's sake? He couldn't expect any pity from her after what he'd done to her career.

So, this was it. For thirteen years he'd been carrying the burden of this secret within him, haunted at every turn that it might come out into the open or, worse, some malfunction or aberration in the girl's behaviour might drive it out. Now the time had come for the truth. There was no flunking it. He had to face up to the harvest he'd sown all those years ago.

Sophie heard the doorbell from the depths of sleep, then a woman's voice downstairs. Mother? Had Mother come back? She sat up, alert. They'd gone into Dad's study, the room below hers. She listened but couldn't make out what they were saying. From the tone they seemed to be disputing something. Oh, no, not that all over again.

She lay with her ear pressed to the floor. It wasn't Mother: it was that woman Helen. Fragments of their conversation filtered up through the boards. They were talking about her.

Jake watched from the doorstep as Helen returned to her car and drove off. She'd given him forty-eight hours to think about it.

One glance as the X-ray plates had told him there was no hope of bluffing his way out. Then she'd offered him the olive branch.

'Let's work together on this,' she'd said. 'I've got the technique taped. I can insert the gene exactly at the right address. I've tried it in rats, mice, rabbits, cats and I'm working on a chimpanzee right now. Every subject has been a success. But you've gone one step further, Jake. And your subject is the one I need.'

A desperate thought had flashed across his mind.

'You've told anyone else?' he'd asked.

She'd smiled. 'I've taken the obvious precautions. But let's not think like that. We're in this together. Let's think of ourselves as collaborators, like the old times.'

'What exactly do you want, Helen?'

'I want Sophie.'

First, she wanted to run full-scale physiological tests on the girl. Were there morphological changes in her brain? Differences in metabolism? Abnormalities in the structure and functioning of the pre-frontal lobes? Specific neurochemicals unusually active? High levels of thyroid or adrenaline?

'Out of the question,' he'd snapped.

Second, she wanted to run in-depth psychological

237

tests. Were there signs of irrational behaviour, inappropriate responses, possibly even schizophrenic tendencies – particularly now, during the critical twelve-to-thirteen period that had proved so explosive in the lab animals studied?

In a word, she wanted *access*.

'No way, Helen.'

'Are you quite sure, Jake? Think again. Blacker's only got to see those plates. Or the hospital board. Or Alex. Or Sophie herself.'

'*No*, God damn you!'

He knew what a vital breakthrough it would be for her. It could be years before she got official authorisation to do what he had already done without consulting anyone. And here, on a plate, was a viable experiment, with a full thirteen years of track record behind it. He could see where it was leading, too. She openly told him that every major American department of state, from Defense to Education, had shown close interest in her work, and she made veiled reference to a NASA programme for genetic enhancement, specifically aimed at designing space colonists for the next century. The drug company funding her research at Chicago, too, was pressurising her to find a means of making that leap across the chasm from animal to human . . . And, above all, there was her professional reputation. Such was the stuff from which Nobel Prizes were won.

What if he said yes, under the strict condition that under no circumstances would Sophie ever get to know the truth?

He could stipulate no tests until she'd taken her Finals, but would Helen really wait that long? Or he could agree to a single series of brain scans; he could fix that up at the Infirmary, where he could be assured of some degree of discretion, offering Sophie some pretext that wouldn't reveal the purpose. But once

238

you yielded to blackmail, you were never free. Helen would demand one series of scans after another until she had what she wanted, and then she'd move on to the psychological tests. What the hell should he do?

He looked up into the sky. The moon was full, and corridors of stars stretched into the cold, black void. He was one small, insignificant particle in an entire galaxy. He shivered. What had he done? What rashness was it to step outside his small part, to reach out and pluck upon the harp strings of the universe? Such hubris would surely meet with punishment. Was this the beginning?

SEVENTEEN

Absently, Jake watched the milk boil over. When the wall phone rang, he knocked the receiver off onto the draining-board where it cracked a glass. He took the call and promptly forgot who he'd been talking to and what he'd agreed to do. Sophie sat at the table, eating cornflakes and reading a book.

'What was Helen doing round here last night, Dad?' she asked without looking up.

He started.

'Why?'

'Why what?'

'Why, uh, weren't you asleep? He forced himself to sound casual. 'No, she's over here with Herbert Blacker, on a sabbatical. She wanted to see if you'd join in some study she's doing on high-IQ kids.'

Sophie groaned. 'Not another, Dad. I suppose you told her no?'

'Well, Helen's an old friend. It's up to you, of course.'

'What's she looking into?'

'Trying to correlate intelligence with brain structure, or some such thing.'

The girl laughed shortly.

'But everyone knows that's nonsense! Tell her to pop over to Princeton and look at Einstein's brain. Structurally, it's perfectly average. Anyway, I thought she was working on genes and intelligence. That's what her paper was on.'

'I really don't know.' He smiled. 'You might just do her a favour. One quick scan, at the hospital. I'll set it up.'

She cast him an odd, pained look.

'Dad,' she said quietly, 'you don't need to bring that up. You know it's all over.'

He put a hand on her shoulder, spotting the lead.

'No harm in making sure, darling.'

'I don't see what it's got to do with *her*.'

'Call it killing two birds with one stone.'

She frowned and was about to say something, but held herself back. His mouth was dry and his hand shook. He couldn't keep up the deceit much longer. She was too bright. And he loved her too much.

'I'll think about it, Dad,' she said and returned to her book.

Something was going on. Dad had behaved exactly like that after Danny had died and he'd gone on pretending everything was all right. It was no good asking him. If she wanted to know, she'd have to go and see Helen herself. Why not? It would be interesting, anyway, to talk to her about her work.

During a break between lectures, Sophie slipped out of the biochemistry building and crunched her way through the salt-strewn path to the Department of Medicine. A board in the hall directed her to level E for the Genetics Research Unit. She took the elevator to the fifth floor, where she asked a technician where she could find Helen Lorenz. The man hesitated, clearly puzzled at what a young girl was doing there, then pointed to a laboratory three doors down the corridor.

Standing on tiptoe, she peered in through a small security window. The lab was empty. The door was operated by an electronic pass-card system, but she noticed the latch hadn't completely closed. She nudged it with her foot. It opened.

Inside, she glanced quickly around at the strange

equipment. Some she recognised: an electron microscope, cryostats, racks of test-tubes and droppers, Petrie dishes and gel slides with their curious ghost-like stains. In one corner hung the fur coat she recognised as Helen's and, on the bench beside it, jotting pads and files and sheets of computer print-out. She'd leave a note.

She was tearing out a sheet from the bottom of the pad when her eye caught the title-slip on a file: *S.M.C.: Agarose # 1.* Underneath, the next file was marked, *S.M.C.: Hybridisation.* She froze.

These were *her* initials! Sophie Mary Chalmers.

She lifted the cover of one file with her fingernail. She caught her breath. Those gene-stains were clearly, unmistakably, human.

Sickness clutched her stomach. She felt giddy and faint. She didn't want to see any more, know any more. Abruptly she turned and rushed to the door. She flew down the corridor and, not waiting for the lift, fled down the stairs, across the foyer and out into the bright, crisp morning air, not stopping until she was back in the safety of her own faculty building, where she hid in the lavatory and sat with her head in her hands, shaking and sobbing.

Jake drew up alongside the pale, long-legged young girl and threw the car door open.

'Hop in,' he called. 'How was Lambert's lecture today?'

Sophie didn't answer, merely climbed in and gazed stonily ahead. What was up?

'Where shall it be?' he offered cheerily. 'Somewhere new?'

'I'm not hungry,' she said.

'Come on, darling, you've got to feed the old synapses—'

The girl's face cut him short. She was as white as a sheet, her eyes wide with worry.

'I want to know what's going on with Helen Lorenz, Dad,' she said. 'It's *me* she's come over to look at, isn't it?'

He chuckled dismissively.

'Whatever gives you that idea?'

'Don't pretend! I saw what she's doing.'

'You *saw*?'

'I went to see her in her lab. She wasn't there. But I saw her desk.' Her eyes were filling with tears. 'Dad, *please*.'

He reached out and, drawing the poor child towards him, hugged her tight. Oh God, this was worse than he'd ever imagined. How could he ever have thought of deceiving her?

Yes, she must know. Now.

'It's all right, darling, it's all right. I'll tell you. Everything.'

He drove far out of town, to a stretch of downland they often visited in the spring in search of rare wild flowers. Now the slopes were covered with snow, with the higher ground grazed bare by westerly winds off the Atlantic and the lower tracks smothered beneath deep drifts. They drew up on a crest of a hill with a view that commanded the entire Bristol channel. Beyond lay the open sea, stretching to some point in the misty distance where horizon and sky became one.

He opened the car window an inch and turned to face his daughter. He felt moved to tears with pity and love and shame.

'Sophie,' he began, 'I want you to remember that, above all, I love you. I love you more than anything on this earth. Everything I have done is for your sake.

243

To give you the best possible start in life. To encourage you to fulfil the whole, beautiful promise within you.'

Sophie sat tight-lipped and very still, her violet eyes unblinking. He took a breath and went on.

'When your mother conceived Danny, it was a joy beyond all imagining. And then he was born, with his problem. We were terribly upset, of course, but we loved him with all our hearts. We knew his life would be short but we were determined to make it as happy as we could. As a doctor, though, I was angry. Angry that, with all our expertise in science and medicine, such disabilities should still exist. And perhaps worst of all, that so many disorders like his should involve the terrible curse of mental retardation.

'As you know, I was working with Helen in the Genetics Research Unit. It seemed natural to set out to try to isolate the genes responsible for intelligence, to find the genes that were lacking, or possibly just switched off, in Danny's and other such cases.

'That was fiendishly difficult, as you can imagine. You and I have often debated what intelligence actually *is*, and we agree it depends on the level you choose to tackle it on. Is it definable as the age at which a child speaks, reads, thinks conceptually? Or is it a *kind* of mind – say, divergent rather than convergent? Or again, should one look for it in the association cortex and consider it some function of the number and connectivity of the cells there?'

She hadn't moved a muscle.

'You're with me? Of course.' He swallowed. 'Well, I made a series of guesses. I said, "I'm looking for a single gene coding for a protein that controls the connection between neurons. OK, then: what messenger-RNA is specific to the nervous system and not expressed in other tissues?" Well, there are several thousand. By various means I reduced this to about fifty.

Then I took a sample of C-S fluid from one of my Down's children undergoing a spinal operation and isolated all the mRNA molecules I could find. I matched these with my target fifty.

'It took years, but finally I found one that was *present* in a normal child but *absent* in the Down's child. Was this the missing product in the mentally retarded brain? After endless frustrating false leads, I eventually hit upon it. A cluster of genes on the long arm of chromosome 13.'

Sophie's eyes were widening, but he couldn't read her reaction. He plunged on; it was too late to stop now.

'I extracted the gene from my own white blood cells and micro-injected it into fertilised rat embryos. I got rats of an astonishing intelligence. They weighed more at birth, they put on weight faster, they opened their eyes quicker, fed on solids sooner, grew better coats, and at the age of six weeks they were out-performing trained adults in maze tests. In a nutshell, I'd found the human intelligence gene!

'Sophie, you can imagine my excitement. More than half the cases of mental retardation are genetic in origin. This opened up extraordinary possibilities for gene therapy! I could see the day when wards like mine didn't exist, when we no longer had to go round patching up Nature's mistakes, when innocent children wouldn't be born with blighted little lives, destined not to run their natural course, when they wouldn't be called upon to plumb the well of human courage and endure what they'd had no part in making . . .'

He paused, remembering how his elation at the time had faded. 'Well, there were immediate difficulties in translating this into something clinically practicable. The gene coded for a neuro-mediator and so it was obviously too late to introduce it into a child after birth, where the neurons were already established. Well, I thought, why not introduce it into the foetus, via a retrovirus? But it wasn't produced by the blood or liver cells ... No, the only way would have been to introduce it directly into the fertilised human egg, and that ... well, at the very least that contravened the medical Guidelines.

'Still, I continued the work in the lab. I wrote papers which generated plenty of international interest, but without much hope of seeing it put to clinical use.

'By now, Danny was about six. For a long time your mother and I had been wanting to give him a brother or sister, but we knew she was the carrier of the syndrome. Eventually, I hit upon the solution. I got approval of the Ethics Committee at the Infirmary to arrange for a rather special *in vitro* fertilisation. It worked like this. Your mother went on a course of fertility drugs. When the time came, she went into hospital and donated six eggs. I fertilised these *in vitro*, and that night, while they'd still only reached the four-cell stage of division, I took out a single cell from each and ran a chromosome spread. From this I identified one good embryo. The following morning, this was re-implanted, and in the course of time that embryo became you.

'But what she doesn't know, nor anyone else until Helen now, is what else I did that night in the labs.'

He took her hand and squeezed it. It was so cold and lifeless. He pressed it between both of his. She *had* to understand.

'Imagine, darling, you were me. Imagine you'd spent your whole life patching up Nature's mistakes. Then you own child was born a mongol. Every day you were surrounded by defects and deformities, and no one seemed to possess the stature or the mind, or possibly just the opportunity, to make any real break-through. But here you had a new, viable human life, lying there on a dish. You had a chance to do more than just cure diseases – you could actually do some positive good. You could create a living being that was more than just another normal, ordinary person, one of the myriad of others who just tread the treadmill of life, who take their measure of pleasure and pain and then die without leaving the world any better off for their existence . . . Instead, you could create one who could be exceptional, who could see above the heads of all the rest of us, who could lead the world forward, discover cures for incurable diseases, even change the whole course of human understanding . . .'

He put his head in his hands. This was awful.

'Sophie, Sophie, I *had* to take the chance.

'It was a terrible risk. I knew the gene had found its right address in the animals I tested, but would it do the same in a human embryo? Most of all, how would a *double* presence of the gene express itself? I didn't know. I *couldn't* know. But I had to try it.'

He sat back. He felt reconciled to whatever the outcome might be.

'Early that morning,' he went on more quietly. 'I put the glass dish under the microscope once again. I filled a micro-fine hypodermic with a solution containing that human intelligence gene, the gene I had extracted from my own blood cells. And I micro-injected it into each of the three remaining cells.

'I watched with bated breath as you flowered inside your mother's womb. You can't know the joy, the *excitement*, I felt at the first signs of life, of healthy, normal life. You grew perfectly, and you were born perfect. And you have grown up perfect in every way.

'You have always known you are special, Sophie.

Now you know why. You *are* special – specially wonderful. Be proud of your extra talents, just as I am proud of you and how you use them. And remember most of all, I love you.'

Sophie said nothing for a full minute. She sat bolt upright, and only from the flicker of her eyes could he deduce that she was working out the implications of what he'd told her. Then she turned slowly to him, her face filled with anguish and perplexity.

'*So what am I?*'

He leaned forward. 'You're Sophie. My angel.'

'But I'm not *me*.'

'What d'you mean?'

She shook her head in despair.

'I'm someone else, too. Someone else inside me. A double person, a double mind. I've inherited two genes from you, instead of just one. I'm ... more *you* than me.'

'No! You're *you*. Entirely yourself.'

'I'm not! You've just told me I'm not! I'm special because I'm a genetic oddity. I belong on your ward with the rest of them. I'm ... I'm a freak. A *freak!*'

With a howl, she flung the door open and stumbled out. He jumped out too.

'Wait! Sophie, wait! Listen!'

'Leave me alone!' she yelled, backing off. 'You cheated me! You robbed me of – of being *me!*'

She turned and, with her arms clasped round her head as if to ward off blows, broke into a run, zigzagging like a hare across the open field that fell away gently towards a small copse. Keeping his distance, he followed her tracks through the shallow, snow-filled ruts. Some way down the slope he stopped to retrieve one of her shoes and, further on, her scarf. She had reached the copse and was rounding a headland when, for a brief moment, she was lost to sight. He raced forward. She had disappeared, leaving only a trail of footprints that led, stumbling and tripping, to a small stone crofter's shed.

Inside he found her crouched in the corner, choking with tears. He reached forward, expecting her to claw him off, but instead she rose and threw herself into his arms and clung there passionately with all her fervour, her whole body heaving desperately and her face burrowed deep into his chest.

'Oh Dad, Dad,' she sobbed hysterically, 'say it's not true!'

She was shaking uncontrollably. He clasped her tighter.

'It's all right, calm down, everything's OK.'

'I don't know ... I don't know whose thoughts I am thinking.'

'Your own, darling, your *own*.'

'Where do *you* end and *I* begin?'

'No, listen—'

She struggled to pull away.

'*Who is me?*' she cried.

He grasped her shoulders and shook her.

'Listen!' he shouted. 'Hold on to reason! Use your mind! Whatever goes to make you up, *that* is you. That's how we all are. That kid in my ward with the alpha-globin gene missing isn't any less himself because of that. Think of Danny. He had an extra chromosome from your mother. Did that make him *more* than himself? Was he more part of her than himself? He was *Danny*, no more, no less ...'

He talked on, hardly drawing breath, forcing her to see reason, knowing that only the power of human logic could save her. But her face had drained of all blood and her eyes were rolled back, and from her throat came a strangled growl that forced itself up through her clenched, frothing teeth. Christ, an epileptic seizure! He forced his fingers between her teeth and tugged her tongue clear of her windpipe. Her shaking grew more and more violent as her muscles locked tighter, until, with a final sickening spasm that racked every nerve of her body, she suddenly went limp in his arms and lost consciousness.

He laid her on the dusty straw floor and, kneeling beside her, loosened her clothes around her neck. A quick check told him her pulse was steadying and her breathing returning to normal. She remained out for thirty, maybe forty seconds, and when she came round, her face had already begun to regain its colour and her eyes were clear and focused. She looked about her, half surprised to find herself on the floor. She tried to struggle to her feet.

'I must have fainted,' she slurred. 'What happened?'

'Lie still, darling. Don't move just yet. I think you had a *petit mal* seizure. It's quite common.'

She pressed a hand against her forehead.

'Dad, am I going mad?'

'Of course not! You're as sane as I am.'

She managed a weak smile. 'That's what I was afraid of.' She paused. 'You know all that business you've been telling me—'

'Leave it just now . . .'

'I think,' she went on in a small, reflective voice, 'that if I'd been in your place, I'd have done just the same.'

He knelt over her and stroked her fair hair.

'Thank you, Sophie,' he replied quietly, deeply moved. 'I do love you.'

'I love you too, Dad.'

The sky had darkened from the east, bringing with it the threat of more snow, and an eerie stillness gripped the bare, frozen hillside. With his arm tight round her shoulder and hers locked round his waist, father and daughter picked their way back up to the ridge and the clearing where the car was parked.

Neither spoke. Sophie limped a little on one foot. Jake had wrapped his sheepskin around her and he walked with teeth gritted and muscles clenched against the cold. With his eyes on the ground, he steered along their former tracks where the snow was at least partly trampled down. It was only when he glanced up to check their direction that he saw the fleeting figure far ahead, running, now falling, then clambering up and running again ... the figure of a boy, somehow strangely familiar in the way his arms lashed the air as he ran ... now reaching the crest of the ridge, pausing to look back the way he'd come – exactly *their* way, but where were his tracks? – and then abruptly disappearing.

Sophie was stumbling and, despite the sheepskin, shivering badly. Bending down, he swept her up and, with her head pressed close to his breast, carried her in his arms up the rest of the hill and over to the car.

That night he put her to bed early and sat holding her hand until she fell asleep. The crisis had passed and she'd spent the evening quietly and calmly. She had been the one to raise the question again; she understood now why Helen wanted to run a scan, and she wasn't averse to it. In fact, from a scientific point of view, she, too, was curious to know the result. Did the extra gene express itself in any altered structure or metabolism of the brain? He'd felt almost shocked she could react so coolly and logically, and so soon after knowing the truth, and though he'd said they'd leave it till the morning, his spirits had risen. Yes, the human mind was capable of anything. She'd overcome

251

her initial, primitive, emotional reaction by the sheer strength of her superior intelligence.

He went downstairs, strangely elated. The weight that had been oppressing him for thirteen long years had finally lifted. He felt renewed with hope and love. He'd lived all this time like an early navigator, sailing the brink of the world, terrified he might at any moment fall off the edge. Now a storm had driven him over the limit, and he'd found the world was round after all. They'd lived through the nightmare and come out safe the other side.

He took a drink into his study; he'd do a little work before going to bed himself. Finding he'd left his briefcase in the car, he slipped on his sheepskin and hurried out into the night. The freezing air seared his windpipe and the icy gravel splintered at his footfall. He'd retrieved his case and taken a few steps back towards the house when he remembered he'd left a file on the back seat. As he turned, he heard a sudden grinding sound from high above him. He looked up just in time to see a large white-grey chunk of something falling out of the black sky. It landed on the bottom step with an explosive crash and burst into a thousand fragments. One piece struck him a glancing blow above the ear. Leaping back, he scanned the roof high above. Following the pitch to the top of the gable, he could just make out the gap where a stone finial was missing. There was no wind. Had the frost prised it off? He'd check it out in the morning. Meanwhile, he'd get that file.

But his legs wouldn't move for him. He stood rooted to the spot, shaking in every limb, as the shock wave hit him. If he hadn't decided to turn back to the car, he would have been on that step. And he would be lying there now, his skull shattered into fragments along with the boulder itself.

He looked up over to the left. A light had come on in Sophie's bedroom and her pale, oval face was pressed to the window-pane, her eyes wide with fright.

In the morning, Jake went up into the attic. Brushing away the cobwebs, he unbolted the small door that led onto the roof. Inch by inch, he climbed along the gulley leading round the low parapet that ran along the edge of the steep, tiled roof, until he reached the front of the house. Yes: a stone finial, an arm's stretch away, had sheered off in the frost. From a superficial look, the rest of the stonework seemed safe except for the far chimney, the one directly above the conservatory, where the pointing seemed badly eaten away at the base. One of these days he'd better get a builder to check over it.

He was about to begin the return climb when something caught his eye on the edge of the parapet ahead. He froze.

A footprint in the snow! Small, but indelibly printed. A *child's* footprint?

But no one had passed through that attic door for months.

A sudden wave of vertigo gripped him, and the whole world about him, the tree-tops and the drive-way far below, began to revolve sickeningly. Clutching desperately at the slippery, sloping roof, he fell to his knees and crawled painfully back along the gulley, not daring to look over the parapet or anywhere except the foot of mulchy snow ahead of him, until he regained the attic door and clambered in head first to safety.

EIGHTEEN

Sophie started violently at the knock on the bathroom door. She spun round. On the other side, her father's voice sounded anxious.

'Sophie? You OK in there?'

'Fine,' she called quickly. 'I'll be down in a minute.'

He seemed to hesitate for a moment, then his steps retreated down the stairs. She turned back to the mirror and leaned closer, studying the image in the steamed-up glass. Slowly she began stroking the back of her finger along her cheek, tracing the line round the point of her chin and up and across to her lips. She'd seen this face in the mirror every day of her life, but who did it really belong to? Whose mind lay behind those eyes? She felt a stranger to herself.

That afternoon, in an hour or two's time, she was due to be going to her mother's. Only, in fact, she wasn't. Dad didn't know, but she'd said yes to Helen Lorenz. Yes to the scan.

Two days before, Helen had tracked her down at the bio-chemistry department and caught her between lectures. She'd taken her on one side, out of anyone's hearing.

'Your father has told me you *know*, Sophie,' she'd said. 'The trouble is, he's absolutely refusing to let you take part in my study. Of course, if the facts ever came out in public, he'd be struck off the register. He'd never get another job. Now, we wouldn't want that, would we?'

Within a minute, Sophie had agreed. All right,

she'd said; just a couple of routine scans, and only a single session. This afternoon.

She thought back to the moment of truth on the hillside. Poor Dad. He'd needed her so badly to forgive him. Was what he'd done really wrong? The reasons were justifiable – Danny and a ward full of genetic mistakes. And generations of mistakes yet unborn. Didn't they count for more than one single individual, as yet a few small cells lying on a Petrie dish? She understood. Yes, she would have done the same. He'd acted from the right motives, from loving motives. He'd wanted to give her the best start in life he could, for *her* sake. He loved her, and by refusing Helen he was risking his career to protect her. If she loved him, shouldn't she try and protect him, too?

With Helen, it was different. She was just cashing in. *She* had no loving motive. All she cared about was the experiment. She just saw Sophie Chalmers as a human laboratory animal. And if she didn't get what she wanted, she'd betray Dad to the authorities. He'd lose his job, he'd be in disgrace, he'd have to leave the hospital and abandon all those children . . . How *could* she?

She felt her rage spiralling out of control. She was choking, suffocating. She gripped the side of the washbasin, panting but unable to find enough air.

I hate her! I hate every bit of her! I'd like to make her choke, I'd like to make her suffocate . . .

Stop! she told herself. *Think.* Be calm, be logical. One step at a time. Do the tests. Don't let Dad know. Just do them, get them over, keep quiet, get rid of Helen and everything will return to normal.

But even as she watched, she saw the face in the mirror before her crumbling. Her whole self was fragmenting. How much longer could she hold the pieces together? Downstairs, her father was calling her to lunch. She buried her face in her hands. Oh, God, what had she agreed to? They were going to scan her brain, to probe directly into her *mind*. What terrible things might they find there? What other self? And what would they do to her then?

From the car, Sophie spotted the red saloon with the registration number that she recognised, parked discreetly up a cul-de-sac. Her pulse lurched. There was no escape. She looked across at Dad. He sat whistling to himself as he drove, so lively and carefree. It was a small thing to give him.

As he drew up outside Mother and Arthur's house, he hesitated.

'That business,' he began. 'I think perhaps it's best if you don't—'

'Don't be silly, Dad,' she said. 'It's our secret.' She wrapped herself tight around his neck and hugged him. He stroked her hair.

'If you want to duck out early,' he said gently, 'just call.'

She shook her head. If only it could be that simple. No, she had to go through with it. And hope that Mother didn't see through her excuse and call him. She broke away and jumped out of the car.

'I'll go round the back,' she called. 'Don't wait.'

'All right. Don't forget, darling, call me if you need me.'

'I won't. 'Bye, Dad.'

She skipped lightly up along the side path and stood waving until he'd driven off. Then, careful that no one in the house spotted her, she retraced her steps and, once back in the street, hurried round the corner to the cul-de-sac. The red saloon flashed its lights. Biting her lip, she stepped forward. She felt like a prisoner surrendering.

Helen threw the passenger door open.

'Well, that's good. You're a co-operative girl, Sophie. We're going to get on well, you and I.'

Sophie climbed in and stared, tight-lipped, at the road ahead. Speaking wasn't part of the agreement.

Helen shrugged. It didn't really matter if the girl kept up a stony wall of silence, so long as she did what she expected of her. She'd give her a couple of scans today. If they showed up anything abnormal, she'd repeat them the following week. She'd just say they hadn't come out properly. Their agreement said nothing about re-runs. With luck, she could spin it out like that until she had everything she wanted.

She glanced around the Radiology Unit. Coloured lights and a low humming sound indicated that the various pieces of electronic equipment were on and functioning. The young radiologist stepped forward.

'Sophie,' she said, 'this is Dr Mangold. He's kindly giving up his Sunday afternoon to help us.' The doctor held out his hand. Sophie didn't take it. 'Well, now, time is short, so shall we begin? Roger, we'll take the CAT scan first. Sophie knows all about computerised tomography, don't you?'

'Ready when you are, young lady,' said the man with a sympathetic smile.

The CAT scan was a quick, simple operation. Sophie merely had to lie quite still on a narrow couch for a few minutes, with her head inside the annular chamber. The instrument whirred and clicked, taking X-rays of her brain in five-millimetre slices from her crown to her chin. These would be stored in the computer's memory for fuller analysis later, but now, at the CRT console, Helen watched the pictures flick up live on the screen. As they progressed deeper into Sophie's brain, the general outline changed shape and, within

257

it, the differential densities of fluids and tissue showed an altered pattern of light and dark.

The result became quickly clear. In terms of organic structure, the prodigy's brain was perfectly normal.

She helped the child off the couch.

'Well, Sophie, you may have an exceptional mind but there's nothing exceptional about the structure of your brain,' she said. 'Now let's check the metabolism. I don't expect you've seen a SPECT scan done before, have you?'

Sophie remained silent. She allowed herself to be led to a chair where the radiologist asked her to roll up her sleeve and hold out her arm. Behind, Helen prepared the hypodermic with the radio-isotope of iodine. Sophie turned and seemed to take in the label at a glance: *1-123 N-isopropyl-p-iodoamphetamine*. No doubt, thought Helen, she could see this marker was allied to the amphetamines and so might induce visual disturbances, but there was no point in making her unduly anxious.

The radiologist administered the injection. Sophie winced but stayed tight-lipped. During the twenty minutes they waited while the isotope reached the brain and circulated through its micro-vasculature, Helen kept up a constant chatter, trying to enthuse her in the science of the process. She explained how the 'contrast' bonded avidly to the sites for a group of natural amines, the brain's main neuro-transmitters. Roughly, a greater preponderance of receptor sites at the synaptic junctions indicated greater connectivity and, in turn, greater intelligence. The isotope emitted gamma rays which were picked up by a special camera and converted by computer into a three-dimensional picture, thrown up on another monitor. Where there was a high density of sites, these would glow luminescent on the screen. The information would, once again, be stored in the memory, and by manipulating the controls she could navigate through the entire brain at leisure, slice by slice, revolving and turning it so as to view it from any angle, inside and out.

The radiologist then led Sophie forward and made her place her chin on a padded rest while he gently adjusted a frame to keep her head steady. Then he set the gamma-camera in motion, starting from the front and tracking slowly round her head in a complete circle.

'Now, Sophie, I want you to calculate something, please,' Helen requested. 'Play around with some binomials.'

As she studied the screen, her pulse began to rise. The first slices captured the pre-frontal lobes. In the centre of each hemisphere a small patch seemed to be glowing with strange, unusual brilliance. She switched to a higher resolution. The patches suddenly magnified to fill the screen. They appeared to be pulsating rapidly, at around four cycles a second. She moved the cursor to the centre of the right hemisphere area and glanced at the lumen level recorded in the margin of the screen. She felt her throat go dry. This was two degrees of magnitude brighter than she'd ever seen on any of her previous studies!

Behind her, Dr Mangold caught his breath.

Step by step, the camera rotated, building up its picture of the metabolism of the complete brain. It had reached half its travel and was recording the amine sites in the hindbrain when the screen began to flicker and blink. A strange, grinding note came from the motor and a warning signal flashed up at the foot of the monitor screen. She shot the radiologist a querying glance; his face registered growing alarm. She turned back to the screen and quickly revolved the angle of view to reveal the underside of the cerebellum. The picture was disintegrating in a thickening snowstorm. On each side of the central worm a small area glowed preternaturally white. What were they? She struggled to mount the lobes, starting from the outside: the inferior semi-lunar lobe, the slender lobe, the biventral lobe and . . . the amygdala.

With a crack and a sputter, the screen flashed searingly bright, then went dead, leaving only a phosphorescent ghost image of the rounded, tonsil-shaped organs, that clung for a moment, faded, then disappeared altogether.

Sophie was wriggling free of the head-frame. She was ashen, wild-eyed. Helen came over and reached out to soothe her, but the girl backed away towards the door.

Helen caught Dr Mangold's eye as he hurriedly checked contacts and tapped dials. He shook his head.

'Electrostatic interference, at a guess, but God knows what.'

'Can we fix it and run that again?'

From the door, Sophie's cry split the air.

'No!'

She shrank away from Helen's approach, her eyes blazing.

'Don't let's waste the chance, Sophie,' coaxed Helen. 'We're half way there. Let's finish it, huh?'

The radiologist chipped in, scratching his head. 'Not today, for sure. The thing's kaput.'

'Well, then,' said Helen firmly. 'We'll make another time.'

'No!' hissed Sophie. 'You promised.'

Helen smiled as reassuringly as she could.

'Sophie, this is *science*! You can't expect the answers all at once. You know how long it takes to do an experiment properly.'

But Sophie's face had suddenly gone as blank as

260

the screen. She stood very still, very erect, her eyes unfocused.

'Would you take me home now, please?' she said quietly.

Sophie reached for the car door as they pulled up in the street outside home. Helen laid a hand on her arm and smiled.

'Thanks, Sophie. I'll be seeing you again.'

Sophie shook her head.

'No, you won't.'

The hand tightened its grip. 'Come on, can't you *see*? You're a pioneer! You're part of the most exciting experiment that's ever happened! In years to come—'

Sophie pulled away and glared at the woman.

'I may be an experiment to you. But to me, I'm *me*.'

Helen's face hardened. 'I thought you were a girl who loved her father,' she said.

Without a reply, Sophie wrenched the door open and fled up the driveway to home. Behind her, she heard the car start up and, after a moment's hesitation, drive off.

She leaned on the doorbell until her father came. She fell into his arms.

'Hey, what's the matter?' He held her away to examine her. 'You look terrible! What on earth have they been doing with you? I'll phone your mother right away.'

'No, don't,' she said, recovering quickly. 'I'm all right. We – we went for a long walk, that's all.'

'In those clothes? I *will* ring her—'

'It's OK. I'm fine. Honestly.' She took a deep breath and forced herself to sound normal. 'What's been happening? Shall we have supper early? I'm starving, aren't you?'

*　　*　　*

Helen parked at the rear of the tall, modern block where she had rented an apartment and picked her way through the slush to the front door. Fumbling for the key, she felt a sudden dizziness and steadied herself against a column supporting the concrete canopy. A car's headlamps momentarily swept across the front of the building, throwing her shadow in clear outline against the wall ... no, two shadows, close together, the second one not hers, different, shorter, thinner— She spun round, but the whole front area was empty. The car was disappearing round the back into the car park. Of course: two headlamps would cast two images, wouldn't they?

She reached to insert the key but her vision seemed to have gone blurred, just as it had at the end of the session with Sophie. A touch of migraine, no doubt brought on by the general stress of those past few days, or perhaps the stuffiness with all that machinery in the radiology room.

Once inside, she felt better. She hurried across the foyer, exchanging a greeting with the night porter, and took the elevator to the seventh floor. Astonishing, she thought as she watched the numbers rise, that concentration of receptor sites – where? – in the amygdala of the girl's brain.

Whatever means she had to resort to, it was imperative she really got her teeth into this phenomenal child.

The night porter looked up sharply from his small television, tucked away in his basement locker room, and in a quick reflex palmed his cigarette. What was that sound? From the television came the muffled roar of a crowd and the clang of a bell announcing the start of round five of the big fight. Turning down the volume with some reluctance, he looked about the long, dimly lit room: the boxes of meters lining

262

the walls, the foil-lagged pipework snaking along the low ceiling, the mops and buckets in the corner, the bicycle propped against the tool chest, the packing case with spares for the generator ... everything was as it should be.

Then he heard a motor whirring. The service lift! Who could be using it at this hour? The governor, paying a check-up call? He ground out his cigarette between his fingers and slipped the butt into his pocket. Fanning away the smoke, he switched off the television, adjusted his peaked cap and padded heavily out into the service area.

The illuminated numbers above the elevator doors rose slowly: five ... six ... seven. Grabbing a handful of unused garbage bags, he headed for the concrete stairs that wound steeply upwards round the lift shaft. If he wasn't at his post at the front desk, he'd better be out delivering to the flats when the governor found him.

He reached the top floor, perspiring heavily. Strange: he'd met no one on the way up, and the lift still stood at the seventh floor, and it was empty.

Helen pushed aside the plate of cold meat and cheese; she didn't feel hungry. She'd tidy up, take a bath and have an early night. She took out a roll of kitchen cling-film and, covering the food tightly, slipped the plates into the fridge. She moved her boots away from the radiator, where they were drying out, to prevent the heat damaging the leather, and emptied the refuse into a large black garbage bag. She unchained the back door and hauled the bag outside onto the service landing where it would be collected in the morning. Leaving the door open, she went back inside into the sitting room for the carton of empty wine-bottles from the small party she'd given the previous day for some of her old department colleagues. As she returned with the carton, she noticed her vision had begun to fuzz and blank out at the corners again, and as she bent down to pick up the new bags the porter had left, her head buzzed painfully. There was only one solution to a migraine: darkness and rest.

She was reaching down to close the bottom bolt of the door when she noticed a muddy smudge on the white vinyl floor. She started. That wasn't from her own feet: she'd changed into moccasins the moment she'd got home. The mark was wet, too. Had someone come in while her back was turned, while she was boxing up the bottles in the other room? The night porter, perhaps? No, he'd already been past: she'd found the new bags lying outside when she'd open the door.

Christ, someone was in the flat!

She stood absolutely still, listening. Upstairs, a television commentator was shouting excitedly; in the hallway, the clock struck the half-hour; to her side, the tap gave a sudden, short dribble. This was being stupid! Of course there was no one. Maybe something had leaked from the garbage bag . . .

She poured herself a glass of water and took it to the bedroom. The migraine was intensifying. She undressed in the semi-dark, with only the light from the bathroom to see by. Slipping on her dressing-gown, she sat down at the dressing-table and began brushing her hair. Through the open door behind her poured the flowery scent of the foam as the bath steadily filled up.

The whorls and starbursts were encroaching on the centre of her vision now. She laid down the brush and sat for a moment with her eyes closed.

Suddenly she froze.

A floorboard, creaking, *right behind her*!

264

She had hardly opened her eyes when all of a sudden this ... this thing whipped over her face ... a sheet, sticking and clinging ... the cling-film! ... tightening over her mouth and nose, winding round her head, once, and twice, and then again, and again, masking her, cocooning her, sucking at her flesh, stifling her scream, smothering her breath ...

She half rose, but sharp elbows pressed her down, she skewed awkwardly to the side, upsetting the dressing-table, crashing the mirror to the ground, falling backwards, clawing with her fingers at the mask clamped like a leech over her face, clawing, too, at the hands winching the cocoon tighter and tighter and tighter ... and through the blurred, distorting layers of film, the figure of a small man, no, a boy, in a torn raincoat, a boy with thin, tight lips and piercing eyes ... and her head exploding, her chest ablaze, her breath gagged in her throat, her nose and mouth and windpipe all sealed, sealed, choking, suffocating ...

Plick!

Sophie stirred for a brief moment, then sank back into sleep.

Patter-crack!

She sat up with a start. For a few seconds there was silence, then it came again. Something spattering on glass. Gravel. Someone was throwing gravel up at the window.

In that instant, without thinking or guessing or even wondering how she came to know, she *knew*. Her heart leapt. Throwing off the bedclothes, she rushed to the window and tore aside the curtains.

Of course it was him. He'd come back at last. After all this time.

The boy was standing in a flower-bed, jumping up and down and waving. Behind, the lawn stretched away to the tall, naked willow at the end and the wide, circular patch bare of snow beneath it. He beckoned her down. He wore a strange, triumphant grin.

Grabbing her dressing-gown, she fled quickly down the stairs and into the kitchen. She threw on the light and unlocked the French windows. An icy draught sliced through the warmth indoors. The boy hesitated on the doorstep, suddenly uncertain of his welcome. He looked terrible. His raincoat was stained and ripped, his face was white as marble, his cheeks bore deep scratches, a wet gash ran along the back of his hand, but his dark eyes glowed as brightly at ever.

Valentin!

'You crazy fool!' she whispered, both excited and horrified at the same time. 'Do you know what time it is? What will your people say?'

She couldn't leave him in the freezing cold, so she pulled him in and shut the door. She fired an endless stream of questions at him, though all along she had this strange feeling she only had to think actually to know the answers. But she went on talking compulsively. She was so glad he was back, and safe, but she was anxious, too. She wanted him to stay but also to go.

Valentin barely said a word. He stood there, shivering and growing dejected, his look of triumph gradually vanishing. Overcome with pity, she took his hand and, sinking into the large farmhouse chair, drew him down towards her, laid his head in her lap and stroked his tousled dark hair to soothe away his anguish. All the while, he hugged her knees tight and nestled closer, ever closer into her.

Sleeping lightly, Jake heard Sophie go downstairs. He lay listening out for her steps to return. A minute or two passed, longer than she'd need to pour a glass of milk from the fridge and drink it. Worried she might not be well, he got up and went downstairs after her. Half way down, he heard her voice, speaking softly. *Who the hell was she talking to?*

The kitchen door was slightly ajar, throwing a thin shaft of light into the hallway. She sat in the farmhouse chair, her back to the door. She seemed to be talking to someone just in front of her, but he could see no one else in the room.

'It's all right, it's all OK,' she was saying in a comforting tone, rocking her body back and forward.

He squinted through the crack of the hinge. No, the room was quite empty. Had she ... a *cat* on her lap?

'Do you hear, Valentin?' she went on softly.

He started.

'Valentin?

He remembered that name from her secret diary. A boy, not a cat. And then a remark he'd overheard Graham make to Alex around the time of Danny's death came back to him with a jolt. *Children who lose a brother or a sister ... quite often you find them inventing imaginary friends.* Was this Valentin an imaginary friend? Surely not children of Sophie's age. Or ... Wasn't that all over and done with?

He bit his lip. *He* was at the root of it all. It was his fault that the child was disturbed. Everything traced itself back to him. Yet what could he do now, though, except trust to love and understanding, and just hope?

Careful not to make a sound, he tiptoed away and, troubled, retraced his steps slowly back upstairs.

NINETEEN

Jake looked uncomfortably around the room. What was he doing at a students' junior common room drinks party? He was a good twenty years older than anyone there. He sipped his Bulgarian wine and tried to concentrate on what the earnest young philologist was saying at his elbow. Sophie stood a few feet away, drinking orange juice and talking to an auburn-haired art-history student called Maryanne whom she invited back home to tea from time to time. This girl had perhaps come the closest to a friend in all the time Sophie had been at the university. Was it, he sometimes wondered, because she was slight in build and so closer to Sophie's own height?

It was demanding, he knew, to share lectures and tutorials, laboratories and common rooms with others seven or eight years older than herself. In her first team she'd been treated as an oddball, and her brilliance had aroused resentment and envy. Things were still tough for her: she was too young to join actively in college sports or to share many of the others' social interests, while her mind so clearly outshone any of theirs that the only relationships she really found rewarding were with graduates and tutors. Perhaps her greatest problem, though, was simply that she was young. She had read, but she hadn't lived; she knew a great deal about the world, but she hadn't experienced it. Inevitably she sometimes felt immature beside the young men and women around her. Still, she'd been used to standing apart all her life, and she'd always managed to cope. Her genuine nature had carried her through, and here at this party, as he could tell from the easy way people came up and spoke to her, she was fully accepted and well liked, too.

What *was* he doing there? She'd asked him along. The invitation had read, *Sophie Chalmers and guest*. The real question was, why had he accepted? Wasn't it, in truth, to keep an eye on her? But why? Was he worried about her after the previous night's experience, or was he simply a fond, possessive father chaperoning his twelve-year-old daughter to a party?

He looked at his watch: this was eating into her evening work time. He glanced up to find her violet eyes fixed intently upon him. She broke away from her friend and came over.

'Wanting to go?' she asked.

'No, no, not if you'd like to stay. Jeremy here was telling me about various aspects of . . . his subject . . .'

'Jonathan,' corrected the young man stiffly, backing away, 'Don't let me keep you.'

'See you around, Jonathan,' said Sophie, dismissing him with a sweet smile. Turning to her father, she whispered, 'Come on, let's go.'

They slipped away and hurried through the tired, begrimed snow to the car. As they headed back home, Sophie looked across at him.

'Thanks for coming,' she said with feeling. 'I hope you didn't feel too left out.'

He smiled. 'I'm very touched you invited me.'

'Don't be idiotic! Who else should I ever want to go anywhere with?'

'Sophie, I do recognise a girl has to . . . grow up.'

'Dad, please.'

'I just want to say you've always been a very sensible girl and you should feel free to do whatever you want. I'd be the first to welcome any of your friends.' What he really meant was that he'd rather she had a real boyfriend than an imaginary one.

He felt her hand on his.

'Dad, will you stop? You don't need to say any of this.'

He squeezed the hand. 'I know, Sophie, I know.'

He slowed down as they approached their home and pulled into the driveway. He gave a sudden exclamation.

'Hey, what's going on here?'

A police car stood parked outside the house. As they drew up, a uniformed officer stepped out of the car and, putting on his cap, came over.

'Dr Chalmers? PC Marsh, sir. Might I have a word?'

Jake listened, stunned, as the policeman broke the news about Helen. They'd been able to pinpoint the time of death to between nine and nine thirty the night before. She had been discovered by the night porter who had entered her flat after the neighbour below reported water pouring through the ceiling. She'd died of suffocation, following a brief struggle. No witnesses had come forward reporting anyone suspicious seen in the vicinity.

Jake was stunned. This was terrible. He'd only seen her just the other day. Who could have done such a thing? And why? What kind of motive?

His mind raced. Helen's words rang in his ears, that time she'd showed him the X-ray plates with the proof of Sophie's unique genetic make-up: *I've taken the obvious precautions* ... Would her death trigger off instructions given to a solicitor, or some colleague back in Chicago, or perhaps even Herbert Blacker? Would the finger of suspicion point at *him*, for having a motive? Worse, would the whole story now come out and the nightmare be set to spiral on for ever? Or had she been bluffing and, through this accident of fate, her discovery had died with her?

The policeman had turned to Sophie.

'I've been given to understand,' he was saying, 'that you were one of the last people to see Helen Lorenz alive. You were with her yesterday afternoon.'

Jake interrupted with a short laugh.

'There's a mistake here, Officer. Sophie was at her mother's house all afternoon. I took her there, and her mother brought her back.'

'About what time would that be, sir?'

'Oh, seven, seven fifteen.'

Sophie stepped forward into the pool of brightness cast by the light over the kitchen table. She met his eye. Her face was white.

'It's not true,' she said quietly. 'I arranged to meet Dr Lorenz outside Mother's house. She was waiting there when you dropped me off, Dad. She took me to the hospital. She did some tests, and then she brought me back here.'

Jake saw the policeman off shortly afterwards and came back into the kitchen to find Sophie sitting at the table with her head in her hands. He put an arm round her shoulders.

'Why, darling?' he said simply.

She replied in a small voice, without looking up.

'She told me if I didn't, she'd report you to the hospital board and they'd give you the sack.'

'Christ,' he muttered. The heartless bitch, manipulating a child like that! And Sophie had gone through with it, to save him. He knelt down beside her and took her by the hand.

'What kind of tests?' he asked gently.

'A CAT scan and a SPECT.'

What? Roger Mangold gave you a SPECT?'

She gave a small, sniffly laugh. 'Well, the machine broke down half way through. Just when I was thinking how much I really hated that woman.' She looked up abruptly. Her eyes were wide with fear. 'Dad, you don't think I'm – somehow – to blame?'

'*You*, angel?'

'You know, like Lizzie?'

'No. Definitively no.'

'I wished her dead.'

He looked deeply into her anxious, pale face. A familiar sick dread gripped his stomach. Oh Christ, not again.

'Listen to me, treasure,' he said firmly. 'There can be absolutely no causal link between your feelings against Helen and the tragedy last night. It's just a coincidence. Two unconnected events just happening to coincide. Remember our random number algorithm? Coincidences do occur, surprisingly often. We shouldn't let them surprise us. They stand out merely because of the vast number of non-coincidences that pass unnoticed.'

'But still.'

'But still *nothing*. Tell me, why do they always have to be *bad* events – accidents, deaths, things going wrong?' He tried to lighten the mood. 'OK, try and make something *good* happen to someone you really love.'

She smiled faintly and, after a moment's thought, she got up and poured herself a glass of water. Then she went off without a word to her study.

Jake fixed himself a whisky and stared into the glass thoughtfully. This was a hell of a shock. He'd known the woman for years now, off and on, he'd admired her work and, to the extent that the situation permitted, he'd actually liked her. It was unforgivable to blackmail a child, of course, but he couldn't help grieving for her. Who could have done it, and why?

Herbert Blacker paused to scratch his head as he emptied the contents of Helen Lorenz's desk into a large packing-case. It was all very puzzling. Why had she really come back to Bristol? The labs didn't possess any chimps and, as he knew from seeing her one night working on a sample of chimp blood, she'd had to bring over her own material to work on. Was it just a case of expatriate nostalgia? He'd seen it before: out they went, chasing the megabucks, only to find they actually missed the idealism and uncommercialism of the English academic way of life. Yet, maybe that wasn't so true in Helen's case; seldom had he seen such ambition.

Most of the work seemed to bear the same reference: S.M.C. Simian something-or-other, no doubt. He flipped through a file marked, *S.M.C.: Chromo Spread*, and glanced at a photographic plate showing a standard chromosome spread of a chimp. So remarkably human. In fact, humans shared ninety-nine per cent of their DNA with chimpanzees. It made you think.

He riffled through several more files, pausing over another containing X-ray plates of gene fragments that looked strongly like the human intelligence genes she'd been working on with Jake Chalmers years ago. A chilling thought struck him: could she have been splicing *human* genes into chimpanzees? Was that why she'd been so secretive about her work? And did that, in turn, provide any kind of motive for her death?

That was for the police to solve, not for him to speculate over. Hurriedly packing the rest of her possessions away, he taped up the case and hauled it over to the door. He'd have it stored in the basement until such time as her next of kin came and claimed it.

* * *

Sophie looked up from the microscope and rubbed her eyes. For once, she couldn't concentrate. Too many questions were clamouring for attention in her mind. Leaving a note on her lab bench in case her tutor came by, she put on her quilted raincoat and hurried down the stairs and out into the pale afternoon sun.

She'd had lunch, as usual, with her father. First thing that morning, he'd gone round to Dr Mangold. To his relief, he'd told her, the radiologist had simply assumed this was part of Helen's study of high-IQ children and he had no inkling of *the other business* – 'our secret', as Dad called it. 'We're safe,' he'd said with a wink. *He* might be safe, secure in the knowledge that he'd never be found out now, but what about *her*? She could never be safe: she carried the secret around with her, inside her, expressed in every cell in her body . . .

She bit her lip. This wasn't constructive. No point in going over ground that had already been resolved.

And yet. The more she thought about it, the more the web stretched to entangle her. There was Mother, for instance. What would she say if she found out that her child wasn't the child she thought she was, but a cheat, a fake, a *freak*?

She stumbled on, hiding her face from passers-by in case they saw the tears. She found a bench tucked away in a small square overlooking the city below. Her hands clenched in her pockets, she struggled to force her mind to master her mood. *Look at it logically*, she repeated silently over and over. *Think it through, reason it out*.

She'd never got over having to choose between Dad and Mother. But she'd *had* to choose: they'd forced her to. It was all because of her in the first place. If she'd been a normal child, there'd have been none of the fights over her unbringing, none of the terrible rows

274

that had ended in divorce. Instead of a broken home, they'd all now be together, as one family. Of course, Mother appeared to be happy with Arthur, but that was only a brave front. And, in his own funny way, Dad missed her, too. If she, their child, had driven them apart, couldn't she somehow bring them back together again? Perhaps there was a way. Suppose she went through with her degree for Dad's sake and then gave up studying altogether and became like an ordinary child, the child Mother always wanted her to be. Wouldn't she come home then?

Far below, through the low mist, a shaft of sunlight glinted off a glass tower block. Above, dripping roofs gave proof of the thaw in the snow's long grip, and in the naked branches of the chestnut trees stretching down the hill, rooks fought and pigeons preened. Cars drove this way and that, people walked purposefully up and down streets and in and out of buildings. Everything had its place, everything knew what it was. Except her. She was alone with herself, alone with a self that wasn't *her*.

A bad self, too. Whatever Dad had said to reassure her, she *knew* things happened around her. Helen's murder was more than coincidence. She recalled her own curse the very morning of her death. *I hate her! I'd like to make her choke. I'd like to make her suffocate* ... And how had Helen died? By suffocation.

And Valentin. Was it coincidence that he seemed to show up whenever things happened? She shivered. Such a funny feeling he gave her. She *knew* things about him, without needing to ask. She did feel sorry for him, though; he had a bad home life. His parents had separated and he wasn't allowed out much. To see her, he mostly had to climb out at night and sneak over the back garden fences. He said she was his only friend.

275

She stood up. She'd take the long way back to the labs, and on the way she'd resolve all her fears logically and decide on her course of action, just as Dad had always taught her.

As he was shutting the door of the shed, Jake heard a muffled chord striking deep inside the house. Carrying the basket of logs round to the back, he paused for a moment outside the living-room window. Against the fast-falling twilight, the room shone out in a rich, warm orange. This was Alex's visiting afternoon, and Sophie and her mother were at the piano, playing a duet together. He recognised it as the Brahms they'd often played in the days when they'd all been a family.

He set the basket down on the gravel for a moment and listened. Sophie sat upright at the top end, looking like a grown-up young woman from that angle with her fair hair now curling at her shoulders and her head tossed confidently back as she laughed aloud, her hands leaping and flying over the staccato arpeggios. Alex, beside her, seemed almost struggling to keep up.

He smiled. Obviously no problem there. What an astonishing girl she was, to know what she now knew and to keep it to herself without letting it upset her relationship with her mother. Her reaction to the news had astounded him from the first. After that initial outburst, she'd become totally calm and reasonable. It thrilled him to witness how an exceptional mind like hers was capable of overriding its lower, unreasoning impulses. He recalled his visit to the Radiology Unit and witnessed with his own eyes the physical evidence of that mind at work. Mangold had played back part of the SPECT tape for him, and he had been stunned by the astonishing activity recorded in the forebrain. Pity that electrostatic interference had put a stop to the test before the radiologist had managed to get a full picture of the hindbrain. Still, who really needed proof of what was so abundantly clear?

As he was bending down to take up the basket again, his eye fell on the rose-bed behind him. Someone had been stamping around! Footprints dug deep into the mud, churning up the melting snow and the straw he'd laid down to protect the plants. Clumps of earth left a trail to the French windows into the kitchen.

He swallowed thickly. This couldn't be Sophie. A prowler? He thought back to the other evening, hearing her talking to that imaginary friend. Had there really been someone there, after all? How could he have missed seeing the person? If so, who the hell was it? Welcoming young men into the house was all very well, but a stranger so late at night was intolerable. He'd speak to her about it when he returned from his case conference that evening.

The duet ended with a virtuoso showpiece played *fortissimo*, and Sophie fell laughing into her mother's arms. Then she sprang to her feet and, declaring it was time for tea, went to the kitchen. Her mother followed and began stocking up the cupboards with the spare provisions she'd brought.

'You're low on biscuits,' she observed. 'Remind me on Sunday to give you some to take back.'

'Thanks,' said Sophie, pouring out three cups of tea. 'Will you take Dad his?'

'Why don't you, sweetheart?'

Sophie took the cup over to the door. 'He should come and join us,' she said, though she knew he never would.

'He's got a case conference to prepare, you said.'

'He could always write it in here. He usually does.'

'I expect we'd disturb him.'

She took the tea into his study and set it down on

277

the desk. Dad gave her a long, searching look, then drew her to him and kissed her. She hesitated at the door for a moment, then thought better of broaching the subject and returned to the kitchen to find her mother cracking eggs into a bowl in preparation for making scones. She watched for a moment in silence, thinking.

'Can I ask you a question?' she asked eventually. 'Do you love Arthur?'

Her mother looked up and gave her a grave smile.

'There's love and love, Sophie. You'll learn that.' She must have seen that this didn't satisfy her daughter. 'Well, yes, I suppose I do.'

'More than you loved Dad?'

Alex stopped what she was doing.

'Your father was ... is ... quite wonderful,' she said. 'But time changes people. Or perhaps it brings out the people they really are.'

'Their real selves?'

Alex nodded, then smiled gently.

'I know you understand intellectually, Sophie, but until you've experienced love of that kind, you can never really know why it happens. And why it sometimes ends.'

'Why did it end?'

Her mother glanced at her, as if judging how much of the truth to impart. She returned to the bowl, stirring the eggs into the flour with a wooden spoon. As she spoke, her voice was sadder than Sophie had ever heard it.

'Your father's a remarkable man. He ... well, it goes back a long way. To his childhood. As a young boy, he worshipped his father. His mother died, as you know, when he was just leaving school. That was the start of your grandfather's problems. The business ... his drinking habits ... everything went downhill.

278

Your father's been wonderful, but he's never quite got over the . . . disappointment. He can't forgive failure. Everything has got to strive for excellence. For him, that's success.'

She paused, apparently pursuing some other line of thought.

'Anyway,' she went on after a moment, 'when you came along, Sophie, with the superb mind that you possess, it was an answer to his prayers. He set about making you quite simply the *best*. That's where he and I began parting company. I'm all for excellence, of course, and for giving a child every encouragement to develop its potential, but I felt you were being force-fed, driven to achieve everything absurdly early at the expense of your – yourself as a *child*. "You're robbing her of her childhood," I'd say to him. We had terrible disagreements. It became a conflict of wills and, rightly or wrongly, his way prevailed. I was for balance, for the golden mean. What did the Romans call it – *aurea mediocritas*? For your father, that meant, literally, mediocrity.'

She managed a smile, but she was clearly very moved. 'Still, you are the proof of the pudding, Sophie. And you couldn't have turned out a lovelier girl, and I couldn't be a prouder mother.'

Sophie reached out and touched her mother's hand.

'If I'd been normal—'

'Sophie, you *are* normal.'

'No, but if I'd been treated from the very, *very* beginning like an ordinary, average child, then would we be still together, all of us, in one family?

Her mother reached out and stroked her cheek tenderly.

'Don't vex yourself, darling. It's impossible to say. That's a hypothetical question.

'But just suppose.'

Alex hesitated, then gave a brave smile.

'I think it's time the oven went on, don't you?'

Alone in the house, Sophie sat cross-legged on Danny's old bed, watching one of Dad's videotapes. She'd been browsing through his collection and come across an old *Horizon* programme. Drawn at once to the title, she'd taken it upstairs to watch. The programme reported on the new forms of life being bio-engineered in top-security laboratories across the world; they ranged from monstrous freaks, such as a hideous, shaggy sheep-goat chimaera, to useful new bacteria designed selectively to combat crop pests. There followed a studio discussion among a panel of scientists and environmentalists. Sophie watched, repelled and yet fascinated, as the issue inevitably turned to the ethics of genetic manipulation. More than once she reached out to switch it off, but she hesitated under a compulsion to know more. More about herself.

The dangers, the environmental spokesman was saying, were both of practice and principle. Practically, no one could foresee the effect of releasing new life forms into the environment. What would happen to the delicate ecological balance, developed over millions of years? What if these super-bugs got out of control? Or if they mutated into yet different forms of life? No triumph was won without a price.

And then there was a matter of principle, the man went on to say. Where did you draw the line?

'The line I draw,' he suggested, 'is between genetic *therapy* – such as curing muscular dystrophy or haemophilia – and genetic *enhancement*, where genes are deliberately altered.'

The scientist intervened abruptly.

'Man has been deliberately altering the genes of plants and animals by selective breeding for millions of years,' he said firmly. 'Walk round a supermarket. Virtually everything you see on the shelves is bred for the purpose. No one says, "Let's go back to eating wild hens, or bread made from prehistoric strains of wheat." '

The environmentalist was growing impatient.

'But I'm talking of tampering directly with nature—'

'Go to Crufts dog show,' riposted the scientist, 'and ask yourself how "natural" the dogs on display there are.'

'— I mean, tampering with the actual building-blocks of life. Maybe enhancement is legitimate if it takes us to a position we could get to anyway by normal selective-breeding methods. That is, if it merely jumps steps we could otherwise take if we cared to. Then super-productive cows or low-fat pigs might be acceptable. But not entirely new species, new organisms. That is man playing God.'

The scientist gave a slow smile.

'Man *is* God,' he said quietly.

Sophie reached forward and switched it off.

She glanced at herself in the mirror. She thought she even *looked* different. Yes, no triumph was won without a price. And today she'd learned that yet another price had been paid for the triumph of her: the family. Burying her face in her hands, she let out a long, quavering sigh. It was all coming to a head. The dam was about to burst.

She skipped down the stairs. Quite suddenly, for no apparent cause, she'd felt the weight lifting off her mind. She was back on course. You only had to apply your mind, to reason it out, and the fears and feelings disappeared. How else could she have expected to react, watching a programme like that?

The light from the porch outside shone through

281

the panes in the front door. Otherwise, the hall was unlit. Reaching for the main hall-light switch at the bottom of the stairs, she sensed a movement in the shadows behind. As she snapped the light on, she glanced in the mirror on the wall straight ahead. In it, she could see that the corridor leading to the utility room was empty. The creak of a floorboard made her spin round.

There, in the corridor, in front of the utility-room door, stood Valentin. He wore his shabby raincoat, a scarf and mittens, and a grin was spread over his face. She shot a glance back at the mirror. There was still no one there, but by the time she looked back to check, he had moved.

'Christmas!' she exclaimed, shaken. 'You gave me a shock! How did you get in?' Valentin wiggled his mittened fingers like a conjuror. 'You picked a window lock!' she guessed. 'You are *awful*!' She couldn't help smiling; the look of mischief in his bright, dark eyes was infectious. 'And hungry, too, I bet. All right, come into the kitchen. We'll see what we can find you.'

'Sophie?' called her father's cheery voice from the hall as the front door shut. 'I'm home.'

Beside her, Valentin shot to his feet.

She looked up from her study desk and motioned him to stay.

'It's only Dad,' she said. 'He won't bite.'

A sudden flash of cold ferocity on the boy's face took her aback. He stepped back into the corner of the small, book-lined room, out of the direct light from the table-lamp.

A moment later, her father came in. He looked exhausted. He gave her a kiss and glanced briefly at what she was writing.

'How did the meeting go?' she asked.

He let out a sigh and rubbed his eyes.

'I sometimes think it's the parents we should be treating.'

'Dad,' she began, 'I'd like you to—'

'Hang on a moment, darling. I've got to get a drink or I'll die.'

He left the room. Valentin stepped forward, his dark eyes narrow and his lips hard and thin. Sophie stood up and reached out a hand.

'Stay. I'd like him to meet you properly.'

The boy pulled away and eyed the door warily.

'Well,' she said, 'I'll see you out, then.'

But Valentin was already at the door. Checking the way was clear, he slipped out. She followed him into the living room just in time to see him vanish through the door into the hall. A moment later, she heard the front-door latch click softly. She crossed the room and went into the kitchen.

Her father stood at the tap, topping up his whisky with water. He took a long swig.

'That's better,' he breathed with relief. 'Rehumanised.'

A puzzled look suddenly crossed his face. She followed his gaze to the pair of mittens lying on the table.

'They're Valentin's,' she said. 'He must have left them just now.'

'Valentin?' he returned quickly.

'I wanted to introduce him to you, but he shot off.' She saw the look on his face and smiled. 'You don't need to say it. I know he's scruffy, he slouches, he bites his nails, but you needn't cut him dead like that.'

'I didn't do anything.'

'You didn't even say hello. Be nice to him next time, Dad, please. He's had a miserable life. His parents split up when he was young, and—' She stopped. 'Don't look at me like that. I'm not one of your patients.'

He held her under an intense stare.

'Sophie, are you telling me I'm supposed to have met this Valentin of yours?'

'Just now,' she said, surprised. 'Well, you didn't exactly *meet* him, but you saw him, didn't you? Well, didn't you?'

The silence lengthened before his expression eased and he gave a falsely reassuring smile.

'Of course.' He rubbed his eyes. 'What am I thinking of? I'm sorry if I was rude.'

She was watching his eyes carefully.

'That's OK,' she said quietly, then looked at her watch. 'Well, I'd better get back to work.'

The boy turned away from the window with a scowl and slunk off down the side of the lawn, in the lee of the bushes. At the foot of the garden he turned and looked back. The man was on his own now, standing in the middle of the room, staring into nowhere, just drinking.

He fingered his penknife. No. Not yet.

But he had to do something. It was bursting to come out.

TWENTY

The day broke startlingly bright for February, spreading across the city a premature hint of spring. On their run through the park that morning, with their breath still steaming on the crisp, dawn air, Jake had noticed the first crocuses nudging through the frosty ground, heard the first blackbirds declaiming from the bare branches of the chestnut trees and smelled the first imperceptible rise of the sap. A sense of elation swelled within him. The worst was over, and fresh hope echoed from every stone and blade of grass.

Though it was Saturday, he was working a full day on the ward to help make up for the time he'd lose at the paediatrics conference taking place in Cambridge over the following weekend. Sophie was working on an experiment in the labs, and they met for lunch just as they did every weekday. With the first real sun of the year warming away the stranglehold of winter, father and daughter strolled through the alleys and courtyards that criss-crossed the older part of the university campus.

They found a bench and sat down to eat their sandwiches. Sophie pulled out a book and skimmed it while at the same time carrying on her conversation with him, an unselfconscious trick that still astonished him. She sat with one leg tucked underneath her; he had many photos of her in that typical pose, taken over the years – mostly over the past three of the four wonderful years in which they'd lived alone together. She said she'd heard there was a film being shot down by the main campus gates and suggested they took a look on their way back.

After a while, they got up and sauntered through the grounds to the main entrance. There, with the sombre granite Royal Fort as a backdrop, they found a film crew busy setting up for a shoot. Drawn up in a loose circle stood several Transit vans, a catering bus and large luxury caravan. A small crowd had gathered to watch as a team of men in fur-trimmed anoraks laid tracks for the camera and ran cables from a mobile power plant. Most of the group stood around apparently idle, while a few went about their work speedily and efficiently with, it seemed, hardly an order given or a word exchanged.

Standing to one side, Sophie watched for a moment.

'Do you suppose they communicate like ants?' she asked.

'How do you mean?'

'Like those extraordinary ants that use a pheromone to terrorise other ants into submission and then drag them off to become workers.'

'A biological theory of power?' he smiled. 'Interesting.'

'It's not so far-fetched. Didn't people around Hitler say they could *smell* his power?'

'Ionisation, at a guess. Charismatic men like that are known to possess strong electromagnetic fields. As if they're in a constant state of high emotion.'

Her brow puckered in thought.

'I wonder if Hitler made things ... happen around him.'

'Go bump in the night? Like London when he blitzed it?' She didn't echo his smile. 'Well, you know cranks associate PK with high emotional states. Frustrated rage, mostly.'

'Jung wasn't a crank. He made his pipe explode.

286

His wife had forbidden him to smoke, and he was extremely angry.'

He gave a short laugh.

'Jung didn't get it right all the time, remember.'

The subject was dropped without resolution. Jake looked about him. The crowd was swelling. Studious undergraduates laden with books and sportsmen in rugby tracksuits stopped to watch, adding to the group of secretaries and workmen and other passers-by that had already collected. A lighting engineer tested the reflectors, a sound recordist checked the microphone boom and a focus puller marked positions with a tape-measure. Beyond the track, two men in overalls were giving a final dusting to a 1950s Oldsmobile roadster. Jake guessed from the accents that this was an American film; a technician informed him that it was a love epic, set in an Ivy League college.

Sophie was waving at someone on the other side of the crowd. People moved back and forth in a constant flow, but he couldn't see anyone he recognised. 'Who's that?' he asked.

'My friend I told you about,' she replied. 'Valentin.'

His senses sharpened.

'Where? Show me.'

She pointed to a group of people beside one of the vans. 'Over there. Behind that woman in a red coat.'

'I don't see any boy.'

'Dad, you need glasses. *There*.'

Jake took a deep breath. Should he pretend? Sophie was tugging his sleeve and pointing.

'He's moved round behind that man in overalls. Now you can see him. The boy with dark hair and that old mac. He's waving back.'

Ah, yes. There was a figure there. Twenty or thirty yards away. A dark-haired boy in an old raincoat. He must have been obscured by the others.

Jake blinked. 'I see him now.'

'He's patting that dog.'

Yes, indeed: a boy, bent down, patting the black retriever.

'I must be dreaming,' he laughed.

'Beckon him over, Dad. I want you to meet him.'

He beckoned. The boy stood up and slowly shambled over. She'd been right: he did look scruffy and unkempt and he slouched appallingly. He must have been twelve or thirteen – her age – with dark, curly hair and strange, penetrating eyes.

She was whispering at his side.

'Try and be nice this time, OK?'

'Yes, Sophie.' He held out his hand as the boy arrived. 'Hello, I'm Jake, Sophie's father. And you, I gather, are Valentin.'

The touch of the boy's hand was like nothing he'd ever felt. A small jolt passed through him at the contact. It was as if he were a lightning conductor earthing a charge.

For Sophie's sake he tried to make pleasant conversation, but Valentin seemed riveted on the film. Jake eyed him critically. Didn't he have anyone to sew up his mackintosh or mend his shoes? How had he come by those terrible gashes on his hands?

'Where do you go to school, Valentin?' he asked the boy.

The boy seemed startled by the question. As if lost for an answer, he turned to Sophie. She thought for a moment, then blurted out an answer.

'Clifton Middle. Don't you, Valentin?'

'And what's your second name?'

Again, Sophie replied, growing noticeably flustered.

'Levinsky,' she responded.

'And you live round here, Valentin?'

The girl sighed crossly. 'Mulberry Crescent, number thirty-two,' she said. 'Dad, this isn't an inquisition.'

'I just like to know who our visitors are. Especially the nocturnal ones.'

She shot him a puzzled glare, then turned to Valentin and began chatting to him. The boy hadn't spoken a word yet. What was wrong with him? Was he mute?

Jake leaned forward and addressed him directly.

'Fascinating how they make movies, eh?'

'Boring,' interjected Sophie. 'Look at them all, just hanging around for the actors to come out.'

The boy's face gradually lit up. He grinned, showing a set of pointed teeth, and his strange, dark eyes gleamed. His voice was low.

'All those people,' he said slowly. 'Hundreds of them, thousands of them, all seeing you, all knowing who you are.'

A moment's tense silence fell between them. Restless with the inactivity, the crowd was beginning to thin out, but Valentin still stood with his eyes glued to the set-up, taking in every detail. Jake looked at his watch; he had time to spare before he had to get back, but he wanted to have a word with Sophie about the paper he was delivering to the conference in Cambridge and he really didn't feel he could discuss it while this boy was hanging around. He glanced again at the wild, tousled lad. What the hell did she see in him? He had nothing whatever to offer her. He didn't even begin to make an intellectual match for her – in fact, he looked a poor specimen even for his own age. And shifty, too. No doubt she felt sorry for him, but from her point of view he was, frankly, a lame duck. With the pressure of Finals mounting, could she afford to take him on? Would she allow herself to get sidetracked into an unsuitable friendship and waste precious time she needed for her work?

He was about to suggest they left when Sophie spotted a friend in the crowd. It was Maryanne, slight and auburn-haired. She was taking photos of the film crew and their set-up. She pointed her camera playfully at them.

'Take one of us,' called Sophie. 'Go on.'

Throwing one arm round Valentin's shoulder and the other round Jake's waist, she drew them together in a group.

'OK, smile!' said Maryanne. She took a picture, then, throwing them a friendly smile, turned away to continue her photographing.

'She's brilliant,' confided Sophie. 'She's always selling her pictures to the papers.'

Not this one, Jake thought tartly. We don't want to see a snap with the headline, 'Prodigy Sophie's Secret Pal' or some such rubbish. He looked at his watch again.

'I think we'd better be going,' he said crisply. 'Ready?'

Sophie turned to the boy. He stood a few feet away, absorbed again in the action on the set.

'We're off, Valentin. See you.'

As they turned to go, Jake stopped.

'Has your mother met him?' he asked suddenly.

'I was going to ask if I could bring him along tomorrow,' she replied, then added more quietly, 'I know what you're thinking, Dad, but it's OK.'

The boy looked from one to the other. His eyes seemed to harden. Then, quite abruptly and without a word of farewell, he turned and darted away. He dodged past an old man with a stick, jinked between two parked cars, dashed across the road and, without a backward glance, vanished out of sight down a small side-alley.

Sophie was smiling. She tapped her forehead.

'He's nuts,' she said affectionately.

Jake had finished clearing away the Sunday lunch and sat at his study desk, working on his paper for the conference.

No doubt there'd be critics who said a medical doctor shouldn't meddle in clinical psychology, but that was the trouble with medicine today: too much compartmentalisation. Who else could see the issue from his vantage point? The paper was titled, 'The Psychosomatics Of Gene Expression – Some Clinical Observations'. In it, he was putting forward a case for the influence of psychological factors on the time and manner in which illnesses with a genetic component manifested themselves. Suppose you had an inborn tendency towards heart disease, could you prevent the onset through adopting a particular attitude of mind? He was treating a boy now with multiple sclerosis who appeared to have acquired the illness only after being told it ran in his family. Did one treat his complaint or his belief? The ground here was tricky; the evidence was always blurred and the explanations never rigorous enough for a scientist. And yet the basis was sound: the body *was* the mind, and the mind the body.

Sophie sat in a leather chair by the window, one leg tucked under her, reading two books simultaneously. From time to time she glanced at the clock on the mantelpiece, looked out of the window and sighed. It was well past three. She caught his eye over the top of her reading glasses.

'You should mention that man with terminal cancer who literally *laughed* himself better,' she suggested. 'It would give you a chance to get in a few jokes. You're always saying how deadly boring conferences are.'

He cleared his throat.

'While I'm away,' he began. 'I'd feel happier if maybe—'

'Don't worry. Suzanne's great. Anyway, I couldn't go to Mother's because of the computer.'

'We could always set it up there.'

'Dad, it's only for two nights. Besides, Suzanne's got Jeremy to look after, too, and she's fixed up to bring him.' She cast a glance out of the window and snapped her books shut. 'Ah, here he is. About time, too.'

Jake rose from the desk. Through the window he could see Valentin skulking in the shrubbery that stood between the house and the street. Funny little tyke, he thought. You could never feel quite sure what he was thinking.

He reached for his car keys.

'Ready, darling?'

On the short drive to Alex's, Jake glanced over his shoulder. Valentin was sitting in the back seat.

'You told your parents where you are going?' he called over his shoulder. There was no reply. 'Valentin?'

He glanced in the rear-view mirror. No Valentin. He did a double-take. In the mirror, the back seat appeared quite empty. He turned and looked over his shoulder again. There was the boy, still sitting with his face pressed to the window. Jake checked back in the mirror. Yes, of course, there he was, just not very . . . *emphatic*. He rubbed his temple. He'd had this head- ache behind his eyes off and on since lunch-time the day before. He'd been up too late, working.

Sophie was looking at him steadily, unblinking.

'You all right?' she asked.

'Fine, fine. Just my eyes tired.'

'I said you needed glasses.'

'It'll be OK when I've finished this wretched paper.'

As he drew up outside Alex and Arthur's undistin-
guished modern house, a sudden wave of disgust swept
through him. A rusty bicycle, robbed of its wheels,
lay discarded on the front lawn and the pebble-dash
rendering on the walls was chipped and peeling. It
looked no different from any other house in its row,
and no doubt the people who inhabited it were good
and kind-hearted and no more nor less harassed or
quarrelsome than any other family of their kind, and
yet it made his heart sink. The uniformity proclaimed
in every line, the ugliness of the metal-frame windows,
the primness of the net curtains, the banal symmetry of
the façade ... He shuddered with an almost physical
loathing. Here was Alex's principle of trading down
to the lowest common denominator demonstrated in
practice. It wasn't to do with money or the lack of
it. The finest could thrive in the poorest circumstances; equally, the most sumptuous surroundings
could stultify the will to excellence. It was a matter
of where you set your eye, whether on the ground
at your feet or on the horizon at the limits of your
vision. How could anything exceptional arise from
such deliberate ordinariness? Yes, without question,
Sophie must remain at home while he was away and
Suzanne must come and stay. One afternoon a week
was already enough contact with such mediocrity.

Hey, he thought, cool down! What's brought this on?

Valentin was climbing out of the car. Was it to do
with the boy? Did he resent Sophie giving her time
and care to somebody who was clearly unworthy of
her, to somebody who might be lovable and pitiable
in his own way but who none the less could only ever
diminish her?

He caught Valentin's eye, and started violently. He'd
never witnessed such pitiless cold malevolence in a face

293

before. This whole affair would definitely have to stop. He really would speak to Sophie this time.

She had run ahead up the front path and was ringing the doorbell. Jake followed. The boy hung back by the front gate. A curtain parted and Arthur's eldest daughter appeared briefly at the window. A few moments later, the door opened and Alex appeared on the step.

Sophie reached up and gave her mother a kiss.

'Hi, Mother. I brought Valentin, as you said.'

Alex looked around. She caught Jake's eye and gave a short nod in greeting. The boy stood just inside the gate, against the tall privet hedge. Alex looked past him – no, right *through* him.

'What have you done with him?' she was asking.

Sophie laughed and, running back down the garden, dragged the boy forward by the hand.

'Come on, Valentin,' she scolded playfully. 'Stop playing the Invisible Man.'

Alex faltered. She blinked once, then again, she peered forward, screwing up her eyes, then quite suddenly her face broke into a broad smile of recognition.

'Sorry! I've been in a different world all day.' She steered the two children indoors, then turned back to Jake. A look of concern flitted across her worn features. 'Are you OK, Jake? You do look pale.'

'Alex—' he began, then halted. With a brief, self-deprecating smile, he said, 'Overworked – you know how it is.'

She laid a hand on his arm.

'Don't overdo it, love,' she said almost tenderly. She glanced indoors after the two children. 'I'll drop them back later.'

Late that evening, Sophie came into his study to say

good night, looking weary and drained. He wrapped his arms round the slim, lithe young girl and kissed her fair head. How could he not worry for her? Was it being *over*protective to want her to be selective in how she bestowed herself? Was this boy, who'd suddenly and for no obvious reason become such a part of her life, *worthy* of her?

They stood in the centre of the room, with her arms round his waist and his around her shoulders, rocking gently back and forward. For a moment she stood very still.

'What are you thinking, angel?' he asked gently.

'I was wondering if he is ever as happy as we are.'

'That boy?' he asked, feeling the sting.

She smiled. 'He stole the show this afternoon. He did a brilliant impersonation of Rachel and her funny voice. Even Mandy had to smile, the sourpuss.'

He sought a charitable response.

'We all work out compensations.'

'Compensations?'

'Well, the boy does seem to get . . . overlooked.'

'He's shy. Until you get to know him.'

'We *don't* know the boy! He just turns up. Have you met his parents? Maybe we should have them in for a drink.'

She pulled away, laughing.

'Don't be so stuffy! And stop calling him "the boy".'

He shook his head. 'I don't know. There's something . . . odd about him.'

'The trouble with you, Dad, is the only children you see are sick ones, in your ward. We don't *all* have problems.'

'Even so.'

Sophie looked up into his eyes.

'I like him,' she said fervently. 'He's funny, I know. But he seems to fit. To belong.'

'He'll only get in the way of your work,' he responded roughly.

'No, he won't. He often comes when I'm working. He sits perfectly quietly, taking care of himself. I feel . . . well, I feel better when he's around. As if he's part of me.' She hesitated. 'This sounds stupid, but when he comes by it's like getting back something I've lost.'

Jake took her hand. Yes, the loss of her brother must still be hurting deeply.

'I understand,' he said gently.

But was that all she felt for this boy? Was she, maybe, mixing up her feelings for him with something else? He knew what she was really describing. She might be twelve going on twenty, she might have a mind that eclipsed those of her most brilliant tutors, she might be the most exquisite creature of his imagination, the most astonishing product of his creation, but she was still a girl, a girl approaching puberty, a human child prey to all the swells and urges that washed the shores of blunt humanity. The more he thought about it, the more he saw that the fact was plain, undeniable. He had foreseen it happening, he'd faced up to it in end-less imaginary scenarios, he'd fabricated safety-nets of logic for himself and layer upon layer of comforting rationalisations . . . Now it was here at last, and it hurt like hell.

He clasped her tighter to him. Her bony chest felt like a dagger.

Sophie, his Sophie, had a crush on this wretched boy.

TWENTY-ONE

'Here you see the optic nerve of a frog,' the lecturer was saying, pointing the marker at the screen. 'The severed end is growing back along the pathway to the tectum. There you can see the axons spreading out and making synaptic contact, guided by the chemical co-ordinates of the concentration gradient.'

At the back, Sophie glanced up briefly, then returned to her book, tilting it so as to read it in the light reflected from the screen. It was perfectly obvious how retinal cells aligned themselves: years ago Gaze and Feldman had demonstrated the chemical gradient at work. She shifted uncomfortably in her seat, aware of a dull throb growing in her head. The lecture hall was a basement room, windowless and stuffy, and the heating, as always, took no account of the warmth of the day, inside or out.

The lecturer had called for lights when she heard a loud *psst*! right behind her. She turned. The main door at the back was open an inch. Through the crack, she could make out a familiar face.

What on earth was *he* doing here?

'Go away!' she hissed, waving him back. 'Buzz off!'

The tall, well-developed girl in the next seat on the bench cast her a strange, mistrustful look. By now, Valentin had opened the door another inch. He stood just beyond the threshold, grinning broadly.

'Wait outside, then,' snapped Sophie in a hoarse whisper. She caught the girl's eye and shrugged apologetically. 'Sorry.'

The girl followed her eye. For a moment, her

face registered blank puzzlement, then suddenly she seemed to recognise something.

'That's the kid I saw hanging around earlier,' she muttered back. 'I wondered who he was with.'

The boy had to be got rid of at once. Sophie rose quietly and went to the door, but he'd already taken a step inside the room. She gripped him by the collar.

'What are you *doing*, you fool?' she whispered harshly. 'Why aren't you at school? You can't come in here.'

'Why not?' responded Valentin, not lowering his voice. 'You do.'

'Don't be stupid! You know it's different.'

She tried to push him out, but he wouldn't budge. She looked back down the hall. Heads were turning: three, four, six, ten ... Soon everyone was watching. She felt herself blushing to the roots of her hair.

At the far end, the lecturer had stopped. He cleared his throat.

'Come in, come in,' he called waggishly. 'Take a seat. Everyone welcome. Children half-price.'

A ripple of laughter spread through the hall. Valentin gave a small, unselfconscious wave. More laughter.

The lecturer held out his pointer. 'Perhaps you'd like to come and give the lecture, too?' he offered ironically.

Valentin actually took a few steps forward before Sophie managed to grab him and force him down onto the bench beside her. She sat bolt upright, clenching her teeth and fighting back the tears, as the class gradually went back to work. Valentin seemed quite at ease. For a while he tried chatting to the tall girl next to him and every now and then he gave a small salute of greeting to the students turning round. He was enjoying himself, but Sophie was dying of embarrassment.

298

The mean wretch. She'd kill him when they were alone.

'Leave it to me,' fumed Jake when Sophie told him at lunch-time. 'I'll speak to his parents.'

'Don't, Dad,' she pleaded. 'You'll get him into trouble.'

'Then maybe he'll learn not to come troubling *you*.'

'Things wouldn't be the same without him.'

'They'd be a darn sight better. He's interferring with your work, Sophie, and I won't have it.'

He dropped her back at the labs, then returned home. He'd taken the afternoon off to finish his paper; he was due to deliver it that coming weekend, on the Sunday morning. For an hour he ploughed through his case-study notes, but his mind wasn't on it. He looked out of the window to the shrubbery, side-lit by a watery sun. The bloody little brat! he thought. It was time he put a stop to the whole thing. He reached for the telephone book. What had she said? Levinsky, wasn't it? Thirty-two Mulberry Crescent?

There was no Levinsky listed at a Mulberry Crescent address.

He went back to his notes and wrote a paragraph. He rewrote it once, and then again. Pushing the work aside, he rose to his feet. Damn and blast it! There was only one thing to do. Grabbing his car keys and sheepskin, he headed out of the house.

A short drive took him to Mulberry Crescent, a horse-shoe street of well-to-do brick houses built at the turn of the century. He drove slowly round the loop back to the main street. The numbers stopped at thirty. He got out and checked on foot. No, there was no number thirty-two. He spotted a newsagent's round the corner and enquired inside. They delivered to every house in Mulberry Crescent, but not to any

Levinsky. He knew most of the boys in the neighbourhood but he'd never heard the name Valentin.

The puzzle began to intrigue Jake. Maybe he'd
mistaken the street name. He asked the newsagent
for a street directory and checked the index. Nothing
look similar.

There was always the boy himself. Clifton Middle
School stood down the street from the church. As
he drove past, he felt a momentary pang of guilt.
He hadn't been to a service since Danny's funeral:
with Sophie's problems clearly containable, he hadn't
felt the need. He parked in the street outside the
school and went in. A handsome, elderly woman in
the administration office asked if she could help him.
He gave her a disarming smile.

'I'm trying to trace the parents of one of your
boys,' he said. 'His name's Valentin Levinsky.'

The woman looked unsure, but consulted a list.

'We have a Matthew Levin,' she offered. 'Seven
Russell Avenue.'

'Maybe I got the name wrong and that's his brother.'

'Matthew's an only child.'

'No Valentin anything?'

The woman skimmed the list again and shook her
head.

'I'd have known the name anyway.' She smiled. '*Blood
and Sand?* Before your time. Rudolf Valentino. Magic.'

Jake returned to the car and sat drumming his
fingers on the steering-wheel. Where could he look
next? He'd exhausted all his leads and found them
utterly false. Who the hell *was* this boy who'd wormed
his way into their lives uninvited, masquerading as
Valentin Levinsky of an address that didn't even exist?

He checked with Sophie on the way back from the
swimming-pool that evening. No, he hadn't mistaken

the details. Nor could she have, either, with a memory like hers. The conclusion was obvious: the boy had told her a pack of lies.

'Impossible,' she said, growing distraught. 'I *know*.'

'You only know what he's told you,' he insisted. 'Have you been to his home? Have you met his parents or his friends? When have you seen his name written anywhere? Well?'

'I don't know,' she mumbled.

He reached for her hand and squeezed it. No point distressing her.

'I don't want you to have anything more to do with that boy. He's not worth thinking about. If he comes round again, send him straight to me. I'll see he doesn't come again.' He brightened. 'Right, enough of that. Tell me how you got on with those interneuron binding sites.'

She allowed herself to be coaxed into discussing the afternoon's work in the laboratory, but he could tell that her thoughts were still on the boy, and that she was troubled. When they reached home, he left her at her computer in the living room, with a cup of tea and a plate of biscuits to keep her going until supper, and went outside to fetch wood. He'd make a good big fire and they'd settle down after supper and read a play together – maybe *Women Beware Women*, as they were working their way through Middleton at the moment.

Putting on his sheepskin coat and wellingtons and taking a torch, he carried the empty wood basket round the path by the side of the house. He paused for a moment outside the shed. The smell of frost hung sharp in the air and the clouds lay low and dark, yet the days were perceptibly lengthening. Another four months to her Finals, and then he'd take her on a long, slow Grand Tour: Paris, Vienna, Venice, the Renaissance cities of North Italy, Rome . . .

He opened the shed door. A foul smell hit him. He took a step inside. Something hit him in the face. Something solid, soft and furry and stinking rotten. He leapt backwards with a cry of shock and disgust and fumbled frantically for the torch.

He flashed the light into the darkness. Two eyes glinted back at him. The eyes of a cat hanging from a beam, nailed up by its back legs. Its head, half severed, was still tarry with blood and its face bore a terrible, frozen grin.

Doubling up, he staggered away and retched violently into the shrubbery.

He knew who'd done it. He knew, too, how he'd catch him. The school could identify the boy from his photo. And then he'd sort the little bugger out.

On the pretext that the Infirmary was looking for a photographer for the commissioning ceremony for the new NMR scanner, he got Sophie to give him Maryanne's phone number. First thing in the morning, he called her at her flat. She'd already had the film developed and printed; she'd happily give him a print – and the negative, too, in case he wanted copies made. They arranged to meet at her faculty after lunch that day.

It was turning two o'clock when he dropped Sophie back at the biochemistry labs as usual and drove hurriedly to the art-history building. There the auburn-haired girl handed him a large white envelope. He thanked her most sincerely and, climbing back into his car, headed off towards the Infirmary.

At the first set of red lights, he tore the envelope open and pulled out the print, but the lights changed and he'd almost reached the hospital before he had a chance to look at it.

There he was himself, his arm on Sophie's shoulder.

There, too, was Sophie, squinting into the sun. Behind stood the crowd of people – two workmen in overalls, a student wheeling a bicycle, a technician bending to check a cable connection.

And that was all.

Where was Valentin?

Cold, sick tentacles spread through his veins.

Now, hang on a moment, he told himself. Take this thing slowly.

A car behind was hooting, but he barely heard it. Carefully, trying to control his shaking hands, he looked at the photo more closely. He broke into a sweat. The cars were piling up, hooting louder. He didn't care. 'There's a logical reason for this,' he was saying aloud to himself. 'Something's gone wrong in the development.' He fumbled for the strip of negatives and held them up to the light. He found the one – the only possible one – of their group. He tilted it so that the light reflected off the surface. He turned it this way and that, examining it meticulously for any possible flaw. *Something was wrong with the camera.* But the workmen, the student, everything had come out perfectly. Sophie, too, was complete in every detail. She even had her arm out, stretched round invisible shoulders . . .

Was he going mad?

Cars swirled around him, now hooting furiously. A police car pulled up behind and briefly sounded its siren. He jerked back to life. Turning the ignition key, though the engine was already running, he pulled away. A few yards away, he stalled: he'd left the hand-brake on. The police car came alongside and the officer leaned across and glared. He nodded back, he gesticulated, he wanted to break down and sob, *Yes, yes, I know, Officer, but don't you realise, the boy didn't come out! He isn't there!*

*   *   *

From the hall, the last sonorous strokes of eleven o'clock died away and the grandfather clock resumed its slow, stately tick. Snatches of a Haydn quartet filtered in from the living room. In his study, lit only by the lamp on his desk, Jake sat re-examining the print through a magnifying glass. No smudge or hint of a shadow suggested the presence of the boy. The emulsion seemed perfectly coherent, without any visible flaw. He examined the negative. In the morning, he'd check under a microscope at the hospital, but even under the magnifying glass he could spot no irregularities or any kind of ghost image in the silver salts.

He reached for the whisky bottle and refilled his glass. It was okay; sooner or later he'd find the answer. There *was* an answer, of course. Everything had its reason.

But what? His mind turned back to his conversation with Sophie just the other day, about the electromagnetic fields known to surround certain particularly charismatic men. Christ's halo, Buddha's aura, the tongues of fire on the apostles' heads, the coronas around living organisms photographed by the Russian scientist Kirlian, the auras surrounding people that mediums claimed to see, weren't these all simply radiation in the subvisual spectrum? Light, as we knew it, was a small band of some three or four hundred nanometres, lying between X-rays and gamma rays at the upper, ultraviolet end and heat, radar and radio waves at the lower, infra-red end. $E = hf$: energy is proportional to frequency ... The jolt he'd received when he'd shaken the boy's hand ...

Could this boy be able to transmit some kind of electromagnetic field, detectable by the human eye but not by photosensitive film? Wait! Come to think of it, not everybody *had* seen him at first. He himself hadn't, that time when Sophie accused him of cutting him dead in her study. Even at the movie shoot, where he'd met him properly, he'd hardly been able to make him out at first. He'd had somehow to *learn* to see him. He'd almost had to *make him up*. And Alex — not even Alex had spotted him at once. Was the boy being 'overlooked' because, quite literally, he *wasn't being seen*? Sophie had had to point him out first every time, and from then on people saw him just as readily as they saw anyone else. What was going on in their brains? Were they learning, over the space of a few seconds, to decode an entirely different form of message falling on the retinal cells? A message that a camera film, without a learning ability, simply couldn't register?

Rubbish! This was science fiction. People weren't light bulbs. What made us all visible was the light we reflected, not the light we generated. How could a human body absorb full-spectrum light and reflect it back at a non-visual wavelength? And if non-visual how did people actually see him when they did? And, to be bluntly practical, even supposing a living organism were capable of reflecting only, say, ultraviolet, what about his *clothes*? You didn't see this rag-bag walking around headless and handless until, *hey presto*, out of the blue materialised the eyes and nose, then the dark, curly hair, that grinning face . . . This wasn't the goddamn Cheshire Cat!

Cat. His stomach lurched and he took a slug of the whisky. He toyed for a moment with a vision of an Invisible Boy. H. G. Wells' poor man had had to go around naked. Not on frosty February nights . . .

He pushed the glass out of reach. He'd drunk too much already. With some relief, he reached for the paper he was still in the middle of writing. At least this was secure ground; he knew where he was here. He slipped the photo into the drawer. He was a scientist and he'd approach the puzzle scientifically. He'd run some tests – discreetly, of course, but enough to wrap it up conclusively. The evidence of the senses was notoriously fallible, but not the evidence of science. The whole function of science was to sort out the true from the false. Science wouldn't let him down.

As he was taking up his pen to resume work on the paper, he heard Sophie's footsteps crossing the hall. A moment later she came in and, going up to his desk, stood behind and put her arms round him.

'How's it going?' she asked.

'I can see the light at the end of the tunnel.' He stroked her hair. 'Bed-time for you, darling.'

She nodded and kissed him on the cheek.

'Don't stay up too late, will you?' she said.

He looked up. The voice, the tone: it could have been Alex speaking. He turned and kissed her.

'I shan't, I promise.' He hesitated. 'Sophie, I'm sorry if I reacted a bit harshly about that boy . . . Valentin. If you like him coming round, then let him. Maybe we could have him to supper and get to know him properly? If his parents wouldn't mind. What do you think?'

'I thought you didn't want to encourage him.'

His laugh rang hollow.

'So long as he *behaves*, I can't see any harm. Can you?'

'No, Dad.' She drew away. 'Good night, then.'

The boy crouched beneath the window, shifting uncomfortably. His leg throbbed painfully where he'd gashed it on a nail, climbing over the fence. He loosened the handkerchief he'd tied round it and felt the blood trickle down his sock. He raised himself an inch.

The man sat at the desk with his back to him, resting his head in his hand. His neck was exposed. The boy clenched his teeth. He could feel the pull growing. He was approaching the moment of his calling.

He glanced at the window. No trouble. It wasn't open, as it had been *that* time, but that wasn't the idea. He scanned the wall above. Couldn't be easier: first the window-ledge, the drain-pipe, then across to the small bathroom window an arm's stretch away and conveniently left open. Then inside, dropping to a crouch, listening at the door, tiptoeing along the corridor, first the girl's room, see that she is sleeping soundly, no need to disturb her, she knows what he's doing, anyway, then into the man's bedroom, over to the bed, slipping in under the frame, lying in wait, waiting for the moment when he'll come to bed, his feet going back and forth on the carpet, first with slippers, then bare, then the bedsprings bearing down, almost crushing him, the light going out, the man's breathing slowing, lengthening, deepening, and then at last the moment itself, sliding out from under like a snake, gathering to a crouch, waiting for the head to angle itself just right on the pillow, opening the penknife without the barest sound, bringing the blade forward, sizing up for the stroke, judging the distance, the weight, the depth . . .

Smothering a smile, the boy rose quietly to his feet and reached for a joint in the drain-pipe to haul himself up. As he put a foot on the ledge and let it carry his full weight, a streak of pain tore through his injured leg. With an involuntary cry, he fell back and, clutching the drain-pipe to save himself, loosened it from the wall, bringing chunks of mortar clattering down onto the flagstones.

Jake heard the cry and the spattering sound that

followed. He was through the back door and round the side in a flash, just in time to see the unmistakable figure in the oversized mackintosh disappearing over the wall. He called out into the darkness after him, half in anger and half in the hope of coaxing him back, but all that he heard was a bucket clattering over, way down at the far end of a neighbour's garden.

As he turned to retrace his steps, something white on the flagstones beneath his study window caught his eye. A handkerchief. In the light from the window he saw it was drenched with blood. Fresh blood. He chuckled grimly. He didn't need ultraviolet sight to see the boy was made of flesh and blood like the rest of the world.

He was about to drop the handkerchief in the garbage bin when an idea occurred to him. Suppose he wrapped it carefully in dampened gauze and sealed it in an airtight polythene bag, maybe he could keep the blood fresh long enough to take a look at it under a microscope. He'd pretty soon tell if a little mutant was roaming the streets of Bristol.

Claiming a crisis on the ward, Jake dropped Sophie off early the following morning; for once, she'd have to take her lunch in the labs' canteen, but he'd pick her up in the usual way at the end of the day. He drove fast to the Infirmary, parked badly across two bays and hurried straight to the pathology labs. There he took the small, tightly wrapped polythene bag out of his briefcase and quickly set to work on the handkerchief, carefully extracting as much of the serum as he could. By the end of an hour he had produced two sample quantities, thinly diluted but, nevertheless, adequate for grouping. That would throw up any obvious anomalies; a proper genetic screening would take much longer and have to come later. But he wasn't going to take any chances even with the grouping.

Leaving one phial to work on himself during the lunch hour, he took the other to the Haematology Unit where he persuaded a young technician he knew well to rush it through for him as an urgent job. He'd come down in the afternoon and collect the results personally.

During the lunch break, he went back to the pathology labs and ran his own basic blood-grouping test on the first sample. He obtained the result almost at once. It was, admittedly, as he had expected: the boy's group was AO, the most common. Nothing strange there. On the way back to the ward for the afternoon duty, he dropped in on the Haematology Unit. It was hardly necessary, but he'd said he would.

The technician met him with a look of bemused triumph.

'I said to myself, "I bet Dr Chalmers lands me with a right sod of a grouping," ' smiled the young man. 'And he did. But I cracked it. On the very last drop of serum.'

Jake felt numbness creep through his veins.

'Come off it,' he scoffed. 'I gave you an AO.'

' "AO", he says! Here, take a look.' The technician brought over a tray of glass slides. From a glance Jake could see there was clotting on every sample except one. And that was one of the rarest groups known. 'Just as I expected,' the man went on, satisfied with himself. 'Nothing's ever simple with you lot up in Genetics.'

Jake thanked him and, taking the print-out of the results, left the room. He stood in the corridor outside, leaning against a window-ledge for support. He was shaking badly. Now this was definitely *not* possible! One blood source had to mean one blood group. The principles were unassailable, the error must be human. But whose? Not his, he could swear that. And surely not the technician's: the man performed nothing but blood groupings all day long.

What had the man said? *Just as I expected.* Hadn't his own result been what he, too, had expected?

Christ, no! Science was *objective.* You ran the tests to discover the answers: you didn't supply the answers yourself. They were there, unchangeable, locked into the thing you were studying. OK, some uncertainty principle might be at work on the level of elementary particles, but not of whole bodies! How could we ever regulate our daily lives otherwise? We had to be able to know, to be certain. Science gave us that knowledge, that certitude. Science was consistent. Rational. Wasn't it? *Wasn't it?*

He felt sick and giddy. The sands were shifting beneath his feet. Nothing he touched seemed substantial any more. The world was mirrors, the objects in it mirages. Expect to fall ill, and you would fall ill. Expect to be the biggest or best, and you'd become the biggest or best. Expect to be healed, and you'd take up your bed and walk ... 'The Psychosomatics of Gene Expression': wasn't that exactly the subject of his paper?

Suddenly he began to shake with laughter. It was all perfectly hysterical. Here he was, standing in a hospital, crammed to the roof with equipment to analyse, measure, dissect, formulate, and you only had to take one step aside and say, *I don't believe,* and down it all fell like a house of cards.

Puff! Just like that.

A hand on his arm made him turn. 'Puff!' he said brightly.

'Dr Chalmers, are you all right?' It was a nurse from the main paediatrics ward.

He pulled himself together. His mouth was dry, his hands trembling. He shook his head and forced a normal smile.

'Thanks. I'm fine.'

310

He watched as the nurse went off down the corridor, casting a worried glance over her shoulder as she went, then turned and walked slowly away. While he stood waiting for an elevator, he examined the print-out more soberly. As he came to the data showing a positive identification, he gave a violent jolt.

The blood group was the same rare kind as Daniel's had been. And as Sophie's was.

Witnesses, you had to have witnesses. Not Sophie, it couldn't be Sophie. But Graham. This was more Graham's field. *I can't explain over the phone*, he'd whispered to the psychologist, holding the receiver pressed to his mouth, *but you have to come, Graham, it's absolutely imperative you come*. It might be his own phone and this might be his own study, but he'd had to whisper. You always had to whisper, because you never knew. You might have left the boy talking sweetly with Sophie in the living room, you might *think* you had, but how could you be sure?

Taking out his key chain, he carefully unlocked the bottom drawer and took out the Polaroid camera, complete with fresh film, its expiry date carefully checked, and a new bar of flash bulbs. Repeatability: that was the trick to sort out reason from unreason. If it happened only once, then it was an aberrant reading, or a gremlin in the works, or some blip or burp that all electronic machinery was prone to. Then he'd rip up the print, burn the negative and the world would look just as it had ever looked: ordered, reasonable, *comfortable*.

He rubbed his hands. Right, he'd winkle out the little gremlins! Puff!

At the crunch of tyres on gravel he shot out of his seat and hurried out to the front door. He didn't want the doorbell ringing and *Let me introduce you, this is Graham, he's a psychologist* frightening the little brat away. Not till he'd had a chance to speak to the man. To prepare him to be witness.

Graham leaned against the fireplace, his legs crossed, listening indulgently. He refused a drink and remained standing. He examined the photo carefully and yes, he said, the phenomenon was indeed bizarre. But Jake could see he was obviously only playing along while he diagnosed his psychological state. Lesson one in dealing with a madman: always agree.

'Thoughtography,' suggested Graham easily, though scrutinising him hard. 'Do you know there's an American called Ted Serios who can *think* images onto photographic plates?'

'Graham, we're talking about the natural world, not the supernatural.'

'There's a difference?'

'I didn't ask you here for a metaphysical debate—'

The psychologist studied the photo again more carefully. Suddenly he looked up and snapped his fingers.

'It's a *tulku*,' he pronounced.

'What the hell's a *tulku*?'

'A form materialised by thought.'

'What are you on about?'

'Tibetan monks claim to be able to create *actual people* through some highly concentrated form of meditation. They call them *talkus*.'

'This is England, Graham, not bloody—'

'Ever heard of Alexandra David-Neel? An English explorer out there. She learned the trick. She created a monk who accompanied her on her travels. He ate, slept, talked just like a real monk. Well, he *was* a real monk – or rather, he became so. That's the point. They're ideas, materialised. The more they are seen, the more real they become. Until they reach some threshold level. And then they actually exist.' He smiled. 'This monk became very boorish and quarrelsome, though. She had a hell of a job *un*creating him. Took her months. She nearly didn't make it.'

A moment's silence fell. Jake swallowed.

'Crap,' he said.

The psychologist continued to smile, unperturbed. He glanced pointedly at the lecture paper on the desk, the title page clear to read.

'When I did my doctoral thesis on schizophrenia,' he went on, 'I became so involved in the symptomatology that I began hearing voices and thinking I was being followed—'

Jake leaned forward, feeling the rage swelling.

'Are you calling me a schizo? Are you saying I'm deluded? Inventing? Take a look for yourself! This boy is *real* all right. He's just ... scientifically ... a conundrum. You're here to verify the evidence. The facts.'

'Facts are flexible, Jake. It's a question of where you draw the line. We call a person insane when the line they choose to observe doesn't conform to ours. Maybe this boy is at that very line. Or even just over it.'

'Oh, come on, Graham,' retorted Jake roughly, picking up the Polaroid camera. 'You've been listening to yourself for too long.'

Without saying more, he led the way across the hall into the living room.

Sophie was sitting with her elbows on her desk, peering thoughtfully at the screen of her computer. Valentin, in a large grey sweatshirt and ink-stained jeans, sat at the desk backing hers, reading a comic magazine.

Hi, Uncle Gray,' greeted Sophie.

'Hello, Sophie. Long time no see.'

'Forty-seven days, two hours and nine minutes,' returned Sophie promptly, with a self-mocking smile. 'You haven't met my friend Valentin.'

Graham drew up a chair to the desks so that he was at the same level as the two children. He gave the boy a friendly smile.

'I've heard a lot about you, young man,' he said. 'I know a Levinsky, works in my department. Couldn't be your dad, could he?'

The boy shot a quick, questioning glance at Sophie.

'No,' he replied in his curious, low voice.

'Live locally, do you, lad?' Graham went on casually.

Sophie intervened. 'If you're wondering about Mulberry Crescent,' she said bluntly, 'that's where his mother lives. She left his father about four years ago and married this other man. His dad lives up by the bridge.' She followed Valentin's gaze to the camera Jake was carrying. She looked from one man to the other. 'What's all this about?' she asked, sensing something.

Graham smiled easily. 'Your dad wants to finish up an album,' he said.

'But not a Polaroid!' she protested. 'The quality's terrible.'

Jake raised the camera.

'Fresh film,' he said. 'Let's try and see. Anyway, I don't have any of young Valentin.'

Sophie turned to the boy with an ironic smile.

'You don't know what an honour this is,' she said.

Positioning himself a few feet away, Jake squinted through the view-finder.

'Right,' he called. 'Graham, you go in the middle, behind them. Sophie, get closer to Valentin. That's it. Ready? Hold it.'

Taking care that all three were well within the

frame, he pressed the button. The flash bulb popped and, with a whir, the film plate was expelled. Careful not to touch the surface, he laid it carefully on the desk where they could all watch the image under the light as it slowly came up. He watched the boy carefully. Right, he thought, I've got you now! Explain *this* away!

A brownish blur began spreading inwards from the edges of the small square of emulsion, gradually taking form as the background. Shadows became hair, three shadows of hair; pinpricks of dark became eyes, three pairs of eyes; noses and lips and teeth and ears, three of everything, three heads, three smiles . . . three *people*. Graham. Sophie. And Valentin.

Jake looked up, dazed, giddy.

Graham was smiling, his eyebrows raised. Sophie was laughing. But Valentin's face bore a different look. It was set in a hard, cruel smirk.

TWENTY-TWO

The school administrator puzzled over the photo for a moment, then shook her head. No, that boy was not a pupil at Clifton Middle. Why didn't he try Queen's Road?

Jake did. No one recognised the boy at that school, either.

He hurried back to finish his morning on the ward. He couldn't concentrate on anything. He'd be in mid-sentence when he'd suddenly lose track of what he was saying, and at least twice he found himself repeating the same instructions to the sister. The conundrum was haunting him. It was Thursday, and he was due to leave for Cambridge the following evening. How could he go, leaving Sophie behind at home, without unmasking the boy?

It was a difficult morning, with two new admissions and a crisis over a small boy with PKU. Just as he'd resolved that, the police officer arrived and asked for a word. In the corridor outside he confided to Jake that they'd come to a full stop on Helen Lorenz's case; no one could suggest a satisfactory motive and, without direct witnesses, the only evidence was circumstantial. A footprint had been found in the kitchen-floor lino-leum, which Forensic judged had been left by an Adidas trainer, size five – a child's size. Did Sophie, he asked, wear trainers of that size and make? No? He apologised; they were asking everyone, however remotely connected. Could Jake throw any light of any kind on *anything*? No, Jake regretted, he couldn't.

Distressed to be reminded of the tragedy and his

mind in turmoil over the puzzle of the boy, Jake was late meeting Sophie from her morning's lectures. He found her sitting on her briefcase on the Department steps, engrossed in a book entitled *Advanced Cytology*. As the day was bright, they spent the lunch hour in Tyndalls Park. She'd found a note from her tutor in her pigeon-hole, sent a week before but misrouted, inviting her, along with a few of her fellow students, to one of his group-discussion evenings at his home that night. Could Jake drive her over when he picked her up at the end of the day? She handed him a slip of paper on which she'd written the address. The house was on the other side of town.

'Don't worry about fetching me back, Dad,' she said. 'I'll get a taxi. Last time it went on till after midnight, remember? Oh, Valentin said he'd look in this evening. Say I'm sorry, will you? Tell him he can come over at the weekend instead. He can keep me company while you're away.'

'Look, angel, I'm not sure—'

She squeezed his arm.

'You're not being silly again, are you?' Her tone grew more concerned. 'Something's the matter, isn't it? You were really funny last night.'

He checked himself. What could he say until he *knew*?

'Everything's fine. Show me that book you were reading. I don't think I know it.'

Having dropped Sophie at her tutor's that evening. Jake drove slowly back over the Clifton suspension bridge, trying to keep his eyes on the tail of the car in front. The sides of the gorge fell sheer to the ravine 250 feet below, and even from the car he felt a twinge of vertigo as he shot a glance over his right shoulder and saw, far, far below, the slip of river, reflecting the last cold rays of the sun as it meandered through the muddy tidal flats out to sea. To his left, heavy black rain clouds were rolling in from the east. Ahead rose the two tall, slender piers, from which thick-plaited cables looped in a graceful curve down to the pedestrian rail before sweeping up steeply to the second pair of piers behind. The bridge was swaying perceptibly in the wind. He shifted uncomfortably in his seat, feeling penned in by the seat-belt. What really held the bridge up? Belief? Not his, for sure.

At the other end, relieved to be back on *terra firma*, he accelerated. He'd better hurry if he was going to be properly prepared for the boy.

He'd hardly passed the Academy when a kid chasing a football darted out in front of him. As he slammed on his brakes, he felt something snap. He was flung violently forward, cracking his forehead on the windscreen and crushing his ribs on the steering-wheel. Tyres squealing, the car screeched to a halt with its rear slewed dangerously across the road. He'd missed the kid, who grabbed the ball and ran off quickly into the park.

He sank back in the seat, shaking violently. The seat-belt had snapped. One end was still clasped by its fixing to the floor, the other lay loose across his lap. He examined the break. A few frayed strands showed where it had ripped under impact, but clearly the rest had been severed, cut cleanly by a knife or razor blade.

Someone had deliberately sabotaged this belt. Someone was trying to terrorise him.

Who, and why?

Alone, in a room, that's how it would be. Just the two of them, him and the boy, face to face, a bit of coaxing and cajoling, and then the investigation could start.

318

Jake emptied his pockets onto the table-top, casting a grim glance at the Polaroid as he took it out, and, slipping off his tweed jacket, put on a loose-fitting jersey. He crushed some ice in a teatowel and sat on the sofa in the living room for a minute or two with the ice-pack pressed to his painfully throbbing forehead. Then, braced by a large drink, he began his preparations.

He was dealing with a boy who was deeply disturbed. Cornered, he might turn wild. He would certainly try to run away. The first thing was to seal off the exits. Jake locked the front and side doors, pocketing the keys. To control the point of entry, he left the French windows in the kitchen ajar. He left the lights on in the kitchen and in Sophie's study, though he closed her study curtains so that the boy would have no cause to doubt she was in. In the rest of the house, he switched off the lights. He wanted to draw him into one area, where he could keep him under control while he won his cooperation to the tests.

Discreetly out of view from the garden, he placed the equipment he'd brought with him from the hospital. Two cameras, loaded with high-speed film; a photographic plate, sensitive to ultraviolet light and sealed in a light-proof envelope; a magnetometer, to measure changes in the ambient magnetic field; a syringe for drawing a blood sample to resolve the contradictory evidence there and to supply material for genetic testing; and finally, a tape recorder to preserve a record of everything that was said, partly to furnish the unequivocal facts of who the boy was and where he lived but also as a safeguard in the event that he himself was ever accused of professional misconduct. He was a doctor, after all, dealing with a minor without the knowledge or permission of the child's parents.

As a final touch, he put on a Handel tape in Sophie's study and took up his position.

The boy glanced into the car as he passed. A severed length of seat-belt lay tossed aside on the back seat. It hadn't worked. But now the man *knew*. He'd lost the advantage of surprise. He gritted his teeth. Falling to a crouch, he slipped noiselessly across the gravel.

From the front, the house was in darkness. Above the turrets and gables, a small, bright moon shone through briefly between banks of restlessly prowling clouds. Skirting the building on the grass verge, he noted the man's study was dark, but light and music came from the drawn curtains of the girl's study next door. What trick was the man playing? He knew the girl wasn't there; hiding in the shrubbery earlier, he'd seen the car return empty.

Through the French windows he looked into the kitchen, brightly lit, warm and inviting. No one was around. The door was ajar. He was just about to slip inside when the phone suddenly rang. He retreated a step into the darkness and waited. It rang on and on. No one answered it.

Someone was in hiding and didn't want to reveal his position. Someone was waiting for him.

With a half-smile, he slipped away and retraced his steps round to the study at the side. He knew that window. He'd enter where he was least expected, and strike from there. Reaching for his penknife, he felt the window clasp. It was open: an invitation. Gradually he eased up the sash, careful not to make a noise.

He hesitated, listening, all his senses honed. Traffic growled in the distance, a plane cruised high overhead, a dog barked two houses down, but apart from the soft strains of music that filtered out through the open window along with the smell of leather furniture and wood polish on the warm heated air, the house was in complete silence.

Gripping the knife, in a single agile movement he swung himself through the window and landed softly on the carpet.

The shadows came alive.

A hand reached out and grabbed him by the shoulder. A figure followed the hand, framed against the window, the eyes gleaming like coals in the dark.

'Got you!' hissed the man.

The boy cried out. He fought to free himself, but the man had spun him round and was grasping him by the wrist in an unbreakable grip. He lashed out with the knife, stabbing and slashing wildly in all directions. The blade bit into something firm, the man gave a howl of pain and released his grasp. The boy darted for the door. Stumbling over chairs and books, he burst through into the hall and fled into the darkness of the house.

Jake snapped on the desk lamp. Blood poured from the closed palm on his left hand. It wouldn't open by itself and he had to use his other hand to unfurl it. A gash ran from the little finger to the thumb, across the palmar fascia and slicing deep into the abductor pollicis. He tested for movement, but the pain was too excruciating to enable him to tell if the critical ligaments had been severed. Shaking with nausea from the shock, he stumbled into the kitchen and plunged the whole hand into the ice-pack. Securing the teatowel around his wrist with elastic bands, he went off in search of the boy. Jesus Christ, he'd sort the little bastard out now.

He stood in the hallway, trying to hear above the thump of his pulse and the throb of his hand jamming his senses.

'Valentin?' he shouted. 'Come here!'

Nothing.

He softened his voice.

'It's OK,' he called into the silence. 'I won't hurt you. I only want a talk.'

A muffled creak. Was it coming from the back stairs? He blundered down the passage and kicked open the door to the utility room. Beyond, the narrow back stairs led up to the bedrooms above. The door connecting to the kitchen was ajar, and in the light he could see straight away that the small room was empty. A sudden, shuddering thud behind him made him jump violently. He whipped round; it was only the deep-freeze turning itself on. Shaking, he reached for a torch and retraced his steps. He'd take the front stairs. As he turned, he flashed his torch quickly around. He frowned: the door to the cupboard with the household cleaning materials was open. He hadn't left it like that, had he?

With the adrenaline burning in his stomach, Jake gripped the torch and began his search of the house. Just let him get face to face with the boy and then he'd deal with him. But as he took the first steps up the stairs, a flash of cold fear swept through him. The boy had a knife – and the use of both hands, besides. For God's sake, he swore: You're a fully-grown man and he's only a *kid*!

The boy crouched behind the door, his knife in one hand and the aerosol can of oven cleaner in the other. Beneath an orange square with a black cross, he could just read the warning on the can: *Caution – contains sodium hydroxide*. On the bedside table lay the light bulb he'd taken out.

He heard the footsteps coming slowly up the stairs. As they reached the top, they hesitated. A board creaked in the doorway. A torch beam flashed round the small bedroom, the light momentarily resting on the wardrobe and the area under the dressing-table, and moved on.

Then he made his mistake. He stifled a small cough. At once the footsteps turned back. A hand holding a torch reached for the light switch and turned it on. Nothing happened. The man took a step inside, raking the ground before him with the torch like a blind man with a stick. The boy held his breath. The beam was creeping closer. Any minute it would find him . . .

Gently he eased the plastic lid off the can and lobbed it across the room. It landed by the wardrobe in the corner with a soft clatter. The man took another step forward, holding his torch out at arm's length and pointing it in the direction of the noise. The boy tightened his grip on the can.

Now! Do it now!

He darted out, keeping low. Pointing the aerosol directly in the man's face, he jabbed his finger down on the nozzle. An acrid spray jetted out into Jake's eyes. With a howl of agony, he dropped the torch and, his hands flying to his face, stumbled back into the corridor. The boy followed, stabbing the air with spray. He could feel the sting on his own eyes as he walked through the acid mist. Then, throwing the can aside, he went for him with the knife. The first blow was somehow absorbed by his jersey, the second was taken by a heavy, glove-like object he was wearing. Deflected, the knife jerked out of the boy's hand.

The man had backed away to the very edge of the stairs. He hesitated for a second, then took another step backwards. Backwards into the void. For one moment, as he frantically clutched at the banister post, it seemed he might recover his balance, but the boy came forward and landed him a violent kick in the stomach. The man toppled and, with a howl of rage and pain, tumbled backwards down the stairs. Vainly grasping at the banisters as he went, he fell and slithered head over heels in a tangle of arms and legs until he landed at the bottom with a blunt, dull *crack*, and suddenly all was silent.

The boy retrieved his knife and crept cautiously down the stairs. In the light from the living-room door, he could see the man lying motionless, sprawled on the hall tiles at the bottom, his head lolling at an awkward angle, exposing the naked flesh of his neck, and a thin tapeworm of black blood trickling from his ear. Not daring to step over the body in case it suddenly came to life, he climbed over the banisters and dropped to the passageway below. Then, with the knife tight in his hand, he crept forward.

Now at last he had him. Now at last he could fulfil the purpose for which he had been summoned.

Blurrily, through the scorch of agony, Jake saw the eyes. Feral, pitiless, pure hate and rage. Burning out of the dark, burning into his own, mesmerising him like a snake. And he saw the blade of the knife, polished as a mirror, glinting in the half-light. Behind, the shadowy form of the boy, crouching, his hand poised.

Move, he thought, and the knife moves quicker. Struggle, and the blade strikes. Any sudden movement, and the blade is more sudden still. Wait. Think. Hold on. Find an edge, find a chink, find anything to tilt the balance.

This is a nightmare. This is happening in my mind. In my belief. It's not real. Puff!

Why was the boy hesitating? Why didn't he strike?

The dark eyes were sucking out his life force. His will was ebbing. The boy was draining him of his vital juices, like a spider drawing nourishment from the living prey.

Puff!

He had the sudden sensation that there was some invisible point in the space between them at which their minds clashed and, for a split second, he had shifted the boundary a fraction. *Tulku*: the word revolved in his mind. This is a *tulku*. He had made him up. He had to *un*make him. He needed a password, a curse, a name in which to deny him, to refuse him, to *unsee* him.

He heard the whisper escape hoarsely from his throat, as if from far off.

'The mirror, look!'

The boy caught a breath. He faltered.

'The mirror, behind you! I don't see you!'

With a small gasp, the boy shot a glance at the mirror on the wall behind him. It was enough. Galvanising every nerve and muscle, Jake swung his ice-pack hand up, catching Valentin a blow on the side of his head, and with a rapid twist of his body rolled free and scrambled to his feet. His eyes still streaming, he backed across the hall towards the front door. Within a second the boy had recovered his balance and was coming at him again. Jake fumbled frantically around for a weapon. His hand lit upon a shooting-stick in the umbrella stand. He wrenched it out and, grabbing it by the base in his right hand and, wielding it wildly about him like a flail, he gradually drove the boy back into the kitchen. Momentarily blinded by the light, he stumbled into the table, sending the equipment he'd laid out crashing to the floor. But the boy was already beating a retreat. For a second he darted forwards and scrabbled quickly among the fallen objects for something, then edged back towards the French windows. Momentarily Jake faltered, unnerved. Against the pitch dark outside, the windows reflected the whole room like a bank of mirrors – the table and chairs, the cooker and cupboards, Jake himself ... but not the boy! He simply wasn't *there*!

He'd tipped the balance, he was triumphing!

He blundered on into the garden, swiping with the heavy metal stick, until suddenly, with a snarl of fury, the boy turned and took flight. He zigzagged like a hare down the garden, darted through the skirt of the great willow tree, scrambled up onto the roof of the shed, slipped over the wall and was lost into the night.

Hurling the stick after him, Jake groped his way back into the house. Double-locking every door and window, he fumbled his way over to the kitchen where, bending forward over the sink with his head under a running tap and gently sluicing his scorching eyes, he gradually felt all his strength ebb from his legs and he slipped to the floor in a cold faint.

Sophie! Sophie must be warned! The boy was evil. What if he got to her first?

Despite the pain, Jake fumbled on his hands and knees for the slip of paper on the floor where it had fallen with the rest of the contents of his pockets. He managed, by squinting, to dial the number. It was engaged. He found some pain-killers in the bathroom upstairs and bandaged up his wounded hand. Despite the pills, agony flooded him in tidal waves, leaving him dizzy and nauseous. He steered himself downstairs and tried the number again. It was still engaged. He dialled for five minutes. What if she were calling for a taxi right then? Swallowing a tumbler of whisky, he eased his aching body into his sheepskin coat and went to the door. He'd intercept her before she left. The taxi would drop her in the street; who knew if the boy wouldn't be lying in wait to catch her on the way up to the front door? Until this thing was sorted out, it was imperative she be kept way. He'd take her to stay the night with Suzanne, or with Alex. This was an emergency.

Rain had begun to fall, steady and thick. The night was dark and the steps slippery. Jake climbed painfully into the Volvo and manoeuvred it with difficulty into the street. Driving, he had to reach across with his good hand to change gear and he sat forward, peering through the rain-spattered windscreen as the wipers beat restlessly back and forth and the seat-belt warning alarm kept up its relentless buzz. He'd reached the end of the street before he realised he'd forgotten to switch on his lights. For a while he kept his speed down, fearing a police car would stop him – he'd drunk well over the limit and, besides, his vision was still dangerously fuzzy – but as he turned into Queen's Road, he grew more confident and began to pick up speed.

At the toll signs on the approach to the suspension bridge, however, he slowed down again, remembering he'd emptied his pockets, and pulled up for a moment into the kerb. Leaving the engine running, with his foot on the clutch, he groped about round the dashboard tray. There was generally some loose change swilling about in there.

He was reaching up to turn on the interior light when a sound froze his blood.

Breathing, coming from the back seat.

Unthinking, he shot a glance in the rear-view mirror. He saw nothing. His nerves were just on edge. Then he realised. He jerked round, but too late. Something black whipped over his head – a band, a belt, the *seat-belt*! It tightened round his throat, ramming his neck violently back into the head-rest, winching tighter and tighter, crushing, throttling ... Gasping, choking, he clawed with his good hand to free his throat, he writhed in the seat and reached back to grab the hands, but they gripped him with ever more demonic strength and held him pinned to his seat, stretching him back at full length so that his feet jammed on the pedals as he fought for breath. The engine revved wildly. Suddenly his foot slipped off the clutch. The car engaged gear and bucked forward, mounted the pavement, shot ahead for a few feet and crashed into a stone pier. The impact flung the boy behind him forward and for a moment his grip slackened. In one swift movement, Jake jerked round and lashed out with his fist, smashing him in the face. Sudden, blind anger overwhelmed him. With a terrible roar, he set upon the boy. In a burst of supreme strength, oblivious of his own pain, he grabbed him by the hair and rammed his head against the window. The boy screamed. Again Jake brought his head cracking down on the pane. A jet of blood spurted from the boy's nose. Wrenching free, he fumbled desperately for the door catch. He managed to evade Jake's reach, restricted as it was by the seats between them, and evade it just long enough to snap open the door and tumble out onto the ground, where he picked himself up and fled towards the bridge.

Jake followed at a shambling jog. Already he felt his temper cooling. For a moment he felt sorry for striking the child. He lumbered after the fleeing figure as it darted ahead, taking to the pavement that ran across the long, high bridge.

A few yards in, the gorge fell sharply away into complete darkness. The wind grew stronger, driving the rain in slanting streaks, visible momentarily in the oncoming headlamps of cars, then almost immediately expunged. On the other side, a figure in a white raincoat was wrestling with an umbrella and, some way ahead, two joggers were steadily disappearing into the distance. On the left, he could see a curtain of rain making its way down towards the estuary, rolling up the last light of the evening sky, but in the chasm, hundreds of feet below, not a light flickered nor a glint returned from the river to prove the darkness was not infinite.

'Stop!' he called, gaining ground on the boy. 'Stop, Valentin! It's all right!'

A car threw up a sheet of spray, drenching his shoes. The boy stopped for a moment, turned, then ran on again. Jake jogged on, calling hopelessly into the driving rain. Gradually he caught up until they stood face to face, twenty feet apart, boy and man, hunter and hunted. Suddenly, all Jake's anger and fight melted away. The poor creature looked so wretched, cowering at the foot of one of the vast, wrought-iron piers.

Jake took a step forward, holding out his hand.

'Listen, Valentin,' he said in a gentler voice. 'Let's stop this. Enough is enough. If you've got a grudge, tell me. Let's sort it out together, properly, like civilised people. Do you hear me? Valentin?'

He took another careful step forward, watching the boy's reaction closely. It was like approaching a wounded tiger cub. After every step he paused and spoke a few more soothing words. He was almost within an arm's reach when the boy suddenly let out a terrified whimper and cast desperately about him. He looked up at the pier rising into the dark above him, and with a sudden, agile leap, he sprang onto the wide safety rail and began clambering up the ironwork.

Jake ran forward.

'Stop, for Christ's sake!' he cried. 'Come down!'

But the boy was maniacally climbing on up, gripping the rivets and bolts and feeling for toe-holds among the nooks in the slippery, ornate Victorian ironwork. The bridge swayed in the wind. Below lay what seemed a bottomless void. For a moment the boy's foot slipped and he scrabbled frantically before he found a hold. Jake felt sick. Should he go after him and try to haul him down, or back off and let him find his own escape?

He looked up. For a second, their eyes met. In place of hate, he saw pure terror.

He reached out. In desperation, the boy stretched up for a new hand-hold, he groped the air, his foot was slipping . . . Jake could see his foot was slipping . . . he put out his hand to support him, to catch him, and for a split second he thought he'd got him safe – but the foot began to slip, the boy's whole body began to slip, Jake clutching more desperately, only having one hand that worked, but the shoe came away, it came clean away in his hand, and suddenly with a scream the boy slid past him, his hands spreadeagled, scrabbling helplessly at the slippery rivets as they passed. The rail momentarily broke his fall. He stood, teetering, fighting to regain his balance, but, just as he was straightening, the momentum of his fall seemed to catch up with him and carry him on, sending him toppling backwards with a terrible, long, dying cry down, down, down into the pitch-black void.

As he stepped back, dumb with horror, Jake saw he still had the boy's shoe in his hand. Something made him look twice. His blood froze.

It was an Adidas trainer. Size five.

Sweet Christ.

Grasping the shoe by the toe, with all the strength of his revulsion, he flung it far, far over the edge, where it was swallowed up at once in the darkness.

TWENTY-THREE

Jake coaxed the crumpled car back home, taking side-streets to avoid the police. The headlamps were shattered, the bumper bore onto the tyres and the fan shrieked as it grated against the radiator. Sophie would have to come home by taxi; that would give him time to tidy up the damage, too.

First he turned on all the lights in the house and made himself some strong, sweet coffee. Then he set to work righting the kitchen table. As he collected up his possessions, he noted that the Polaroid photo was missing. So that was what the boy had stopped for as he'd beaten his retreat. Why should it have been so precious? Well, it was gone now, gone with the poor lad. He found a dustpan and brush and cleared away the fragments of glass where the syringe had shattered on the hard floor. As he picked up the magnetometer, he noticed its dial had cracked in such a way that a splinter of glass had jammed the pointer on the reading at the time of impact. The magnetic field it recorded was way over any normal limit.

He covered his cuts and dressed his hand carefully – he'd have to wait until the morning to see a specialist neurologist – and, swallowing another few pain-killers in a tumbler of whisky, he settled down to wait for Sophie to return.

Calmly. Quietly. It was all over now.

The boy was dead. And he was guilty of his death. He'd met violence with violence. If he hadn't bludgeoned him in the car, if he hadn't given chase, if he'd backed off at the last minute instead of making a clumsy attempt to save him . . . Oh, *Christ*.

Should he go to the police? What if someone in a passing car had reported seeing a man wrestling with a boy? But if anyone *had* witnessed it, why hadn't the police turned up? Would someone spot the body on the mud flats at first light, or would the retreating tide carry it away out to sea? Then, what about the boy's parents? At this very minute, in some small home by the bridge, a father would be waiting up for his son, just as he himself was waiting up for his daughter, and the son wouldn't appear. The man would phone the mother, the boy's friends, the police. No one would know. There'd follow a terrible chain of anxious days and sleepless nights. Would they ever find the body? If so, would they match the trainer? Would they then conclude it was suicide, perhaps out of remorse? Without doubt, they'd be round to see Sophie. There'd be questions and more questions, visits from social workers and child psychologists . . . Think how she'd suffered when Danny died and how it had triggered off her troubles. After four years of healing, and with just four months to go to her Finals, was it fair to subject her to the distress?

No. Let the boy not achieve in death the destruction he'd tried to wreak in life.

Jake could see it all clearly now. He'd got it round the wrong way. It was Valentin who'd been obsessive about Sophie, and with the passion of which only a child was capable – total, unconditional, *amoral*. A child was born a barbaric, self-centred little animal; its whole development was a process of growing to civilisation, learning to temper its actions by moral constraints and adapt its behaviour to conform to general social codes. Valentin had been Sophie's age, but in the very degree she was advanced, so he was retarded. He had the emotional responses of an infant. Clinically, he was a psychopath.

He'd reasoned like a psychopath, too. Helen had hurt Sophie, and so she had to be punished. Instead of taking civilised action, however, such as reporting her to someone in authority, he'd taken animal action. And killed. He would have killed Jake, too, if he'd managed it. He'd tried before with the seat-belt – perhaps, too, with that stone finial that had come crashing down from the roof? What had been his motive? Jealousy. Again, the instinctual, irrational response: to kill. The line dividing man from animal was very fine. Most children passed it around the age of two. Valentin never had; he had remained arrested on the far side.

What of the strange phenomenon of the boy himself? Could the power of his frustrated passion have built up to such a strength that it had manifested itself physically? Did this explain that astonishingly high magnetic field surrounding him? Jake went to his bookshelves and tracked down a series of experiments conducted in Leningrad some years before on a woman who claimed to be able to make objects move psychokinetically. They'd noted the presence of a strong electrostatic field in tune with a pulsing magnetic field. Now, two such fields vibrating transversely to one another produced electromagnetic radiation. Could the boy somehow be altering the wavelengths at which light reflected from his own body in such a way that sometimes, briefly, he actually *shifted over into the subvisual spectrum*? It sounded crazily far-fetched, but in principle, Jake had to admit, the science was plausible.

He would never know. Nor, perhaps, would he ever find out exactly who the boy was. Was his name really Valentin Levinsky? Did he actually live alone with his father somewhere over by the bridge? Perhaps not even Sophie knew for certain. The only absolutely sure fact was that he had gone back into the night from which he'd emerged, and he'd gone for good.

A taxi was drawing up in the street, a door slammed and Sophie's footsteps came running up the gravel drive. Jake was at the door as she reached the porch. He drew her in and, closing it behind her, hugged her with all the strength of his love as he felt all the strain and tension ebbing from his weary soul.

She caught sight of his bandaged hand and pulled away.

'Dad!' she cried. 'What've you done to yourself.?'

'The car had an argument with a wall. Everything's all right.'

'But your head! And there's blood on your neck.'

'Just a scratch. Nothing to worry about, darling.' Silencing her anxious protests, he led her into the kitchen. 'Tell me how it went this evening.'

As she glanced about the room, a puzzled look flashed over her face.

'Did Valentin show up?'

'No.'

'Funny. I can almost . . . feel him here.'

He gave a short laugh. 'No, no. He's not here. Goodness knows where he is now.'

'Now?'

'Or ever.' As he squeezed her hand, he felt his eyes smarting with tears. 'God, I'm glad you're here, my darling. Here and safe.'

The dawn air was pure and crisp, and across the park the mist hung like skeins of silk. Jake stood with his stop-watch beside the old bandstand, watching the figure in the primrose-yellow tracksuit as it broke into a sprint by the shuttered tea-house and bent its steps in a wide curve back towards him. Sophie arrived breathless, tossing her fair hair and laughing. He consulted the stop-watch.

'Three minutes eighteen, give or take.'

'Give.'

'Three seventeen point six, then.'

'The year I was born, in tenths of seconds,' she computed effortlessly. 'Same as Valentin.'

He started, but kept silent. She shot him an anxious glance?

'What's the matter, Dad? Is your hand hurting? You know, you want to look out you haven't cut a nerve.'

He nodded. 'I'll get it seen to this morning.' He began walking back towards the main gates. Scanning the trees and shrubbery, he sighed. 'Just look, spring is really on its way at last.'

'You're in a funny mood today.'

He shrugged. 'Just happy to be alive. My mother used to say, count your blessings every day.'

'You can't have very many if you can count them.'

'I can count ours.'

Her violet eyes smiled with a trace of irony.

'But we're well into six figures!'

They turned through the gates and he lengthened his stride so that she could jog alongside.

'Let's do something this afternoon before I go off,' he proposed. 'There's the Hockney drawings at the art gallery.'

'But you haven't finished your paper.'

He tapped his forehead. 'It's all in here.'

She pointed to an imaginary sheet of paper. 'You want it all down *there*.'

He smiled and took a deep breath of the fine, chill air. Everything seemed different today. Clearer.

'I've been thinking,' he began. 'Maybe I'll extemporise. How about this?' "Gentlemen," I shall open by saying, "each of you sitting there possesses beneath your skull two fistfuls of pink-grey tissue, wrinkled like a walnut and something of the consistency of porridge, and capable of storing more information than all the computers and libraries of the world put together. Even if we could put them all together to make a single global computer-library, a single *organism* of knowledge, we couldn't conceive what it would be like, how it would behave or think and of what, if stretched, it could really be capable. We can only be sure it would be beyond our conception. The human mind, I maintain, gentlemen, is infinitely more powerful than we have ever begun to conceive. Infinitely more beautiful, and infinitely more destructive, too." '

She danced ahead of him, laughing.

'You can't use words like "beautiful"! They're subjective, based on feelings and beliefs.'

He felt himself fumbling towards a new understanding that was gradually taking shape even as he spoke.

'Yes, Sophie. That's the point I'm trying to make.'

'Then I'm missing it.'

He struggled to articulate more clearly.

'Science is measurement. As such, it has only occupied itself with things that can be measured. Now, feelings, beliefs and ideas are simply not amenable to this. Human emotions do not conform to an input-output model; that's where the behaviourists came unstuck. You can't look at ideas through microscopes. There's no scale of atomic weights for beliefs. Pure science has quite simply ignored these as being outside its field of enquiry and, *de facto*, beyond truth.'

'Is this part of the text, Dad?'

'Hang on. Now, it goes back as far as Descartes and the mind-body split, and it seems increasingly clear to me that it's a fatal wrong turn. The body has become a legitimate province of science, while the mind has been relegated to the pseudo-sciences – psychology, sociology and the rest. The distinction is convenient, but false. Once you accept it's false, you can begin to see how a whole immaterial world should exist in parallel to the material world – equally valid, *scientific*, if you like, and obeying the same kinds of rules. Take natural selection, for instance. Beliefs and ideas have lives of their own. They are born, they develop and grow, they propagate by spawning new offshoots or by colonising more minds. Minds are the soil in which ideas, like genes, are expressed. My point is that we have systematically neglected the power of our minds. The two worlds, you see, are interactive, interdependent. Ideas that take root in our minds can directly influence our bodies. My paper looks at one example only: how the mind controls gene expression. Remember that small boy I treated for multiple sclerosis? It was his *idea* he'd get MS that actually lit the touch-paper and triggered the genes into action.'

He paused, awed by the inevitable conclusion.

'But it goes beyond that. Through the action of our mental faculties, I believe we can actually become *materially different*. We stand now at a crossroads in our knowledge. We are approaching the millennium. The next century will see the epoch of the mind sciences. Mind will be God, thought will be power. Thought-power will provide our instruments of healing and our weapons of killing, our source of welfare and our means of warfare. As I said, infinitely beautiful, but infinitely destructive, too.'

Sophie was eyeing him carefully.

'Are you being deliberately contentious,' she said after a pause, 'or do you mean all this?'

He held her eye.

'I mean it, and I believe it to be true.' He paused. 'We have gone as far as logic and reason and scientific tests of validity can take us. These are beliefs, like any other. Disbelieve, and we open the door to another kind of reality. This is where science and religion meet. And where they part.'

They stood facing one another in silence for a long moment, then Sophie reached forward and took him by the hand.

'Dad,' she said quietly, 'why has it taken you so long?'

Jake threw his suitcase into the rear of the hired car and turned back to the porch to say goodbye to Suzanne. At her side stood her nephew, Jeremy, a bright, self-assured eleven-year-old whom she was looking after for the weekend while her sister went away. Before all this, he wouldn't have wanted the boy there, distracting Sophie from her work, but now he almost welcomed his presence; it would make the house *feel* better.

He gave Suzanne's arm a warm squeeze.

'Sunday afternoon, then,' he said. 'Just drop Sophie at her mother's, and you go off home. Alex will bring her back here, as I said, and anyway I'll be home well before then.' He ruffled his hand through the boy's curly head. 'Sophie will show you how to work the computer games.'

'Thanks,' said the small boy.

'I've left a note for extra milk both days—'

'Don't worry about us,' insisted Suzanne. 'We'll be fine. You look after that hand of yours. Mind you take care driving.'

'I will. And thanks.'

With a wave he went to the car. Sophie stood beside the open door. He held her in his arms, relishing the feel of her strong, lithe body. She clung ever tighter to him.

'I wish I was coming with you,' she said.

'I'll be back before you know it, darling.'

'It's silly, I know, but I just feel . . .'

'Ssh.' He stroked her fair hair. 'Suzanne will take good care of you.'

'It isn't that.'

'Next time, then, I promise. You'll see – these conferences are excruciatingly boring.'

Sophie released her grip. From the pocket of her dress she pulled out a small bunch of snowdrops, tied together with an elastic band.

'Last of the year,' she said. 'To remind you of home.'

He kissed her tenderly on the cheek.

'Thank you, angel. I'll treasure them.'

She turned him round abruptly and pushed him into the car.

'Go on now, or you'll only have to drive too fast. Call when you get there. Don't forget.'

'The moment I arrive. 'Bye, my sweet. Work well.'

Engaging the automatic, he drew slowly forward down the drive. At the street he slowed and wound down the window to wave. Sophie returned a small wave. As he pulled away into the street, he cast a final glance in the mirror.

There was a troubled, haunted look in her wide eyes.

Sophie lay in bed, unable to sleep, staring up at the pattern on the ceiling cast by the moonlight. Down the corridor, Suzanne was letting out a bath. The central heating gurgled in the pipes. In the distance, a police car tore through the night, its siren howling. She shivered. She'd felt uneasy ever since Dad had left. Something was somehow . . . missing. For a while she fell into a light sleep, disturbed by strange dreams, but

woke and stirred restlessly until finally she decided to
go downstairs and find a book to read.

As she slipped on her dressing-gown, she glanced
out of the window. To the right, the sky was a smudge
of orange above the city; to the left, inky darkness. In
the centre, at the foot of the garden, stood the weeping
willow tree, grazing the ground. In front spread the
lawn, a black-velvet pool, reflecting nothing.

As she stared out at the willow tree, she began
to notice that strange, familiar, metallic taste in her
mouth. Her forehead began to pump, in and out,
slowly at first but more and more powerfully. The
low-hanging fronds of the tree seemed to stir in sympathy. No, something was stirring behind them, *within*
them. The pulsing grew more forceful. She couldn't
drag her gaze away. It was locked onto a small patch
that grew brighter, while everything around it became
more blurry. It seemed to sway back and forth, back
and forth, in time to the pumping in her head. (Why
was this happening again? What was going on?) The
fronds were now swishing crazily, as if someone was
violently shaking the tree. Then suddenly they parted,
and as they parted, they grew still. From the opening
emerged a head, shoulders, an arm, a leg. The figure
of the boy, crouching. Dark-haired, angular, animal-
like. He looked about furtively, then stepped abruptly
out into the open, onto the black-velvet lawn. He took
a few steps forward, then looked up. Straight at her.
Into her.

Sophie smiled. What trick was he up to now?

But this time it was no grin that met her, but
a grimace. A grimace of pain and longing.

With a small cry, she turned and fled down the
stairs and into the kitchen to let him in.

Poor Valentin: she'd never seen him so distressed. He

clung to her as if she were the very source of his life. He mumbled incoherently, and she found it impossible to understand what was really the matter. At one moment he seemed to be under the illusion he'd somehow failed her and kept desperately saying 'sorry'; at the next, he raged venomously against 'that man'. Then his mood changed again and he grew tender and pleading. *This* was his home, he said, and, please, he wanted to stay there, with her, for ever.

She was filled with pity. He'd been thrown out by his cruel father and he had nowhere to go. Of course he could stay. Dad would be back the day after next; he'd go and see the man and sort it out. Meanwhile, what the poor boy needed was a haven where he belonged.

Jeremy was staying in Danny's old bedroom and Suzanne in the spare room, and so she put him in a sleeping-bag on the floor beside her own bed. Just as she was falling asleep, she reached out and felt for his hand. His touch melted into hers. It was good to have him home.

TWENTY-FOUR

Jake hated conferences: stuffy lecture halls with dreary speakers and uncomfortable seats, twenty-four-hour bars, too much food, too little exercise. And the loneliness. It hadn't really hit him until now how lacking in sex his life had been since Alex had left. At home, it didn't seem to matter, but here, away from his roots, it stung. Leaving the gathering just now as supper ended to return to his room, he'd found himself in the lift with two other delegates, one escorting a secretary, the other a pretty assistant, both heading off for an early night.

As he entered the room, he caught sight of the snowdrops in the toothmug beside his bed. What the hell did he want with complications? He had enough to worry about as it was. He glanced at his watch. She was bound to be up still.

Kicking off his shoes and loosening his tie, he threw himself on the bed and reached for the phone.

Sophie answered. Her voice was animated, as if he'd caught her in the middle of a conversation.

'Hi, Dad, how's it going?' she asked at once.

'It's going.'

'That bad? Talk to anybody interesting today?'

'Just had supper with Pete Greenwood. That man has a mind like a laser. He's on the verge of cracking cellular oncogenes.'

'Cambridge again, see?'

'You can do your thesis anywhere, Sophie. What counts is getting the right supervisor. I've been thinking about Charlie Evans at Oxford.'

'What about Jeremy Parnassus at UCLA?'

'Let's not try and settle this on the phone.'

'How's the hand?'

'Hurts at night, but I'll live. Tell me how you've been. How's everything at home?'

'Same as usual. Suzanne is giving the place a spring clean. Jeremy's stuck up in Danny's room all day, watching TV.'

They spoke for a good twenty minutes before he eventually drew it to a conclusion.

'Well,' he sighed, 'you'd better be going to bed.'

'You, too. You've got to be on form in the morning.'

'I must say that eleven on a Sunday morning is a heathen time to give a paper. I think *this* is where science and religion really part.'

'That should be your opening line.'

'Right, it shall be! Now, go and have your bath. I'll call again in the morning.'

' 'Night, then, Dad.'

' 'Night, darling. Love you.'

'Love you, too.'

Jake slept fitfully. The hotel bed was too short and the mattress too soft. The room had been newly carpeted and the smell took him sharply back to the dank flax fields on the farm in Ireland where his mother had once taken him to show him her birthplace. He thought of her wise, knowing face, made hard and defiant by years of brutal and ignorant treatment, and he asked himself, if he were to come face to face with her now, would she forgive him? Forgive him his sin of omission in her, forgive him his sin of commission in Sophie? He thought of his father, too, and wondered if there was a force for justice at work in the world and whether, in his ruin, the man had met his just punishment. And then, as for himself, in his mortal guilt, should he meet his own retribution, and would it come at an unknown time and through unseen hands, without permitting him the chance to plead his cause? Tormented in both body and spirit, he lay tossing and turning into the early hours, when he took a Valium tablet and finally succumbed to sleep.

The shrill ring of the phone in the morning barely roused him. It was the conference organiser. The professor from Montreal, scheduled as the last speaker of the day, had received an urgent call from his hospital and was having to catch an earlier plane back to Canada. Could Jake switch times with him and give his own paper at four in the afternoon instead?

Grudgingly, Jake agreed. He took a shower and shaved, ordered up breakfast and then called home. The phone barely rang before it was answered.

'Hello?' said a boy's voice.

It was Suzanne's young nephew.

'Hi, Jeremy,' said Jake. 'How are you doing?'

'Fine, thanks.'

'Is your aunt there, please?'

'She's cooking breakfast.'

'Sophie, then.'

'She's upstairs.'

Jake hesitated. Well, the boy was a responsible lad. He could be trusted with a message.

'Will you tell your aunt I'm going to be late? I don't expect to be back before nine tonight. Could she stay till then?'

'All right.'

'You won't forget, will you?'

'No.'

'What time did I say?'

'Nine.'

'Good lad. Send Sophie my love. I'll call when I get a moment.'

344

Odd, thought Jake briefly as he put the phone down. It didn't sound as if Jeremy was speaking from the kitchen. The only other phones were in his study and his bedroom. Perhaps Suzanne had roped him in to do a bit of spring cleaning.

Valentin put the phone down. He smiled to himself. When Suzanne put her head round the study door, he was innocently looking at the books on the shelves.

'Wasn't that the phone?' she asked.

'No.'

'Oh.' She looked uncertain, but he stared her out. 'Valentin, I don't think you should be in Dr Chalmers's study.'

'Sophie doesn't mind.'

'It isn't Sophie's room. Come on out.'

He shot her a glare of hate. At once she raised her hand and clutched her forehead. He could have given her a real headache, but he had to save his energy. The man was coming back in the evening, and he was going to be properly prepared this time.

Sophie glanced at her watch and reached to switch off the computer. Three o'clock: time to go to Mother's. Shutting her study door, she slipped across the hall and hurried up the stairs. From the landing she could see Suzanne and Jeremy in the driveway below, loading their luggage into the car. She took the narrow stairs up to the attic. There, Valentin was examining the lock on the door leading to the roof.

'We're going now,' she said. 'Change your mind and come.'

The boy shook his head. 'I can't.'

'But you enjoyed yourself last time.'

'I've got to get ready.'

'Ready?'

'You know.'

'I'm not sure I do.'

'For when he gets back.'

'Dad?' She gave him a sympathetic smile. Poor boy: not everyone's father was a tyrant. Dad would understand. He'd happily let him stay until things were sorted out. 'Don't worry about Dad. He's a push-over.'

Valentin gave a small start. 'A push-over?' he echoed.

Suzanne was calling them from downstairs. Sophie held the door open and beckoned him.

'You'll have to leave the house, anyway. Suzanne will go mad if you stay here on your own.'

'I could take care of her.'

'Suzanne's the last person in the world who needs taking care of. Anyway, she's going off home now.' She led the way down the steep back stairs. 'My mother will drop me back around seven. What will you do in the meantime?'

'Things.'

She laughed. 'You could always go to the park. There's usually a football game on Sunday afternoon.

She locked the front door behind them and, giving Valentin a friendly squeeze, climbed into the back of Suzanne's car alongside her young nephew. As they drove off, she turned and waved. Valentin stood for a moment in the driveway, then disappeared into the shrubbery.

Valentin waited for the sound of the car to die away, then re-emerged from the shrubbery. He slipped quickly round the side of the house, and within seconds he was climbing back inside through the study window he had deliberately left unlocked.

He stood in the hallway, listening to the sounds of the house. For the next four hours, it was all his. His to explore, his to penetrate, his to set up for the trap.

346

The tape recorder was the easy part. Working with the hammer and chisel, though, wasn't so nice, and twice he hit his thumb and raised angry blood blisters.

But only one thing mattered: getting it right this time. And no mistakes.

Jake left the lecture hall through a press of hands and, bracing himself against the biting Cambridge wind, hurried across the car park and climbed into his car. It hadn't been what they'd expected but it had gone down well. He drove contentedly, without hurry. It was a quarter to six as he hit the motorway to London; with a bit of luck, the Sunday-evening traffic into the capital wouldn't be too heavy and, if he made good time round the Orbital, he should be home around nine. In good time to catch up with Sophie before she went to bed.

Putting on a Sibelius tape, he settled down to enjoy the drive home.

Sophie jumped out of the car and, leaning back in, gave her mother a kiss.

'Thanks,' she said. 'That was great.'

'See you on Wednesday, sweetheart.'

'Right you are. 'Bye, Mother.'

She ran up the driveway to the house. The lights were on. Dad must be back, though she couldn't see his car. She stood waving on the porch until her mother had driven away. Slipping her key in the latch, she opened the door and went in.

'Dad?' she called. 'I'm back.'

There was no reply. She looked in his study. No briefcase on his desk. No sheepskin hanging in the hall. She pushed the door open into the kitchen.

Valentin was sitting in the farmhouse chair in the centre of the room. His jersey and jeans were white with some kind of dust or ash and on one hand he had a large sticking plaster. In the other he held something at which he was gazing in rapt admiration. The photo Dad had taken the other night.

'Where's Dad?' she asked.

The boy grinned. 'On his way.'

'How did you get in, then?'

'The window.'

'Really! I do think you could have waited. Dad wouldn't be too happy.' Slinging her book-bag into a chair, she poured herself a glass of orange juice from the fridge and carried it through into the living room. 'Vain creature! Is that all you can do, sit there admiring that ugly mug of yours?'

She sat down at her desk and, switching her computer on, was soon immersed in updating her McKusick catalogue with several new mutant phenotypes that had been recently proven.

Jake stopped at a motorway service station to refuel and phone home. The phone gave the 'unobtainable' sound. He called the operator, who checked and told him the line was out of order. Puzzled, he returned to his car and selected a tape of Rachmaninov. Maybe young Jeremy hadn't replaced the receiver properly. Still, he'd be home in an hour and a half.

Time passed, and Dad wasn't back. Sophie was growing anxious. Why hadn't he phoned? He'd have known before she left for Mother's if he was going to be late. Had he had an accident?

At seven fifty, she decided she'd just check that he'd left the conference all right. She went to the kitchen and, glaring at Valentin, now sitting idling over a comic magazine of Danny's he'd dug up from somewhere, she reached for the phone.

It was dead.

She was rattling the cradle up and down when her eye fell upon the cable down by the skirting-board. It had been cut.

She turned to Valentin. He wore a smug grin.

'Did *you* do this?' she snapped.

He nodded slowly, almost proudly.

'But *why*?' she demanded, incredulous.

He frowned at the question, as though it was somehow unfair. What on earth was he up to? She strode over to the door.

'You'd better not have tampered with the others,' she said crossly.

'No,' he said.

'I should hope not.'

At the door, she turned. Valentin had taken out the Polaroid again and was staring intently at it.

'No,' he repeated quietly. 'Not now. Not any longer.'

Something in his tone stopped her short.

'What do you mean, Valentin?'

He looked up, his grin spreading.

'I don't need you now. Not any more.'

She shook her head. What rubbish the boy talked! Hurrying out of the room, she went to her father's study and picked up the phone. She had dialled the number before she realised it, too, was dead, the cable neatly snipped down by the floor. Furious, she flew up the stairs into his bedroom. The same there.

She spun round to find the boy standing in the doorway of the bedroom.

'You'll darn well catch it when Dad gets back!' she warned. 'Mind out. I'm going next door to use theirs.'

Valentin held his arm across the doorway.

'*He*'s going to catch it when he gets back,' he said with a knowing smile. 'Isn't he?'

'What d'you mean?'

349

'You know.'

'I *don't* know! And I'm not wasting any more time trying to find out. You're a stupid fool, Valentin. You think Dad will let you stay now?'

She went to push past him, but he kept his arm firmly blocking her passage. She tried to knock it aside, but he stood his ground. She stared uncomprehendingly into his eyes for a moment, then her anger suddenly touched flashpoint and she threw herself on him, pummelling and biting. She'd always thought of him as small and weak, but in fact he was built of leather and steel. She wrestled and tussled and finally broke through. She'd reached the top of the stairs when he brought her down in a flying tackle. Kneeling with his full weight on top of her, he pinned her shoulders to the floor and began closing his hands round her neck. His dark eyes burned with a fury of hatred she'd never seen before.

'Get off me!' she yelled. 'I'll scream.'

'Scream, then.'

She knew no one would hear, anyway. She wrestled for a moment, then went limp.

'I'm sick of this stupid game,' she said. 'Let's stop.'

His grip tightened round her neck.

'No!' he hissed. 'This was your idea! You started it. You brought me here. You're . . . *responsible for me.*'

He was deranged, unbalanced, mad. What could she do? She couldn't overpower him, so she had to outwit him. Don't challenge a madman's logic! *Agree* with him!

'Yes, all right, I am,' she choked.

He shook her violently. Then, equally abruptly, without any warning, his manner changed again. Releasing his grip, he put his head in his hands and let out a long, despairing sigh.

'No, no,' he mumbled. 'We mustn't fight. We are *us*.'

350

He looked so pathetically wretched that she couldn't help reaching out to him. He took her hand and, pressing it against his cheek, sought her eyes.

'I did it all for you,' he said in a voice desperate to be understood. 'To please you. Because you wanted it.'

'Of course,' she said tenderly.

'Because I *am* you. You made me.'

'I . . . what?'

'It's because of what *you* are that *I* exist!'

She checked herself. What was he saying? The look in his eyes made her shiver. *Agree*, she thought. *Say you understand.*

He turned to her, suddenly more desperate than ever.

'You won't get rid of me, will you?'

'Of course I won't, my poor sweet.'

'Promise?'

She bit her lip. What was he asking her?

'I promise,' she said gently.

Abruptly he gave a small, rough laugh.

'Well, you couldn't, anyway. Not now.'

What was he on about? 'Ssh,' she hushed quietly and drew him closer. He nestled into her embrace, hugging her as tightly as if they were one.

Sophie cradled the tormented boy in her arms as the minutes ticked away. He muttered inaudibly, but he gradually grew calmer. If only Dad would come! She could only make out fragments of what he was trying to say.

'I did my best,' he slurred. 'I tried my hardest. You can't be angry.'

'Why should I be angry with you, Valentin?'

'I nearly did it. Very nearly.'

'I'm sure you did.'

351

The boy pulled away and looked her full in the eyes.

'But I got *her*. You can't say I didn't get her. Eh?'

'Her? Who?'

'You know. That scientist woman. Helen somebody.'

She smiled. 'You got her round your little finger, you mean.'

'No,' he grinned, '*really* got her.'

Sophie felt her smile freeze on her lips and her body lock rigid with horror.

'You *what*?'

'Did her in. Like you wanted.'

With a sudden thrust, she pushed him violently away.

'It was . . . *you*!'

Instantly his manner switched. His expression lost its sweet and sorry defencelessness and took on a vicious, blustering look.

'No, Sophie. *You* did it. Through me.'

She gasped. *Her?* Had she wished the woman dead and willed him to do it? What was he, then? Was he *part* of her? Could she have possibly . . . ?

Her hand flew to smother a cry and, sick with the terrible realisation, she staggered to her feet and backed down the stairs into the kitchen. She was over by the French windows when he entered. He stopped in the doorway and eyed her with malevolence.

Go! Get out of there! Run, scram, flee, hide, get help, stop Dad!

She flew at the French windows, wrestling with the locks frantically, but they wouldn't open. She was all fingers and thumbs. Quick! Quick! She heard the squelch of his trainers crossing the floor. She heard a rattle in the knife-box. Vainly she turned the locks this way and that. He was coming for her. She turned. In his hand he held a very large knife. He was on her. He touched her throat with the point. She froze. Then he beckoned her gently, slowly, carefully, away from the door and led her at knife-point back into the room, where he sat her down at the table. Without taking his eyes off her even to blink, he went round the other side of the table and sat down facing her. Laying the knife on the table between them with the blade pointing towards her and, beside it, the photo he worshipped, he placed his hands on the edge of the table, fixed her with an unflickering stare and settled down to wait.

The grandfather clock in the hall chimed nine. Where *was* Dad? He must be warned! He was walking into a trap.

Think! she told herself. Be clever. Use your wits. But how could she outwit the boy, when he . . . somehow *was* her? His moods were now fluctuating wildly, unpredictably. At the moment, he was morose and kept shaking his head and saying, 'If only you hadn't done that, Sophie,' in a tone of false regret.

She tried chatting as if nothing were amiss, but he couldn't be lured. She tried returning to their earlier conversation, but he no longer wanted her comfort. She tried suggesting she showed him a computer game, or made him his favourite Welsh rarebit, or fetched a book to read to him, but he wouldn't be drawn. When she casually moved to get herself a glass of milk, his hand darted forward like lightning and grabbed the knife, tilting it so that the blade caught the light and flashed in her eyes.

Finally, she played the only card she could think of. She rose to her feet. Instantly the knife was in his hand.

'I've got to go you-know-where,' she said shortly. 'Wait outside if you don't trust me.'

Suspiciously, he followed her into the hallway to the small lavatory under the stairs. She went in and locked the door. Humming loudly, she gentled eased the window up and, careful not to make a sound, climbed out. Valentin was knocking on the door, calling for her to hurry up.

'Won't be a moment,' she called back.

Reaching in through the window, she flushed the lavatory. As the sound from the cistern swelled to its peak, she took to her heels. She pelted round the side of the house, across the gravel drive and, not daring to take the open drive itself, disappeared into the shrubbery. Within a moment, she was crouching beneath the wall that bordered onto the street, her pulse thumping violently, listening for any sound from the house.

After a while, she rose carefully to her feet. She only had to step up onto an old tree-stump and she'd be over the wall. She knew the direction from which Dad would be coming and she'd recognise the hired car, and she could jog along until she met him. She'd done it. She was free.

A twig snapped. Barely two feet away.

She hardly had time to draw breath to scream before a thick loop of rope, the old tow-rope from the shed, whipped over her head and tightened in a slip-knot around her chest, pinning her arms to her body and toppling her off balance onto the ground. A hand pressed itself against her mouth. She bit hard into the flesh and heard a muffled howl, then a violent blow struck her on the side of the head, jerking her skull up out of its roots. Dazed, her vision swimming, she became aware that she was being hauled along by the shoulders through dead undergrowth and onto the gravel, before gradually the stars in the sky began to spin and burst and everything became engulfed in darkness.

The final trio of *Der Rosenkavalier* was swelling to its

ultimate climax as Jake began the gentle ascent home to Clifton. He drew up in the driveway but, carried by the music from one peak to another, he stayed inside the car for a moment to hear the last, humorous quip on which the opera ended. Exhausted but smiling, he dragged himself out of the car and stretched his limbs. God, it was a long way to drive. England looked a pinprick on the map until you tried to drive across it. Still, it was only nine fifteen: not bad time to have made.

He took his suitcase out of the boot and, still humming the rising melody with its mounting, dotted rhythm, he stepped across the gravel, avoiding the fresh puddles and, taking out his latch-key, let himself in at the front door.

'Hi!' he called, 'Sophie? Suzanne? Yo ho!'

No reply.

Had the wretched woman lured them all upstairs to watch television? He dumped his suitcase down in the hall and went on into the kitchen. Odd, he thought: with Suzanne there, the place usually smelled like an old English farmhouse, full of the aromas of baking and roasting and ironing.

'Sophie?' he called again.

He glanced into the living room. It was empty. No light came from her study. He listened. The house was strangely silent. Perhaps they were hiding. He felt too weary for a game.

As he went back into the kitchen, his eye fell upon a photograph on the table, *That* photograph. The one Valentin had taken.

His world spun upside down.

Holy Christ.

He gripped the table edge in naked terror.

'Sophie!' he yelled.

Wildly, frantically, desperately, he charged through

the house, kicking open the doors, stumbling up the stairs, bursting into one room after another – her bedroom, Danny's old bedroom, his own bedroom, the spare room, up the narrow attic stairs (why were the attic lights on?), then slipping and skidding down the back stairs into the utility room, back into the kitchen, the living room, Sophie's study, unlit but perhaps—

She was still at Alex's. Of course!

He grabbed the kitchen phone. It was dead. Yes, he remembered the fault on the line. But ... what was that? The wires *cut*?

Wait!

A voice! *Her* voice!

He stood very still, listening with his senses honed. Yes! He could hear her. A small voice, as if she were in a cupboard. Where, oh God, where?

He followed the tiny sound into the utility room. It seemed to come from *outside*. Grabbing a torch, he pushed open the door that led into the small glass conservatory. The smell of damp compost and mouldy clay pots hit him.

'Dad!' came the small voice. 'I'm here! Over here! Help!'

He flipped the light switch, but nothing happened. The place was dark, but no Sophie to be seen. Where the hell *was* she?

'Dad! Here!'

Under the bench somewhere. What on earth ... ?

He flashed his torch into the darkness.

Pots. Slug bait. Sacks. Weed killer. Bulbs. Seed trays. And, on top of a sack of potting compound, playing slowly and clearly, a tape recorder.

'Dad! Over here!'

Sophie squirmed her way along the dust and wood-chippings. Wriggling to her feet, she hooked a pair of shears off the shelf and, falling back onto her knees, worked until the blades were in position, then leaned back so as to pin the handles between her back and the stone floor. Sawing hard, she finally managed to cut the cords. Two brisk slices of the shears severed the rope binding her feet, and a moment later she was at the shed door.

It was locked.

The shears failed to prise door from frame. At last, groping blindly around in the dark, her hand fell upon the small hand axe that Dad used for chopping kindling. It took ten smart blows to shatter the boarding around the lock and enable her to force the door open.

Dad's car was back! She ran towards the front porch, then thought again. Better go round to the back, in case. She sped along the side path into the garden. Keeping out of the light to avoid being spotted, she saw at once that the living room and kitchen were empty.

And then she heard the grunt. It came from high up. She looked up, tracking the sound.

On the roof, etched against the orange night sky, his body bent in the effort of heaving against the vast black chimney stack, stood Valentin.

She glanced quickly down at what lay directly below. She saw everything, exactly.

Letting out a scream, she rushed forward.

Jake heard a patter on the glass roof. It sounded like pebbles.

Pebbles?

He looked up sharply, flashing his torch into the night beyond.

A figure on the roof. *That* figure!

The boy!

At that second, the door from the garden burst open. Sophie stood in the doorway. A sudden shower of pebbles or sand spattered on the pane immediately above.

'Dad!' she screamed. 'Get back!'

'Sophie!' he cried.

'*Get back!*' she repeated.

But he couldn't move. He was paralysed. Rooted to the spot.

Sophie threw herself on him. Just as she did so, there came a loud groaning, cracking, splitting sound from high above. She struck him full in the chest with the flat of her hands and with a violent thrust sent him staggering back against the far wall. At that very second, the lid of the world fell in. Bricks, masonry, rubble in tons crashed in through the roof, shattering, splintering, crumpling everything beneath it. One fleeting glimpse of the girl, arms outstretched, with terror, love, pity flashing across her pale, oval face and her violet eyes, and then a vertical wall of brick and glass engulfed her, crushed her, buried her like a broken flower under a canopy of rubble and dust.

And, far above, as if in echo, there came one long, terrible, terminal cry of pain.

TWENTY-FIVE

Jake stood in the chill morning air, still wearing the suit in which he'd delivered his lecture, heedless of the cold and damp. He hadn't slept, and he'd never sleep again. The sun hurt his eyes; how could it be shining when the light in his life was extinguished? In the distance, the city was going back to work; hadn't they *heard*? A robin alighted momentarily on the rim of the pile of rubble, cleared in the centre where the small body had lain, crushed and broken. Beyond lay the path, its gravel churned up by boots and shovels. His own hands, heavily bandaged, bore the weals of his mindless frenzy, flayed by the rough bricks, spiked by nails and lacerated by glass as he'd hurled himself in a mania of despair upon the pile that had buried his child.

Indoors, he could hear Graham trying to comfort Alex. He could hear her feet pacing restlessly back and forth as, shattered and distraught, she tried to get to grips with how it had happened. Chimneys didn't just fall like that, there'd been no wind, no storm, just this sudden, cruel act of God, leaving behind those eternal outraged questions that would never rest: why *their* child, why *then*, why *there?*

He hadn't told her it was Valentin's doing. He hadn't mentioned the boy at all. How could he, when . . .?

The avalanche had brought down the whole frame of the conservatory, pinning him for a time beneath a roof spar. After he'd clawed his way out and frenziedly torn aside the wreckage crushing the child, as he had raised the frail, mangled body into his arms, a towering, unslakable rage had seized hold of him. Roaring like thunder, he'd stormed into the house and up the main stairs, he'd blundered along the landing and up into the attic, holding out his bleeding, torn hands so as to grab, throttle and maim, and, careless of his own life, even wanting to die in the act of vengeance, he'd charged out onto the roof and scrambled up to the broken stump of chimney.

Beside the chimney he'd found a hammer and chisel. But the boy?

The boy had vanished. Utterly. Into thin air.

Later, in the first light of dawn, he'd gone back and examined the roof. Half way up the main stairs, he'd seen the unmistakable mark of a muddy trainer, clearly going up, and recalled that the driveway had been wet on his return. He found another, fainter print ascending the attic stairs. Across the linoleum on the attic floor he'd found a trail of his own footprints, coming *away* from the roof, wet with the grimy mulch of the gulleys, but no comparable tracks to show that the boy had come back down.

Gradually, as he walked round the garden among the daffodils, feeling the sun already warm upon his shoulders, everything began to fit into place with frightening clarity.

Valentin had come back to life.

How?

He'd been *brought* back.

By whom? By him?'

Or . . . by *Sophie*?

Had it, in fact, been not the strength of Valentin's feelings that enabled him to transcend normal physical laws, but the strength of *Sophie's*?

Was it possible that . . .

. . . that *Sophie had created Valentin?*

Was Valentin really a figment of her mind, made flesh? The unconscious expression of her suppressed rage? Could it really be that her rage and resentment at Daniel's death, irrational though she had recognised it was, had laid the first brush-strokes of his being? And later, her rage at discovering she had been genetically manipulated, her rage at being robbed of the sense of who she really was, her rage at feeling she was not *herself*, all these had made the creature more real? That Valentin was her rage made manifest? And evil?

Sophie herself, consciously, was not capable of evil. She might have had thoughts of hate that afternoon when he confessed to her, but she had reasoned it out with him and accepted his explanation. Driven underground, her feelings must then have finally burst out – and, fuelled by her double intelligence, burst out with double intensity. He thought back to the rats in the laboratory, and shuddered. Unconstrained by reason, those animals had acted on their immediate impulses and turned on one another, maiming and massacring. Sophie, however, possessed supremely the faculty of reason. Had she, through sheer force of her superior reasoning, suppressed her rage, compelling it to erupt somewhere else? Everything eventually found its level. Feelings had to be felt: they couldn't be reasoned *away*. And she *had* exhibited fierce feelings, hadn't she? Remember that time she was given the SPECT scan: he hadn't told her what Mangold had said about the phenomenal activity he'd glimpsed in the amygdala just before the machine broke down – just like the evidence Helen had come up with on that rat-tissue slice all those years ago. Hadn't Sophie herself said that it had broken down *just as she was thinking how much she hated Helen?* That same force had nurtured Valentin as the embodiment of all her buried resentment and fury. Evil. Hate made flesh.

He shivered. He'd been arguing at the conference for the power of mind to influence matter, but this was way beyond anything he could have imagined. Here he was, saying that Sophie's feelings had actually *materialised* the boy. It *had* to be. Wasn't *that* why people had never properly seen him until she'd 'introduced' him? What they saw after that was a projection of her mind. The more they saw him, naturally the more they believed in him – and the more he was believed in, the more people saw him. What had Graham said about *tulkus*, those forms materialised by thought? *The more they are seen, the more real they become.* What Sophie's mind had conjured up, the world took for real. And thereby it *became* real.

But another, crueller implication stopped him dead.

Who had been the object of her rage, of her hate? Who had been the target of Valentin's murderous mission? First Helen, yes. But then?

Himself.

The terrible conclusion was inescapable. Sophie had hated him, subconsciously, with every bit as much ferocity as, consciously, she had loved him.

No, no, Sophie could never have hated him!

Yes, yes, she had. She probably never realised it and, with an intellect such as hers, the suppression was almost certainly invincible, but it was, none the less, true. His child had raised up a champion to avenge herself on him. The creature turning on its creator.

But wait!

At the final moment, hadn't she shown her love was stronger – no, absolute? Hadn't she made the supreme sacrifice and laid down her life in exchange for his? Love, redeeming hate? In that act of unconditional forgiveness, she had abolished her hate and reversed the impulse that had given birth to Valentin.

The figment could exist no more as fact. Without her mind to nourish his reality, he had lost his existence. Without purpose or function, he had returned whence he had sprung. Vanished into nowhere. The creature had died with its creator.

Oh, Sophie, *Sophie!*

This was Jake's retribution, his punishment for tampering with nature, for playing God. Sophie, his own creation, the child to whom he had given life, had turned on him to destroy him. Yet she had died to save him, giving her life for his.

What man could possibly live with that?

The funeral took place in the church where, barely four years before, Daniel had been laid to rest. The day was insolently fine, with the first buds bristling on the hedgerows and the air alive with the clamour of birds.

Jake walked slowly up the broad stone steps on Alex's arm, pausing towards the top to catch his breath. He felt an old man; his hair had turned quite grey and his body seemed like a heavy, alien burden he was condemned to haul around.

He let Alex lead him into the church and down the aisle to the pew at the front. In the row behind sat Arthur with his four children and, beyond, several colleagues from the hospital. From across the aisle, Herbert Blacker, his old professor, cast him a glance full of sympathy and reconciliation. On all sides he saw Sophie's friends from her school days, children from the neighbourhood, tutors and fellow students from the university, many of whom he'd never even met. He felt deeply moved and, in a way, slightly surprised; somehow he'd never imagined she'd been so popular or moved among such a wide circle of friends.

The slow, sonorous toll of the bell stopped and the

priest took up his position in front of the coffin lying before the altar, and from the organ loft sounded the opening chords of the funeral Mass.

Herbert Blacker stood by the open grave as the small coffin was slowly being lowered in. A few feet away lay another grave. Its headstone bore the name Daniel Chalmers.

Damn bad luck, the professor was thinking. That fellow Jake Chalmers was a bit too unbalanced for research work, true, but he was a fine physician. Deserved better than he got – one child disabled, the other a prodigy, and then to lose them both in their early years. Special pity about the girl. The word went round that she'd had one of the foremost minds of her generation. She'd looked all set to leave a lasting mark on science. The human race was all too short of outstanding brains like hers.

He shook his head sadly as he watched the coffin come to rest at the bottom of the pit. Tragic, the sight of a child's coffin. In the centre, a large engraved brass plate bore the girl's initials. He could read them without glasses from where he stood: S.M.C.

It was only when the first clods of earth thudded down on the wooden lid that Herbert Blacker stopped abruptly in the middle of his train of thought.

S.M.C. Those initials rang a bell.

He'd put it out of his mind and was following the main body of mourners back down the path to the lodge at the cemetery entrance when he halted abruptly in his tracks.

S.M.C.: that had been the title of Helen Lorenz's files. He'd assumed it stood for 'Simian something-or-other': she'd been working on chimp DNA.

Or had she?

He remembered the thought that had gone through

his mind at the time. *Humans shared ninety-nine per cent of their DNA with chimps. It made you think.*

It certainly made him think now.

Within an hour, Herbert Blacker was standing in the dusty basement of the Department building. Helen Lorenz's relatives had shown no interest in collecting the packing-case that he'd filled with her work and sent down for storage. Beneath a naked light bulb, his pulse mounting, he went through the files one by one. *S.M.C.: Chromo Spread. S.M.C.: Hybridisation. S.M.C.: Agarose #1.* His hands were shaking badly and his shirt was drenched with sweat as he put down the last of the papers.

He understood.

A slow smile gradually crept across his face.

Maybe the human race might one day see another Sophie Mary Chalmers. But then, why just one?

Jake returned to the cemetery that evening. He brought the very last of the snowdrops, to match Sophie's gift to him. He cleared a space among the other flowers and laid his own small offering carefully at the base of the tall headstone, upon the freshly turned earth. Three small bunches of twelve, one for every year of her short life, and three because it was a prime number. He took great pains arranging them in perfect symmetry. Sophie had always loved symmetry.

Everything has to be in its place. Doesn't it, my darling?

He closed his eyes for a moment, feeling her presence so strongly, imagining that she was beside him or looking down from somewhere above, trying to picture her oval face with its violet eyes and its knowing, clever smile and wondering what she would be saying if she could speak to him now. 'Don't pull such a sad face, Dad,' she'd say. 'Cheer up! I'm OK. Love you.'

Briskly he rubbed away a tear and looked at the snowdrops. They captured the whole innocence and beauty of the girl.

He stood back and scanned the grave, noting the bunches of flowers and the wreaths with their black-edged cards. And, to the side, one that he hadn't noticed before: square and bordered in white, a card and yet not exactly a card . . . more like a picture, a photo . . .

He bent forward. He blinked. A sick panic gripped his stomach. He reached to pick it up, but recoiled in horror. There was no mistaking that photograph. There they were, the three of them, just as he'd taken them. Sophie on one side, Graham in the middle and—

Sweet Christ, how had it got there?

Valentin.

No! It was impossible! The boy had vanished, returned to thin air. *Hadn't he?*

Suddenly the rest of Graham's words flashed through his mind . . . *the more real they become. Until they reach some threshold level. And then they actually exist.*

Giddy, he stumbled forward, clutching at his heart, as a bolt of pain shot through his chest. Grasping the headstone for support, he looked up. In the distance, between the cypress trees, silhouetted faintly in the dying sun, he saw a fleeting image. It stopped momentarily. It met his gaze across the rows of gravestones and the rising film of mist. Then, with the ghost of a smile, it turned away, retreated down a winding path and disappeared from view.

Fontana Paperbacks: Fiction

Fontana is a leading paperback publisher of fiction. Below are some recent titles.

- ☐ CABAL Clive Barker £2.95
- ☐ DALLAS DOWN Richard Moran £2.95
- ☐ SHARPE'S RIFLES Bernard Cornwell £3.50
- ☐ A MAN RIDES THROUGH Stephen Donaldson £4.95
- ☐ HOLD MY HAND I'M DYING John Gordon Davis £3.95
- ☐ ROYAL FLASH George MacDonald Fraser £3.50
- ☐ FLASH FOR FREEDOM! George MacDonald Fraser £3.50
- ☐ THE HONEY ANT Duncan Kyle £2.95
- ☐ FAREWELL TO THE KING Pierre Schoendoerffer £2.95
- ☐ MONKEY SHINES Michael Stewart £2.95

You can buy Fontana paperbacks at your local bookshop or newsagent. Or you can order them from Fontana Paperbacks, Cash Sales Department, Box 29, Douglas, Isle of Man. Please send a cheque, postal or money order (not currency) worth the purchase price plus 22p per book for postage (maximum postage required is £3.00 for orders within the UK).

NAME (Block letters) _____

ADDRESS _____

_____